By the same author

SEMANA SANTA

DAVID HEWSON

EPIPHANY

HarperCollins*Publishers*

HarperCollins*Publishers*
77–85 Fulham Palace Road,
Hammersmith, London w6 8jb

Published by HarperCollins*Publishers* 1996
1 3 5 7 9 8 6 4 2

A catalogue record for this book
is available from the British Library

ISBN 0 00 225363 1

Set in Linotype Minion by
Rowland Phototypesetting Ltd, Bury St Edmunds, Suffolk

Printed and bound in Great Britain by
Caledonian International Book Manufacturing Ltd, Glasgow

We do *not* know the past in chronological sequence. It may be convenient to lay it out anaesthetised on the table with dates pasted on here and there, but what we know we know by ripples and spirals eddying out from us and from our own time.

EZRA POUND, *Guide to Kulchur*

Acknowledgements

Vivienne Schuster, my agent at Curtis Brown, gave me, as usual, the definitive advice when I began: just write it. Nick Sayers, my editor at HarperCollins, proved equally consistent in knowing what I was trying to say even when I couldn't put my finger on the exact words. Jane Barringer finecombed the final manuscript. Connie Hallam took on the amazingly long-winded job of persuading most of the past idols I wanted to quote to let me reproduce a few of their words of wisdom. As for Jagger and Richards ... well, frankly, on reflection, I wasn't that bothered anyway. Sometimes the Midnight Rambler rambles a little too much. Barry Hampshire, who first introduced me to the arcane pleasures of playing in a rock and roll band nearly a quarter of a century ago, provided some welcome solitude at the Flower in Hand Hotel, Scarborough, just when I needed it. And, always there, my wife Helen held everything together at home while I seemed to spend the best part of 1995 commuting between Seattle, San Francisco, Kent and Spain.

It was a long trip but I hope you all think it was worthwhile.

DAVID HEWSON, *June 1996*

DESERT ROSE

Fission

It is not because angels are holier than men or devils that makes them angels, but because they do not expect holiness from one another, but from God only.

WILLIAM BLAKE

Christmas Eve 1975, Palo Alto, Northern California

'Things sparkling.'

Five-year-old eyes flash through the window, fix on gold and silver mannequins behind the glass, moving to a clockwork time, one with a baton in its hand, one bowing at a tiny violin.

'See, Florrie. Things sparkling.'

The pet name grates on her. She feels stupid here, in this foreign country, in this foreign costume, the white hems dragging around her ankles, stupid golden wings hanging on her back. Conscious of her awkwardness in this strange and unfamiliar place.

She looks at her brother, trying to shift her anger, her inward, nameless grief to him, looks into the window, sees two small, ghostly figures reflecting back at her in the thin winter sunlight, their robes rustling in the faint breeze. *So cute, so cute,* the passers-by said, and every word infuriated her. *So cute, so cute,* their mother had stopped, looked, admired them, taken out the little Kodak Instamatic, taken their picture in front of the window, said just a minute – just a Mummy minute, she thought – just wait here. There were things to do and it was so busy in the store.

She felt the coldness rise up from inside.

'Don't be stupid, Miles. It's hard I know. But try.'

Her voice has the authority that springs from another twenty minutes on earth. She is the older twin and that has always been

3

between them, something solid, something so palpable it need not be mentioned. Twenty minutes, twenty years. No difference. The gap is tangible. She feels superior, always, even at five years old, and more. Feels *responsible* and blames him for the burden.

Behind them, a huge truck lumbers down University Avenue, clouds of diesel spewing in its wake, the noise booms in their heads, loud, painful, shocking. The dust cloud hovers in the late-afternoon air, then slips slowly down the slender thread of Californian gravity. Specks of black begin to mark their perfect white robes, like rot marks on the soft skin of half-ripe peaches. She can feel the light, faintly chill winter wind stirring the wings fettered to her back. The golden tinsel leaves make a metallic rustling sound that hovers around her. The smell of diesel mingles with the aroma of cinnamon floating from a bakery two doors away.

Miles feels for her hand, small pudgy fingers straining to link into hers, looking for safety, assurance, warmth. She shuts her fist tight, as tight as she can. Refuses him entry. It feels good, right, proper. It feels grown-up.

'Why is she taking so long? Why? Florrie? Why?'

There's the whine, slender, high-pitched, insistent, nagging away at the back of her head, an actor that never misses its cue. She closes her tiny eyes, shuts them tight enough to feel the muscles in the lids start to scream, bunches her arms in front of her, thrusts her tiny fists beneath her armpits, lets her loud silence wash over them, then, her head turned away from him, opens her eyes again, stares silently into the window: gold and silver, red and green. A gaudy Santa Claus stares back at her from behind a bright, brassy saxophone. Children's recorders peek out of gift boxes in the seasonal display. Sheet music lies scattered around the instruments, like leaves that have fallen from some invisible tree.

From inside the shop, his face somewhat obscured by the flashes in the window glass, a young man peers at them. He holds a guitar by the neck, gently, as if it has some kind of life of its own, a precious life, with its own discrete, intrinsic value, a life that needs preserving. There is a white plastic name badge on the lapel of his cheap, cotton jacket. She makes out the letters, a name that flits around her thoughts, fighting for recognition, then floats away, drifts lazily to the back of her head.

He looks back at them, puzzled, maybe a little concerned, and then

4

smiles pleasantly: two tiny angels stock-still in University Avenue on the day before Christmas. Then he turns, he is hearing a voice (she can tell this even without placing the source of the sound, and wonders, perhaps it is Mother, perhaps she has finally found what she wants, remembers they are there, waiting for her, outside), and is gone.

'Florrie?'

Higher now, like the kettle coming to boil on the Aga in their kitchen back home, back in the cool green never-ending landscape of Cambridgeshire, where the sounds are different, the smells are different, where things have a comforting familiarity that threatens no one, not even the young.

Where we should be now, she thinks. Not in this foreign place where no one knows our names and the smiles, that are everywhere, have the quality of cheap Christmas decorations: skin-deep, temporary, ready to be blown away by the first gust of wind.

Sometimes (and this began before they caught the aeroplane, this began back in the greenness long long before in a bedroom that was not hers or his) sometimes she can feel this stoniness deep down inside her, this black, hard feeling that comes and goes. Sometimes it's so hard it frightens her, makes her think things she cannot believe: her father dead, her mother crazy, car crashes, aeroplanes falling from the sky, the world coming to an end.

And her brother gone. That one comes a lot, comes more than any of the others.

Sometimes it says things too, in a loud, clear voice that is not quite man and not quite woman. Words she does not understand, words she has heard but knows she must never repeat out loud (but this does not stop them ringing around her head, first in the voice that comes from the hard place, then in her own inner speech, round and round and round they spin).

In the beginning she just let the stoniness lie there, cold within her stomach, until finally it decided to go of its own volition.

But there are occasions, more and more of them these days, when she likes its presence there, waits for it to come. *Wills* it to come and enjoys the strength that flows through her whenever it is alive. Like now.

'Florrie!'

She looks at him and he wishes he had never spoken. There is a blackness in her eyes he recognises and does not like. He holds his wrist close to his body, out of habit, and remembers what it feels like when she burns it, the soft flesh twisting like fire under her grip.

'I'll tell,' he says, flatly, automatically, in a voice that is already weighed down with defeat, with knowledge, a small, dull threat that carries no substance, floats away on the breeze down University Avenue. 'When Mummy comes out of the shop, I'll tell.'

She smiles and underneath his thin white gown he shivers. These tinsel wings feel heavy. He is tired and cold and lonely.

Her face contorts, like a bad actress, the way, Miles thinks, girls always do when they want to unleash some small act of cruelty.

'The little angel Gabriel,' she says, in a slow, deliberate voice, and there is a pricking in his eyes that he hates, wants to stop, but cannot control.

She reaches forward and touches his cheek, gently. Her hand is icy cold yet he thinks he can feel patches of sweat there, moisture against the grain of her skin.

'The little angel Gabriel,' she says again, and he feels her finger and thumb start to pinch, hard, relentless, into his cheek.

Along the low, flat-roofed shops of University Avenue, the wind gathers suddenly, scattering the leaves on the street, blowing old news-papers and discarded trash into tiny, swirling hurricanes of litter, making the last-minute Christmas shoppers reach for their hats, wonder why they are here, on the day before Christmas, when they could be home watching TV, getting ready for church, or just mixing a stiff cocktail and thinking about surviving the days, the years, the dwindling life ahead.

From across the street, the two little kids in fancy dress, standing stock-still in front of the window of Moore's Music Store, seemed, for a moment, to merge, their golden, tinselled feathers locking in the sudden gust, fusing into a single, ethereal creature.

She encircles him with her wings, and suddenly he is in darkness. The joy feels so hot when she hears him sobbing, hears the voice chanting wild nonsense

three quarks for Muster Mark

inside her, giving her the words to whisper in his ear, words that fan his terror until she can feel his keening as a wild, loud vibration against

6

her skull, a shrill, painful wail that gets louder and louder until there is no other sound.

The stoniness comforts her with its secret complicity, its invitation into the conspiracy, and she can almost see its shape, like a film between this world and another, a perfect, seamless sheet of gleaming glass, hard, shiny, with no entry or exit path, no point of possible failure, no hidden corners in which to conceal a lie.

His keening ends. Now she can hear her own words spilling through her lips, sliding through her teeth, the spittle frothing from her mouth as she races to let them out, not even knowing what they mean.

She feels him quiver, knows the time is right, then lifts her golden wings. The wan Californian sunlight illuminates his face and for a moment she flushes in triumph, feels her victory and a bright, hot, adult heat.

Yet this time there is more there, more than she expected, more than she wanted. His eyes roll back and forwards out of control. There is a sound coming from his throat that is more animal than child.

She lifts her tinsel wings high away from his crouching body, so high that her arms begin to ache. Like a tiny bird, trapped in its nest, he rises, eyes darting wildly from side to side, looking for an escape route, then flies, a fluttering rush of white and gold that races away from her.

Inside, the stoniness is flooding away fast, like a swiftly receding tide. The voice is silent. She cannot remember what it sounds like any more. The day is cold. Her wings weigh painfully on her back, her shoulders slump forward pathetically.

When, finally, her mother returns, she is five years old once more. No explanations, no reasons, nothing but tears and the beginning of some dread new, adult sensation that seeped into her world so easily, so effortlessly, that she wondered if it would ever leave.

Miles is gone and what terrifies her, what makes her feel the world tremble under her feet, is the memory of her last thought as he flew from beneath her wings. The sudden, certain conviction that this was final and held no possibility of reversal.

That however many times she said sorry, however long she spent alone in her bedroom counting the Huckleberry Hound pattern on the wallpaper over and over again, he was gone forever.

That in fleeing her, he had also fled the world.

ONE

The Emerald City

LORENZO: The man that hath no music in himself,
Nor is not moved with concord of sweet sounds,
Is fit for treasons, stratagems and spoils;
The motions of his spirit are dull as night,
And his affections dark as Erebus:
Let no such man be trusted. Mark the music.

WILLIAM SHAKESPEARE,
The Merchant of Venice, act 5, scene 1

Without music to decorate it, time is just a bunch of boring
production deadlines or dates by which bills must be paid.

FRANK ZAPPA

Awop-bop-a-loo-bop alop-bam-boom.
LITTLE RICHARD

Christmas Eve 1995, Seattle, Washington State

Past the sex bar with the glittery sign – half the bulbs gone but still
readable – that says '100 beautiful naked ladies (and one ugly one)',
past the city's leading parrot emporium, the Christian country farm
shop, the grubby line of pawn and porn stores, the fish stalls where
the big Pacific salmon fly through the air for the gasping videos of
the tourists, down three floors, past magic shops and feminist book
stores, oriental paper-folding speciality counters, the little table where
you can try lumps of red-hot chilli pepper jelly that sit like little traffic
signs on slices of thin brown bread, beyond the noise of the crowds,
the barking of the importunate bums, the sound of a piano being
played on the pavement (Bruce Hornsby, slightly off key, but a good
impersonation all the same), deep in the bowels of Pike Place, this
subterranean proto-community of shopping mall escapees and floating, flaking nineties human jetsam, Paul Dunsany sits at the mixing

9

desk, playing with the controls in front of him, listening to find some way he can sort order out of the aural mess that keeps coming through the cans clamped tight over his ears.

Another bunch of kids who think they're the new Nirvana. Even down to the blond rinse on the lead singer. Another bunch of kids who've got it wrong.

He watches the tape turning on the old U-matic eight-track, sees, for a brief moment, the flakes of magnetic scurf on the thin brown plastic jump and dance every which way to the electronic tune that spits off the head, turns up the bass mix and thinks, with some difficulty, about Ry Cooder, tries to remember some snatches of distant, lovely guitar. Beyond the smoke-stained glass the kids stare hopefully at him, waiting for a prompt, waiting for some small miracle. Checked lumberjack shirts, unshaven, unmemorable faces, long, dirty hair. The usual uniform. The Seattle uniform, born of these grey, industrial streets.

He shrugs his shoulders, harshens the mix a little more and mentally tots up the bill. Maybe a hundred and twenty dollars for the entire session and if you coarsen the tape up enough, make everything hum to its limits, they'll go away thinking it sounded better than it did when they played it.

'That's great,' he says finally down the mike, trying to hide the boredom in his voice. 'Buy yourselves a coffee. Take a walk. You get the tape when we get the money.'

They shrug, obey, start to clear away their kit: two cheap Strat copies, an unidentifiable bass, and a $200 electronic drumkit. Boop boop, Dunsany thinks to himself. Boop boop bippy boop. Probably punched into the system's microchip by some teenager in Tokyo. Welcome to the age of digi-music: three chord tricks and drum rhythms out of a Sega machine.

You're getting too old for this, he says quietly to himself, for the third time in this brief day. Just pull together a hundred grand, put in a new electronic studio, let Frank and the teenage computer genius run the whole thing, sit back, play real music, relax.

A hundred grand. A dry little laugh forms somewhere on the skin at the back of his throat, makes its presence known, acknowledges his recognition, then disappears in silence, too lazy to waste the energy on converting itself into sound, too jaded to form even a puff of air from the lungs.

Dunsany starts to curse the drum machine again, the tinny electronic sounds ringing in his ears, then stops. The black phone by the console is ringing. He looks through the control room door into the dingy little office. The teenage computer genius has his head halfway down the big colour monitor making love to some sequencing program, dead to the world. Frank is nowhere to be seen. Dunsany sighs, picks up one of the three Christmas cards by the desk, waves away the cigarette ash into the air, then reaches for the phone, grabs it and says, 'Pike Studios, music for your ears, other parts catered for at daily special rates.'

There is a pause down the line and automatically, without knowing why, he reaches for his face, his index finger slowly tracing the smooth thin line of a scar that runs down the right side, from below the eye almost to the chin. It is nearly invisible now, marked mainly by the absence of bristle. Dunsany turned forty-two the month before. Someone brought in a cake at the Zanzibar, put it in front of him once the set was over. He took one taste, smiled, declined. Too old these days for pot cakes; the taste of Redhook, fragrant, cold, amber, seems more appropriate, more fitting. His hair is short now, bushy and light, chestnut brown, but just over the ear, just on the collar. He wears round, owlish tortoiseshell glasses, his cheeks are starting to become heavy. More like a trendy account exec in some ad agency than a musician. Changed days, changed people.

'Paul?'

He hears the voice and this time it is real, the scar is starting to hum, to set up a faint cold pain on the surface of his skin.

'Paul? You read the papers? You fucking believe it?'

It takes him a moment to work it out, to come round. To picture this voice that sounds so close down the line, but has an echo, inside the timbre of the tone, that seems so distant, in time, and in some other way too.

'Hal?'

'Who else?'

It seems like years. It *is* years. Still the Boston twang is there, less marked than two decades ago, but present, welded into the voice, the person, indivisible, a marker beacon that can flash down the phone line and identify itself without being asked.

Dunsany struggles for something to say, tries to picture the person on the other end of the phone in his mind. It disturbs him: the image

11

he has from twenty years ago remains much stronger, much more real than that from the last time they met, half accidentally, in some restaurant down on the waterfront, watching the ferries float across the Sound, struggling for the words that might still connect them, whenever . . .

Paul Dunsany fights to find the words that might breathe some life into their dialogue. 'So how're things, Hal? How's Louise? Still making megabucks, raising kids to keep the schools busy in Bellevue?'

'Fuck the small talk. You get time to read the papers these days or you still playing at being the fifth Beatle?'

'You know sometimes, Hal, you really show your age. No one gets off on being the fifth Beatle these days.'

'Really. I'll try to remember that. You have any idea why I'm calling?'

There is a strange note to his voice, one Dunsany has hardly heard before. Somewhere in the depths there is the timbre of fear, the high, unmistakable pitch of panic.

'Illuminate me.'

'Jesus. It's been everywhere these last five days. On the TV, on the front pages . . .'

'I get busy sometimes.'

'Yeah. One day you might grow up and recognise there is a difference in this world between activity and work. That's a sign, my friend. First sign you're growing up.'

'I'll try to remember that.'

'I doubt it. Quinn. Now I know you got a problem with your memory from way back when, but that name mean anything to you, old pal? Ring any bells up there these days.'

Dunsany catches his breath and now the scar is really hurting, screwing up the skin on his face so tight he can feel the migraine starting down at the nape of his neck. Something swirls through his inner mind, a mix of shapes and colours and people.

'Quinn is out of my life. You know that. He should never have been in it in the first place.'

'No. Well he was. He was in all our lives, whether we liked it or not. And now he's about to make a little comeback. Isn't that nice?'

Paul Dunsany can feel his stomach tightening, and puzzles over it, wonders why.

'After this, Paul, I want you to go out and buy a newspaper, spend a few minutes back in the real world, and try to work out what the fuck is going on in the big bit of space outside your head the rest of us call home.'

'Quinn is there for life, Hal. We can forget about him.'

'*Was* there for life, Paul. Down in la-la land you may be able to ignore these things, but the rest of us have to deal with this curious kind of parasite you get around these days called attorneys. Attorneys do bad things, Paul. Things we don't want. They read books, screw up laws, get money out of the government that lets them fuck around where they should keep their noses out. Read the papers, Paul. Quinn is out. Today. It's big news. Not quite like giving Charlie Manson parole, a million-dollar pension and a free set of kitchen knives to do with as he pleases. Not *quite*. But we're getting close.'

'That's not possible.'

'There you go again, discounting the existence of attorneys. Sure it's possible. Why do you think these people are there? They caught Quinn these days and he'd be lucky to escape the chair. But they didn't. They caught him twenty years ago, when life didn't necessarily mean quite what it does today, particularly if the judge was wearing the wrong colour socks when he passed sentence. Some goddamn attorney has been going through the court records, picking holes in the proceedings, and the outcome is he walks. Not exactly a pardon, but if he's out I guess he won't be bitching. Let's face it, we both know, we *all* know he deserved what he got. And more.'

Dunsany wondered about that one: did he know that? Or was it just something he accepted?

'What do we do?'

'What *you* do is nothing. You just sit tight. Talk to no one. If someone wants to talk to you about this, you let me know. You work Christmas Day?'

'Pike Place Studios – we never sleep. Yeah. Some kids have booked some time, so I'll be here.'

'That's good. If I need to, I'll call. We all stick together on this one there'll be no problems. I'll see to that. Unlike you, I did something with the money we took up here and that can pay for plenty. And don't worry. I won't be asking for contributions. All I want is for us to be able to agree about how we're playing things.'

Dunsany tried to think about the consequences. It was impossible, like trying to reach for two notes on the fretboard that are beyond reach, however hard you stretch.

'Thanks,' he says, finally.

'Thanks nothing. We play everything right and this means nothing to us, Paul. But you know Quinn. Whatever tricks your memory plays from back then you *know* he could bring us all down if he starts talking to the cops or the press or *anybody*.'

'Yeah,' said Dunsany, and asked himself inwardly again, did he really know that, was it really true?

'And Mouse?'

This seemed so long ago. Dunsany could feel the years swirling around him.

'You mean Margie?'

The voice on the end of the line paused. He couldn't work out how much this Hal Jamieson liked being corrected.

'Yeah,' Jamieson said. 'Margie. You know where she is? What's going on there?'

'No,' Dunsany said, shaking his head pointlessly, where no one could see. 'That was all so long ago, Hal. This whole thing was so long ago. You think any of us could keep in touch that long?'

'No. But I had to ask. You know that, don't you?'

'Yeah,' Dunsany said, and didn't even think about it.

'So what time does a musician get to work these days?'

And finally, as if it had worked its way up from somewhere deep and half forgotten, there was a note of friendship in his voice, a note mixed with a sense of apology and bewilderment at the way things had gone after so long. 'If I have to call, that is. I know you bohemian guys keep strange hours.'

Out of force of habit, Dunsany looked at his watch. It was 9.45 in the morning. Three hours' sleep since finishing at the Zanzibar. He needed a half-decent coffee that tasted as if some time in its life it had made more than a passing acquaintance with the substance known as caffeine. He needed to think. He needed to get rid of the bandload of young jerks, who had now gone back to playing and were starting to strike up 'Santa Claus Is Coming to Town' arranged by Bruce Springsteen.

'Tomorrow, ten on. Till whenever.'

'And Paul?'

'Yeah?'

'Go out. Get a paper. Get sober. Get real. You may need it.'

Dunsany nodded, put the phone down, lit a cigarette, let the ash drop steadily from the tip down into the crevices of the mixing desk.

'Quinn,' he said, quietly to himself. And twenty years disappeared from his life like a puff of smoke.

TWO

Joni and the Detective

All the tears
All the rage
All the blues in the night
If my eyes could see
You kneeling in the silver light
If you're out there can you touch me?
Can you see me? I don't know
If you're out there can you reach me?
Lay a flower in the snow

ROBBIE ROBERTSON/MARTIN PAGE,
'Fallen Angel'

The little shuttle train ran round and round its circular path beneath Sea-Tac airport, taking her from the gate to the terminal, and all she could do was stare into the deep, dark glass of the windows, watch her reflection, impassive, tired, pale, her golden hair a mess of curls, and wonder: why? This was such a long way from London, a long way from the only place she could even begin to think of as home. She felt drained, a little heady, after the nine-hour flight, and it was hard to concentrate. It was hard even to *think*. Time ran backwards in this strange, foreign place, and while her body told her it was close to midnight, the watch on her wrist said it was five to four in the afternoon.

When the train came to a halt, Joni Lascelles joined the crowd falling out of the door, walked to the baggage carousel, waited for her plain cheap black case to disgorge from the mouth, and wondered how you began to orient yourself in this new place, this new continent. This was the first time she had made this great trek, the first time she had sat on the plane, watching the world turn to ice as they flew across the roof of the earth, from one ocean to the next. There was so much invested here, and it went beyond money, it went far beyond that, and yet she was unready, she was unprepared. It had all happened so

16

quickly, the rapid arrangements after the funeral, the frantic dash to shift responsibilities in the little lawyer's office where she worked, the calls to America to find help, to track down people you could just look up in Yellow Pages back home.

Why was she doing this? Why did it have to be her?

The little case dropped onto the carousel, she picked it out, went to the gate and waited for the shuttle bus to downtown. This should have been exciting: a new place, a new world. It smelled different: moist, chemical underneath the dampness, but with something salty and elemental that came in from the sea too. The day wore a shroud of grey, luminescent fog. You could see no more than a few hundred yards. It was impossible to judge this place except by its smell, and that was industrial exotic, something so odd, so far from what she expected, that it seemed unreal. There should have been pine trees, grizzly bears, vast rivers, towering, snow-capped mountains. Instead, this grey shroud, and the smell of diesel and factories, overlaying the salt mist from the sea.

There was a wreath hung on the outside door of the airport and underneath, as if anyone could forget, the words, 'Merry Christmas to all Sea-Tac Customers and We Wish You a Happy 1996'.

She looked at the circle of leaves, the red flowers, and thought: they see Christmas, I see a funeral. The world interpreted one thing, she interpreted another. A picture formed in her mind of the tiny 1950s crematorium in north London, a pale pine coffin disappearing down the ramp, taped organ music, three mourners, apart from herself, and two of those were from the hospital. A life that ran for fifty-three years, from the Blitz, through the Cold War and Elvis, through Suez and Jackson Pollack, through Stalin and Gorbachev, Bernstein and the Beatles. A life that went into some strange kind of stasis, some enervating pool of amber, just when it should have been at its best, just when it should have been flowering. And all this, turned to dust, removed from the world, in a few – she could count them – seconds that ticked away inside a tiny brick building that could have doubled as a municipal bus station waiting room.

But where she has gone, there lives no hunger. Where she has gone, there lives no pain.

Joni Lascelles stepped on board the shuttle bus, paid her fare, then watched the greyness slip past, punctuated, as they approached the city, by the huge, hulking, half-seen outlines of office blocks, and on

17

the pavements the shapes of pedestrians, hurrying through the blanket of mist, not wanting to stand still, to let it swamp their lungs. The tiredness lifted a little as she saw the people on the street, and she was able to think, dispassionately, from a distance, about her own life, and its shape, the work ahead. And it was the work that mattered, nothing else. There may be other things that happened here, and she knew what that thought meant, even though she didn't want to elaborate upon it, give it form. These strange, short, frantic liaisons, that went from nothing to passion to boredom in days, weeks at the most, were part of her, were some in-built facet of her character that she couldn't control, couldn't begin to understand. If they happened, they happened. But the work came first, came before anything else that mattered.

The bus dropped her outside the hotel. It was old, the stonework marked by smog and pitted by the ocean spray. She walked through the narrow front door, registered under the half-interested gaze of the desk clerk, went to her room, lay on the bed and watched the ceiling, waited. It was the night before Christmas Eve. Time no longer existed, or if it did, it had changed, had lost its form, become mutable, untrustworthy in the flight across the world. She looked at her watch, then started to unpack, did half the job, then lay on the bed and slowly drifted off to sleep.

It was almost 10 am and she had been awake since four, lying on the bed thinking of nothing in particular. Tom Cordobes was ten minutes early and made no apology. He watched her take some notes and a pad out of the case, then, with a motion that almost seemed furtive, stuff the cheap black Delsey underneath the bed. He sat on a wicker chair, took out a cigarette, and waited. Finally, she sat down on the bed, a battered low coffee table between them, smiled wanly and said, 'I'd rather you didn't.'

Piercing blue eyes impenetrable as the sea fog that now blanketed the city.

'If you don't mind.'

Tom Cordobes grunted, tapped the unlit Marlboro on the little hotel room table, then pushed it back into the box. He suddenly felt old today. He wished he hadn't driven all the way north, up through Oregon, that long, long road through nowhere. But it kept down the costs. You could always fly then try hiring something, but then if the debt went bad, and these days it went bad too often, you just wound up even more out of pocket. And there was no way he was going to be flying to London to chase the ticket on this one.

'You sure sound English,' he said, then tried to cover the grimace with a smile. Might as well start off with a dumb statement. Tom Cordobes was five eleven, pushing sixty years of age, and had the heavy build of a younger, more muscular man now starting to run to waste. He wore a pale, creased suit, light-brown leather shoes, well polished to the extent that they almost hid their age. His face was tanned and leathery, lined like old hide that had been left out too long in the sun. He had a greying Zapata moustache that dated back to his days as a motorcycle cop. Tom Cordobes acquired things then never quite remembered to let them go. The moustache was one of them, along with the collection of Roy Orbison records and the mobile home outside Milpitas, way south in California, that had served as both residence and office since the city taxes in San Jose went so sky high it just didn't make sense any more, so high it just seemed obvious to unhook the answerphone, the PC and the fax and plug them in back home. You live cheap enough you don't need to earn that much money, Cordobes said to himself at the time. And as the police pension seemed to get smaller and smaller with every bill that fluttered onto the breakfast table, he began to forget which part of the equation came first.

He pushed his business card across the table. The Pequod Hotel, on the corner of Third and Lenora, was not the sort of place he expected to meet some fancy English lady lawyer. This was the kind of area the real estate agents called 'upcoming', which in his book meant the arty-farty types were queuing up to renovate the lofts but still kept tripping over bums as they humped their futons over the doorstep. Outside the street was grey and dirty – what little he could make out through the dense, opaque fog that had swept in overnight from Puget Sound. The traffic noise was muffled by the gloom, but intense all the same, even through the closed window. He'd been hustled three times by nondescript low-lifes in the three-hundred-yard walk from his parking space. The room was big enough but it looked like it had been furnished from a garage sale: one large double bed with a sagging mattress, two chairs, a battered coffee table, above them a cheap, yellowing chandelier that didn't cast enough light to bring the dust in the corners into proper view.

'You pick this place yourself, Miss?'

She looked at him, curious. It was so direct he almost felt like blushing.

'It was booked by the office travel service.'

Nothing more.

'Well, don't you go walking around here on your own. Couple of blocks over, when you're down there with the tourists around Pike, no problem. This place is still, how do you put it, improving. And it's got some way to go.'

'Thank you,' she said, and passed a business card across the table. He looked at it: Lascelles and Soames, solicitors, with an address in London that meant nothing to him. Above it, Joni Lascelles, senior partner.

Senior. These seniors are just getting younger by the day, Tom Cordobes thought to himself.

In another age, when he'd been swanning round Palo Alto in a squad car, feeling like he was king of the castle, he'd have called her a 'girl' and no one would have argued. No one ever did argue with Tom Cordobes in those days, not if they wanted to stay happy and whole.

Joni Lascelles was slim to the point of angular thinness, about five feet eight, and wore tight, dark-blue Levi's and a black, rollneck sweater. There was a slender silver bracelet around her wrist and what looked like an expensive watch. She wore no make-up and that made her seem somehow even more striking: round, large, slightly staring light-blue eyes in an open, attractive face, eyes that never seemed to leave you. And a mouth that was always half open, even when she wasn't speaking, a full, expressive mouth that, like the rest of her features, seemed almost exaggerated, almost too big. Her head was a mane of bright blonde curls, dyed no doubt, but with a confidence in the colouring that meant it didn't really matter. This was what she wanted to look like, this was her statement, and it said, even to some-one of Cordobes' age: hippy chick. It said: this could be '68, except she was cleaner and smarter and more knowing, except that she had *chosen* this look, not had it forced on her by some insistent rush of peer pressure. Somewhere in her bag, he just knew this, was a pair of round, opaque wire-rimmed shades and when Joni Lascelles put them on she would look just like some face straight off the cover of one of the albums you used to find dope traces on when you raided the hippy kids' homes: serene, staring, and maybe a little wild underneath. Cordobes couldn't decide whether she was attractive, maybe even beautiful, or whether there was something blank, some nothingness in her face, the way some kids had these days, that meant you didn't really want to look at all, because it just might be a waste. Whatever she was, she wasn't plain. And she wasn't senior, no more than twenty-five he guessed, maybe a lot less, it was getting harder and harder to tell.

He realised he'd been silent, thinking about her looks for too long, felt her eyes sweep over him, felt like blushing again. Then she smiled, a big, broad, open smile, with perfect, lustrous white teeth gleaming at him, and he couldn't stop himself returning it. When she smiled, Joni Lascelles was just plain lovely. It was like having a big, bright beam of warmth suddenly open up on you and Tom Cordobes didn't even pause to question its sincerity, he just couldn't stop himself wondering how often this little miracle happened, and whether there was some lucky guy somewhere who got it turned on for a private showing now and then.

'I got distracted somewhere along the way,' Cordobes said.

'That's OK,' she said, still smiling, all that blankness just gone from her face from the moment it happened. Some women could just charm you out of the trees when they felt like it, Cordobes said to himself, but it was a real long time since he'd met one of them. Mostly these days the only lovely young women he met were screaming at him for busting up their marriage. The way the business goes.

'You'll be wanting to know about payment.'

She reached into her bag and took out a blue plastic wallet, the kind you got down the bank. It was stuffed with dollar bills. She counted out a handful then put them on the table.

'There is the thousand-dollar retainer, as you requested. After that I'll agree to the two hundred and fifty dollars a day plus expenses you outlined on the phone.'

Cordobes scooped up the bills and wished it was always this easy.

'There's a lot I need to know, Miss. Like how you came to be asking me to do this in the first place.'

'Research,' she said and left it there.

'You care to elaborate? I mean, there are things I don't have to know but there are things I do. And right at this moment I don't feel I know an awful lot. Like, why me, for instance? Don't get many commissions from London in Milpitas these days. I'd like to think it was an honour.'

She pulled an expensive lacquered fountain pen out of the attaché case and started to make notes. He felt like he was being prepared for some kind of medical check-up.

'You were a police lieutenant at Palo Alto during the Quinn case.'

'Yeah. How you know that?'

'As I said. Research.'

'You that good at research, why you need me?'

She thought about it. She seemed to like the question.

'It's one thing getting someone to run through old newspaper files and match them up with today's state register of licensed private investigators, Mr Cordobes. We can do that down the line from London. Now we need some actual investigation and that really isn't our area.'

'So what is your area? You a criminal lawyer? What?'

She shook her head. 'We're a civil law firm. I don't know what you call it over here but we work on family estate cases. Probates. Wills. That kind of thing.'

'Sounds kind of boring.'

'Really.'

'If you don't mind my saying, that is. You sure this isn't a newspaper thing? I hear say they got the *National Inquirer*, loads of those tabloid animals all out there looking to find the mighty Quinn and unload large sums of money on him just to find out what happened back then. If that's the game you're in, Miss, you should be telling me right now. I got rules to work to and if they step over into the privacy area things can turn pretty nasty for me if it all goes down bad.'

She walked over to the bedside table, picked up a bottle of sparkling water, unscrewed the cap and poured herself a glass.

'You'd like some?'

He grimaced. 'You ever hear what W.C. Fields said about that stuff?'

'You mean about fish fucking in it?'

And this time he really blushed, somewhere deep beneath the walnut tan, and they both knew it.

He said nothing.

'Yes, Mr Cordobes,' Joni Lascelles smiled at him. 'Several times, I think.'

She sat down again and put the glass on the plastic table top. He could hear the little bubbles fizzing madly and found himself waiting for them to subside before he could continue.

'It's an old joke. A bad joke. Sorry.'

'No problem,' she smiled. 'I'm of age. And to answer your question, no. Our client is not a media organisation. Our client is exactly the sort of client we always have. Boring as it may be. An estate that may or may not be contested depending on what we can learn about what happened in Palo Alto twenty years ago. I'm sure I don't have to remind you of something. That while your newspapers may regard Quinn as some kind of mass butcher there was only one proven death in Palo Alto at the time and the police couldn't charge him with it in any way.'

'Not *charged*. No. That's not the same as not guilty.'

'Actually in a court of law that is *precisely* the same.'

'You're the lawyer. I'm just an ex-cop who had to deal with all that shit and I'm telling you that Quinn was up to his neck in stuff that would curl your hair. We didn't even get to know the half of it, you want my opinion.'

'No,' she said, and he was almost taken aback by the hardness in her voice. 'That's exactly what I don't want, Mr Cordobes. Opinions count for nothing in the kind of case we're talking about.'

'Will stuff? Probate? That kind of thing?'

'That kind of thing. We have an estate that needs to be settled and will be settled if no further information is forthcoming from Mr Quinn. If, on the other hand, he were to prove willing to make a simple statement, without prejudice, without naming any guilty parties . . .'

'Ah,' said Cordobes, and at last he thought he was maybe getting it.

'Then,' she continued, 'the estate would be settled differently.'

'It's the difference,' he said, 'between being dead and being missing. Someone's dead, you can rule them out of the will, someone's still missing, you need to make some kinda provision or something.'

'Exactly. Not that any of this concerns you. All we require of you is to find Mr Quinn, to organise an interview if he is agreeable, and that is that. We're willing to finance this for two weeks at the agreed rate and if nothing is concluded by then we will give up on the idea.'

Cordobes nodded. 'Hell of a time to try to do this. Over Christmas.'

She stared at him hard. 'What choice do we have? At some stage

Quinn will surely talk to someone. If he makes the statement for money to the media it will probably invalidate it in the court's eyes. Either we speak to him first or not at all.'

'Yeah. I can see that.'

Joni Lascelles stopped making notes and put the pad down on the table.

'Can you do it?'

Cordobes shrugged. He was getting too old to bullshit people.

'Like I said to you on the phone, I know people at the Obispo pen. They're good people. They hate seeing Quinn get out *at all*. And that makes them a little scary about talking too. See, there's not just the media who may be chasing this guy. Plenty of crazies would love to take a pop at him given the chance. Make a nice hunting trophy for the study and I don't see many people objecting.'

'So?'

'So, like I said on the phone, I got a pretty good steer from inside Obispo that the man is on his way here. But that's all I got. And by *here* I mean Washington State, which is one big place to hide. It's a start, not a great one, but it's a start.'

'So what do you do next?' she asked, and Tom Cordobes realised he didn't like interviews, particularly not ones with such young people, not at all.

'What I do next is I chase connections. My guess is he's got to be coming here for a reason, someone's got to be paying for it. His parents are both dead. I took a look at some of the records on file. I may be old, Miss Lascelles, but I got a PC too. There's some money in the estate there for him but not enough to live from. Maybe I start chasing connections, looking for people who moved from Palo Alto up here around the mid-seventies, maybe something comes through. Best I can suggest for the moment.'

Joni Lascelles was nodding and smiling enthusiastically. 'Good. That's exactly what I thought. From what I've read, Quinn was part of a defined sub-culture. That sort of thing can help.'

She smiled at him and it was hard to shake off her eyes. 'You mean he was a hippy?'

'Right,' she said, and he could feel the eagerness spilling over now as she spoke, could measure the way she failed even to notice his interest. 'And look at the timescale. A late hippy at that. Haight Ashbury was way in the past by 1975. Things had moved on. That wasn't

24

a general scene he belonged to, it was a timewarp, something stuck in the past like a fly in amber.'

'Yeah,' said Cordobes, grinning, grinning so hard, with that new knowing look in his eyes, that he could feel the air growing slightly chill as he spoke. 'And you know that's interesting. A nice young lawyer that studies recent history. Now that's unusual. That's really something.'

The room went quiet and Tom Cordobes really didn't mind. Not at all. He thought he liked Joni Lascelles, maybe could learn to like her a lot, he could use the work, and before he left the Pequod he made sure to leave the number of the twenty-five-dollar-a-night motel on the edge of town where he was staying just in case she needed him between his regular, scheduled reports.

But he would have hated it if he'd left the nice young lady lawyer with the impression he was dumb or something.

THREE

The Barn

Be not too liberal; it doth belong
To dogs alone to fuck the whole day long.

FRIEDRICH NIETZSCHE

In 1975, before they built the sprawling Gresham Woods shopping mall and changed the water table of half of Palo Alto and Menlo Park, the San Jacinto creek still, on occasion, contained moisture on the long, winding journey down from its source in the Los Altos hills. The little *arroyo* meandered lazily all the way down through dry, empty scrubland straight to the big highway of El Camino Real, the old Spanish settlers' road, where it disappeared under a culvert close to the CalTrain line from San Francisco to San Jose and beyond, then wound up in the public drainage system somewhere beneath University Avenue. The river bed was usually bone dry by the time it reached the highway, except where the Gresham Woods, a few acres of eucalyptus trees, their bark peeling in the California sun, their leaves filling the air with the constant, cloying scent of throat sweets, made enough shade over a couple of local springs to keep a little mud, and maybe even a thin line of brackish water trickling over the rocks.

The creek ran through the middle of the woods, its stony sides tumbling a good twelve feet down to the bed, and the line of the watercourse neatly divided Palo Alto from Menlo Park. The trees provided a little shelter for the itinerants who found their way here from the city, usually hitching rides on a passing freight train. The bums littered the stony bed with shopping carts, empty bottles of Thunderbird, beer cans and plastic bags. If you got close enough, skirting the playing field where the hearties of Stanford came to play soccer and rugby (this being Stanford, ordinary football was OK, but not enough to satisfy the sporting curiosity), you could blunder into

26

the obvious presence of their shady, nether world. A strong stink of shit and urine came out from under the piles of plastic bags that littered the feet of the eucalyptus trees; it fought a daily battle with the heavy scent of the leaves and the fog of gas and diesel fumes that billowed off El Camino. No one would have relished the chance to say which won.

It was ten in the morning and Roscoe Sutter – known to the inhabitants of the Barn, always, since the moment they had moved in, as Muttley – was hungrily biting into the remains of a greasy cold burger he'd found by the roadside close to the Oasis bar. Tomorrow the church folk came to University Avenue and got all sentimental and gave the bums a real Christmas dinner. He hadn't been there before – these last two winters had been spent in the city until things got too rough – but the word was out on the grapevine: free food, warmth, maybe some clothes. He'd be there when the handouts arrived but just right now a cast-off burger from the Oasis would suit him fine.

Roscoe Sutter sat on the ground with his back to a tree and ate without thinking, his fuddled mind only half registering the unfamiliar noise that burbled up from the foot of the creek, the gentle sound of running water. There was a movement off to his left, on the path that led across the train tracks, and, against his better judgement, he turned to look. A long-haired kid in baggy jeans was shuffling along the path, hands stuffed deep in his pockets, lost to the world. Roscoe could feel the anger start to bubble inside him, find its way into his throat, found he couldn't fight it anyway. The college kids didn't do much except taunt him. No one had beaten him up since he left the city, which was a change that took a little getting used to. But there was something about them that just got him going and once he started there was no stopping.

He began to mumble wordlessly, just loud enough to let the kid hear. It was a habit Sutter couldn't control and one that had won him his nickname in the Barn. The kid listened to the shapeless stream of bad-tempered muttering, then started to mimic it back through the shadowed half-light of the eucalyptus wood,

rassenfrassenrassenfrassenrassenfrassenrassenfrassen

mimicked it so accurately that it just made the old tramp get worse and worse and worse. Muttley, the cartoon dog, always there, always

27

on cue. And no Dick Dastardly to keep him in check. Hal Jamieson wondered who'd come up with the name in the first place. Michael? Probably. He came up with most things, except the dope (which was Hal's forte). He set the mark they'd come to live by in the Barn and no one quite knew how it happened.

Hal Jamieson quit mumbling when Muttley was out of earshot, took a deep breath between his teeth and wondered if he could keep it long enough to reach the front door without getting another blast from the shit cloud in the woods. He didn't make it. Smoking too much again, he thought, and half choked on the laugh.

The Barn had been many things but never a barn. That was Michael's name, once again, and somehow it just stuck. In 1973, when the real-estate developers started to look at the land around the San Jacinto creek and abutting El Camino with some seriousness, the area had gone into a period of temporary blight. No one wanted to risk buying property there but nor did they want to sell, just in case some old patch of rocky scrub turned out to be ideal for a new drive-in Wendy's or, if you got real lucky, the next Nordstrom store. The area just began to live in some kind of stasis until the tides of money floating from east coast to west decided to stop shifting and settle down somewhere. Except no one knew quite when or where this might happen, so the few properties that hid in the woods, down little private dirt track lanes, just sat and waited and got more grubby, more forgotten, by the day.

The Barn was a single-storey wooden building that had once served as a farm provision store back in the twenties, when orange juice was the hottest provision the Valley had to sell. This was a time before microprocessors, a time before the Internet. All the Valley had then was fruit, and it poured OJ into San Francisco and beyond, every drop of it grown in the well-kept orchards that crept up the Valley, along the flat, glacial bed, watered by the mountains that stood on each side, brown-hewn ranges that looked as if they could live forever. Over the years, as fruit gave way to other industries, as Stanford grew and new companies like Hewlett-Packard and Xerox began to emerge from the garages of college professors who wanted more to live on than an academic salary, the provisions business went belly up, the store got converted into a home, almost, and a succession of owners came and went, none of them staying too long. It wasn't that the place was ugly. It was a brown, timber shack, with one big living room, three bedrooms leading off it, a little narrow kitchen, a single bathroom, and a couple of outbuildings. But there was much worse around and some of that got prettied up with a coat of paint, a white picket fence, and soon sold for tidy bucks to the new tide of academics and professionals who started to come into the Valley in the fifties in ever-increasing numbers. These were new people, professional people, people looking to the future. But they liked the Valley. They liked the way the old towns and villages looked a little European, they liked the way the area had style and class and some sense of establishment you didn't get in the growing suburbs of the city. Old was good, when it came to property anyway. But it had to be the right kind of old.

The problem was the Barn proved the old real estate agent's saying over and over again: what matters most is location, location and location. The big, sprawling rich man's campus of Stanford was less than a mile away, with its elegant college buildings, its well-kept grounds, and that flat, ordered air that said: come here, boys, and you *will* succeed, whatever. But that was just too far for the Barn, which sat on the wrong side of the old Spanish road, unwashed, unkempt, in the depths of woods that smelled like a cross between an underground men's room and a drug store counter. The sun somehow rarely made it through that big tall covering of eucalyptus branches, there was no real road there, just a meandering dirt track, and every thirty minutes or so, just when you least expected it, there was the thunder of wheels, the roar of a steam whistle, and CalTrain sent some giant iron monster lumbering down the track so slow and so heavy you could feel the floorboards shake.

In 1968, an air force lieutenant newly returned from Vietnam, looking to offload some money he'd made from pushing dope into the ranks, came across the plot for sale in a real estate directory, phoned someone he knew in the development business, guessed the deal was good for a risk, and bought the house and two acres of eucalyptus wood around it. He lived in Austin, Texas, and never visited the site once, not even when it was plastered on every newspaper front page, every TV screen in the country. Three years later he sold it for a seven hundred per cent profit and counted himself an intelligent, and lucky, man.

In early 1975, the air force lieutenant had not been so sure. There was a significant sum invested here and no sign of a return. So he contacted a local agent and told him to find a tenant: any tenant provided they paid up front and didn't want any stupid clauses in the contract giving them things like security, rights, or anything that could stand in the way of a quick sale if the market suddenly started to go sky high.

Michael Quinn had seen the ad in the local newspaper. Like everyone else he knew at Stanford, he had lodgings. Lodgings were clean, they kept your parents happy, they provided a service. But they also came with rules, restrictions, caveats. Fences that surrounded you, dictated what you did. In the space of two days, Quinn had retrieved the details for renting the Barn, raised the first year's rent from some of his fellow students in electrical engineering with surprisingly little difficulty, and had signed the tenancy agreement himself, keeping everyone's name off the piece of paper just in case something should go awry, what with all the dope and other stuff that might be passing through. Not that anyone intended to live there, full time anyway. It was just a place to be when you didn't want the wrong people watching.

The only rule was that there *were* no rules, Michael Quinn said the day they moved in. And that had pretty much been proved right.

Hal Jamieson pushed open the door. It was hardly ever locked. There was nothing much of value there except a battered hi-fi system, a good record collection, and, on average, a couple of thousand dollars' worth of dope, depending on how well he'd been doing scoring in the city, and whether you looked at the value in terms of what he paid, what his customers paid, or what, to use the terminology of the cops, was the 'street price'.

'After the Goldrush' was playing on the hi-fi, Neil Young's high-pitched voice cutting through the gloomy interior of the room. In the far corner, hunched over the cover of the album, long, straight, blonde hair spilling onto the solarised picture of the singer, someone was rolling a joint. He peered harder.

'Mouse,' he said to himself into the near-darkness. A round, expressionless face stared back at him, mouth agape. She was already seriously stoned, as usual, but it didn't make much difference. Mouse – he didn't know her real name just then – was someone Quinn had just acquired, out on the street, someone who knew nothing about the college, someone who put out the trash, someone Quinn liked to fuck when he felt like it. More, she wasn't even a student, just worked in some diner some place, and she used the Barn as a home, not as a pleasure dome like the rest of them. She did some cleaning, she did some menial stuff. It kind of paid back even if the conversation rarely got beyond bands and dope.

She nodded towards one of the bedrooms. 'He's in there. Reading.'

Mouse made it sound like an act marginally worse than watching *Mary Poppins*.

Hal Jamieson walked into the bedroom. It stank of sweat and stale humanity. Michael Quinn sat on the bed hunched over some big obscure book that looked like it came from the lab library. Jamieson glanced at the page and caught a sub-heading about quantum mechanics, shook his head and wondered what Quinn got out of this stuff. Then he reached into the pocket of his coat, pulled out the little crumpled envelope, held it out in front of him and let Quinn peer inside. Ten little pills, dark red and harmless-looking.

'Some new kind of acid on the street,' Jamieson said. 'They call it Desert Rose.'

Quinn looked up from his book at him and, not for the first time, Jamieson felt a little shiver run through him. Michael Quinn – somehow they all accepted, all *knew* there was no foreshortening of his first name – looked like he should have been singing in a church choir: skinny body, close-cropped blond hair, an angelic face, ice-blue eyes that blazed at you no matter how much dope you put in there. Jamieson wondered if there was anything Quinn wouldn't do if he felt in the mood for it. Some of the things he'd seen in the Barn had pushed it for him, had made him wonder where the barriers were. Made him realise that for Quinn, more and more, there *were* no barriers.

'You should read more books,' Quinn said. 'They make the dope taste better.'

Then he dipped his hand into the envelope, picked up a tab, gently placed it on the tip of his tongue, smiled, displaying neat, sharp, slightly yellow canine teeth, and swallowed.

31

FOUR

Pike Place

Our inventions are wont to be pretty toys, which distract our attention from serious things. They are but improved means to an unimproved end.   HENRY DAVID THOREAU

> They said, 'You have a blue guitar,
> You do not play things as they are.'
> The man replied, 'Things as they are
> Are changed upon a blue guitar.'
>
> WALLACE STEVENS,
> 'The Man with the Blue Guitar'

The teenage computer genius had his head deep down an Apple 9500 PowerMac, cans clamped to his ears, listening to something that made a grin break straight across his pale, waxy face, stretching the thin brown moustache on his upper lip to a kind of limit where it looked ready to give up the ghost and let the skin underneath take over. His name was Jamie Earl Dexter and he had recently turned twenty-five but this didn't make any difference: in Pike Place Studios – where his official title was recording assistant, production – he was, he would always be, the teenage computer genius.

His eyes were tight shut and he was humming in that loud, out-of-tune way that people do when something good is coming through the cans. It was only when he sensed something in the air, something out of place down in the depths of Pike Place, that he opened his eyes again, dimly recognised the scent of perfume, looked Joni Lascelles in the face, went bright red, and started to jabber.

'*Lady alert, lady alert,*' Genius babbled in an ever-rising pitch. 'Jesus. Frank? Frank? *Lady alert!*'

Paul Dunsany came out of the control room, cans around his neck, the lead coiling down to his waist, looked at her, caught the amusement in her expression, smiled, shrugged his shoulders.

'Genius,' he said.

Genius was sweating profusely, the fat moving gently underneath a grubby Pearl Jam T-shirt, and he looked ready to burst into tears.

'Genius. If you want me to call the paramedics just say so but first of all let's try to fix this ourselves. Just calm down. Take it easy. Breathe deeply. You can make it, boy, really you can.'

Genius's fat face was all aquiver. 'I shouted "lady alert" and Frank never came. Never.'

Dunsany walked over, placed a comforting hand on his shoulder, looking at Joni Lascelles all the time. You got so used to spotty youths shambling through the studio that, in the end, that was all you expected. Paul Dunsany was the second man in Seattle that day to see Joni Lascelles smiling and find it hypnotic, something so piercing there that it was impossible to ignore.

'Hello,' she said, and straight away Genius felt his brows narrow. He knew this didn't sound like Seattle. Not even out there in Bellevue or Redmond where the upscale folk lived.

Paul Dunsany smiled back at her and couldn't work out why he was feeling so uncomfortable. She was so poised, she looked so *thin*. And confident too. There was some rock-hard confidence in the way she stood there looking at them that didn't really brook you walking away until this was done. Her hair just tumbled back out of her head in a profusion of blonde bubbles. With the round shades on her face, she looked so in place. Then she took them off and he stared into big, round, blue eyes that didn't break the return of his gaze for a moment.

'You're an *artist*?' Paul Dunsany asked.

Genius thought his brows were going to knit together and stay that way. The boss just didn't talk to people that way. Not even down the Zanzibar when some of the girls got hooked into the liquor and looked like they'd come across real easy for him once they heard him play, once he pulled out some old number, maybe JJ Cale, maybe a Cooder thing, and crooned it all slow and sly and quiet in that low, deep voice, with nothing except the guitar, not a keyboard or a synth, least of all a digitised drum pattern, in sight. Genius spent half his life – the half that didn't involve painting electronic crotchets on a high res screen – dreaming about women and the more he dreamed the further away they seemed to get. The boss just seemed to let them wash over him, hardly noticing. It seemed one hell of a waste.

33

The lady was laughing. It was a nice noise. It made Genius smile so he stared hard at the screen and tried to hide it.

'You need to be an artist to get in here?'

She was looking at Paul Dunsany with her head tucked into one side of her neck. A funny little habit, he thought. Like she was examining him, checking him out.

Dunsany shrugged again, then felt the scar on his cheek start to burn, rubbed it, wondered what the hell was going on here. 'Not exactly. We pick up all types. Genius here, now he's a real artist.'

Genius could feel his scalp going red underneath the matted covering of greasy brown hair.

'He can do things with that computer you wouldn't believe. These days he runs the place, believe me. Just not the sensitive type of artist. Huh, Genius?'

'Shouted "lady alert". Goddamn Frank never did come,' Genius grunted, then shoved his face back in the screen.

Dunsany stowed the tape he'd been working on – a jingle for a new soft drink called Karma that was supposed to increase your memory and cut your cholesterol, for Christ's sake, sung by the city's leading Ella Fitzgerald impersonator – and took a really good look at the woman. Joni Lascelles was wearing a dark-blue woollen jacket, biggish silver earrings dangled from her ears, and with her big head of hair she looked like someone he saw in the magazine ads when they were doing a sixties retrospective, except that there was a brain going on behind it all, that much was obvious.

'The man in the health food store sent me,' she said in a voice that was low-pitched, slow, quite deliberate.

'Ah,' said Dunsany. 'Marti the Mouth. The one-man Pike Place broadcasting system. Tell me. Do I owe you money? Is there a warrant out there for something? Mostly, the ones Marti sends me want money these days. Way of the world.'

'Not money,' she said, catching the hint of tiredness, of resignation in his voice. The studio looked shabby. Maybe, she thought, all studios looked shabby. But there was money trouble there too. You could just feel it.

'In that case you can sit down,' Dunsany said. 'Even if you're not an artist.'

She didn't take the hint, just folded her hands on the counter. They were long hands, long, white, delicate fingers. No rings, he noticed,

34

and wanted to pinch himself for even thinking about this. You didn't get this kind of heat in the head at this age. It wasn't right. It wasn't appropriate. If something happened, you just sort of waited and waited until it arrived, so strong, so insistent, you couldn't say no. Paul Dunsany looked at her and felt the years rolling away in more ways than one, and didn't like the sensation.

'I'm looking for advice,' she said, and then put the shades back on, for no good reason as far as he could see, given the dingy illumination in the room. 'I write. Back in England, I write rock, culture pieces for some of the papers, some magazines. I got here for Christmas on a cheap ticket and I was just looking for some advice on where to go. Music places, art places, I could mention in an article.'

'Ah,' Dunsany said, bundling the jingle cassette into a Jiffy bag, and wondering what it was about this woman that seemed so odd, so intriguing. 'The *Seattle scene*. People in England still interested in that? I'm an old man, you see, I don't keep up on these things, but I thought we were supposed to be following you guys again these days, not the other way round. Grunge is old. Just go down Pioneer, look in the clubs. You can feel it.'

She was knitting her long white fingers together on the counter. And he wondered to himself: is this nervousness? Is this really what it is?

'It wasn't grunge that interested me,' she said, and he found himself really wishing she would take off the shades, let him see the person he saw before. 'I wanted to go further back than that. I wanted to do something about what's left of the hippy culture. What came out of California in the sixties, the seventies. What influence it has now. They said this was the place to ask.'

Dunsany thought about it briefly, wondered if he was really hearing this. 'The what?'

She said nothing, startled by the suddenness of his reaction.

'You go around using language like that in this city, lady, people can get very offended. This is *not* the place. Go down to San Francisco, you got real freaks down there, stuffed exhibits – beads, patchouli oil, Dead sweatshirts – for all I know. Probably some historical archive, a theme park maybe. This is Seattle. We're . . .'

He searched for the word but it was just out of reach.

Genius looked up from the screen and his round, flabby face looked deadly serious.

'We're real,' he said. 'This is 1995, 1996 nearly. We're real.'

And then he went back to pushing the mouse, his eyes glued to the screen.

She didn't say anything and Dunsany knew, straight away, that the shades weren't coming off, not now, not for a little while. There was some pale, hazy sense of disappointment hanging around her head, the blonde curls shining in the dim light of the studio, and you couldn't miss it. Dunsany suddenly felt sorry for her, felt awed, maybe a little shocked, by the idea that a person like this could be, in any sense, in some kind of despair, be marked by some form of loneliness.

'You came all the way from England?' he asked. 'For this? At Christmas?'

It was Joni Lascelles' turn to shrug. 'I guess it seemed a good idea at the time.'

'Jesus. I never knew you English people were so impetuous. You know anybody here? You got any plans?'

She shook her head. Dunsany sighed. He was used to the way people drifted in and drifted out of the city, out of his life. Sometimes it seemed like this was what life, what America was truly about: drifting, picking up what flecks of joy you could along the way. But usually they didn't look like this: so self-assured, so striking, so apparently certain of themselves, even with this fragility, this brittle edginess underpinning her. There was some sense of purpose there. It was hard to imagine this woman drifting anywhere she didn't want to go.

'Bad research,' said Genius without taking his head out of the screen. 'You wanna be a writer, you gotta work out your research. Even I know that.'

'Yes,' she said. 'Bad research. It happens.'

And even Genius thought he might start feeling a little sorry for her in a while. The city was a cold, damp, miserable place to be alone. Hell, it was a cold, damp, miserable place to be *with* people most of the time.

Dunsany felt underneath the counter, pulled out the club flyer and passed it over to her.

'You get so you need it, find your way down to Pioneer and look us up in the Zanzibar. As the song says, strictly for the lost and lonely. Only no Nirvana, no rap, no techno stuff.'

She looked at the piece of paper. There was a colour photograph of a band. Dunsany was in the centre, holding a pale-blue Fender Stratocaster.

'You play?'

Dunsany's eyes widened and he looked more than a little amused. 'They generally roll me on stage in a wheelchair if I'm too tired to make it in the Zimmer frame. I no longer trash hotels these days but if I'm feeling really chipper I'm apt to make a very nasty mess in the bathroom. Comes of age, you know, like incontinence and dentures. I'll spare you the really squalid details.'

She was laughing with him now and he liked it, liked the way she stared at him, so up-front, so open, so surprised. And liked the way she took off her glasses then, let him see the blue flashing there, so alive, so attractive that he half wished she had never bothered, half wished she'd said no and just walked out of the place for good. It might just be for the best.

'I'll try to fit it in,' she said, then put the flyer in her bag.

'That would be ... *nice*,' Dunsany said, trying to phrase the word in an English accent.

And inwardly he said to himself, as she made for the door, one last look behind her, that it was exactly the right word. In the fog, the grime, the soullessness of the city, there was a spark of something there that would be *nice*.

He took the jingle tape out of the Jiffy bag, went back into the studio control room whistling the tune, and thought he might just sit down and do some more work on it. Improve it a little. Why not?

Genius wondered about saying something, wondered about whether to take his face out of the crotchets and minims on screen (which were now dancing to the sound of a digitised pig squeal recorded somewhere in Arkansas).

But he didn't. Genius didn't know much about women so it didn't seem right to say what he was thinking. And what he was thinking was that the nice-looking English lady who might have popped off the front cover of some dopehead album of the sixties could turn out to be bad news. Very bad news indeed.

FIVE

The Rush and Desert Rose

'Tis a superstition to insist on a special diet. All is made at last of the same chemical atoms. RALPH WALDO EMERSON

A drug is neither moral nor immoral – it's a chemical compound. The compound itself is not a menace to society until a human being treats it as if consumption bestowed a temporary licence to act like an asshole. FRANK ZAPPA

What we do is as American as lynch mobs. America has always been a complex place. JERRY GARCIA

Four and a half hours before Rosamund Seymour's screams had started a police operation that was to galvanise first the Palo Alto police department, and later much of America that Christmas, Michael Quinn began to feel the first effects of the alkaloid start pumping through his veins.

Desert Rose was an experiment. But then acid was an experiment, so according to the reasoning of the Berkeley chemistry student who had fabricated the prototype hallucinogen in a small lab in a remote rented industrial unit outside Oakland, what the fuck did it matter? Not an iota. Not a hair inside Nixon's nose. Not least because the kid had not the slightest intention of taking the stuff himself.

Thanks to the presence of a couple of new chemistry and botanical volumes that had found their way into the amateur drugmaker's life, Desert Rose was a psychotropic cocktail that mixed the old with the new: a scientific distillation combined with a botanical hallucinogenic compound. It mixed lysergic acid diethylamide with two natural, chemically related alkaloids: ergot, a parasitic fungus found on rye, which had been stolen from the Berkeley agricultural lab; and an equally narcotic alkaloid from the seeds of a tropical morning glory plant, imported from Mexico. The tyro chemist mixed the three, added a little dye and holding compound, then used his small tablet-making apparatus to turn the results into something you could put into an envelope and wholesale for five dollars a unit. It didn't have the approval of the Food and Drug Administration but then, since each element in the cocktail was a known and safe hallucinogen in its own right, who needed it?

It tasted dry and metallic, left a hard, slightly unpleasant feeling at the back of your mouth, made your palate go dry. And then you just waited. This was acid. You always waited, wondering if you'd notice the second it happened, or whether it would just sneak up on you from behind and hit you over the head.

The moment Quinn knew something was different was when the book in front of him, a previously impenetrable text about quantum mechanics, finally began to make sense. The day before he had attended a lecture by a visiting English professor, some guy called Seymour, and listened half baffled, half fascinated, knowing there was something important there, something that could help him, but finding the key, the thing that unlocked the necessary interior vision, remained beyond him. It wasn't, strictly speaking, electrical engineering. But something, over the months, had been telling him that everything around him, everything that interested him, all came down to the same stuff in the end. Maybe it was all mathematics: you could write the universe on the board with a piece of chalk. Maybe it was all quantum mechanics, some giant soup of electrons, atoms, molecules and queerer particles that held everything – the Dead album on the sofa, the mucus in his lungs, the rings of Saturn, Gerald Ford – held them all together in some seamless, speckled cloud.

What the big, aggressive-looking, red-haired English guy had been going on about was electron interference and when Quinn heard him again in his head it threw some little switch inside, made him take out the book that now sat on his lap, the words beginning to move, beginning to form silver curlicues around their edges, to dance to some music he couldn't yet hear, and start to dip into some kind of elemental, existential brawl where physics, morals, religion and something he tried to think of as reality kept locking heads and trying to beat the shit out of one another.

You looked for proof, the English guy said, and you had it as far back as 1801 when Thomas Young performed the slit experiment (and you could hear the dummies in the lecture room snigger a little at that). Didn't matter. Quinn couldn't stop listening, couldn't think of anything else as the English guy had gone on about what happened, how Young had shone a light towards a mask with two narrow slits and a screen behind it. You make the slits narrow enough and close enough together, what you saw was not two bright lines on the screen but a kind of pattern, like waves.

Quinn had seen the dummies in the room doing the 'big deal' look but he couldn't do much else except listen to the English guy's low, laconic voice, droning on a little, daring them to understand.

He lost track of the book, swam in his own thoughts. In the next room Mouse put on some music, the high-pitched Canadian again. What was happening, the guy said, and they verified this easily later, when you got the equipment that could detect right down to the individual photons, could *prove* things, what was happening – *round and round and round we spin* – was that they could *prove* that the single source, the single element, this minute essence of light was interfering with itself on the other side of the filter, that the pattern, the fringes were made by the selfsame particle crashing, colliding with itself over and over and over again.

And what that meant (he couldn't believe you could tell all this in such a slow drone, couldn't believe it was something you didn't want to scream everywhere) was that the particle was travelling through both slits at the same time. Was in two places – no, more than two, was everywhere – all at once. That he, they, everything, every particle, every mote and tiny separate speck of the universe was here and not here. No rules, no boundaries, no divides, nothing to contain, define, them in this thing *(things?)* they called the world.

Quinn looked down at the book and it was alive, the letters and illustrations raced around the page like veins of coursing mercury, filigreed and shifting through more dimensions than had existed only a few moments ago, in and out of the paper which now seemed like parchment, like skin, covered in pores that breathed through the spaces, the holes that flowed through the atom, the electron, the proton, the neutron and whatever else existed (or didn't) in the celestial soup.

The song came to an end but the notes, the high, high voice stayed in his head, going round and round, leaving some kind of mark, some electrochemical stain on the cerebral nuclei there. Quinn gave himself up to the hallucinogen now, let it become his reality, his universe, and he knew there was no stopping it, felt a last, sudden thrill before he let go, like breathing deep before jumping into some giant, astral rollercoaster, wondering when the ride was going to come to an end.

He looked at his hand, the pale skin, the pores, the slight film of sweat there, and felt he could jump through, could break through the skin and dive down deep into the matter there, beyond anything they knew, anything they read about in the books, down to the tiniest particle, the tiniest sub-element there was, something that was here and there and everywhere simultaneously, beyond logic, beyond chaos, beyond (and the slow, bored tones of that English voice came back to him, were the last he would hear before the metamorphosis, before he was transformed)

three quarks for Muster Mark

beyond substance, beyond time. Something in the multiverse.

Michael Quinn could feel himself changing, could hear the pulsing of the blood through his veins, the tiny, myriad chatter of his own essence, the particles that made him, linked him through time and space to Herod and Hitler, Samarkand and Arcturus, matter and anti-matter, made him one, made him countless all in the same breath, in the same instant in time, the same time in an instant.

He stood up and felt the solar wind brush against his cheek, felt the sinews, the bones, the pulsing veins and arteries of his physical shell groan and strain as they moved. The room was lit with colour, shades that went beyond the normal spectrum, beyond adjectives, colours that whirled and span and danced in front of him. There was such energy in the world, in the universe, such vibrant, screaming energy he had never known, yet still he could not see far enough, still he could not drill down to the essence, the tiny silver key that unlocked the gates of perception.

The music led him on, hypnotically, like a magnet, through the door into the gloom of the living room, the sounds getting louder and louder in his head, Quinn more and more aware of where the energy, the physical energy in him was now focusing, where it sought release.

She sat on the sofa, silent, motionless, almost in a stupor, almost as if she had been waiting for him. He touched her hair: it crackled underneath his skin, there were flecks of gold in it that had never appeared before, something magical there, something almost holy.

Quinn let his hand run down to her cheek. It felt as if she were on fire. Through his fingertips he felt – no, *received* – the pulse of blood in her veins, the soft brushing of the capillary hairs, the secretions of sweat from her pores, the microscopic chanting of the particles dancing, dancing everywhere, every time.

She didn't even look at him, just let his hand move over her skin, let the long, thin index finger find her lips, and he can feel the grease there, feel it drag his momentum, brush lightly across the creases there, slide inside. The wetness, the softness, the gentle caress of the pores on her tongue, astonish him, he feels the energy in his groin focus now, turn harder, feels her hand there, is unaware of his movement, unaware of how he slips down to kneel by her now, feels her mouth move away from his hand, brush lightly on his neck – there is a foetor, a miasma of her inner odour, drifting up in a cloud of particles from her throat – move down, hard, short fingers, tearing, grasping at his shirt, the front of his jeans.

When she takes him into her mouth, his head arcs back automatically. He stares high into the darkness of the room and lets himself drift beyond the world into some new place where there are no words, only feelings, sensations, revelations.

When it happens, there is no sense of time. Michael Quinn does not know how long he has been screaming, cannot put a name to the sensation that grips his body, his essence, cannot know whether this is pain or ecstasy, the promise of life, a covenant with death.

He looks down to the source, the focus of the energy that pulses hot beneath him. The girl's face looks deathly pale, her eyes are closed, she is taking him still hard from her mouth and there are stars coming into being there, being born, pearly white, a galaxy that flies into the air, soars for the universe, blossoms, then falls to the pitiless grasp of gravity, falls to earth, flecks her hair, her skin, falls like precious drops onto the precise yellow-white ivory of her teeth, sparkles on the cheap golden necklace that hangs over her throat.

There is a sound booming in his ears, a choir of unearthly voices

three quarks for Muster Mark

chanting slowly, atonally, in perfect unison.

He sees the largest pearl form at the corner of her mouth, overlaying the skin, the light glistening from its depths. There is a grim, a sickly sensation in his stomach, like nausea, no, like vertigo, as if he were standing on top of a tall building, the tallest, there is none taller, standing at the very edge and looking down beneath his toes, down into the pearly lake, the pearly sea that sweeps from horizon to horizon, from the beginning of time to the end of it, and beyond. The structure, hidden, flimsy beneath his legs, collapses and Michael Quinn falls through eternity, falls into the pearly white sea, is swallowed by it, engulfed, subsumed, feels its substance, its matter, its particles, looks them in the face, sees them grow larger and larger until there is nothing left except one.

And it has no face, it can have no face, this apparition, gold and white with wings that flutter gently from its back, flutter in the pearly white sky that cannot exist, cannot be real, in this time in any time. One protean essence that stands at the heart, at the soul of creation.

Michael Quinn stares into this shifting thing in front of him, is aware from somewhere of the smell, this humanness in the pearly white fabric around him, knows there is nothing more, nothing smaller, nothing more fundamental, listens to the voice of the thing, quiet and young and compelling

godnotgod

and hears it say, *What the fuck?*

Creation turns to blackness. When he awakes – a second, an hour, a millennium has passed – the girl is nowhere to be seen.

The smile is sticking to his face like a rictus, the rush is over. He walks to the little kitchen, reaches into the drawer, takes out the long cheap knife someone bought at Woolworth's.

This change is permanent. The knowledge sits within him like a leaden thing in his stomach. When he grips the handle he can feel the particles vibrating under the black, plasticised surface, when he peers at the metal he can see into its structure, discern the complex molecular make-up of the alloy that holds it together to create the face of its earthly presence.

He goes to the bathroom and takes a long leak. She has been here before him. He can smell it on the air. In the cloud of human odour, heavy and tangible in the air, he can feel, can *see* the faint, leathery trace of ingested dope. He shakes the drops of piss into the bowl, watches them fall into the water, remembers what preceded them, looks and sees the swirling helical structure of the DNA in the traces of semen that articulate with the pale yellow stream that flows from him, feels no sense of wonder, no awe at these revelations.

Michael Quinn packs the serrated kitchen knife into his jacket, walks out of the door of the Barn and enters a world that is born anew.

It is late morning now in Palo Alto and half a mile away the last-minute Christmas shoppers are starting to work their way down University Avenue.

SIX

Schrödinger's Cat (1)

We should not say that one man's hour is worth another man's
hour, but rather that one man during an hour is worth just as
much as another man during an hour. Time is everything, man
is nothing: he is at the most time's carcass.

KARL MARX

When Hal Jamieson first came north, that dread, slow, frightening
flight from California, he never thought about the name. There had
dimly been some plan, some idea to form a corporation with the
money, look for something to do, hang around the nascent world of
computer programming, pick up some skills and see what happened.

There was enough money there to last two, maybe three years, if
they generated a little income from somewhere along the way. And
that was all that mattered. These were different times, different days,
and if you wanted to rent an office in some nondescript block downtown for three hundred dollars a month, incorporate yourself as the
Schrödinger Cat Company and then tell people you really wrote
software, what the fuck? After a couple of years, the calls from cat
owners looking for pet food started to fall away, the software slowly
began to drift out, first for the early Apple machines, then on to the
first IBM PCs, and gradually, almost unknowingly, Jamieson found
himself rolling down the great and growing mountain of personal
computing, gathering snow all the way.

It wasn't exactly Microsoft but then it wasn't some brief, sparkling
mayfly in the humungous PC explosion either. In 1979, the first full
year they had real products to introduce into the market, the Schrödinger Cat Company had a turnover of \$379,600 and net earnings of
\$5,200 (largely because Jamieson had taken so little out of the company
to live on, had worked selling encyclopaedias door to door at night
to make ends meet, and had used amateur, freelance programmers,

some of them no more than thirteen, working from home, to get the stuff beyond the beta stage and out onto the streets).

Five years later, when Apple launched the first Macintosh, SCC – the name was somehow always shortened now and few could remember, least of all understand, its origins – was first among its rivals to market with a bitmap painting program for the new platform. Mac-Gogh took some time to make it – Jamieson could not believe Apple had fouled his pitch by bundling a free paint program with the machine itself – but within two years most anybody who owned a Mac also owned a copy of MacGogh and a good proportion had paid $249.95 for it. Even Jamieson was puzzled quite why, since there was little you could do with the thing except draw little cartoons that kids loved, but when he looked at what was happening to his bottom line he didn't really care.

In 1987 SCC grossed $34 million, with net earnings of $4.7 million, moved to fancy new offices out in Bellevue and took a listing on Nasdaq. Jamieson and his original shareholders all became millionaires overnight, as, shortly, did anyone who had worked for the company for more than three years and exercised his or her stock options.

And like Topsy, SCC just kept on growing. MacGogh was not Jamieson's idea but it turned out to be the smartest thing SCC ever possessed. At first it was just a plain bitmap paint program – you painted a dot on the screen with a brush, or associated those dots into patterns, later maybe gave it a colour and that was it. But when the Macs began to get more powerful, and they ported the product line to Windows, things started to happen. You didn't just paint dots, you manipulated them. This was digital technology, it described everything not as an analogue series of continuous, contiguous elements, but as a collection of discrete dots, points, pixels, tiny atoms of information. And that meant that these clever kids Jamieson – now president and CEO – kept employing, kids who were as happy with higher maths as they were with programming, electrical engineering or even quantum physics itself, these kids could write algorithms, tools that bent the atoms in the digital make-up of the picture, changed cyan to magenta, solarised a photograph, blurred out smudges, invented a new kind of reality.

In the beginning it was something of a joke. A newspaper artist would use the Mac to marry distorted photographs of a politician with a line art drawing. Cod cartoons, gimmicky ads, they all became the fashion until the art departments got bored with them, moved on to something else, and just accepted the software – now MacGogh Pro Version 7.0, retail price $795 and up – as something that lived in the studio, like a scalpel or a roll of masking tape, something you used when you needed it, without trying to show off too much.

In 1994, when Apple rolled out the PowerMac, ten years after the first little Mac 512 hit the streets, SCC launched a native video manipulation package, VideoGogh Pro, street price $1,500 or so, and all the work-station manufacturers took one look at it and felt deeply sick at heart. It was too late to do the image manipulation work that made Tom Hanks shake hands with Richard Nixon in *Forrest Gump* – Silicon Graphics had won that one – but Jamieson didn't care that much. In a decade SCC had gone from painting a single monochrome dot on a nine-inch monitor to manipulating millions of pixels, in millions of colours, at movie studio resolutions. And even though the amount of information you needed to do this was huge, even though breaking one single continuous tone movie frame into its constituent digital atoms could fill the hard disk of a single conventional PC many times over, suddenly it didn't matter any more. Anybody with five thousand dollars to spare could go out and buy some hardware and software, plug in a high-res VCR, roll the pictures onto the screen and change, improve upon reality. No more voices out of synch, no more hairs in the gate. Now you could drill down to the very photon behind its pixel, talk to it, put it right on a few things, *correct* it.

Spielberg loved it. George Lucas loved it. Most of all, Wall Street loved it. In late 1994 Jamieson went on a buying spree, snapping up the more promising little fish in the graphics world left stranded in the crocodile jaws of falling retail prices and the aftermath of the recession. It gave him a pretty good stranglehold over the professional end of the graphics market – with only Adobe as competition – and, with an eye to the future, he also picked up some Internet publishing packages and networking solutions along the way. He bought low, dodged a couple of public interest investigations by the Justice Department, and either pulled out every cent of wasted overhead from what he acquired or sold the remnants on for a profit. In May 1995 SCC reported net earnings of $124 million on revenues of $837 million. In the space of a year, even without another acquisition, SCC seemed bound to break through the one-billion-dollar revenue mark. It didn't matter that much to Jamieson – what was one dollar either side? –

but to the markets, to the press, to his competitors, the very idea had some kind of magic about it. Becoming a 'billion-dollar' company was some kind of big American milestone that had to be marked. Jamieson thought about it for a while then PX'ed his old Cessna 340 pressurised twin for a brand-new Citation jet, swallowed hard and let himself get talked into basing it on the general aviation lot at Sea-Tac. It cost SCC around $350,000 a year in fuel, parking and maintenance alone, all for no more than two hundred hours in the air, but it kind of went with the image. And Jamieson liked flying there too, liked the confidence the controllers gave you when the weather was turning foul, the way they just eased you onto the ILS and got you down through the shit.

It was a dull December day. The fog had lifted and in its place was a low blanket of pale cloud that seemed to stretch forever. The traffic had been bad. The traffic always seemed to be bad these days as he drove from the rich, green, leafy suburbs of Mercer Island out onto the highway that ran beside the lake, then south to Sea-Tac, past forest and water, past flat, low industrial estates and the sad, jumbled, out-of-town shopping precincts that seemed to mark every near-airport location he'd ever known. His favourite departure was when the wind was coming out of the north, on a clear fine day. That way you rolled up the runway, lifted off the wheels, circled back over the city, appreciating the gorgeous perfection of its location, by the blue waters of the sound, with a world of green and rock and, in the distance, snow rolling out all around them. But this wouldn't be one of those days. All he'd see would be the rain, the moisture, spattering the screen, making the city look like a dull, leaden mass a couple of thousand feet beneath his wheels. This was the way it went if you wanted to fly in these parts. Eight times out of ten you spent most of the way up and the way down just looking at the instruments, because looking out of the window got you nowhere at all. Then every so often, Seattle surprised you, took your breath away, made you think there might be a God out there after all. But if there was, why did he keep this all to himself, so often?

Jamieson parked his Lexus in the GA lot, pulled his flight bag out of the back seat, looked into the mirror. He was short, five six, and beginning to put on a paunch. He wore a Liz Claiborne cashmere sweater, Klein jeans and polished black leather cowboy boots. His head seemed a little too big for his body, and it was never still, turning, twitching on his shoulders as if looking for something, always.

Jamieson pushed open the car door, felt the cool damp air hit him. The cloud ceiling had lifted a little now. Maybe up to six hundred feet or so, enough for an instrument departure. Five minutes of controlled panic on departure, climb to altitude, cut the autopilot into the GPS, slot the new Dylan CD into the portable player he had in his flight case and then relax for a couple of hours. Flying didn't bother him. It was like everything else, the technology made it easier. When he picked up his first private licence ten years ago you did everything by hand, you used slide rules and navigated by eye. Nowadays, now he had his instrument rating and could let others take the strain, you just programmed the entire flight plan into the GPS, flicked in the autopilot, listened out for the occasional waypoint check.

Easy, easy, easy.

Jamieson threw his case onto the flight despatcher's counter and said, 'Hello, Bob.'

The despatcher smiled back. He had thirteen software millionaires on his books and every one was different. Some looked like nerds, some looked like they'd just walked out of the FBI. Hal Jamieson was like none of them. He could have been the lead singer from some seventies rock band who'd gone MOR and started doing regular spots in Vegas. That big round face still looked young, if you didn't go in too close, bronzed and always smiling, those big white teeth flashing at you. His black hair hung down in ringlets, right down to the shoulder, always clean and shiny, always perfectly curled, real rock star stuff, even down to the single gold earring that shone in the bright lights of the despatch office. Jamieson's forehead was starting to do what foreheads do when some men hit forty, starting to crawl further and further up his scalp. But when you blow-dried your hair the right way it didn't show too much, for some people it didn't show at all. If you had women around when Hal Jamieson took out his bright new Citation they'd just fall over him for a ride and there were more than a couple of ribald cracks running down the despatcher's room about what might, or might not, have happened at thirty thousand feet, with the Citation on autopilot and heading east, way out into the empty air high over Spokane.

Sometimes you saw Jamieson in the papers, with his dark, good-looking wife, no family though, you wondered about that. He put money into charities and sports teams, sponsored community things, came across as a real nice society man, caring, not the sort to patronise.

SCC was the first software company in Washington State to adopt a positive employment policy towards gays and ethnic minorities, long before this kind of thing became mandatory.

Just some old hippy, the flight despatcher said to himself. A rich old hippy and if he likes to screw around up there in his Citation, then good luck to him.

Hal Jamieson scribbled out a flight plan, tossed it over the counter and tried to keep smiling. It didn't come easy.

The flight despatcher looked at it, checked the details – some of these millionaire pilots were a little lacking in the administration department on occasion – nodded, then faxed it through to the control room.

Then Jamieson walked outside, back into the cold damp air, stepped over to the Citation, unlocked the door, felt the coldness of the air inside, and started to run through the external pre-flight checks, only half thinking about what he was doing, half wondering about the weather en route. He'd looked at the actuals when he left. It was clear and sunny in San Jose and set to stay that way.

SEVEN

The Eucalyptus Woods

We are always talking about being together, and yet whatever we invent destroys the family, and makes us wild, touchless beasts feeding on technicolor prairies and rivers.

EDWARD DAHLBERG

Rosamund Seymour stepped out of the music store onto University Avenue and began to curse herself on several fronts. The sun was hurting her eyes after the gloom in the store. She had spent too long there, had become lost, absorbed, in the racks and racks of albums, all so cheap, so comprehensive, the rows of sheet music, the bustle, the energy of the place, which swamped her, in a way she found annoying since it was so predictable, it was just the kind of thing she hated about herself, because, she knew deep down, Daniel had already started doing the hating for her.

Even at Christmas, England kept its pace, maintained its decorum, and Cambridge just got busy, not frantic, overheated. Here people just let go and, for a brief period – how long, she wondered, how long had she left them outside telling them she would only be a minute, a Mummy minute, Flora had said quietly as she stared into the window – she had let go of them and then let the store swallow her up. Daniel's tedious academic meeting would be over by five, the Christmas service, two angels supplied from across the Atlantic, was due to start in the chapel an hour later. She looked at the small gold Cartier watch on her wrist, felt the weight of the bag on her shoulder with its albums, its gifts, the camera, and sighed . . . so little time.

And behind her, at the back of the store, Paul Dunsany, his clean long hair flowing onto his shoulders, the faint smile never leaving his face, looking so young, so wide-eyed and artless, checked his cheap watch, caught the attention of Mr Moore, the store owner, at the

51

counter, waited for him to nod, the little moustache and bow tie bobbing in unison, then went behind the counter and picked up his shoulder bag, let himself out the back door, wondered whether he should go home, straight home, or maybe make a diversion, wondered a second more, went to the old bike, kicked it into life, decided to find a burger and a beer at the Oasis, then head for the Barn.

Flora Seymour stared up at her mother, so tall, so tall. The light was funny now, she had been crying and it made the thin pale sun refract, splinter in front of her, made it fracture into strange component colours

three quarks for Muster Mark

as the photons raced and sang through the painful saline moisture of her tears.

'Florrie?'

The street was so flat and long, the buildings so low and innocuous. This was a large town that masqueraded as a small one, big, smart America pretending that it was just a little village, and Rosamund Seymour felt out of place, lost, wished she could be in some big city street, where the wind sent the litter racing along the gutter, and there were crowds, real crowds, not straggles of passers-by who seemed to be wandering from nowhere to nowhere.

She felt the sudden, unmistakable snatch of fear – and saw Daniel's red face, red hair furious in front of her – and a strange sensation in the pit of her stomach, a pain that felt like she was hollow inside. She was a tall, striking woman, large-hipped, matriarchal. She towered over the child, her bright Laura Ashley skirt billowing around the girl's face in a multi-coloured swirl powered by the light breeze that had now built up along the length of the avenue. Flora looked at the colours, red and blue and purple and green, and some she didn't know, had never seen before in her short life, wished they could swallow her, consume her whole, alive, entire, wished there was a world inside them into which she could disappear.

And then the breeze stiffened again, swept the bright, gaudy fabric out of the way and she found herself staring upwards once again, staring at her mother's face. There was fear there too, it was something new, something she should not have been able to recognise, something fired by an unspoken *(unthought?)* exchange between them, the word-less mutual transfer of some vague, misshapen anxiety.

'Where is Miles, Florrie?'

What surprised her, what made Rosamund Seymour even more afraid, was the complete absence of anger in the question. Ordinarily she would have been curt, severe with them, clicked, automatically, into the little lecture about trust and growing older (and left out the part about grown-ups who disappear into music stores for one minute and reappear a quarter of an hour later).

Instead, she was almost pleading.

The little girl was stock-still, silent, the tears now coursing down her face in two thick streams that stood out on her cheeks. Rosamund Seymour blinked. The light seemed too bright, seemed to make the white of her gown blaze in the sun, seemed to make the golden wings, murmuring in the breeze, glow like living things, on fire with their own inner energy.

She bent down, stared Flora in the face, tried to prevent herself crying too, felt the prick of tears at the edge of her eye, leaned over, brushed the moisture from the girl's cheek in two sweeping outward movements with the side of her thumbs (how many times, thought Rosamund Seymour, how many times have I performed this exact movement, this little act that seems to capture the very preciousness of being a mother?).

'Flora,' she said. 'You don't need to be afraid. I'm not cross. Nothing's wrong. We just have to find Miles. You have to tell me where he went.'

And once again Rosamund Seymour watched, slightly in awe, the way the child responded. It was as if there were two children in the same body, one pushing, striving, screaming to be older, so much older, one desperate to return to being two or three, when nothing mattered, that dread word responsibility was never uttered. The remarkable thing was that you could see it in her face, could see the features, so striking, so open, marked, even beautiful, you could see them disappear, become subsumed in the shapeless, amorphous pudginess of the toddler.

The toddler Flora looked up at her, glanced to her left and pointed to the street corner. Rosamund Seymour straightened her back, told herself to be calm, not to be stupid, not to let the girl's nameless, groundless fears infect her, took the child's hand and walked up

University Avenue. The Laura Ashley dress billowed around the angel in the breeze but never quite managed to smother the bright painful white of her gown or the prismatic glow of the gold on her back.

She had good eyesight. The avenue was long and straight and, for an American thoroughfare, narrow. Miles was dressed to stand out. It should have been easy. It should have been so simple. But there was nothing to see. Up and down the long, flat avenue Rosamund Seymour scanned with her perfect vision and all she saw was the afternoon trickle of late shoppers, arms piled high with pre-wrapped gifts in bright wrapping paper, sprouting satin ribbons, perfectly tied bows.

She looked at Flora again.

'Where did he *go*, Flora?'

The girl pouted, the sides of her mouth screwed up in a way she knew so well that she could almost come to hate it.

'No. Don't cry. You're not in trouble. I just want to know. Where did he *go?*'

Flora pointed down a side street, the first turning off to the right after the music store. It was called Petersen, was the width of a village lane back in England, a century, a millennium away, and there was nothing here except a line of low, single-storey offices and homes, one small Chinese restaurant with pictogram characters painted on the window in red. A sweet smell, pungent came out of the front door. She could imagine Miles walking down here, his golden wings billowing in the wind, the tears drying on his face, something like determination beginning to grow in his wheeling, confused mind.

She looked down Petersen, all the way down the long, straight narrow street. The houses and offices disappeared after a block, there was a long stretch of empty scrub, then everything was swallowed up by the woods, dark, grey-green woods, full of nothingness, no buildings, no people.

Rosamund Seymour looked at the woods and started walking. She didn't even notice the tiny hand in hers, didn't notice that it now gripped her and not the other way round.

There should have been someone to ask. There should have been an old couple, straight out of one of those folksy American paintings – those aren't real, Rosamund, some little inner voice taunted, this is real but those aren't – there should have been Ma and Pa walking hand in hand down the road, smiling, thinking about Christmas, thinking about the family gathering around a big wooden table, smiling and laughing, and they would look at her, she would feel the warmth, the humanity in their souls, and they would say yes, I saw him, I saw the little kid with the white robe and the wings, the kid with the funny accent, and we took him in, we gave him milk and cookies and he's there now, he's right in the house, sitting in front of *Sesame Street*, asking us whether Big Bird's a boy or girl and whether Maria, who's so pretty, so really pretty, has a boyfriend or not.

She could almost see them, almost convince herself that if she thought hard enough and long enough, strained with everything that was inside her being, she could create them, make them pop up out of the sidewalk, smile with those ancient, pearly white teeth then make it all right and good and wholesome.

But there was no Ma and Pa. They walked the length of Petersen, along the broad, perfectly laid-out pavement, past the little offices, past the scrubland with the real estate signs and the warnings of future development from the city council, right to the very edge of the woods. There was a smell here and somewhere in the back of her mind she registered what it was – shit and throat sweets – but there was no one to ask. No one except a scruffy black tramp, leaning back against the peeling bark of a tall, thin tree, a shopping cart by his side, surrounded by empty cans and bottles and piles of old paper. She thought to ask, she would have asked, but as soon as she got close, she could hear something coming from him, some low, deep grumble that was so inane, so full of an animal craziness

rassenfrassenrassenfrassenrassenfrassenrassenfrassen

that she didn't dare go any nearer.

The woods were dark and seemed to stretch forever. The leaves of the tall trees so high above them seemed to blot out the late-afternoon sun completely, making the forest bed a black and unwelcoming carpet of shadow. When she stepped into the blackness, hardly noticing the small, sweating hand entombed in her own, even the breeze disappeared, there was nothing now but the darkness, the stillness, the stench, and the dappled shafts of light that flitted in front of her on the rare moments they broke through the leafy canopy above.

There were woods back home where she took the children for walks, away from the tense, silent atmosphere of the house, to a place where they walked for miles, where they listened to the birds, looked for mushrooms, raced through blankets of golden leaves each autumn, searching for sweet chestnuts to roast in the huge, warm kitchen Aga and fill the house with their heavenly scent. But these were not good woods. There was no bird sound. There was nothing wholesome in the strong, rank aroma that drifted on the still afternoon air.

It was like being drawn to something, being led, invisibly, unknowing. Within seconds, she was inside the wood, enclosed by it, hardly knew how she got there, hardly knew whether she was on a path, set certain between the thin, pale towering trunks, or had strayed into the spent earth that was littered with dead branches, dry, rustling leaves, and dark, seedy piles of trash, old clothes and worse things, things that she tried not to look at, tried not to acknowledge.

There was a flash in the dappled light in front of them, a flash of gold and she knew, before she had named the shapes in her head, before she had had a chance to try to think, what it was. Flora saw too and she was whimpering, a low, slow steady noise, metronomic and pulsing, the kind of thing Rosamund Seymour associated with mental hospitals and crazy people and that world beyond worlds where madness lived, knocking on the walls trying to escape.

What remained of the wings lay still and broken on the ground, shattered by some nameless force, the perfect gold of the feathers now a confused snarl of deep burnished colour in the dim light of the wood. Their shape – like a teardrop she thought, why had she not noticed that before, how much they resembled a teardrop? – was imprinted on the woodland floor, like a stencil over the leaves and garbage and shit that surrounded them, innocence overlaying decay.

She did not want to look further but there are some things that happen automatically, some actions that run to some hidden, unwritten rule that you couldn't dodge, however hard you tried, however hard something inside shouted and screamed at you not to look, to turn around, call the police, do anything but go there, open your eyes and *see*.

No, said Flora to herself (for she had already seen), no it was not me, I did not do this, I am not responsible.

Rosamund Seymour lifted her eyes and looked around her, looked at the woodland floor beyond their immediate presence, the trees, the shining, peeling bark, into the middle distance and beyond, but there was nothing, no sign of a small, five-year-old boy wearing the white robe of an angel, no wings now, flightless, pinned to the ground by gravity, the face, the radiance, the holiness of an angel.

No sign, and for a moment this was a relief, and then her eyes caught it, caught the small, pale shape attached to the peeling bark of the tree, almost invisible in the gloom, almost camouflaged against the eucalyptus.

She dragged Flora there, unconscious of her presence, her hand clenching and clenching the tiny fist it contained until the girl screamed, felt the punishment, the weight, the anger of the world begin to fall upon her.

The hand, the tiny pale hand, covered in dirt, its fingernails grimy, mud making black crescents of the tips, was still and waxy. It had been severed at the wrist, they could see the tendons, pearly white and yellow in the caking red gore of the flesh which hung down loose and fibrous, not a clean cut this, not the slice of a butcher's knife, but something altogether more cruel, more savage.

The palm was pinned to the bark. Through the back of the hand, a rusty nail (which Lieutenant Tom Cordobes of the Palo Alto police force later finds is a cast-off from the CalTrain track) had been hammered through the flesh into the soft, fragrant wood. There was little blood around the wound. It looked, she thought, like the clean, clinical lesion you might see in church, in some peaceful, cheating image of the crucifixion, little blood, little pain, little agony.

Rosamund Seymour stared at the five small fingers, outstretched on the bark, slightly bent, slightly curled, as if in surprise, turned her back on the tree, on the wood, walked out, out into the sunlight, clutching her daughter by her hand, not knowing she was there, not knowing anything, merely feeling the blackness swim in her mind, letting it overwhelm her thoughts until there was nothing there, nothing at all.

Except the sound, the noise, and that seemed to come from somewhere else, this constant, ear-splitting keening inside her head.

The cop car was there three minutes after the first call but it was an hour before anyone could understand what she had to tell, and another hour before they found what there was to find in the woods.

By 8 pm on Christmas Eve 1975 the TV crews were starting to arrive in Palo Alto and all holiday police leave had been cancelled. The search for Miles Seymour had begun.

EIGHT

Chimes in the Fog

The difference between false memories and true ones is the same as for jewels: it is always the false ones that look the most real, the most brilliant.   SALVADOR DALI

Tom Cordobes was sitting in his ancient Buick by a tangle of low, smoke-coloured warehouses close to the end of runway 17 at Seattle-Tacoma international airport, watching the grey gloom begin to fall steadily from the sky and mark the end of the damp, fog-filled afternoon, thinking about the past two decades, wondering where they'd gone.

The cheap Japanese airband receiver he'd taken out of the trunk was now chattering and crackling away in the passenger seat, most of the noise coming from the diminishing movements of scheduled traffic – New York, Anchorage, San Francisco, LA, even a flight in from London – feeling their way through the beacons and networks of invisible aerial highways that comprised the instrument landing procedures for the Sea-Tac zone.

Twenty years is a long time, and Tom Cordobes remembered events by their nature – their colour, their sound, their smell – not by some exact date on the calendar. And these were a big twenty years, twenty years that managed to embrace a couple of divorces, getting busted out of the cops, trying to run your own business, which meant walking that narrow line called the right side of the law, but not walking it so casually you never got to earn a living. Twenty years ago Tom Cordobes was just getting through his first divorce. He hated the idea of *not* working over Christmas. He wanted something to keep him out there, shuffling the streets, thinking about anything except the deep, open, empty space back home, on the other side of the bed. And so, insidiously, without his even noticing, the days had become just like any other time, and if there was something different out there for the rest of the world – choirs and kids carolling and people reeling out of their offices at five in the afternoon drunk as skunks and convinced they could still drive home, no problem – then that was just part of the pattern on the gaudy fabric that made up the face of the world. Not something that affected, controlled him.

The memory had come back unbidden and it made him feel cold, made him feel freezing in the old car, in the nascent, northern dark. A tiny white hand, pale, marked with dirt, nailed to the peeling bark of a tree in a lonely, fetid forest. The image deep within his head was radiant. Almost beautiful. And then from somewhere else, somewhere Tom Cordobes couldn't even begin to figure, another flash of recall: as he was looking at this sad little piece of a human child there was, in the middle distance to his right (and he was even sure of this, it *was* to his right), a huge, mechanical rumbling and screeching of metal on metal, the blast of a deep, powerful whistle, movement, slow but certain, passing, passing, passing. Then, from somewhere else, somewhere full of pain and humiliation that seemed a lifetime away, the sound of a bell, chiming long and loud through the fog.

Triggers. Cordobes had thought about the case from time to time over the years. Thought about it even more when the English girl came up with the job and the name Michael Quinn came back into his life once more. But there was a difference between *thinking* and *remembering*. There was a difference between the facts that lived inside his head, like pieces of paper inside a filing cabinet, ready to be taken out, inspected, put back where they belonged, and the real stuff. The images, the sounds, the smells of that time that began close to the dying days of 1975 and came to such an abrupt, such a public end when 1976 was scarcely born.

The trigger came and the memory that shot out when it did left Tom Cordobes gripping the scarred steering wheel of the ten-year-old Buick so tight the blood drained from his hands. It began, not on some day like any other, it began right now, on Christmas Eve, twenty years ago, almost to the minute. And for a moment, the distance between now and then, between being and not being, seemed to disappear, seemed to dissolve into nothing but some shambling, formless chaos, a mess of lives and accidents and happenings that made no sense at all.

Cordobes retained the instincts of a cop. He didn't like to think outside the boundaries, he didn't like to roam out of the loop. You got somewhere, in an investigation, in *life*, by knowing what you are, what you can do, and you stuck with it. No good dreaming of things that never come to pass, particularly dreaming those dreams in a mobile home in Milpitas. You lived in the space you knew and let the rest of the shit roll over you.

And most of the time it worked. Most of the time.

Cordobes shook his head as if to clear it, swore mildly under his breath, reached over for the airband radio and turned up the volume. Turn it up loud enough, he thought, and all the mess, all that big swirling cloud of stuff, would just roll back into the distance, like fog dispersing under a breath of wind.

The radio crackled halfway through a call. '. . . inbound from San Jose estimating Sierra One in five and we'd appreciate a vector straight onto the ILS if you guys have the time, sir.'

His face flared instantly, Tom Cordobes slammed both his big hands straight down on the wheel so hard it bounced, and yelled, 'Fuck!'

He had been sitting on the periphery of the field, listening to the radio, for three hours solid and the one moment the bastard came was the moment his head was somewhere else.

The radio was silent. Cordobes kept his mouth shut, didn't even breathe to make sure he got every word. Eventually the controller, sounding bored and more than a little tired, came back on the air. 'Say again callsign traffic inbound from San Jose. We had two of you guys calling at once there.'

Cordobes immediately reached for the pen and notepad on the passenger seat, found himself straining to hear every sound that came out of the radio.

'Citation November Nine Nine Two Five Sierra Whisky, currently at level . . .'

He scribbled the registration number down on his pad, closed his eyes and felt a sudden rush of relief. It had been a long shot, that sudden burst of memory had nearly cost him the game, but at least he was beginning to get somewhere. Maybe . . .

Five hours earlier, as half the nation's media had parked themselves outside the gates of the Obispo pen, an armoured truck had driven out, turned straight for the freeway and headed for San Francisco international airport. Behind the dark, tinted windows sat two prison officers and an unemployed city actor trying to eke out his normal wages as a barman serving the thirsty downtown financiers from behind the counter of the Occidental Grill. It was a simple deception. Cordobes could see it all happening in his head, could watch the familiar landscapes that lived around him, like wallpaper stuck to the wall of an invalid's bedroom, provide the backdrop to the deceit. From Obispo, the truck drove along the flat, arid land of the Valley to San Francisco airport where the actor, who bore a passing resemblance to the last-known picture of Michael Quinn which was snatched inside Obispo ten years previously, was smuggled into a waiting Learjet. The media got enough footage to make some minor mystery headlines on that night's news and went home, if not quite happy, a little sated. And elsewhere, the real game began in earnest.

When the media train had snaked its way onto the freeway to follow the decoy, a Bell Jet Ranger helicopter had flown into the helipad at the rear of Obispo, two private detectives in dark shiny sunglasses and dark shiny suits managing to bulk out most of the three seats in the rear. The prison governor, who had mixed feelings about the whole thing (he had wanted Quinn out of Obispo as soon as possible but hoped it would be in a box), reluctantly watched as the release forms were signed, Quinn smiled at the credentials of the two goons who had come to meet him, and the Jet Ranger had kicked up a big cloud of pale brown dust, then leapt into the sky in a roar of turbine fumes.

It had taken ten minutes to get Quinn out of his cell and into the helicopter. All the usual release procedures – offers of counselling, forwarding address details, financial status check – had been waived on the back of some order from the prison department in Sacramento. Some of the prison people said the assholes in Justice were probably crapping themselves Quinn was going to sue the living shit out of them so they were just trying to make it easy. Some of them said there was more to it than that, there was political pressure, and when that word *political* got used behind the walls of Obispo you got two reactions: intense hatred, intense fear.

Whatever, Quinn was gone. And in the ten minutes it had taken him to clear the prison, one of the officers had stopped by with the chopper pilot, given him a cigarette, said nothing much of moment, just talked about the weather and how, one day, it would be real nice if he could afford to take his wife on a helicopter ride somewhere, maybe over the city, seeing the Golden Gate from a thousand feet and going, 'Wow, wow, wow.'

'You do that kind of thing?' he'd asked the pilot and the head behind the Ray-Bans had just shook slowly.

'Nah,' it drawled. 'We just do commercial traffic outta San Jose. Taking these PC company jerks places they can't stand going in a stretched limo 'cos the traffic's too bad.'

'Yeah,' said the prison guy. 'Guess you're going back there.'

And without thinking the big head behind the Ray-Bans nodded. The pilot remembered what the despatcher had said when he sent him out on the job, cursed himself silently, then thought, fuck it, they want a secret agent to do this shit, they should get a fucking secret agent.

He stared at the prison guy and said, 'Those rotors gonna be going again real soon, sir. I advise you to stand well clear.'

And the prison guy smiled, went back into Obispo, found the mobile cellphone in his private locker, went into the end trap in the staff restrooms, phoned Tom Cordobes on his own mobile in Seattle.

'He's flying outta San Jose, Tom. Forget any shit you see on the TV. It's San Jose he's going to.'

Cordobes tried to pump him for more but the prison guy was getting tired of it, and the more he heard about what might or might not be happening in Sacramento the more he wished he hadn't done the old cop a favour at all.

'Gimme a break, Tom. I told you it's Washington State somewhere, I told you it's San Jose. That is all I'm gonna tell you 'cos it's all I *can* tell you.'

And then he pressed the off button on the mobile phone.

Cordobes had thought about it for a while, then driven up to Sea-Tac, taken the radio transmitter out of the glove compartment, and sat there listening for some private traffic coming in from the south. It had to be private. No way would someone go to this sort of trouble and pop the media's most wanted man on some scheduled flight. Even if there was a scheduled flight worth speaking of out of San Jose. And it had to be Sea-Tac. That big Pacific low was all over Washington State by now and one short call to the Sea-Tac tower established that it was the only airport north of Portland still open now that Boeing Field had closed its doors for the holiday.

He listened to the exchanges between the tower and the inbound traffic. They might as well have been in Chinese for all he could understand them. But he knew enough to realise that a Citation would be headed for the GA terminal round the back of the airport. Tom

Cordobes turned the ignition on the old Buick, heard the engine cough hesitantly, found himself praying the cold and damp and fog wouldn't work its way into the points and plugs and the distributor, so used to the dry, Milpitas air, and just shock them to death when he needed them most. The car hacked into life and he drove slowly round the perimeter road, through the thickening fog, towards the low GA building that looked a little like an army bunker decorated with stripes of fluorescent lighting. Tom Cordobes realised, as he wound his way through the fog, that there was something in this place, something in this time, that he just plain hated, maybe its northernness, the cold, wet atmosphere. Maybe something else altogether that he couldn't quite put his finger on right then.

Cordobes turned off the engine, waited in the parking lot, listened to the radio some more, made out the aircraft on its final approach to land, then, after touchdown, listened to it getting instructions for the right taxiway. It amazed him anything could get down from the sky at all in those conditions. After ten minutes of taxiing, the Citation parked close to the GA building. Cordobes stayed in the car. He didn't want to be obvious. He could see the lights of the plane beyond the wire, hear its engines dying down with a whine.

Fifteen minutes later, framed in the piercing white lights of the doorway, the tall, lean figure of Michael Quinn – it *was* Quinn, Cordobes knew it straight away, and he was amazed to find something walking down his spine when he saw him – paused briefly for a moment, then walked out into the night. Three figures followed – two big, bulking guys, guys with a shape, with an aura Cordobes recognised even in the dark. Then a shorter, slighter man, his long hair billowing back in the breeze, face too distant to try to catch.

The two big guys walked in front of Quinn and he followed them to a big four-by-four Shogun in the corner of the parking lot. The little guy said something to them and climbed into what looked like a Lexus nearby. It all happened so quickly. Cordobes saw puffs of exhaust fumes, red and white lights on the tailgates. And then they were moving, fast, so fast, out of the lot.

He switched the key on the Buick. It hacked, and hacked again, trying to catch fire. He gave it a good five seconds and nothing happened.

'I do not fucking believe this. I do not fucking believe this,' Tom Cordobes said flatly. He turned the key again, listened to the battery start to complain, start to wind down a little, listened to the ignition choking on the damp night air. The red lights were pulling away out of the exit now, disappearing fast into the fog.

Cordobes leapt out of the car, opened up the trunk, found an old can of WD–40, yanked up the hood and sprayed it every place he could think of. Then he slammed the hood down, climbed back into the car, threw the can into the floor well of the passenger seat and turned the key again, hearing the battery start to fail now, hearing it yawn itself slowly to death.

The engine finally kicked in on the fourth attempt. By the time Tom Cordobes pulled out into the main exit road there was nothing to see except the grey swirling gloom that was beginning to shroud the world, the billowing, opaque nothingness that rolled in relentlessly from the sea.

NINE

In the Rose Garden

What *do* girls do who haven't any mothers to help them
through their troubles?   LOUISA MAY ALCOTT,
                                                Little Women

Bring in the bottled lightning, a clean tumbler, and a corkscrew.
                                       CHARLES DICKENS,
                                          Nicholas Nickleby

When the telephone rang it was six in the evening in Seattle and she
was asleep, dreaming the same dream over and over again, of her
mother's funeral, the cold November day in north London, no words,
no thoughts, nothing running through her head except the certainty
that this burial, this committal to the ground, was a link that ran
through her straight into the future, and somehow shaped her life.
Something that gave her lonely existence some form, some direction,
perhaps even some hope.

Her mother had died in the sanatorium which, for most of Joni
Lascelles' life, had been her home, the place for those uncomfortable,
increasingly infrequent visits, where it was impossible to do much but
talk, try to smile, attempt to offer some small piece of human warmth
across the huge, aching gulf that separated them. Over the years, her
condition had eased a little. As her hair turned grey, as the lines appeared
on a face that still seemed young, unspoilt by the world, she had become
more calm, less prone to violent outbursts, to sudden, unpredictable
silences. Close to the end, they could even talk a little. Not about themselves, not about the family. These things were too close, touched too
many raw nerves. So instead they spoke about the weather, the flowers
in the gardens, the small, quiet kindnesses of the nurses. And how Joni
dressed, how her job, which seemed so important – the law always
seemed important – just kept getting better and better.

To her, it seemed mundane, seemed almost a waste to spend the days pushing papers around a desk, but her mother found the idea of a daughter in the law, a daughter involved in property, so fascinating. She knew, from the way the nurses spoke, that she was, towards the end, the primary source of conversation. That, on the rare occasions she spoke at anything approaching length, her mother bored everyone else in the hospital to tears with her small achievements, her career, her prospects.

Only once did the mask drop a little, and that was six months before the end, when the greyness was closing in on her, making her fade visibly in the daylight until there was nothing there except a dry husk of a human being, waiting to disappear from the world. They were in the garden, the big, well-kept garden, and it was May, a warm day that was a prelude to an unexpectedly hot summer. The roses were out early. They stood, in large, carefully-tended, circular beds, a slow-moving curtain of yellow and pink and red, filling the air with scent, so strong it was almost overwhelming. She had sat by her mother's side, on a plain, slatted wooden bench with a nameplate, 'Given in gratitude . . .', on the back, and they had talked intermittently, with some unspoken discomfort between them. It was not a good day. The tiredness, the wayward look in her eyes, was back, and there was nothing, no medication, no words, that could stop it. It was the kind of day when Joni didn't dare look at her watch for fear of provoking an outburst, a flood of self-pity. It was the kind of day when she wanted to look at her watch more than anything.

So she had talked about the flowers, about the day, the bright, sunny day, anything she could think of, except herself. And her mother had listened, watching, not speaking, watching with a cold, wary eye, a look that Joni recognised and feared, knowing where it might lead. It was a one-way conversation. It went nowhere and, inevitably, it petered out, dried into nothing. So she sat, waited for her mother to respond, said nothing, smiled, a thin, patient smile that was the best she could manage.

'You never . . .' she said eventually, staring into the sea of waving roses. 'You never *ever* mention a man.'

Joni Lascelles closed her eyes and wished she was somewhere, any-where else. On the breeze she could hear the big red London buses groaning through the traffic on the High Road. There was the sound of a train somewhere in the distance. A blackbird screeched, and from the hospital building behind there was the low rumble of voices, those quiet broken voices she had come to associate with the sad, shattered people who lived here.

'Why do you ask?' she said. 'Does it matter?'

She opened her eyes and stared into her mother's face. There was a look there, a look that happened only rarely but that was enough. It was so cold, so chill. So *crazy*. And what frightened her most was the thought that she might be staring into a mirror. That what she saw was her own self, not so many years hence, trapped in the dry husk of a life spent wrestling some nameless, writhing demon in the depths of her head.

'We are *expected*. You know that. We are *expected* to have a man. I was married at your age. And you never mention anyone. *Never.*'

So what do you say, she wondered. Sometimes it was hard to put a name to them, they flitted in and out so quickly. One week, two. Some brief, speeded-up passion that fizzled out as quickly as it flared. Which would her mother prefer? The men who flew through her life, brief, easy lovers, expecting nothing, giving little in return. Or the other kind – there *were* only two kinds, she often thought. The ones who wandered through her life, her bedroom, like mayflies. And those who sought that strange thing they called 'commitment' and then drifted away when they found she was unable to return the urgent, quick need that drove them, unable to see there was much to all of this but the tangle of bodies, lying skin to skin, in a dimly lit bed.

'I know what you're looking for,' she said, and there was something hard and cruel like triumph in her voice, in her face. 'You're looking for *goodness*. You're looking to bury yourself in someone and forget you're alive.'

Briefly, she could have hated her. Briefly, she could have let the mask of sympathy drop and say what she felt: the resentment for this strange childhood, this strange, solitary world that surrounded her for as long as she could remember. But this was her mother, and she was dying, she did not need the doctors to tell her that. It was written all over the old-young face, in the lines, in the desiccated skin, in the greyness. This was her mother and she was being eaten by death. She was allowed her tempers, allowed her cruelties, even when they made the target so accurately, and Joni knew, knew all along, that she relished the pain they caused.

'One day,' she said, and stood up, stared into the sea of flowers, let

67

her eyes grow liquid and drift out of focus until they saw nothing but the colours, and she heard nothing but the humming of bees and the steady drone of traffic from beyond the garden walls.

Six months later her mother was dead, a casket disappearing behind a wall, a tiny monument in a municipal repository for dust. But not dead in her memory. When the telephone rang, she was alive, she was staring back at her from the rose-coloured, perfumed depths of a recurring dream in which the word goodness rang round and round, ironically, sounding like crazy laughter trapped inside a tin can.

The telephone rang and she did not know where she was. Did not know this shabby bedroom, did not recognise the dull, dead light, falling through the window, or the sounds of traffic, and distant fog-horns beyond.

She sat upright and reached for the phone, only realising where she was, what she was doing as she answered the call.

'Hello,' she said, and tried to remember the time of day, knowing her body could give her no clue.

'Dear Joni,' said a disembodied voice down the line, a cracked, old voice, the colour of walnuts.

'Uncle Simon.'

She felt like a girl still when she spoke to him. She always felt like a girl.

'They have dealt with the estate, my dear. I thought I'd better call. Your office gave me the number. Transatlantic business. My, we *are* doing well.'

And, just as always, she did not know which way to take him, whether there really was congratulation, perhaps even pride, in the voice, or something infinitely darker, infinitely more cynical.

'It was work. I had to come. I explained that to you when you called.'

'Yes, yes, it doesn't matter.'

Her head was clearing. She was able to look at her watch, to recognise the time, and, with a little effort, could start trying to fool her body into thinking it was right.

'You didn't need to call. Really.'

'How right you are. But I thought it best. We are family after all.'

She waited for him to go on. There was a little game here. He liked it. She could feel his enjoyment.

'But why tantalise you? She was intestate, of course. People in mental

68

homes can't make wills, not ones that mean anything in the eyes of the law. I sometimes wondered if she really was as mad as she made out, you know. Or whether she just didn't want to leave, to face the idea of our world. Perhaps you did too.'

'I don't want to hear this,' she said. 'You should not be saying these things.'

'No. Perhaps not. Ill of the dead and all that stuff. Anyway, the upshot is she was intestate and, by the time the nursing bills are cleared, you stand to inherit a few thousand. Five. Possibly seven. You have to wait for the solicitor to do his sums. And a few possessions too, though if you take my advice you'll ask for them to go to one of the charities. Nothing there worth keeping.'

'They can store them,' she said. 'They can keep them for me until I come back. Then I'll decide.'

She could see the sour little expression on his face at the other end of the line, five thousand miles away, in a thirties semi in the dull south London suburb where he made his solitary home. It was now two in the morning back home, she could hear the jangling sound of brandy in his voice, and she wondered what really drove him to make the call: mischief, loneliness, boredom, or a mixture of all three.

'Very well. And when *will* you be home?'

When I want, she said to herself. When I damn well feel like it.

'After Christmas, some time. When the work's done here.'

'Good,' he said. She could feel the question, waiting to come down the line, feel him judging how to say it.

'And are you *enjoying* yourself?'

'This is work,' she said, straight away. 'The timing may be awkward but that happens to be how things are. I don't recall there being many things to keep me at home. I don't recall any invitations. Do you?'

'Such a family,' he said, and there may have been a touch of regret there, it was hard for her to judge. 'Where did we go wrong?'

'I have to go,' she lied. 'Things don't grind to a halt here the way they do in England.'

'Oh, the American work ethic. Please spare me. I've heard enough about it from them to last a lifetime. I don't need any more. Well. Merry Christmas then, Joni.'

He was doing his best. He was trying.

'Merry Christmas, Uncle Simon.'

'And a happy New Year.'

She paused and said, 'Yes.' Then heard the phone go dead, looked at the room, the small, cramped room, that seemed to belong to another age, twenty, thirty, forty years past. With a suddenness that she recognised, that was now so familiar, she longed to be out of it, longed to be walking, moving, anywhere, her head down into the slow damp air, arms, legs, moving rhythmically, not stopping.

She went into the bathroom, showered quickly, threw on a new set of clothes, looked at herself in the mirror, the shock of blonde hair so wild, the face that she never liked to look at too closely. Then walked out of the hotel, out into the street, and disappeared into the slow-moving crowds strolling along the sidewalk.

TEN

Louise Gostelow

Love and sex can go together and sex and unlove can go together and love and unsex can go together. But personal love and personal sex is bad.
ANDY WARHOL

Louise Gostelow looked across the main room of the Barn, unsmiling, lit a Camel, breathed deep on the dark, intoxicating smoke, and thought she might drown in her own boredom. There was no one in the place except the stupid hippy girl who sat doped up on the sofa, dead to the world. Nothing travelled between Mouse and Louise Gostelow. It was as if they had been born on different planets.

There had been Gostelows in San Francisco since the mid-nineteenth century. They bought and they sold – land, grain, stocks, shipping, mortgages, insurance, anything they could lay their hands on. And they sold it well. By the turn of the century, they had progressed from being an important Californian family into being a dynasty. They had holdings in railroads and shipping lines, newspapers and, as the century wore on, film studios, radio, then TV stations. And like all dynasties, they knew how to behave, were aware of their status in the fast-swimming waters of Californian society. They married the best people, usually in St Peter and St Paul down the hill from the Filbert Street mansion, and they gave birth to the best children who attended the best schools and colleges, before starting the endless cycle again. And died too. She didn't forget that part. She couldn't because sometimes, when she was in St Peter and St Paul looking at all the flowers and the sad, resigned faces of the line in there, sometimes it was hard to remember: was this a marriage or a funeral? Was there a difference, when you got down to it in the end? Louise Gostelow just didn't know, and hated the idea that one day she was going to find out.

Sometimes the line faltered, sometimes it was tough for someone to keep up the family flag. But when that happened you always closed the gap. No Gostelow ever went broke (but more than a few got bailed out, then found a nice, lazy board seat somewhere else). No Gostelow ever hit the sauce and let the side down in public (but the medical files in private wards of West Coast sanatoriums told a different story). No Gostelow ever divorced, this being a good Roman Catholic family. The males of the line, and a few females too, could put the Kennedys to shame when it came to screwing around. But they handled it all better than a bunch of East Coast Irish upstarts (the Gostelows began in England, in the flat, green countryside of East Anglia, and if they knew their name just happened to be an anglicised version of the Irish gypsy surname Costello they never let it show). These things didn't end in the divorce courts. They just rolled on quietly, discreetly, and usually without issue, since the Gostelows' brand of Catholicism also embraced an enlightened, if somewhat unorthodox, attitude towards birth control.

Louise Gostelow was one of the breed. If you looked at some of the pictures of Gostelow women going back to the late nineteenth century that now hung in her parents' Telegraph Hill mansion you could see the same features on the young faces from nearly a century ago. Her hair was jet black and straight, cut now in a modern, angular Quant bob (none of this hippy chick stuff), close into her neck. Her skin was a light-olive colour, almost Mediterranean. The Gostelows never brought forth an English rose, not even when they imported some fair-haired bloodstock into the line. She was short, no more than five foot four, and there was already a hint of slight heaviness to her figure from the waist down, something she inherited, something she cursed, since it meant that the diets and the health farms just spread out for her in the future, like marriage, like kids, like the routine she'd seen eat up her own parents, and still they probably wouldn't work. But in a sense that didn't matter. Louise Gostelow's most astonishing feature, the feature that turned heads in rooms, just like it said in the books, was her face. She was a classically beautiful woman, beautiful in an old way that you didn't see in 1975, darkly beautiful, with full, curved lips (rarely without lipstick, and that bucked the trend too), and eyes that flashed, amused, teasing, almost constantly. She had no women friends to speak of. Women mistrusted Louise Gostelow, felt something akin to fear about her unashamed sexuality, the naked interest with which she could approach men, speak to them, leave them entranced, aroused, then walk away and make them wonder whether it was all really just a game. Whether she was just the playful society virgin she made out or something darker, something more exciting.

More than a few knew the answer. In the previous six months, since her father had told her who she was going to marry – some quiet boring kid of the Callaghans who was destined for a lifetime career in stockbroking – Louise Gostelow had been trying to fill the space that remained of her single life with every experience she could manufacture. It was one of the reasons she had put up the money for a share in the Barn. The dope soon bored her. The company bored her (once she'd tried it). But this was a place where she could screw the men she wanted to screw, with no prying eyes (she chose her times carefully), and no recriminations afterwards. Sometimes (most times, if she was being honest with herself) she didn't really enjoy it. But that didn't matter. There was a big alarm clock hanging over the head of Louise Gostelow and she could hear the tick-tock going day and night.

That Christmas Eve, Paul Dunsany rolled his ancient Triumph 350 bike down the drive, cut the engine, flipped the prop into the drying mud then walked into the Barn. He could just make out the Christmas lights way off in University Avenue, red, yellow and green against the pale grey of the night sky. On El Camino, the traffic drummed along at a steady pace, a line of cars throwing giant torch beams back and forwards at each other. You could feel something was happening. The world was winding down, just a little, just for a day or so. And it was waiting, knowing that nothing was really going to happen here, in this flat, neatly ordered town of academic suburbia, with its row upon row of timbered single-storey houses, with their wreaths on the door, and fairy lights showing through the living-room window. You didn't expect anything to happen, you just waited in expectation, and then sighed when the holiday was over and the real world came back to claim your waking hours.

Inside, Louise and Mouse sat in silence on opposite sides of the room, Mouse hunched on the sofa, dead to the world, Louise seated, relaxed, in an ancient wooden chair, looking like she was sitting out a conversation at a cocktail party. She wore jeans – they didn't really suit her figure – and a light-coloured sweater. Her hair shone in the dim light of the room and Dunsany could feel her eyes following him

73

as he walked over to the seat next to her, picked up the battered house guitar – a Harmony Sovereign that had seen better days – and automatically began to finger an old James Taylor instrumental, a jazzed-up version of 'Greensleeves'.

'Hi,' he said, and the olive eyes glittered back at him. She was drinking, he could smell the whisky in the glass from where he sat. He didn't much mind. When he thought about it, and he tried not to since it didn't really lead anywhere, Dunsany knew that Louise Gostelow was the only reason he still came back to the Barn. The dope was OK but most of the time it bored him and even with his salary from the part-time job at the music shop it was hard to afford. Dunsany may have made the grade to get into Stanford but even with the scholarship fees it was hard going. One lone, single parent, way south in Santa Monica could not afford to keep him in Afghan Gold. So he just turned up when he thought she might be there, sometimes driving past to see if her little red MG sports car was outside, then driving on if it wasn't. Paul Dunsany fell into the naive category among her admirers; as far as he knew she was just one beautiful society girl with a society boyfriend back in the city waiting for the marriage banns to be read and he tried as best he could to stop himself dreaming it could be any other way.

She put the glass down and listened to the guitar notes floating around the room. Louise Gostelow found it hard to make Dunsany out. He didn't fit in the Barn. He had no vices, no dark, spoiled parts that needed to be indulged now and again, while there was room, while there was space, to let them roam free. She could feel the way his eyes followed her around as she walked, as she breathed. She knew enough to understand the unspoken words that filled the empty spaces in his conversation. And he was good-looking too, hair a little too long, but with an open, round, honest face, the sort of face that went through life trusting too much and getting hurt along the way.

'You play the guitar really nicely, Paul,' she said eventually.

He kept his head down over the instrument and said thanks.

'Is that what you're going to do? When you leave college? Forget about electronics, all that shit we get thrown at us all day long, go play guitar?'

He plucked the metal strings in a neat, closing dominant chord (Paul Dunsany could read no notes, he just felt his way into the sounds), and thought about it.

74

'I dunno.'

'You *don't know?*'

He couldn't work out whether he was flattered or scared by her questions.

'Maybe.'

'Two sorts of people in life, Paul. Passengers and drivers. You got to make the choice.'

'Maybe some of us don't have a choice,' he said, and immediately regretted it.

'No,' she answered, straight away. 'Maybe some of us have more choice than others. But we all have *some* choice.'

'About everything? *Everything?*'

He caught the sadness in her face and wished he hadn't made it appear there. She laughed, a dry noise without much humour.

'Point taken.'

The glass was empty. She wondered how much whisky she had drunk over the last hour and found she couldn't even begin to guess. It tasted cold and metallic at the back of her mouth.

'You still got that old bike?' she asked.

'Yeah.'

'You know something. I've been in more Rolls-Royces and Mercedes than I can remember but not once, not *once*, have I been on a bike.'

He was genuinely astonished. 'You don't say?'

She waited and waited.

'Paul,' she said in the end.

He was fingering the strings of the guitar again, then he looked at her. She could see some adolescent redness in his cheeks.

'When a woman makes a comment like that, you're supposed to say, "Really, well why don't we go for a ride right now?"'

Paul Dunsany blushed then smiled and said, 'Really, why don't we go for a ride right now?'

Her face lit up and he wondered if this sudden, lovely transformation was real or something you just got taught when you grew up rich. Then realised he didn't care. There was something stirring inside of him, something exciting and he didn't dare hope what.

'I got an ulterior motive,' she said.

He just grinned.

'Don't get this wrong, Paul. I just drank the best part of a bottle of Jack Daniel's. My parents have gone down to Catalina for the holiday so they can't come out and pick me up. Would you be a real darling and drive me back to Telegraph Hill on your little machine?'

'No problem,' he said, after a moment's pause, and already he was wondering where this was going, where this would lead, already some hidden little hope generator inside him was stoking up the fire of his expectations, which were more than physical, that went without saying, that was implicit in everything he thought.

'As fast as it will possibly go?'

He shrugged a little. 'As fast as makes sense. I like to stay alive.'

She picked up a little leather bag, pulled out a pack of Camels and lit one.

'God, Paul. You're so *cautious*. What will you be like when you're *old*?'

And he couldn't think of an answer.

She threw on a red wool jacket and they walked out of the Barn. It was dark and cool now. The old bike was lit by a single electric bulb that had been left on in the bathroom. Dunsany flipped up the prop, climbed onto the machine, kick-started it into a low, meaty rumble, then waited for her to climb on the small saddle seat behind him.

'Couldn't do this in an evening dress,' Louise Gostelow giggled, then the bike dipped under her weight, and he felt her hands grip gently around his waist. He opened the throttle and the two big cylinders pumped power through the primitive metal frame of the machine.

'This is good, this is good,' she said, then leaned forward, rested her head against his left shoulder, waited, held on tight, so close he could smell the booze on her breath.

Dunsany rolled the throttle some more, kicked the bike into first and pulled away gently across the hard, compacted dirt of the yard, found the track in the faint moonlight between the eucalyptus trees, then drove slowly, in first all the way, through the wood.

As he passed the low group of outbuildings behind the Barn something caught his eye; something gold and frayed, like metallic sparks scattered on the ground, gleamed briefly in the beam of the headlamp.

Then it was gone, and they rode out into the night, out onto El Camino, then onto the highway into the city, past the waters of the bay, faint silver ripples glinting in the moonlight, past the growing office blocks of the Valley suburbs, past the airport where the last holiday jets were circling high overhead, their engines just discernible over the constant, faithful low growl of the bike.

Paul Dunsany rarely visited the city. This was not his place. There was something foreign, something daunting about it that kept him away, that made him feel he was not welcome. But this night it looked magical, from the first moment, after they had left the airport behind, when he began to see the lights and the hills ahead. It looked like a place of wonder, a place that lived on a different, higher plane from the world he normally inhabited. As he came off the highway, only guessing where to go from her shouted instructions, yelled over his shoulder, he turned down Market, dodging the cable cars that rattled and rang down the street, then into Kearny. The street lights shone down the long, straight street like Christmas decorations. Then he hooked left into Columbus, past the great pale bulk of St Peter and St Paul, right into Filbert, up a hill that seemed to get steeper and steeper all the way, until it petered out into nothing, and ahead was the green, sub-tropical vegetation of Telegraph Hill, and, dimly lit, a set of steps that led to a white building, shaped like the end of a giant fireman's hose, that he recognised, from a rare, rubber-necking visit, as Coit Tower.

He followed her guidance and rolled the bike into the drive of a big timber house that sat on the left side of the hill, set at a crazy angle, huge, old, towering above them, like something out of an Addams Family cartoon. The street was so steep that, when she got off, he struggled to keep the bike upright as he flipped it onto the stand. She laughed.

'What form of transport is this, Paul?' she said. 'What kind of people use it?'

'Poor people,' he said. 'And people who like to feel the wind in their hair.'

She seemed so alive in the mingled light of the street lamps and the big lazy moon that sat above the Coit Tower and looked down on them, half amused, through the feathered palms that stood outside the house.

'I like that feeling,' she said, and she wasn't so drunk now, he knew that, he could keep saying it over and over until it stuck. She wasn't so drunk.

'I like it.'

Louise Gostelow walked up to him, put her arms around his neck, kissed him on the mouth, and her breath had only a faint miasma of booze behind it. The rest was just sweetness, so sweet he could forget any doubts, any forebodings he might have about this strange turn of events.

'I'm hungry. I need to change. You come in. You wait for me. There's no one here.'

He followed; following came naturally. Into the big white timber mansion, into the huge saloon room, with its red velvet furniture and the paintings on the walls that looked so old, with faces that traced the family line close to a century back. There he waited, trying not to think, trying not to hope.

When she returned, she was different. She wore a long flowing Indian cotton dress with a faint pattern and a pale angora jacket. She was elegant and it made him feel small, inadequate, until he looked into her eyes, and they shone, shone so much he didn't need to think about anything else that evening, just follow her, stumbling down the hill, back into North Beach, past places he didn't recognise.

They fell and they fell, and finally they fell into Vesuvio, where Louise told him about Kerouac, and what he drank and how much. Showed him the pictures on the scruffy walls, the poems, the graffiti, the beat history that seemed to sweat out of every pore of the little bar that, in truth, had nothing about it except its past. They drank Jack Daniel's on the rocks and it tasted sweet and heavenly, then they fell again, out into the street, arm in arm, looking through restaurant windows, as she wondered out loud where to exercise her American Express card – Chinese, Italian, Californian? – before they went into a Mexican cantina where they drank margaritas, so sour, so salty, and ate hot, spiced tamales and fajitas, getting the food over their fingers, their faces as the meal wore on.

When they left, she was drunk again. He couldn't deny it. He couldn't deny he was the same too. They tottered along the street and he had no idea where he was, no idea which way to turn. It was late and there was nothing around, nothing in the street except one lone cable car clanking its way home, slowly, like an ancient human being struggling to bed.

She stopped and watched it disappear up the steep, beetling hill, then said, 'Paul . . .'

And she walked out into the street, kneeled down on the road, put her head to the ground, beckoned him to follow.

He looked up and down the street, watching for cars.

'You're always looking for danger, Paul,' she said.

'You have to.'

'Not always. You look for it all the time, you miss so much. Listen.'

He kneeled by the side of her, couldn't take his eyes off her face, her beauty in the night.

'*Listen!*'

From underneath the street came the sound of humming, of something singing, a long, continuous metallic hiss that sent a faint pulsing through the ground.

'You know what that is?'

Her eyes were so wide, so open. He shook his head.

'Underneath the street. There's a cable there that runs the length of the city. It pulls them along. Day and night. No matter how heavy they are. Up and down the hills. All the way. You imagine that? You imagine what it would be like to grab a cable like that running through the world? Let it pull you wherever it wanted to go? You don't ask. You just go with it? You imagine that, Paul?'

He didn't want to look into her face any more right at that moment. It was too intense. Too close to something he didn't like.

'No,' he said. 'There's cars coming, Louise. We need to get out of the way.'

She stood up, a little shakily, saw the distant beams coming down the road, wound her arm through his, led him to the sidewalk. He wasn't looking at her. He didn't want to look.

'Poor Paul,' she said. 'So afraid of danger. You think there's anything in this life that's worthwhile and you don't get danger come attached to it? You really think that, Paul?'

His head hurt a little now from all the booze and somewhere inside of him he could feel some little alarm bell ringing away. It was a noise so distant, so small, so pathetic, it was easy to ignore.

'I don't know.'

She felt beneath his jacket, felt beneath his shirt, felt the warm skin of his stomach, so soft there. And still he didn't want to look at her. Still he feared something magnetic, something that he couldn't resist, in her eyes.

'I want us to go home now, Paul. I want us to go home, to go to bed, I want to fuck. Or is that too dangerous for you?'

Paul Dunsany looked down the long San Francisco street, saw the cable car hop the hill, disappear down the other side, leaving the night to nothing but the two of them and the silver sky. And knew the answer.

ELEVEN

A Lesson from the Gourmet

A considerable percentage of the people we meet on the street are people who are empty inside, that is, they are actually already dead. It is fortunate for us that we do not see and do not know it. If we knew what a number of people are actually dead and what a number of these dead people govern our lives, we should go mad with horror.   GEORGE GURDJIEFF

'You ever bone a chicken?'

Tom Cordobes looked at the little hand on the lab table, looked at the pathologist standing over it, big brown eyes gleaming through bottle glasses, and thought the last thing he needed right then was some guest lecture from the Gruesome Gourmet.

Gordon Broadhead – resident ghoul in the Palo Alto Police Department – doubled up his working life as a county pathologist by doing Mr Menu broadcasts on one of the local radio stations that played Barry Manilow non-stop for the shop-till-you-drop housewife population of the Valley. Sometimes he seemed to forget just which job he was doing when, hence the nickname some depressed detective had invented one night when Broadhead had embroidered a deep and intensely thorough autopsy on the female teenage victim of a hit-and-run accident with an exacting account of how to make the perfect cheese soufflé. At the end of the event, when the detective's stomach was quivering somewhere between his throat and his sphincter, Broadhead had looked at the mess of meat and bones on the table and said, 'It's how you handle the oven that really matters, John, I tell people that time and again but do they listen?'

The cop grunted, smelled a miasmic burp rise up from his innards, and said, 'So what do you think?'

'Think?' Broadhead's brown eyes blinked behind those thick glasses.

81

'*Think?* She got hit by a pickup truck doing sixty down El Camino and you ask me what I *think?*'

And from that moment on Gordon Broadhead was the Gruesome Gourmet.

Tom Cordobes really wasn't in the mood for this. He didn't like Broadhead. He didn't like the way the guy looked thirty-five coming on sixty in his shiny polyester suits and shiny dress leather shoes. He didn't like the way he combed what was left of his hair right over the bald patch as if you wouldn't notice. And he didn't like the way Broadhead seemed to be a professional bachelor, always going to these in parties for the Stanford set, meeting all the right people and never ever, once, mentioning a woman. Cordobes thought that the Gourmet was probably either queer or just not interested and he couldn't work out which was worse.

'Spare me the menus, Gordon. We got a murder inquiry on here and I don't think I'm gonna have time to pop in to Safeway for any last-minute shopping.'

Broadhead gave him an ice-cold stare and put down a scalpel on the lab table next to the tiny hand. Cordobes thought it looked unreal somehow. Like something you might see in one of the toyshops, a part of a favourite doll that someone had left to be mended. Except for the blood and tattered flesh that marked where the wrist had once been. One look told you *that* wasn't made in Taiwan.

'I'm talking business here, Tom. Not food.'

Cordobes hated the way Broadhead didn't just insist on first names but used them all the time. It was overly familiar. It just didn't ring the right bells in the station.

'Well, I'm real pleased to hear that,' he said and smiled coldly. Broadhead looked at him, looked at the big muscled body, thought about how much pent-up aggression seemed to be stored inside Cordobes' tight-fitting suit and wished that someone with a little more style had been assigned to the case.

'First time you bone a chicken something funny happens, Tom. Whoever did this found out the same thing when he tried to cut off this hand here. See, with a chicken it all seems very easy. You turn the thing over on its back, you cut a line down the backbone, then you start to ease away the flesh from the bone. I use an oyster knife. You need something small.'

'Real good tip, Gordon,' Cordobes grunted. 'I'll try to remember that one.'

'Good,' said Broadhead and Cordobes wondered, for a moment, whether he really meant it, really had missed the irony in his voice. 'The problem starts when you get to the legs. To the knee joint to be precise.'

'The problem?'

'You can't cut it. Leastwise, not without some practice. People think these joints are just like two pieces of bone that mesh up to each other, you find the seam, you run your blade through it, it comes apart.'

'Not so, huh?'

'Absolutely not, Tom. This is a very complex part of the skeletal structure. It's a combination of blood, sinew, muscle, tightly bound together. Designed to last a lifetime and take all that work, bending all the time, that stuff.'

'Gordon,' said Cordobes and he really thought his patience was going to run out on him now. 'I'm not investigating the death of a chicken. It's a kid. Five years old. So I'd really appreciate some input. *Now.*'

Broadhead sniffed. 'The point, if you'll give me the opportunity to make it, is that whoever did this with this hand made the same discovery. He – she, who knows? – certainly had no medical training. You can see from all this hacking. He just guessed you could snap the wrist off quickly with a couple of cuts and found you couldn't.'

Cordobes wondered about it.

'You mean he found out it was hard.'

'Hard?' The big brown eyes looked astonished. Broadhead walked over and took Cordobes gently by the wrist. The cop could feel the cold, hairless skin of his hand and hated it.

Broadhead stared into his face and said, 'Don't worry, Tom. I won't bite.'

'I don't normally hold hands on the first date, Gordon.'

Broadhead blushed a little, then said, 'The point, Tom, is that the wrist is an extremely complex, extremely tough part of your body.'

He felt with his fingers round the perimeter of Cordobes' wrist, round the muscle and sinew there.

'You've got to think of it as a bracelet of bone and muscle, working together to do all those complex things the hand can do. You can't just snip it off with a knife like cutting the ribbon on a candy box.'

The pathologist let go of Cordobes' hand.

'What you're saying,' Cordobes continued, 'is that it took him a long time.'

'You bet. You perform an amputation in hospital and you use a saw for most of the work. I've seen a couple of amputations in murder cases before. Normally people just use an axe. It's simpler, it's quick, but even then you'd be amazed how many people don't get to do the job with the first blow.'

'And this guy?'

Broadhead went back to the lab table, then pushed a big magnifying glass on a stand over the hand lying there in a specimen tray.

'Take a look for yourself. This was *hacked* off. Something serrated, maybe like a kitchen knife. Whoever did it had *no* idea what he was taking on when he started. You can see the way the flesh is arranged at the base of the wrist. He had to feel his way around with the knife just to get some kind of way into the carpal tunnel, just so he could get around the bones.'

'How long? How long would it take him?'

Broadhead shrugged. 'Hard to guess to be honest. Depends how strong he was, how fast he worked. Hard to imagine it was under fifteen minutes. Maybe more than half an hour.'

Cordobes didn't like to ask the question, didn't like to think about it.

'And the kid. What would he be doing?'

'What do you think, Tom? Screaming.'

'Maybe he'd pass out or something? Gimme some crumb, Gordon, I got a mother out there who's gonna be asking.'

'I'm a pathologist not a psychic, Tom. If he was lucky he passed out, sure. But there's plenty of evidence from the history books, people getting amateur amputations on the battlefield before anaesthesia, that suggests a lot of them stayed conscious throughout. Search me.'

Cordobes peered through the glass. The hand seemed so unreal, so *silent*.

'What about the blood?'

'Lots of it. Lots and lots of it. You could get this kind of injury and survive though, you know that?'

'I guessed. We checked all the hospitals in the area to see if anyone's had to deal with a kid who lost his hand. Nothing.'

Broadhead thought about it. 'In that case he *has* to be dead. You'd need a transfusion to survive this, that's for sure. No other body parts found?'

'Nothing. Not yet. We got the full team out searching every inch of those woods but it's not easy in the dark. Maybe tomorrow.'

'One happy Christmas for the mother,' Broadhead said and Cordobes was astonished. It was the first time since he'd walked into the room that the guy had acknowledged there was a human side to this thing.

'Why's there no blood on the hand? Hardly any there at all.'

'He washed it,' Broadhead said. 'That's my guess. We'll run a full test, see what traces we can pick up of anything. If there's something there we'll get it. But he washed it for sure.'

Cordobes grimaced. He knew the stats. The clear-up rate for murders started way high in the first few hours after you found the body then just started falling and falling and falling. In his book you had a couple of days or so to get your bead on the guy you thought most likely, then a week to close it. If you were floundering in the dark much longer than that then you were just relying on luck to help you out. And luck wasn't something Tom Cordobes could put much faith in.

'Doesn't tell us a lot,' he said.

'Not yet. Maybe in the morning, Tom. Don't lose faith.'

'Yeah,' Cordobes said and decided he couldn't wait to go outside and light a cigarette, couldn't wait to flush the smell of chemicals and antiseptics out of his lungs.

'One thing though.'

Cordobes put the pack of Marlboro back into his jacket pocket.

'You met the mother?'

'Yeah. Nice lady. When she stops screaming.'

'Is she *clean?*'

Cordobes was mystified. 'Clean? You mean like dope?'

'No. Clean like in "do they wash?"'

'Gordon. This woman is the wife of some fancy English academic over here doing some guest lecture stuff at Stanford. She's got an accent that sounds like the Queen of England goes see her for voice training lessons. We're dealing with real top people here, which is why the Captain's breathing down my neck already. You bet she washes.'

'And the kids too? You said there was a sister.'

85

'Real quiet little thing. What'd you expect? She looks like she belongs on the front of a Christmas card. What you getting at?'

Broadhead puckered up his mouth a little, thinking.

'I'll know more in the morning but if that's the case then maybe something's wrong here. Take a look at the hand. See for yourself.'

Cordobes peered through the glass. It told him nothing.

'It's grubby,' Broadhead said. 'Just look. It's been washed OK but it's still there. Dirt. On the skin. Under the fingernails. And something else too. Some kind of mark. Like a burn. I got to run some tests on that but you ask me that's a power burn.'

'Power burn? Like he got electrocuted?'

'Something like. As if he gripped some live cable or something.'

'That fatal?'

'I perform autopsies, not miracles.'

Cordobes said, 'The kid got killed in the Gresham Woods, for chrissake. God knows what happened to him before some fucker nailed this to a tree.'

'Sure,' said Broadhead. 'But I'll tell you one thing, that's not casual dirt. That was there *before* the hand got hacked off. My guess is that this is the hand of a kid that didn't wash too often. Or that something happened before the hand got cut off to make it real dirty indeed. And he touched some power cord, got burned. Not bad. Least not on the hand.'

'You think you can find out more on that?'

'You bet,' said Broadhead, and Cordobes couldn't help warming to his enthusiasm. 'The burn won't tell us much more than we know already but all that shit under the fingernails is going to tell us lots.'

'Tomorrow? Not now?'

Broadhead thought about it for a moment then said, 'One thing. I looked at that dirt under the fingernails. Put a little of it in a solution. We'll get some tests in the morning but I can tell you one thing.'

Cordobes waited. Broadhead liked to have his moment.

'Wood smoke. It smelled of wood smoke.'

'Like what?'

'You ever walk in those woods, Lieutenant?'

'Not if I have a choice.'

'This is winter. Winter is cold. You walk there and you smell that smell a lot. It's the smell of bums. Bums sitting round little fires trying to keep themselves warm burning any old shit they can. Beats me the

86

authorities let them get away with it. Now do I get some time to do some work?'

Cordobes nodded in silence, walked out of the lab, stood in the corridor and lit a cigarette. There was the sound of someone walking briskly down the hall. He looked and saw the tall, lanky figure of Mike Labatt, one of the detectives on the team coming towards him.

'We got him,' said Labatt. 'Fucked if we haven't got him, Lieutenant. Right there in the woods red-handed.'

Cordobes looked at Labatt. He was only twenty-seven years old and this was the first murder case he'd seen. The kid looked too involved, too excited for his own good.

'Calm down, Mike. You found a body?'

Labatt hesitated, tried to gather his thoughts.

'No, sir, not a body.'

'A body would be useful, Mike. A body would be something to get excited about.'

'Yes, sir,' said Labatt, and Cordobes could feel the undertow of resentment in his reply. These kids, he thought. One day they'd be running the station. Maybe it didn't make sense to piss them off now. The ones you get to like you when you're on the up escalator could sometimes come in awful handy when you're coming back on the down one.

'We found a suspect, sir. He had part of the boy's clothing, part of the costume on him.'

Cordobes looked at Labatt and waited for a moment, wanted to slow this down, the way it was supposed to happen, the way you were supposed to prove you were thinking. 'What part?'

Labatt grinned, like it really meant something. 'Part of the wing, sir. Gold.'

'What else?'

'We're still looking, sir.'

'Nothing else, huh?'

Labatt didn't look like he was taking that as some kind of criticism. Thick skin, Cordobes thought. Useful in a cop.

'Not yet. But he was in the vicinity. The mother remembers seeing him.'

'She does?'

'Yes, sir.'

Cordobes thought about it, pulled on the cigarette, watched the flame burn down to the filter, threw it onto the floor, screwed it out with the sole of his shoe.

'He's a bum. He's the bum the mother saw when she first went into the woods.'

It was a statement, not a question, and Cordobes just quietly loved the way Labatt responded, that sudden look of amazement in his eyes.

'Yes, sir! And he won't say where the kid's stuff came from.'

Cordobes took another cigarette out of the pack, lit it. He didn't want it. The gesture just seemed right. Seemed appropriate. Then he smiled, the kind of knowing smile he liked to use when dealing with people under him.

'Lead on, Detective,' he said.

They walked up three flights of stairs back through the main detectives' room – now full of happy-looking cops smoking cigarettes, cracking jokes to each other and surreptitiously phoning their wives to say yes, maybe, honey, they would be home for Christmas lunch after all.

Cordobes walked into the interview room and ordered the cop in there to get out.

'Sir?' said Labatt from behind him.

'You too, Mike. I just want a little talk with the gentleman on my own.'

Cordobes walked over to the window. From the third floor he looked down into the station parking lot then over towards University Avenue. It was a dark, starlit night. He could even make out Christmas lights in the Avenue, green and white and red in the distance.

Tom Cordobes opened the window to get some fresh air into the room. He sniffed: wood smoke. Then he went and sat down at the interview table. The old black tramp sat opposite him. He wore a red and green woollen cap and an ancient tweed overcoat tied at the waist with rope. Cordobes just couldn't even begin to guess at his age. The man's face was lined and covered in grey stubble. The bum's eyes – bright, white, frightened eyes – stared back at him over the table. Crazy eyes, Cordobes thought. Crazy eyes.

Cordobes sat down, lit himself a cigarette, blew the smoke over the table.

'Name,' he said flatly.

The old tramp started hugging himself through the filthy fabric of the overcoat, hugging himself hard and swaying slightly, to and fro.

'Name,' Cordobes said again, and he could feel it inside him already, feel the little red spark of anger.

The bum tried to speak, tried to spit the words out.

'Roscoe Suh . . . Suh . . . Suh . . .'

Cordobes held his hands high in the air, clenched his fists into huge balls of meat and muscle, then pounded them on the table as hard as he knew how. The sound was like the roar of an explosion inside the little interview room.

'*Roscoe Suh . . . Suh . . . Suh . . .*'

Cordobes stamped his fists again and there was nothing in the room but their sound, that big wordless boom that filled Roscoe Sutter's head with a fear and a foreboding more shocking, more terrifying than anything he had ever known in his small, inconsequential life.

'Well,' said Tom Cordobes, after the sound had died away to nothingness, 'well, "Roscoe Suh . . . Suh . . . Suh", we'd like you to talk to us, we'd like you to tell us where the kid is, we'd like you to . . .'

But Roscoe Sutter was somewhere else now, somewhere back in the woods, where the kids taunted him and did things he didn't understand, where he retreated into himself until there was only the woods and the half-darkness, and the noise that came unbidden, without meaning, out of his throat

rassenfrassenrassenfrassenrassenfrassenrassenfrassen

just came out even when he didn't know it.

Tom Cordobes looked at the old black bum, looked at the way his mind had gone somewhere else, listened to the incoherent mumbling coming out of his mouth, then stood up, walked behind him, breathed deep – you didn't want the smell of wood smoke, no one wants the smell of wood smoke in their lungs – took hold of him by the collar of the old overcoat, pulled hard, as hard as he could, and dragged him over to the window.

Tom Cordobes held Roscoe Sutter with one hand and used the other to unlock the sash lock and push the window wide open on its central hinge. Fresh cool air came into the room and almost got rid of the smell in there, the smell of fear and the smell of the bum, of wood smoke, of shit and piss.

He looked down into the car park. It was empty now. The men were still waiting in the station, still looking at their watches and waiting to be told they could go. Cordobes took Roscoe Sutter's collar by both hands, gripped deep into the old tweed overcoat and pushed him through the window. There was a sound from the old tramp, a gasp, like wind escaping from a deflated balloon, then Cordobes reached forward, grabbed the back of his coat and held him there, seventy feet above the ground, held him as he pivoted out of the window, the ledge cutting hard into his waist, and Cordobes just let him rock, let him rock gently between life and death for a while, the cop's hand holding on just lightly enough to let him know it might not be there forever.

There was a time, when Cordobes had been a military man in 'Nam, when you could do this and go all the way. When you could just let the guy — some dope dealer, some pimp, whatever — fall all the way out of the window, crumple into a heap on the ground below, then send some kids around to clean up the mess. When the blood started to come down from his eyes, Tom Cordobes realised those days were gone.

He heaved Roscoe Sutter back into the room, punched him once, hard, in the guts, felt his nose wrinkle automatically at the fresh smell of piss coming from the bum's filthy jeans then threw him into the chair.

Cordobes picked up the exhibits bag, looked at the little gold pieces of tinsel in it, watched them flicker under the pale, anaesthetic fluorescent light of the interview room, then pushed them in front of the old tramp.

'Where?' Cordobes said. 'Where Roscoe Suh . . . Suh . . . Suh . . . ?'

There was snot hanging from the old man's nose now, it dripped slowly onto the neckline of his jacket, his eyes filled with glassy tears.

Slowly, rhythmically, nodding backwards and forwards all the time, Roscoe Sutter started sobbing, made a low, insensate noise that might have been the sound of a primitive beast discovering how to weep.

TWELVE

The Zanzibar

But then they danced down the street like dingledodies, and I shambled after as I've been doing all my life after people who interest me, because the only people for me are the mad ones, the ones who are mad to live, mad to talk, mad to be saved, desirous of everything at the same time, the ones who never yawn or say a commonplace thing, but burn, burn, burn, like fabulous yellow roman candles exploding like spiders across the stars and in the middle you see the blue centerlight pop and everybody goes 'Awww!'   JACK KEROUAC,
On the Road (1957)

It is not my fault that certain so-called bohemian elements have found in my writings something to hang their peculiar beatnik theories on.   JACK KEROUAC,
quoted in the *New York Journal-American*
(8 December 1960)

There were lots of dingledodies there in the Zanzibar that night and a few of them even went 'Awww' ...

It was Christmas Eve after all.

Roseanne Fitzgerald sat down at the band's table, the one next to the men's room door (where else?) and let the smile slide quickly off her face. It was hard enough keeping it on while you sang through a fug of cigarette smoke to three hundred juiced-up human beings (and here she used the term liberally) across the crowded bar of the Zanzibar. No way was she going to keep on trying to imitate Debbie Reynolds while, three feet away, half the men in Seattle seemed to be lurching out of the can, fumbling their dripping dicks back behind their flies, then doing a drunken little finger wave and saying, 'Hi'.

Frank Grayson was the first to follow her, his hand still tingling a little from the big fat metal strings of the Fender bass. Then Paul Dunsany, his hair too short for the location, looking like a teacher or an accountant, not a guitarist, no, never a guitarist. And finally a big hulking figure, a barn door of a man, with a huge head and a long ginger beard. Joni Lascelles watched him sit down with a thud and wondered how he managed to hide so much bulk behind so small a drum kit.

'Lady alert,' Genius grunted quietly and Joni looked at him, wondered what it was he appeared to resent about her.

After Cordobes, after the call from England, the day fizzled out. She hadn't walked much after she visited the market, walked by chance into the studio. The energy wasn't there, so she slept a little. She woke, not knowing which time zone she was meant to inhabit or felt like occupying. The world had just jumbled itself up into a mush of sensations – tiredness, brief bursts of energy, lassitude, momentary, intense periods of concentration. This period couldn't last for long. It was unthinkable to countenance it, she would never get the work done, and the work was why she was here.

Then something about what happened in the studio came back to her: some glimpse of possibility she didn't want to kindle. There was a close, hidden thing in her relationships with men, something that lay so deeply rooted in her past, in a part of her she did not understand. And that was the flow, the processing of the decisions, the ways she would commit herself almost without thinking, commit herself up to the point of involvement, of sex, without knowing what lay on the other side of the act, without, sometimes, even stopping to think if this came from attraction or boredom or simple curiosity. The moment of discovery always seemed to come after the point of commitment, and the discovery, inevitably, was disappointment. That somewhere in this search, this quest, for something – *goodness? asked a tiny voice inside her* – it all went astray, fell apart in hot, angry recriminations. From which she learned nothing. Only that the next time it happened it would be not one cut, one sore gaping wound less painful.

At night, outside in the city, the mist was a little less thick, and you could smell the ocean cutting straight through it. She walked down First, past the entrance to the Pike Place market, past the line of girlie bars, the trendy, renovated hotels, down into the area they'd talked about, that everyone talked about, down into Pioneer Square. There was no real square that she could discern, just a tangle of grimy streets full of bars, with neon signs outside the door, crowds of people falling out of cabs, and music everywhere: rock and blues and jazz and punk, grunge and techno and some things she couldn't even begin to name. This was the centre, the heart, of Seattle at night, and it looked so tawdry, so down at heel, that it almost seemed as if there was a rule – you do *not* paint this place, you do *not* fix all the broken light bulbs that peer black and empty, like stumps of rotting teeth, from the front of house display. This is not LA, this is not New York. You want glitz, you want perfection, you go there, you fool yourself. This is Pioneer and if it looks dirty and industrial and the bums get so desperate that on a bad night they're asking each *other* for change, then so what?

The Zanzibar was announced by a red neon sign. It sat on the first and second floor of a terraced brownstone building that could have been Victorian if you peeled away the neon and the beer signs. Inside, she had walked into a fug of beer fumes and cigarette smoke. It took a good minute for her eyes to adjust to the dank, interior gloom.

She had sat down next to Genius without saying a word, let the waitress bring her a beer (and a big tan glass of Redhook appeared there out of nowhere almost straight away), then let the sounds wash over her, trying to catch the names, recognising a few – there was Cooder, there was a Stephen Stills song, some Tim Buckley, even an astonishingly sexual version of 'Dock of the Bay' with the girl singer, her long red hair bright under the cheap floodlights of the little stage, stock-still, voice in perfect pitch, full of some deep, nameless emotion that skipped right over the words, right over the notes, and stood there hard and real and forthright in the air.

The girl (no, Joni said to herself after a while, that was illusion, she was older than she looked, she had to be to sing that way), the *woman* took the lead in most of the numbers and it seemed as if she could sing any way she chose, she could be Janis Joplin or Linda Ronstadt, Melanie or Diana Ross. You picked the tune, she sang it. And her expression changed too. She wore some hippy chick outfit, a long yellow tunic, a beaded necklace hanging low down the front, then jeans. But you could close your eyes and listen to her voice and for all you knew she was someone else, maybe black, maybe white, maybe in an evening gown or some half-stoned Woodstock outfit of the kind Joplin wore when she stumbled onto the stage back in '69.

Then, just once, Paul Dunsany took the lead, sang 'Mexican Divorce' the way Cooder had recorded it but with a few extra notes and a heap more emotion. Dunsany's voice had limits in the range but that didn't matter. It had some electrifying kick behind it, some deep, elemental force that seemed to hunt around the fringes of sadness, maybe even grief, then step back a little in awe of what it had seen.

She remembered the night she had been in the Albert Hall in London to see Clapton, not long after his son had died, not long after that outpouring of anguish he'd called *Tears in Heaven* had come out, and when he played it then, in that big, soulless cavern, you couldn't hear a soul breathe, you just sat there, pushing the walls of your private existence and wondering what would happen, what might burst through from the other side, if you pushed too hard.

It was like that when Dunsany sang. Joni Lascelles knew there and then that something was going to happen.

'Lady alert,' Genius said quietly again.

The big man leaned over the table, looked straight into her face, and said, 'Genius. You amaze me. Your powers of observation increase day by day. They figured out yet whether this lady has a name?'

She smiled at the big face in front of her, held out a pale thin hand and said, 'I'm Joni.'

He took her hand. It felt like being swallowed by a bear's paw, but there was something gentle there too and the voice didn't match the figure, didn't match the sweatshirt which had a big logo on it that asked, 'Q: What's the difference between a rooster and a lawyer? A: The rooster clucks defiance.' The voice was too certain, too articulate, too cultured.

'No relation, I assume? Shame, I guess. I play that old record four maybe five times a week and you know it still amazes me. The music and the words. Most of us can do one or the other. Both together? You know that's *real* hard for mere musicians to do.'

She smiled and said, 'Excuse me?'

The big man held back his head and recited, '"All the guilty people. They've all seen the stain. On their daily bread. On their Christian names. I cleared myself. I sacrificed my blues. And you could complete me. I'd complete you."'

She thought about it and said, '"Court and Spark". 1975.'

'Good, good. I think you'll find it's '73 in fact but what the hell. It's beautiful. And Joni, that's beautiful too.'

'I picked it myself,' she said and let the words hang in the air.

'You don't say. I'm Ben Rawlins. Daytime, I try to teach the youth of Seattle sociology at the college here. In the evenings I endeavour

94

to corrupt their souls with this low-down demon music. And a little help from my friends, of course. You know my friends or am I to take it that the world of genetic engineering is truly upon us and you really are Genius's lovely sister?'

She laughed a little, she couldn't help it, even though she could feel Genius twitching beside her.

Dunsany leaned over the table, took a long swig of beer, looked at her, felt the distant heat of some kind of recognition, and said, 'We make Ben play drums because it's the only instrument we know that can drown out his talking. I'm Paul. Genius you know. This is Frank who failed to come to Genius's rescue this morning for reasons I'd rather not know. And this is Roseanne. I should have introduced her first but musicians just aren't renowned for their manners.'

The long lean black bass player didn't seem in the slightest interested. He just hugged his glass of beer and lit himself a cigarette. But Joni was conscious of being appraised by the singer who sat next to Dunsany in a way that was almost proprietorial. When she came off the stage, she had left behind some presence, some public character there and had become what she really was. Joni smiled at her, felt her smile come back, slightly cold, distinctly questioning, then said, 'You must be sick of hearing this but I thought your music was just wonderful.'

'Sick?' The drummer was waving his hands theatrically in the air. 'Sick? "I will praise any man that will praise me." Enobarbus, in *Antony and Cleopatra*. Most sensible guy in the play.'

'I will praise any man who gets me another beer,' said Roseanne and pushed her empty glass across the table.

Joni looked into her bag, tried to do some mental calculations, then said, 'Let me. It's a pleasure.'

'Drinking is a pleasure,' said Ben Rawlins. 'Buying is a chore.'

Then he called over the waitress, waved some dollar bills and ordered another round.

'Joni's interested in hippies,' Dunsany said and she wondered why he did it, wondered if he knew she would bring it into the conversation anyway.

'Hippies.' Ben Rawlins repeated the word like it was something out of a zoological tome. '*Hippies.* You know, I was in San Francisco last week and I walked into Macy's. They got this necktie display. Excuse me, Joni, you'll get my drift but let me explain to the simple people here. A necktie is an ornamental clothing item much favoured by men who wear suits.'

'What's a suit, Unca Ben?' Genius asked in his best Elmer Fudd voice. 'Come to that, what's a hippy?'

'Life is too short to impress upon you all the world's wonders, Genius. Merely accept my word that suits exist and neckties are frequently purchased by the people who wear them. In any case . . .'

'You know any short stories, Ben?' Roseanne Fitzgerald asked. 'Be nice if you brought them out for a walk here once in a while.'

'There are no short stories to explain the existence of suits or neckties. Or hippies come to that.'

The singer looked at the big glass of beer that had just appeared in front of her, picked it up, smiled coolly and started to drink.

'The essence of this tale is, I walked into Macy's, I walked up to the necktie counter and there it was. A set, no, excuse me, a *collection* of neckties designed by the late Jerry Garcia.'

Frank Grayson choked gently on his beer, then, when he'd recovered, said, 'You mean *the* Jerry Garcia. Really?'

'None other. 'Tis shocking to relate but sometimes this world holds horrors in it that simply plead to be told. The venerable Jerry spent some unspecified part of his final years *designing neckties*.'

'Who's Jerry Garcia, Unca Ben?' Genius asked.

'Jesus, be quiet, Genius, will you?' said Frank. 'This is a major revelation for us grown-ups. What the hell they look like, these ties?'

Ben shrugged a little. 'Kind of what you'd expect neckties to look like if they'd been designed by someone whose brain had been doubling as a chemistry lab for the best part of thirty years or so. More than a couple looked like the carpet pizza young Genius parked on my best rug a couple of weeks ago.'

'Wasn't me,' Genius objected. 'I always get the blame.'

'That, dear boy, is what the young are *for*. Couple of them looked like the sort of stuff you get hawked down Pike Place by those guys with suitcases who never quite look you in the face when you hand over the money. Personally, I don't do neckties, but if I did, on reflection I'd probably score down Pike instead of Macy's. At least you know some cute little guy with nylon hair isn't gonna come along and try to take your inside leg measurement while you're turning on.'

'So that's what happens to hippies,' Roseanne said. 'They grow old and design neckties. Amazing the things drugs do to people.'

'There is a thesis here,' said Ben. 'I can feel it coming on. Whatever *did* happen to the great American hippy? The ones that didn't stay the same, didn't drown in their own patchouli oil? Where'd they go? Mars?'

'Search me,' said Roseanne. 'I'm too young to be hip, too old to be punk. Suits me fine.'

'You can count me out too,' said Ben. 'I can put my hand on my heart, Mr McCarthy, and say, in all honesty, "I am not nor have I ever been a hippy." Question of time really. Where these guys find the space to hang out for days on end doing that stuff? Frank?'

'You kidding?'

'I may be stretching things here, but, Genius?'

'Like I said. What's a hippy, Unca Ben?'

'I'll consult my engagements book and see if I can fit you in for a month or so.'

Ben Rawlins grinned, a sly little grin, leaned over the table and looked at Paul Dunsany.

'And now. For our most senior, most respected member of the ensemble. Paul?'

Dunsany thought for a moment, wished the conversation would go somewhere else but knew Ben Rawlins better than that, then said, ' "I am not nor have I ever been . . ." Aw, shit. I'm old, Ben. Between the beer and the Alzheimer's do you really think I can remember everything I was doing all those years ago?'

'Memories are never erased. They merely slumber waiting for the signal to awake them. My ruling in this matter, young lady, is that the venerable Dunsany should pursue this subject with you further. Take her for lunch, Paul. In that little Chinese café of yours or some place. God knows, you got nothing to do this holiday.'

'Lunch would be nice,' she said smiling, and he was glad she said it, he knew it had to come from her.

'Yeah,' said Dunsany. 'See I'm so old they're fixing me dates now.'

'Someone's got to do it,' Ben said. 'What are friends for? So that's agreed then. Go see him tomorrow. He just about *lives* in that studio in any case. Me, I'm gonna take a leak then get back behind the hardware. You guys might not have noticed but we're due back on in four minutes.'

Dunsany stood up and looked into her face. It was impossible to work out what was going on there. Maybe she didn't even know herself.

'It's a joke,' he said. 'Musicians, we don't lead real lives . . . we play jokes all the time. It doesn't mean anything.'

'It doesn't mean I'm invited?' she asked.

'No,' he said. 'You're invited. If you want.'

'I want,' she said.

'I'm really bad at this, huh? Out of practice.' He looked so uncomfortable. Almost like a child, struggling for the right words. 'Noon would be . . . *nice*. Really. I'd like that. You've got to excuse me now. Work, if you can call it that. You staying?'

She shook her head.

'I guess Genius isn't such great company. You know, I lose more girlfriends that way . . .'

'You do?'

'Not exactly. Tomorrow.'

She watched him walk onto the little stage, pick up the blue guitar, check the tuning, watch the rest of them assemble, wait for Roseanne who was still at the table.

The singer got up, straightened her tunic, turned to Joni and said, 'Paul Dunsany is a real nice guy. You won't fuck him up, will you? He's had enough of that.'

She looked a little sad, and more than a little old when she said it, and Joni couldn't help wonder what had, or had not, passed between them over the years. Then she was gone, onto the low wooden podium, and that stage presence returned, she was wearing a broad, genuine smile, her red hair was shaking as she moved, the notes were building into something that rumbled around the band, waiting to appear, waiting to energise the smoky, breathless air of the club.

Joni Lascelles was glad she said nothing. She whispered a quiet goodbye to Genius who looked at her a little oddly.

'I was kidding,' he said flatly, and there was something unpleasant underneath his voice. 'I know who Jerry Garcia is. And I know what a hippy is too.'

She tried to smile and then she picked up her bag, left the club, walked out into the chill of the night fog, walked slowly up to First, picked up a cab and asked for the Pequod. They drove past streets empty except for a few drunken party-goers, past towering buildings that seemed old and anonymous in the street lights.

In her room she showered to get the smell of smoke off her, washed her hair, let the dirty water flow down the cracked tiles in the bathroom, patted on some talcum, patted on anything she could think of to get the smell of the club, the smoke, the drink, the oldness of it all, out of her hair.

When she was done she sat down on the old, creaking bed, reached underneath and pulled out the suitcase. She took out the three things she was looking for and put them on the bedcover. There was a nine-millimetre handgun bought that day from some dealer in the roughest part of the city. He told her how to use it. She wondered if he was telling the truth, wondered if there was any way of knowing, gave up even trying to think about it. Then she looked at the photograph. It was old now, a little creased around the edge, the colours fading after twenty years. Two children, white robes, golden wings on their back, standing outside a music store in California, the boy smiling, delighted with himself, entranced by the world, the girl, same age, staring straight into the lens with a defiance which didn't match her years. Unsmiling, her eyes weighed down with some unspoken, shapeless anger.

Joni Lascelles held the photograph in her hand, stared at it until she lost focus, till the shapes forgot their form on the shiny paper of the print, swam in the liquid tears that filled her eyes and ran in a constant, thin stream down her cheeks.

She brushed them away with an arm, picked up the passport, looked at her picture there, looked at the name. This was what scared her. This was something that was chained to her, impossible to reject, impossible to show. You could change most anything in life these days, your face, your clothes, even your name. But when they gave you a passport you went back to your birth and there was no time for a deed poll, no brief space in the rush that had come upon her when she first heard the news in the papers, when she first decided to fly to America. When she first decided to take on the work.

The passport did not lie. Beneath a picture that was three years old, but still clearly recognisable, it gave her name as Joanne Flora Seymour.

INTO THE FOREST

ONE

Freedom

Violence does, in truth, recoil upon the violent, and the
schemer falls into the pit which he digs for another.

SIR ARTHUR CONAN DOYLE,
The Speckled Band

Nature has not got two voices, you know, one of them condemning all day what the other commands.

MARQUIS DE SADE,
Philosophy in the Bedroom

Michael Quinn awoke with a headache and a tight, congested feeling
behind the eyes. He didn't know exactly where he was. Hal Jamieson
didn't feel the need to say before he vanished into the dense Seattle
night, nor did the goons who drove the car. They just took him some
place way outside the city, way beyond the street lights and the highway, jounced along some rough country track, opened up the cabin
and led him inside.

He didn't like the air. It smelled of pine and freshness, it was a
million light years away from the damp, human fug of Obispo, that
cloud of sweat and piss and worse that had enveloped him the best
part of these past twenty years. When he looked out of the window,
all he could see was green forest, rolling away like a huge ocean swell,
rolling away into nothingness, since the peaks beyond were hidden in
low cloud the colour of wood smoke. This place was high. He could
feel it in his lungs, feel the thinness of the atmosphere, how scrubbed
and lifeless it was. He looked out of every window, in every direction
he could, and saw nothing but the green, nothing but the smoke curling
around the base of the peaks in the distance. No other buildings. No
roads. No sign that man had a place here at all. After the pen, it was
strange. It was almost frightening.

Quinn closed his eyes again, tried to remember what had started the gift, forgot, relaxed, let his mind roam, explore the structure of the scent on the air, finger the molecules of resin there, wander, inside, outside. He tried to remember how long it had been since he had felt the change within himself, that slow, insidious metamorphosis, right deep down in the cells, but he couldn't and it didn't matter. The transformation had started a year before the doctors even noticed, a year before the test became part of the pen routine. And he'd known all along. He could feel it in his blood, a queer, curious change in its composition, its fluidity. He could sense the way it lacked its previous resilience, moved sluggishly, cowering, through his veins, ready to be taken by something that lurked in some dark, hidden, invisible corner of his body.

When the results of the prison tests had come in they had called him into the hospital, sat him in a small, white-tiled room, given him a petite woman doctor, with long brown hair, wire-rimmed glasses and a face that brimmed over with sorrow and sincerity. It took her five minutes of unfocused discursive rambling to get round to the point and then she told him he was HIV positive.

Quinn had grinned at her, an expression that made her feel cold and afraid, and said, 'So tell me something I don't fucking know, you stupid bitch.'

That was what really killed him. They locked you in a pen with a thousand other men, they left you alone just long enough so that the big guys, the ones you just didn't dare say no to, they could do what the hell they liked, and then years later they send some soft-haired bitch in to say you're going to die of AIDS. And look at you as if to say: *sorry*.

It lay there in his blood, deep alongside the corpuscles, quiescent, waiting to pounce. When he tried hard he could even picture it: a central, luminescent core with two molecules spinning inside and a lustrous spherical casing. When he closed his eyes he could see this thing – which to him now had a life of its own – seek out its victims, pick and choose between the passing cells, looking for the T4s it liked best, maybe fixing on a monocyte or macrophage if there was nothing better around. The virus itself gave him no problems. He could almost ascribe to it an identity and, in its single-mindedness, its ruthless search to justify its own existence, find something to admire. When they gave him the AZT he could feel it then, laughing, really pissing itself with laughter, at the idea that this could harm it, this could put back the day when it would decide to explode within him. And he couldn't stop himself laughing with it.

Quinn sniffed again, felt the mucus behind his eyes, felt reassured. This wasn't the virus waking up, flexing its muscles. This was the damned air, the clean, scrubbed mountain air, choking him with its freshness, its scent.

He swore, went to the bathroom, coughed and spat into the basin, then pulled on some jeans and a sweatshirt and started to look around.

In the living room sat one of the goons. He wore a shiny grey suit, looked big enough to take on one of Obispo's best animals, and stared straight at Quinn with a hostility that he made no attempt to conceal.

'Good morning, sir,' the goon said. 'My name is Steve. Mr Jamieson has employed me to look after you. I hope we can reach an accommodation, sir.'

Quinn grinned. His teeth looked too big for his mouth these days and they were an unpleasant shade of yellow.

'Sure, Steve. Sure, we can reach an accommodation. What're friends for?'

'I'm pleased to hear that, sir,' Steve said.

Quinn looked at the man's big lifeguard's face, the strong line of brown moustache, the hair cut too short, plastered to the scalp, and wondered where Hal might have picked him up. He looked like a cheap hit man, an extra from a third-rate Mafia movie, handsome in the kind of way that got you bit parts in Hollywood in between the security work that paid the rent.

'Mr Jamieson asked me to phone him when you got up, sir. He'd like to see you.'

'Christmas party, Steve?'

'I don't know, sir.'

Quinn felt a sudden flash of pain in his forehead and let the anger rise up behind it. The anger came up a lot these days. It was hard to make it go away.

'Cut the fucking "sir" stuff, will you? It's giving me a headache.'

Steve stood up and Quinn suddenly realised how big he was, realised that this was probably the best way Steve had of talking to anybody and was letting him know it.

'Whatever you say, Mr Quinn. That's fine by me.'

Then he walked over to a large wooden desk close to the long rear window, picked up a mobile phone and started to punch the numbers.

Quinn shambled over to the front of the cabin and stared out of the window. Nothing but the ocean of green and grey for miles around. When Hal wanted isolation he knew how to get it. And he had the money these days too.

He went to the front door, looked at it. Big and strong, made of seasoned pine, well made too, with huge supports, work that seemed recent, not the kind of door you could kick down easily or find your way around. He turned to see what Steve was doing, saw the big guy's eyes had never left him, turned the door handle, was unsurprised to find it locked, then smiled across the room. Steve just continued talking on the phone in a low voice, watching him with a dead expression.

Michael Quinn softly whispered a single word from an old soul number: 'Freedom . . .'

And wondered why the hell he couldn't remember who sang it and when. Then Steve came off the phone, pocketed the handset in the side of his light-grey jacket.

'Mr Jamieson would like to see you. He'll be here in forty-five minutes.'

'Really. So we're way out in the boondocks, Steve old friend. Nothing much around here 'cept bears and raccoons, not for miles around.'

Steve just looked blank and said, 'I'm not authorised to give you that information, Mr Quinn. You can ask Mr Jamieson if you like.'

'Yeah.'

'Would you come away from the door, sir, and sit down? I'd like to have a little talk.'

Quinn couldn't believe the guy. Couldn't believe where Hal found him. He did as he was told. When he was seated, Steve took the chair opposite him, gently pulling up the knees of his suit as he sat down.

'The way things look, Mr Quinn, we're going to be seeing a lot of each other over the next couple of weeks.'

'You got the short straw, Steve. Didn't Hal have a couple of hits he could have given you instead?'

The big man ignored it, just went on talking.

'Seems to me for both our sakes we should understand where we are on this. Understand what the rules are.'

Quinn sang the f-word again and still puzzled over where it came from.

'Rules,' he said. 'I was under the impression I just got *out* of jail.'

'Rules,' Steve said. 'Just so we understand each other while this goes on. Won't go on forever, not from what Mr Jamieson says. But while it does, we need rules we both can work by.'

'Rules,' said Quinn.

'You don't go out that door without me. When we go out you don't try to run away or nothing. That should be simple. The door's staying locked and I'm the only one who's got the keys. The windows here are all secure. No other way out except through that door. Mr Jamieson paid for a lot of work over the last couple of days to make sure of that and you can take my word, sir, that's exactly what he's done.'

Quinn put his hand in the air and said, 'I promise not to try to escape. But tell me, Steve, where the fuck do you think I'd escape *to?*'

'Nowhere, from what I hear. You go walking around out there and anyone recognises you my guess you'll be dead within the hour. There's a whole nest of people right now who'd like to see you off the face of this world and more'n likely they'd kill each other for the chance to put you there. You got the weirdos, you got the media, you got all sorts of people. I could bring you the papers if you want. You could watch it on TV. You're kind of a celebrity right now though I think Mr Jamieson hopes that won't last. As long as it does I think it's best for you, best for both of us, if you just stay here, keep your head away from those windows, and let the world forget. While that's going on you can look on me as your jailer, you can look on me as your protector. To be honest, I don't *give* a shit. I'm doing this job and I'm telling you how I'm doing it so's we both get minimum hassle and minimum misunderstandings. Misunderstandings is what gets people hurt these days. You follow me?'

'I follow you, Steve.'

'You want things, I'll see what I can do.'

'What sort of things?'

'Whatever sort of things you want. Those are Mr Jamieson's orders.'

Quinn's eyes lit up. 'What do you think a man would want after twenty years in Obispo, Steve?'

'I never been in jail and I don't intend to. So I don't rightly know. Strikes me you would probably be interested in a woman. Some good food. Some whisky. Maybe some dope. Those things don't give me no problems. You just give me the list, I'll keep you happy, long as you keep me happy. That a deal?'

Quinn looked at the big man and his brown, craggy face. It looked like it had been shaped by a wood chisel, just like the cabin itself. The guy was maybe no more than twenty-five, twenty-eight or so, and he didn't like this work, didn't like it one little bit.

'Sure, it's a deal,' said Quinn. 'And this *is* Christmas, Steve. When does the party start?'

Steve didn't smile one tiny little bit. 'First you got to talk to Mr Jamieson. Then I got to talk to him. Meantime maybe you'd better start thinking about that list.'

Quinn grinned, those big yellow teeth gleaming under the bare light bulbs in the cabin. Baxter looked and found himself just hating the sight of him, hating the weird, half-human look of his head. It was almost reptilian.

'I am already, Steve,' said Michael Quinn. 'Believe me. I am already.'

TWO

Telegraph Hill

San Francisco is a mad city inhabited for the most part by
perfectly insane people whose women are of a remarkable
beauty.   RUDYARD KIPLING,
American Notes

> Hey kids, rock and roll.
> Nobody tells you where to go.
> REM, 'Drive'

Louise Gostelow stood at the bedroom window of the big timbered
house on Telegraph Hill and looked out at the ocean. It was a clear
day. No fog, only a hint of haze. The sun had that bright, clean edge
that spoke of a bite in the air, a crispness that gave everything its own
sharp focus in the limpid yellow daylight. From the window she could
see right round the shoreline, from Fishermen's Wharf, past the Marina
to the long red form of the Golden Gate Bridge yawning out across
the blue water, over towards Sausalito where a scattering of yachts
were now starting to sail, like pocket handkerchiefs scattered on the
bay. It was the kind of view that would steal the breath from anyone
who had never seen it before. But Louise Gostelow seemed to have
woken up with it every day of her life, and if there'd been nothing
but a grey wall and a tiny yard there outside the window she would
hardly have noticed the difference.

Through the second window, up the winding street was the white,
stumpy outline of Coit Tower. She could hear the cars driving past,
looking to park for the view, and she couldn't help wondering why.
These weren't tourists. These were people who'd seen it all before.
And still they came back, still they went through their little ritual, not
thinking, just doing. It was nine thirty on Christmas morning and she
was smoking her third Camel since she got up.

She wondered about the family party down in Catalina, all those seasonal rituals that just seemed to go on and on and on, year in, year out, never changing, never wanting to change. You just did the same thing and then you got older. End of story. And when the change came for her, when her little period of parole, of freedom, ended, and she walked down the aisle at St Peter and St Paul, then the same thing would happen to her, the same slow slide to entropy – do the electrons wind down like tiny clockwork toys? does the earth quit spinning on its axis? – to non-existence, with all the little rituals along the way. In five, ten years' time at the most, she'd be in Catalina herself, drinking too much gin, watching the children, *her* children, open their presents, tear the brightly coloured paper to shreds, screaming, screaming, screaming, play their part in the ceremony that seemed to run around and round, forever connected, seamless through the years, like running a pencil round a Möbius strip, until the leaded point just pressed too hard and ripped the paper in two.

The more the future rolled out in front of her, a narrowing highway leading to nowhere, the more Louise Gostelow thought of the present, its possibilities, its potential, the volume, the intensity of the experience that she could cram into her real life before she woke up one day and found the unreal one, the one with its chains and purposes and responsibilities, was waiting for her by the side of the bed, shackles in hand.

The phone rang. Paul Dunsany, still sleeping, began to stir, naked under the silk and down coverlet of the double bed. She stubbed out the cigarette, and walked briskly downstairs into the huge vaulted lobby. She was wearing a cashmere sweater, a simple gold necklace and dark, velvety slacks. First thing after she had got up she had bathed, washed the smell of sex out of her, washed everything out of her. One more experience down the road.

Louise Gostelow picked up the phone and knew, even before she heard the voice, the deep, smoke-stained female voice, that it would be her mother, could be no one else.

'You could still come down to Catalina, honey,' the voice said, half pleading, half commanding. 'Jim could fix a plane or something. You don't need to be on your own.'

She sighed and the noise annoyed her, the noise was something she had lived with since she was a child and it grated, the way an old ache grates.

'Just once. One Christmas on my own. That's all I ask.'

'I see,' said the voice down the line. 'On your own. I'd like to believe that, Louise, really I would.'

'I am twenty-one years old, Mother. You do not own me.'

'Sure. I don't own you. But everything carries a price, honey. You've got to learn that.'

She closed her eyes. There were footsteps on the stairs and she always hated this part, not the words, not the act, just how some of them looked when it all came home.

'The way you keep telling me how could I ever forget?'

There was an unpleasant, wordless sound down the phone. She could learn to hate her mother, of that Louise Gostelow was sure.

'When we get back, don't let me go finding any nasty surprises there, dear, will you?'

'No,' she said, then just put down the phone, cut the conversation dead, knowing what it would be like at the other end, that pursed mouth, the creased lines around the lips, that hard, soulless expression, saying, without a sound, she'll learn, she'll obey, she'll come into line.

She lit another cigarette, turned round and watched him standing there, looking shy, looking stupid.

'Hi,' he said. He was dressed now: cheap jeans, a cheap plaid shirt. Paul Dunsany only needed a badge saying 'no money' to complete the picture.

'Hi,' she said and walked into the kitchen. He followed her and it was huge, vast and white and astonishing, with big clean windows. The sun shone through them so brightly it hurt his eyes.

'There's some coffee,' she said. 'Help yourself. It doesn't come with breakfast.'

Dunsany poured himself a cup, sat at the long polished pine table and looked at her, a look she'd seen before, a look she hated.

He struggled for the words, struggled for the courage to say them, but also to define, for himself, what they really were, what these feelings really meant.

'I want this to be something special, Louise. I want this to last.'

She stood by the big window over the bay, stiff and upright, the cigarette permanently at her mouth. She stared out towards the sky and the big white stump of Coit Tower on the hill. She didn't look at him, didn't even look towards him.

'Don't say anything, Paul.'

111

And he was so young then, so young he didn't even notice anything, didn't feel the charge in the air.

'I just didn't ever dream . . .'

And at that she laughed, quietly, coldly.

'*Dream?*'

It was still hard to say it, that was the odd thing. After the intimacies of the night, the closeness, nothing closer. 'The two of us.'

'Ah.'

In his mind's eye he could see her naked in the big soft double bed, the smooth olive body, her nipples erect, dark, taut fascinating shapes in the moonlight, he could remember the touch of her skin, their slow, anguished movements, inside each other, feeling, probing, loving. There had been nothing like this before. It was like opening a door onto a different level of being, one that was more than sex, one that came from some deeper, more fundamental bond, a giant thing that sprang from each of them and danced delightedly in the dimness of the room.

'It was OK,' she said and looked at him frankly. There was something going on he couldn't work out, something he couldn't understand. 'I'm not complaining, Paul. It was fine.'

He gulped at the coffee automatically and she winced at his manners, she couldn't help it. Suddenly Louise Gostelow was filled with an urge to get him out of the house, to get him somewhere else, somewhere she couldn't see him. Then she remembered about the car, remembered how much she'd drunk the night before, and cursed herself.

'Paul?'

He was looking at her with a mixture of admiration and puzzlement. The kid really didn't know what was going on.

'Paul, I need you to take me back to the Barn. I got to pick up my car, come back here, do things.'

'Sure,' he said, and he was smiling again, happy again. 'Then what?'

'Excuse me?'

'Then what do we do?'

She sighed. It always seemed to come down to this. There were times when she wished she could shake off that pure white side to her appearance altogether.

'*We* don't do anything. Anything at all.'

'OK,' he said. 'You want some space.'

She couldn't help laugh. 'Space? *Space*? What the hell are you talking about, Paul? We went to bed together, we screwed, that's it. Look on it as something for your scrapbook. One day I'll be up there in a white wedding gown on the social page of the *Examiner* and you'll be able to look at the picture and say, hey, I screwed her, really I did. Once. Twice. How many times was it? I don't recall. I was really loaded last night, maybe you didn't notice. But the guys'll love it, believe me.'

And she was genuinely taken aback by how shocked he seemed, how this possibility could never have occurred to him.

'You think I'd say something like that?'

'All men say things like that, Paul. Don't get me wrong. I *don't* care. It's fine by me. It's nothing more or less than I expect. These things happen. That's fine. Then they're *over.*'

There was something pathetic about him that really went to her, really made her want to hate him.

'You don't get it, do you? You're hoping I'm just some pretty rich virgin who happened on you out of the blue and, wow, that's it, love and roses and happy ever afters? You really believe that, don't you? What sort of world are you locked into, Paul?'

He tasted the coffee and it was cold and bitter. The room, so white, so large, so impersonal, now seemed oppressive. The house was strange, foreign, a place where he did not belong, could never belong.

Paul Dunsany pushed the cup away from him, wished he could feel something like anger but knew there was only sorrow, a burgeoning, deep-down sorrow that would grow and grow and grow.

'But I just don't understand . . . why?'

And some kind of mask fell away from Louise Gostelow's face. She stared at him with a grim, smiling hardness he'd never seen before, a look so unattractive – and it would only last a second, he knew that instantly, straight away she would be back to her old self, the self he couldn't take his eyes off, couldn't stop thinking about, now more than ever – that if he had ever seen it before, nothing, not the ride home, not the night, not the chance of their skins ever touching would ever have happened.

'Jesus, Paul. You can get real dumb. The reason why is I already fucked everybody else in the Barn. Last night you were the only one left. Couldn't you even *begin* to guess at that?'

It was like shutters coming down on the world, coming down with one great big slam, cutting off the corners of the horizon, hemming you in, saying not that way, this, not up, down, trimming your life to fit the way things were and not the way you wanted them to be. It was as if the spectrum of colours that filled your vision just got cut in half, half of them got thrown away into the blackness of deep space and nothing took their place, what you saw, what you felt, just got duller, more muted, less tangible.

'I need a ride back to the Barn,' she said. 'I need my car.'

Paul Dunsany nodded blankly, got up, walked out of the big timber-framed door, down the wooden steps, and waited for her to follow. When she did, he kicked down hard, hard as he could on the pedal of the big old bike, pulled back roughly on the throttle and let the mindless roar of the engine drown out everything else in his head.

THREE

Roscoe Pleads

Conscience is the inner voice which warns us that someone
may be looking.   H. L. MENCKEN,
Sententiæ: The Mind of Men

'You sure about this, Tom? I mean *really* sure?'

Captain Cy Langton was one year away from retirement, running
thirty pounds overweight, and wheezed when he walked. He was a
big, grey man who once thought of taking up the ring professionally
but then decided being a cop offered better prospects, a better chance
of a pension. He didn't like coming into the station on Christmas
Day. Didn't like looking at Tom Cordobes, who bore a strong resemblance
to a man who had just woken up from some big, long session
embracing the whisky bottle and couldn't wait for the next one to
start.

'What you mean, am I sure? Sir.'

There you go again, Cordobes said to himself. Letting the dislike
slip out just like that, just real easy, so's the Captain, who'd rather be
playing golf or fucking the little secretary from records he's been seeing
behind his wife's back these past six months, rather be doing anything
at all except police work right now, just so's the Captain gets all the
cards on the table face up. Cordobes looked at the pictures on the walls,
looked at Langton playing golf on Maui, playing golf at St Andrews,
playing fucking golf – *golf!* – all over the world. A miniature golf bag
pen holder, a souvenir from a tournament in Florida, sat on the
Captain's desk, three pens and a pencil sprouting out the top. In
Cordobes' book real cops didn't play golf, didn't play anything at all.
This wasn't a job for players.

Langton sighed and looked at the report again.

'This bum can't read or write. True?'

'Dictated it to me. Sir. Word for word.'

'Sure, Tom. You know I seen so many of these confessions come across my desk from you these past ten years, I really start to get a hold of your style.'

Cordobes felt the vein start throbbing hard in his head, prayed for some Tylenol, maybe a drink. Why the fuck the old man couldn't just take it, put the report through, go home, watch TV, it beat him.

'Like I said. Those are his exact words and that's what I'll be testifying to in court.'

'Well, that's real neat, Tom. What else you think you'll be testifying to? Seems to me you're gonna *need* something else. All you got here is a confession from a man who can't read or write, a confession that sounds like some extract from a teach yourself policing manual. And nothin' else except some kid's hand. Nothin'. You got no body. You got no link with this Sutter guy and the kid.'

'We found traces of his costume in Sutter's stuff.'

'Jesus, Tom. You seen these guys? You seen how they live? They pick up any old shit they find on the streets just 'cos they might be able to do something with it later. They're running some kinda private refuse department out there. Don't make them murderers. Why the fuck he's supposed to do it? Where's it say that here?'

'Says the idea just came to him when he saw the kid.'

'But why? I took a look at this guy. He jumps six feet in the air the moment you blink at him. What I hear of your interview technique maybe that's understandable, but he don't look the violent type, not by a good mile. You're enough of a cop to know that too.'

'Kid crimes are like that, Captain. Kind of people who do this sort of thing to kids *wouldn't* try it on adults, too cowardly.'

'That's bullshit.'

'It's a confession, Captain. You can't ignore that.'

'You think so?'

Langton picked up the report, held it up to the light, tore it in half then tidied the pieces into the waste bin by the big office desk. Then he stared hard at Cordobes over the desk.

'I just saved your job there, Tom. Don't suppose you realise it, don't suppose you'll thank me for it, but that's a fact. You put your name to this and you'll get hounded out of this force and it's a close-run thing as to whether you don't deserve it. What's happening to your judgement, man? This guy can't even give a convincing explanation of how he's supposed to have killed the kid.'

Cordobes couldn't take his eyes off the waste bin for a moment. He couldn't believe what he'd seen. Couldn't believe the Captain would turn down the opportunity for such an easy way out.

'Sir,' and there was no attempt to hide the aggression now, none at all, 'Sutter said he threw the weapon away, he didn't know where. That is a very common account in homicide cases. A very convincing account.'

'Convincing, my ass!'

Langton's voice boomed so loud it seemed to bounce off the frosted glass of the office door.

'This guy's a bum, for chrissake. Where's he meant to have thrown it to? These guys live in a radius of no more than half a mile around the Gresham Woods. We've had men looking under every leaf and pile of shit there and there's nothing, not a knife, not a shred of clothing, not even a drop of blood. What's he supposed to have done here, Tom? Booked into the goddamn executive suite of the Holiday Inn to do the job?'

'I don't know,' Cordobes said slowly, 'but I *do* know I got a confession.'

Langton banged his hand on the desk. The miniature golf bag with his ball pens and pencils in bounced an inch into the air.

'Shit, Tom. You think I'm stupid? You could beat a fucking confession outta the Pope if I left you alone with him for three minutes. Truth is, it don't mean a thing, 'cept you're too fucking quick with your fists. And I'll tell you one more thing, Tom. I got talking to the Gourmet this morning and he tells me he ain't even sure this hand you found *belongs* to the kid who's missing. Far as he knows, you might even be charging the Sutter guy with murdering someone we can't even prove is dead yet. What you gotta say to that?'

'Broadhead is a faggot and an asshole.'

Cy Langton's eyes rose upwards and fixed briefly on the ceiling.

'Jesus, you kill me, you really do,' Langton said eventually. 'What the hell has that got to do with anything? Don't you have a conscience, Tom? Don't anything ever prick you? You could be leaving the guy who really did this out there to do it again, and all you can think about is that Broadhead's a faggot.'

'Sutter *may* have done it. I'm telling you that. Sir.'

'Well, maybe you'd just better try to put some flesh on that *may* then, Tom, and hope that while you're doing it we don't get some other kid turn up dead while your main man is in custody. You keep the bum there, you go looking for a body. You tell me what you're doing and you *don't* go doing any interviews with witnesses unless you got someone with you. I'll be damned if I'm gonna put my ass on the line just 'cos you can't keep your fists down every time you come across someone who's black or a fag or otherwise don't fit into your preferential person category.'

Tom Cordobes could feel the blood in his temples throbbing in time to his pulse and hoped, really hoped, this wasn't going to go on much longer. There were limits, everyone had limits, and he was getting close to his.

'Sir,' he said, mouth so straight and level it looked like he was in pain. 'And the media?'

'You leave the media to me. They can go round baying for blood as much as they want but if we get someone into court on this I want to be damn sure the DA can put him away.'

'Even if it's Sutter.'

'Even if it's Kriss Kringle himself. That's the law. We keep it, we don't make it. You try remembering that.'

'Sir.'

The old man's face was florid now. He could have put on a red robe and false beard and done a fairly passable stint as Father Christmas himself, if he'd managed to wipe the scowl off his face.

'You go now, Tom. You behave on this one. Ain't no personal fucking crusade. You get those guys out there earning their overtime. This is gonna cost the department a real lot of money. They want some value for it, and from what I seen they don't seem to have had much so far. You find me a body, Tom. That would make me *real* happy.'

'How long can I keep Sutter?'

'How long you want? That guy's got a roof over his head and hot food for the first time since he was last in jail. I don't think he's gonna be screaming to get out anywhere real quickly. If he talks to some lawyers and tries to get smart, explain to him how feelings are running high, maybe he needs protective custody. Mention the lynching word. You can do this stuff real good if you ask me. Explain how we can't go around releasing suspects when they don't have an address with a zip code at the end. You make it up, you talk to him, Tom. Seems to me you can talk to him and get this guy to agree to most anything you like.'

Cordobes nodded. The Captain leaned over the desk and glared into his face.

'And you do this right, Tom. From this point on I am protecting your ass no more. There's young guys out there would love your job if you fall down on this one and the way things are moving now you're *gonna* fall down. You understand me.'

'Sir,' Cordobes hissed.

'Jesus Christ. I'm trying to help you, man. You get kicked out at your age you're gonna be useless for anything else and the pension won't pay for much neither. I know you had your personal problems. We all got personal problems. Goes with the job. But in the end it comes down to you. All I'm saying is whichever way you choose, you gotta live with the consequences. You understand that, you understand that good, 'cos I'm damned if I'm gonna give this pep talk twice.'

'I understand,' Cordobes replied, and in a way he felt he did, in a way he knew that, already, there was a choice, a crossroads there in front of him, and only one path you could take.

There was silence in the room for a good ten seconds and then the phone rang, so loud it made Cy Langton jump.

'Fuck this goddamn new switchboard,' he said, reaching for the phone. 'Got more bells and whistles on it than a space rocket and I'm damned if I know enough to get an outside line most the time.'

He picked up the phone and barked, 'Langton.'

Tom Cordobes was glad he stayed and saw what happened next. What happened was the blood drained from Langton's face, just as if someone had pulled a plug out somewhere in the jowls of his throat. All the anger, all the fire, just faded away until the Captain looked pale enough to throw up. The conversation lasted all of a minute and Langton barely said a word. When it ended, he put the phone down slowly. He looked old and tired.

'You better go over to the Seymours' house, Tom,' he said eventually. 'Take the full homicide team with you. This mess just seems to get bigger by the minute.'

Then Langton stared at the little golf bag, belched a low, puke-smelling belch, closed his eyes and let his head fall down between his hands.

FOUR

Shiny Happy People

From this hour I ordain myself loos'd of limits and imaginary
   lines,
Going where I list, my own master total and absolute

WALT WHITMAN,
'Song of the Open Road'

Lonnie swept the table and he swallowed up all he found
It was forty-eight hours till Lonnie came around.

STEELY DAN,
'The Boston Rag'

The smell of dope hung like an opiate curtain in the fuggy air of the Barn. It made Paul Dunsany feel a little sick. His head, his mind reeled stupidly. They had eaten some food, some kind of bean stew that Mouse had prepared, ladled out silently into bowls and put on the table. They had smoked. And then they had turned on the old General Electric TV, waited as Quinn patiently fiddled with the controls around the back until the colour took on some semblance of reality, sat back, let the pictures roll over them, through the toons, through the news (which they did not watch, did not even listen to), finally settled into watching *Singing in the Rain*, relaxing into not doing, not thinking, not being.

Dunsany wondered why he was still there. Louise acted as if nothing had happened. She smiled at Hal Jamieson's jokes, she hogged the joint (she *always* hogged the joint, Hal said), and she said nothing, let her eyes avoid meeting his without ever making it seem intentional. There was something so secure, so certain about the way she did it that made him feel small, used, dumb. Something that made it hurt just that little bit more until he blocked it out, until he retreated into the dumbness, the stony place where nothing happened, no thoughts, no regrets crept out of the walls.

He watched Gene Kelly dance through the water-logged streets of some set in Burbank, asked himself why he was even looking at this shit, got up and walked out without a word. The air was cool and smelled different. Not better, just different. He took two big breaths, felt the dope headache go back somewhere inside him a little, pause before returning to the attack, climbed on the bike, kicked the pedal and rode down the drive.

They didn't even seem to notice as he left, but there was something nagging him all the same, something in the atmosphere that was strange, wrong.

As he turned out of the dirt track into the side road that led to El Camino two cops standing by the side of their white squad car looked at him through opaque black Ray-Bans, wondered to themselves if they could really be smelling the fragrance of dope through the eucalyptus miasma that was flooding out of the Gresham Woods and blocking their sinuses, gave up on the idea and watched him go. This was a quiet day in the little university town. The students were gone, mostly. The people who remained just stayed inside their sprawling, single-storey timbered homes, watching TV, eating too much, letting themselves get mellow with wine, waiting for the day to wind down. When you came down to it, the cops thought, Tom Cordobes had found the guy and now it was just a matter of stitching together the pieces. You didn't need to chase some doped-up kid on an old motorbike that looked like it was about to fall apart. It was Christmas Day after all.

Paul Dunsany never heard it but they had laughed when he left. After he walked through the door, after he started to pump the pedal on the bike, Hal Jamieson began to giggle in that dope-filled way that people do, and the giggle caught on, even with Louise Gostelow, even with Michael Quinn, even, in a half-hearted way, with Mouse, sitting at the back of the room, alone, in a faded armchair, the upholstery half undone, watching the movie and thinking it was wonderful, thinking it might make her cry with happiness (and that wasn't just the dope, that was something else too).

'He's so fucking straight,' said Quinn eventually. 'Straight as they come. Jesus. What a creep.'

'So why's he come?' said Hal. 'What's in it here?'

He looked at Louise, her face shining through the clouds of smoke, saw her smiling back at him.

'You tell me, Hal,' she said.

Hal Jamieson sat forward on the couch, let his arm roll out in front of him, some kind of mock curtsey.

'The boy' – he let the words spin out into the semi-darkness of the room – 'the boy's in *love*. And with dear Louise, too. My, wouldn't your momma be pleased if you came home with *him*, my girl.'

'Maybe I've been home with him already,' she answered, and there was a look in her face that he didn't like, a look that stirred something he wasn't meant to feel, wasn't supposed to know about, something called jealousy that didn't have a place in this bright new universe because its cause, its parent, had been eradicated, replaced with something more sophisticated, more cool, more open.

'Maybe,' said Hal and he felt the dope start to give him a little cramp in the windpipe.

'He plays the guitar real nice,' said Mouse in a quiet, dreamy, only half-awake voice. 'He's a nice guy. He doesn't want to fuck people around like you guys do.'

'Sure,' said Hal. 'A *nice* guy.'

'The world needs nice guys,' Mouse said. '*You* might need a nice guy some day.'

And they looked at her like she'd stepped out of place, walked into a part of the room she never belonged without realising it. Mouse swept her long greasy hair back with one hand, more out of habit than because it was falling in front of her face, and did what their joint expressions told her to: she shut up.

'You got some more of that acid?' Quinn was seated in the darkest corner of the room. They couldn't make out his face.

'Does your uncle Hal let you down, dear boy?' The Boston hack in Hal's voice seemed more marked than ever. 'What flavour you want? Strawberry, lime, vanilla? Maybe you want to try something new? A little Key West cocktail?'

'I want what I had yesterday. You know the name.'

'Ah,' said Hal, and tried to hide from himself the fact that he'd worried about it, afterwards, worried whether the dope had been bad or just plain disappointing. Worried that it had come from somewhere he didn't understand, didn't fit into the mental register of drugs he carried around with him in his head, always.

'Say it.'

'The name?'

'Say it.'

Hal Jamieson shifted forward into the light and tried to get a better view of Quinn. The kid looked too thin, too theatrically thin. His long, narrow frame filled the corner of the room with an angular, unnatural shape.

'The name is Desert Rose, dear Michael. And I regret to inform you that the Jamieson pharmacy is currently out of stock. However, if you'd . . .'

When it came, it took them all by surprise, even Quinn himself. The thin figure hunched itself up into a dark, shapeless silhouette and the voice just came out of him, so loud, so violent, so demanding.

'*Don't fucking lie to me!*'

Hal sat motionless, stunned. Quinn was rising on the other side of the room, walking towards him. He seemed bigger than usual. Or maybe the room seemed smaller. Whatever. There was something in the air he didn't recognise, something he didn't like.

Quinn strode over in what seemed to be two steps, his face came into the sunlight that fell through the window in a single, solid yellow shaft. Behind the light, half in shadow, Hal could see Louise's face. To his astonishment she seemed mesmerised, engrossed in this sudden fierceness, so unexpected, so wild.

'Don't fucking lie to me, Hal,' Quinn said more quietly, and if he'd just listened to the voice, if his eyes had been closed, Hal Jamieson would have believed it was all over, it was just a momentary explosion caused by nothing, caused by some temporary affliction that would go away, be forgotten, die quietly and sink, in silence, through the cracks of the ancient wooden floorboards beneath their feet. But his eyes were open, and they were locked on the face above him, that curious mixture of innocence and craziness that now seemed to have acquired yet another side to its character, a side he could only guess at except to recognise its wildness, its ferocious, force-filled drive.

Hal Jamieson looked away, tried to think, and for a moment he had the impression – no, it was true, he knew it was true but refused to allow himself to believe it – that the walls of the room were pulsating, as if they were alive, as if someone or something was pushing away at the intimate fabric of their existence, trying to stretch it until you could feel it snap.

'You've got some more, Hal. I *know*.'

And he nodded, though he didn't understand how Quinn *could* know. They left the dope to him. They didn't ask questions except what and how much. For all they knew it came out of the sky or from the Safeway down on El Camino. Its source was irrelevant, only its presence, its existence mattered, not where he stashed it so that no one, not even the cops with their dogs, could ever find it.

'Yeah,' said Hal. 'I got some. I was trying to protect you, Michael. This is new stuff. It's not a great idea to drop too much. You gotta get used to it, get to know it, find out what it does for you. You try something else, huh? I got plenty else.'

'Just fucking fetch it, Hal, and quit wheedling.'

And the way he put it, the way he looked after Hal Jamieson came back with the stash from behind the bathroom cabinet, there was just no saying no. Not even when he handed it round, handed it first to Louise, then to Mouse, and then to Hal himself, watched them swallow, made *sure* they did – and that was something Hal Jamieson really didn't understand – watching them all the time until the little smear of alkaloid was inside them, working, working, working.

They sat around, feeling their throats get dry, feeling the sound of their own blood begin to boom in their ears, watching the patterns start to crawl across the walls and the floor, snaking through all the colours of the rainbow and a few more besides.

When they were all there, and he could feel that point, he didn't need to ask, or even look, Michael Quinn waved his hand in the air, watched the coloured stream of particles flutter in its wake, and told them about what he wanted them to hear, what he wanted them to understand, as much as they could.

Told them about Schrödinger's cat.

FIVE

Hearing Voices

'Seven years and six months!' Humpty Dumpty repeated thoughtfully. 'An uncomfortable sort of age. Now if you'd asked my advice, I'd have said "Leave off at seven" – but it's too late now.'

'I never ask advice about growing,' Alice said indignantly.

LEWIS CARROLL,
Through the Looking-Glass

Whatever else is unsure in this stinking dunghill of a world a mother's love is not.   JAMES JOYCE,
Portrait of the Artist as a Young Man

This Christmas Day even the bums seemed to have deserted the city. There was scarcely a soul on the streets, even though the fog had lifted a little, its place taken by a thin wet cloud that seemed to be drifting slowly down from the sky in a fine, gentle film. She could taste the salt on the air, the damp, dusky salt that washed in from the Pacific via Puget Sound and hung there, solid in the atmosphere, soaking everything. Two days on, there was something curiously familiar now about the city. The streets around the Pequod were grimy, semi-industrial, inelegant. Even the modern shopping centre she'd glimpsed on one of her previous walks did little to alleviate the sense of a city, a community, that cared nothing about its outward, physical aspect. But for all this, there was a sense of acceptance, and she could feel some part of herself starting to share it. The city said: this is how it is. Take it or leave it. And as she strolled past the soot-stained brownstone buildings, navigated the unevenly paved sidewalks, got around to accepting that there was no point in wishing otherwise, Joni Lascelles distantly understood how this rough, imperfect place could, in a way, be 'home' more easily than somewhere that drowned in its own shiny, artificial perfection.

In the city, it was natural to drift. In the city, it was natural to fall from one thing – one event, one person – to another, without worrying too much about the consequences. In the city, life consisted, naturally, of a series of short, often pointless, sequences, linked by their existence, not some common thread of reason. There was, in this chaos, some deep, subterranean sense of order, and it appealed to her, she could feel it whirring away beneath the street and a part of her couldn't wait to grip the wire, let it seize her, carry her somewhere else without asking, then set her down and let her deal with the consequences.

Somewhere off First, close to Pike, she came across the man. He was a bundle of rags, shredded rags, like a human being that had been through some sort of machine, a tattered collection of fibres, hunched against the sooty red brick wall of some deserted warehouse waiting to be turned into a coffee shop and have the new young people come through its doors, smiling, anxious, bright and happy, not seeing the rags on the street, not knowing what went on beyond the luminescent portals of their own carefully tended interior lives.

There was a movement inside the rags, arms seeming to shuffle into place, knees hunching up towards the body to keep out the damp, cool air that waved in off the Sound, you could almost feel the lice teeming inside the wiry fabric of the rags, rushing, rushing, rushing, excited at the idea that someone was there, that someone was passing.

It was like this always. You wanted to pass, you wanted to stare at the pavement, walk straight ahead, eyes fixed unseeing on the horizon. But you couldn't. Something, some hidden force – *it's you, idiot*, said the voice, and she recognised the truth there – just wouldn't let you, made you look even though you knew it might destroy you.

When she looked at the tramp, looked into his eyes, she knew why she had resisted it so long. Because these were not the eyes of some Seattle street bum, living among the trash and the debris and the filth of the gutter in 1995, queuing up in Pioneer Square to hustle the kids as they went into the Golden Gate, the Pioneer Club, the Velvet Glove and the Zanzibar, filled with some mute despair overlaid by anger.

You know who it is, the voice said. And she found that once she had given way, once she had allowed herself to look, some inner notched mechanism of sensory cogs and wheels turned and whirred relentlessly, then said, damned for a penny, damned for a pound, if you're going to look, you might as well look and drink it in for all it's worth before the earth starts to turn to stone and you with it.

Joni Lascelles stared into the eyes of the tramp. The face was different, fatter, more lined, somehow blacker, the skin a different, deeper shade, and she was able to say to herself, this is not, this cannot be Roscoe Sutter, who I only half remember, who I do not even know, a face, a sound, a smell from twenty years ago, half seen, never forgotten, retreating, hurt, murmuring senselessly like a sick animal, retreating down the narrowing whiteness of some antiseptic corridor in a vast, echo-filled building that had seemed to hang over her life ever since.

She watched the face change shape, watched the cheeks become more lined, recognised the frightened rictus grin, saw the black and yellow stumps of teeth staring through the gaping mouth, saw the eyes again, recognised those eyes, then listened

rassenfrassenrassenfrassenrassenfrassenrassenfrassen

to the sound that wasn't really there. Closed her eyes, waited for the voices. And that sudden shift in time as the past cleared and the present dimmed, a moment of release that lasted no more than a few seconds but could encompass, within it, entire revealed episodes.

Joni Lascelles closed her eyes just enough to keep out the grey, damp light of the city, listened and, with her inner eye, watched.

'Flora,' Daniel Seymour said. 'Go to your room. Go and play with something. Mummy and I need to talk.'

The little girl picked up the Huckleberry Hound book and walked past the Christmas tree, its lights blinking white and blue and pink, past the tall white angel, the illuminated wings outspread at its peak, and out of the living room. Even with the hasty decorations the house seemed too white, seemed to be made of bleached skin. It was a house they loaned to visiting academics and it had that characterless, cold feeling that always seemed to hang around temporary accommodation, however well furnished, however much money someone spent on the decorations. You could turn on the heating the day before the new people came, you could air the beds, throw open the windows to let the wind blow through the place. But it didn't matter. This was not somewhere that people lived. This was not a home. It was merely bricks and mortar, an artifice through which they passed and then moved on.

Rosamund Seymour looked at her husband and felt the hatred, the resentment, most of all the *blame*, wash over her. Felt relief that at least the girl couldn't hear – *you forget the walls, these thin American walls, so thin you can hear and you can see too, the sounds making little pictures in your head* – what was happening.

He was a big man. In the winter, when the winds blew straight from the Russian steppes over the North Sea and into the low flat lands of East Anglia, he played rugby and made them watch, made them stand in the painful cold, on the flat, frozen earth, watching these men rage against each other on the field with such violence it made her want to turn away, hide her face in the warm, soft wool of her mother's coat (but not let Miles see, never let Miles see). And in the summer, which always seemed hot and warm and sunny, when the countryside turned so green that the brightness hurt, he played cricket, for hours at a time, making them watch this too, the slow dance of men in white on a perfect grassy stage, a dance that meant nothing to her, except that she had to watch it, had to sip the warm fizzy drinks, eat the home-made scones until she felt sick and ill (and never let Miles see, never let Miles see).

He was a big man and he had a big voice, one she could hear always, even long after he was dead. It came to her at the oddest moments, out of nowhere, and left her speechless, half from fear, half from excitement.

'How could you?' Daniel Seymour bellowed at his wife. 'How could you?'

She was sitting on the couch, the one with the delicate, faint floral pattern, mock-English, maybe the college thought they'd like that, they'd feel at home (she never felt at home, not in the house, not in the little cocktail parties where the small talk ranged from quantum physics and the Helsinki Accord to whether a little-known politician from Georgia called Jimmy Carter could seriously think he might be the next President). She was sitting, feeling his rage well over her, like the spring tide, remorseless, unyielding.

He crossed the room and stood towering above her, bent down, held her shoulders with his huge, strong arms.

'I keep you, Rosamund, year in, year out, I keep you. And all I ask in return is that you look after them, you keep them. You take care of them.'

There is some satisfaction for him in her tears, in her dread.

'I did, Daniel. I did, I did, I . . .'

'Then why is Miles dead, Rosamund?'

And the word itself seemed to be made of stone, to contain some stark, indisputable finality. It stilled them both into silence, a dark, anguished, separate silence.

When the sound of the word subsides in the air, Rosamund Seymour is different, is resigned to what is happening, what always happens.

'Daniel. You mustn't do this. You mustn't look for some way to hate me. Always. Some way to punish me. If we stay together we can survive. But it is for you to make this happen. I cannot . . .'

The air is torn apart by the rush of his arm, the muscles flexed and tense, the violence of the sweep, and upstairs, in her quiet room, where she has long since ceased counting the figures of Huckleberry Hound on the wallpaper, the child starts to cry, in silence, knowing what happens next, knowing how it feels, the touch of his hand, in anger, in some other circle of pain too.

Her mother screams and this is so loud that she can feel the pressure flickering in her ears in both times, in 1975 and now, equally real, equally painful, it pierces through the fabric of the years.

With her inner eye, young and old, she has seen it too. Seen the blow come sweeping down from on high, punching hard into the stomach – *it doesn't show there, he says, he always says, he is good at things that do not show, do not cause comment at the cocktail parties* – and seen her mother double over in pain, her mouth open in shock, amazement that the world can contain so much grief, so much agony in a single day.

Watches too the expression on her father's face. This is not to do with Miles. This is not to do with anything except Daniel Seymour and the death grip he has on his small, enclosed world and those who inhabit it.

'You do not listen, Rosamund. Never. Never. Never.'

He grabs hold of her sweater, jerks her half to her feet, punches again with his free hand, feels himself hardening the more she struggles, the more she screams.

'You do not fucking listen. Miles didn't listen, Flora doesn't listen. The more I tell you, the more you don't fucking listen.'

He is a big man and when he tugs hard at her sweater – she smells the gin, strong, like flowers, like perfume, on his breath – the seams give way, he rips it, in one long, deliberate sweep, from her back. She is wearing a white bra underneath. Her body is reddening from the blows. He reaches down, feels the waistline of her slacks, pulls hard on it, pulls her towards him.

The world is reeling in front of her. Rosamund brings up her knee to try to strike him, he parries the limb, hits her across the face. There is a look, a wildness in his eyes, she knows and wishes she did not recognise.

'Daniel?'

The sound of her own voice shocks her. It seems to belong to someone else, so loud, so desperate.

'Daniel. Not now. Not now.' And then spells the words out slowly. 'We. Need. You. I need you. Flora needs you.'

He pushes her back onto the couch, takes hold of the front of the bra and rips it painfully from her shoulders, reaches for the top of her slacks.

As if in a dream, she brings her legs up slowly, with a purpose, a firmness that surprises him: normally she gives in. Then she brings her knees up to her chin, over her naked chest, the red weals staining the skin, clasps her arms around her legs.

She is not crying now. There is still, calmness inside her head, as if some lever has been turned somewhere, a lever that says 'No!' and says it so loud that he can hear, even Daniel, this strange, threatening man she no longer recognises – and has not for years, the realisation surfaces, like a bubble popping to the surface – who stares at her, full of anger and outrage and shock and violence.

'No more, Daniel,' she says. 'I will not be treated like this. I do not *deserve* to be treated like this.'

He is a big man and she can see his erection through his trousers, sullen, threatening. He watches her see it, smiles, and Rosamund Seymour feels cold. The thoughts race around her mind, the thoughts, the doubts, the suspicions, and the memories of small, puzzling events, tantrums with few words spoken, a mosaic of happenings that meet and then fit, in a few seconds, into a picture, a *comprehension*.

Daniel Seymour rises from his knees and he is smiling, a cold, hard smile she does not recognise. He looks at her once then turns, walks towards the brightness of the tree, tall, erect in the corner of the room, towards the stairs and, in a voice that is neither kind nor cruel, says loudly, 'Flora.'

Rosamund watches as her vision fades into a tiny, blood-red funnel, like the iris closing on a camera.

She gets up quietly from the couch, feels the pain in her torso stab at her once then fade into the background, as if realising its unimportance in this new place. He is close to the stairs now, close to the Christmas tree.

'No,' she says, with little force, with no direction in particular, not expecting the word to have some effect or even that he should hear it. And then without thinking she picks up the heavy glass ashtray from the coffee table, walks over, as he turns to look at her, registers the surprise – no, *amusement* – on his face, feels her fingers grip the glass tightly, her arm draw back and follow the curving arc of the glass missile.

Daniel Seymour was smiling as the glass hit his right temple and the smile stayed on his lips as if frozen there, until the red cloud swam into his vision and a huge dark explosion consumed the linear march of his thoughts. He stumbled backwards, fell against the wall, fell down onto the floor, and she struck again, then again, the ashtray, now dripping blood, rising against the fairy lights in constant repetition. He tried to speak but there was the taste in his mouth, of blood and salt and bile, and now he was rolling, trying to get out of her way, trying to think how to hit back – because hitting back was what a man did – kicking at her legs, her crotch, just trying to hurt her, even though it seemed to make no difference.

He rolled underneath the tree and looked upwards. The branches spread out over him, green needles sparkling in the strange fairy lights, bathed in the redness of blood, lights that seemed to be ebbing in their intensity as his breathing grew more laboured.

She was on him now, she straddled his body, and the oddest thing that was to strike Daniel Seymour, in these last seconds of his life, was how this was pleasant, how this was a sexual act, just as real and fundamental as the days, long past, when she would roll on top of him in bed and sway gently in the night, her breasts dark circles that felt warm and sweet as his fingers reached for them, sway gently, gently until the world burst into some feverish, liquid, shivering spasm.

Rosamund looked at his gaping mouth, listened to his panting breath, reached over, snatched a scarlet glass ball from the tree, pulled with her hand until she broke the cotton that held it loosely to the branch, then stuffed it into his mouth. She could feel the imprint of the pattern on her fingers: holly leaves, holly leaves. She reached down, put one hand on his shattered forehead, one underneath his chin, slammed his mouth shut. There was the noise of something breaking and Daniel Seymour's eyes grew big, so big and white they wanted to see beyond the world. Blood appeared in the line of his lips as she held his mouth tightly shut, a line, then a flood, and locked there, so tightly above him, she watched him swallow hard on the glass, choke on the shards, watched the quivers and spasms engulf him. She had no idea how long it took. When he was still she rolled off the body, lay on the floor feeling her muscles scream at her mind, then got up, walked back to the fireplace, looked at herself in the wide, chrome-framed mirror and wondered what manner of creature it was that stared back at her from the glass.

Upstairs, in the little room with so many Huckleberry Hounds on the wall that it was impossible to count them all, Flora sat on the bed, her face in her hands, no tears, no sound, waiting, waiting, waiting.

When she finally found the courage to walk downstairs, her mother was crouched in the centre of the room, knees up to her chest, head buried between her legs, rocking gently, backwards and forwards, making no noise, and refusing to look, refusing to lift her eyes to the room, to see, to accept what it contained.

The girl sat down beside her and waited, but to Rosamund Seymour she was invisible, there was nothing in the world but the red-filled darkness behind her eyes, a place that was so empty, so barren, so anonymous, that it was somewhere she could finally feel safe from the world.

Joni Lascelles said, 'Mummy.' Then looked at the shape in front of her. This was not Roscoe Sutter, not the shuffling figure she had seen in the police station so long ago. His face was different. He looked nothing like the old tramp in the corridor. Sometimes anything could be the trigger, she thought. But the other thing she discovered, no, the other thing she knew already, was that she could distance it. She could move from one place to another and leave it all behind. For the time being.

The tramp looked at her, something like worry on his face.

'You OK, girl?' the bum said eventually. 'You look like you seen a ghost.'

She felt her eyes with the back of her hand. No tears this time. No tears. She reached inside her bag, pulled out a five-dollar bill, passed it down to the tramp. He smiled, looked genuinely surprised, tipped his hat.

'Merry Christmas, Miss,' he said. 'You have a good one there.'

'Merry Christmas,' she answered and walked down the street, towards Pike, letting the past flood back into her, from places she didn't even know about, then sorting it, filing, stashing it somewhere inside where it didn't show, didn't need to make an appearance until she whistled for it.

SIX

The King of Mercer Island

And you may find yourself living in a shotgun shack
And you may find yourself in another part of the world
And you may find yourself behind the wheel of a large
automobile
And you may find yourself in a beautiful house, with a beautiful
wife
And you may ask yourself. Well ... How did I get here?

TALKING HEADS, 'Once in a Lifetime'

It was the *Seattle Times* that gave him the name, in a profile after the new house was completed, and from then on it just stuck: the king, the king of Mercer Island. A couple of software billionaires had swanned into Mercer before him, built huge, sprawling mansions, boat jetties, even a floatplane mooring. Nothing as big as the Gates place but Gates had chosen to take the millions his teenage dweebs made for him out in the mink-lined Microsoft coffin in Redmond and build his personal Xanadu elsewhere, on the shoreside of the lake, further north, beyond where the tour boats tended to roam too often, with the gawk-eyed visitors leaning over the sides. And that left Mercer wide open for someone with a touch for showbiz, an eye for the bizarre.

The island had escaped the suburban growth of the city through a combination of good fortune and the force of money. It sat neatly midway between downtown Seattle and the fast-growing techno-suburbs of Bellevue and Redmond, a developer's heaven linked to the old money and the new by a couple of bridges that swam happily above the clean, sparkling waters of Lake Washington. This was a big island but it was a precious one too. And when the money started to flow, downtown and out in the suburbs, Mercer, without anyone much thinking about it, had become the natural place for the rich people to live: isolated without being distant, so close to the water, and the tumbling green forests, that you felt you lived in some verdant paradise, and Nordstrom was only fifteen minutes away by car in either direction.

Hal Jamieson had conceived the idea of the house back in 1987, when the Nasdaq listing had become a good racing certainty, and he knew, for the first time, that thanks to God, hard work and a market starting to salivate at the imminent arrival of the junk bond era, he was going to be spending his entire life surrounded by more money than he could ever possibly use. As it turned out, SCC was one of the least junky flotations to come out that year.

This had been a time when the marriage to Louise had been going pretty smoothly. They didn't row too much. Sometimes they even talked about kids. It came to nothing, though they had plenty of fun trying, and for a little while she'd made noises about seeing one of the big-time expensive doctors down near the university, seeing if there wasn't some way round it – eggs in the tube, semen in the syringe – that could make her pregnant after all. Then the flotation happened and suddenly Jamieson's workload went from heavy to phenomenal. All these people who had just bought a chunk of the company felt they'd bought a chunk of him too, demanded presentations, explanations, reports, analysts' briefings. As SCC started to slip immeasurably out of his absolute control – they brought in a new layer of middle management and the idea, he knew, was that one day they'd really run things, really they would – the irony was that he seemed to have to work harder and harder at flimsy, ethereal things, things that didn't really matter. Like meetings. And glad-handing the people from Nasdaq. And all the other bullshit that seemed to go with the job of running a newly public company.

Somewhere along the way Louise slipped from his grasp and, if he'd had the time to look back – the time, who the fuck has the time? – he would still have been unable to pinpoint the moment, and there was a moment, of that he was certain, when it happened. It was like crossing a bridge, turning round and seeing it collapse behind you, with no obvious way of rebuilding what had just been destroyed before your eyes. One day she was not there when he thought she would be. One day he didn't come home without calling. It all just started to slip gently apart, in hotel rooms out to the south on I-5, in the beds of friends who had too little to do and too much to drink, anywhere that seemed convenient, anywhere that seemed to fit.

By the end of '87 he realised she hadn't mentioned getting pregnant for months, and realised too that he was glad, that it was the last subject he wanted to hear introduced into the conversation. And so he threw her the house – no, more than a house, a *statement* – as some kind of consolation prize, some sort of thirty-million-dollar bunch of flowers. He bought the land, offered several times the market value for the adjoining waterside plots of three long-standing Mercer Island residents who succumbed eventually, when they just couldn't say no to such huge sums any more, and handed the whole thing over to her. By this time it was making waves in the papers. But this was an era when excess wasn't excessive and, in any case, Hal Jamieson just didn't look the Gordon Gecko part. His hair was too long, he hated wearing suits, and, in the bars, men could mention his name and exchange a knowing glance: unlike some other computer billionaires they could mention, Hal Jamieson knew how to spend his money. He liked to party. He liked to drink. Most of all, the word said, he liked women.

It took four years to build and she supervised every brick. To his surprise, the project came in bang on budget. Maybe she'd been balling the contractor.

The mansion didn't look like thirty million dollars. It didn't look like anything anyone had ever seen in Washington State. Louise had flown to Europe for three months to think about what she wanted to build. When she came back, she told him she'd bought what she wanted, was having it shipped brick by brick from Palma de Mallorca. It was an ancient *finca* that had once belonged to a cousin of the King of Spain, so square and solid you'd think, at first glance, it could have passed as a castle. Then when you looked again you appreciated the subtleties. The delicate rose windows on what had once been a private chapel. The cupola towers at each end of the main wing. And the tiles, a weathered Mediterranean red that looked wonderful under the Washington sun but sat mute, almost resentful, during the days when the rain and fog came in. That was the problem with the mansion. Hal Jamieson felt it instinctively straight away, and the odd thing was that he felt Louise knew all along this *would* be the problem. That it was plain to her from the outset that the house would always seem out of place during the long days of damp dull weather that hung around the city for weeks on end, like a tropical flower force-fed to bloom in the Arctic.

He didn't understand that one little bit until the day the last contractor moved out and they stood on the perfect, newly turfed lawn, under a warm April sun, listening to the water lap at the newly built jetty, with its newly built motor launch, behind them.

He nodded, smiled at her, wondered where she was these days, what occupied her time, her thoughts, and said, 'It's incredible.'

She looked at him, trying to gauge how much he understood.

'It's money, Hal. You can do anything with money. You should know that.'

'Yeah.'

He looked at the great golden stone, the huge red roof that seemed to go on forever, wondered what had brought him here, what turn in his, in their, existence.

'You need a party, Louise. *We* need a party.'

'I called the caterers yesterday.'

'That's my girl.'

'You'll give me some dates? When you're free? Who you'd like to invite from your side?'

'Sure. I'll get Deborah to fax it to you.'

She said nothing, looked at him, not the house.

Hal Jamieson smiled, felt his shoulders move without being told, remembered what it was like to feel a jerk.

'That sounded really bad, didn't it? Like I was talking to some business people or something?'

'Or something.'

'Louise?'

It would be easier if he didn't feel anything any more, if he didn't look at her and remember all those days and nights when there was nothing in the world but them, their bodies, pale and hot under a single sheet. When she looked just like she does now, not a day older, not an ounce less beautiful.

'Things get crazy. That's what pays for it all. No craziness, no mansions. Seems to be life's golden rule. If you want . . .'

She watched him with the exact same pair of eyes that had first trapped him back in California, first made him want her so much way back then.

'If you want, you have the house. I'll live some place else. It's no big deal. Whatever you want, you can have it.'

'What are you saying, Hal?'

'I'm saying if you want me to go, I'll go. If you want me to stay, I'll stay.'

'What do you want to do?'

He thought about it, thought about the way she smiled when she said it.

'Does that matter?'

'It matters to you.'

As plain, as flatly as that.

'I'd like to stay. Who knows? New house, new life.'

That smile again and then she said, 'Who knows?'

'Yeah.'

He rubbed the sole of his Reebok against the grass. It was so perfect it seemed impossible that it could be a living thing.

'You need a name for it, you know. All houses gotta have names. Dunfuckin. Whatever. No. I'll tell you what. Something Indian. We're supposed to be into this Native American thing right now. They used to live here, after all. Pick some Indian shit, something from the Duwamish centre, they'll come up with something.'

'I thought of that,' she said.

'You did?'

'Yes. In Renton there used to be a waterhole called Skate'lbsh. They thought a supernatural dwarf lived there and made anyone who came close to him grow wealthy.'

'Really.'

He was grinning.

'Louise. I'm wealthy already. I don't *need* some fucking supernatural dwarf to handle my portfolio.'

'I know,' she said. 'I'm calling it Desert Rose.'

A handful of small cumulus scuttered across the sun and that meant he couldn't read, just couldn't even see, her face when she said it.

'You're some fucking woman, Louise,' he said in a half-whisper. 'I'll say that for you.'

Then Hal Jamieson walked over the perfect green lawn, past the perfect stone mansion, climbed into his car and drove off for the night.

SEVEN

Michael Shines

With memory set smarting like a reopened wound, a man's
past is not simply a dead history, an outworn preparation of
the present: it is not a repented error shaken loose from the
life: it is a still quivering part of himself, bringing shudders
and bitter flavours and the tinglings of a merited shame.

GEORGE ELIOT,
Middlemarch

Hal Jamieson drove the Lexus past the narrow, half-hidden driveway
to the cabin, drove a further half-mile up the winding, tree-lined hill,
then pulled it over onto a narrow patch of grass at the brow. From
here, on a good day, he could see back to the fringes of the city, across
mile upon mile of pine and fir, rolling in a vast green sweep down
the hillside all the way to the coast. Today the view was limited to no
more than half a mile, and even that got obscured from time to time
by the swirls of grey smoking cloud that wheeled around these lesser
foothills of the Cascades.

There had hardly been a soul on the road as he drove up from
Mercer Island, up from the waterline into the mountains that sat like
a backdrop to the city, and that suited him. Hal Jamieson had taken
care about how he owned the cabin and the hundred and fifty acres
of empty forest around it. There was a string of shell companies
separating him from the deeds, companies that ran through a series
of states out to Bermuda then on to Grand Cayman, so long and
tortuous it would take years to link him into the property. It was the
first offshore deal he'd set up, as much out of interest as necessity,
and as things turned out it was a smart move. When he heard the
news that Quinn was going to be freed, this was a place where he
could hide him until the storm blew over, until he worked out what
the hell to do next, a place where there would be some respite from

the tsunami of publicity that just had to follow, and with no footprints leading back to him if things somehow went wrong. Except they couldn't go wrong. He couldn't allow that to happen.

Hal Jamieson pulled out a pair of Pentax binoculars and looked back down the road. There was no sign of anyone else. No cars – they would have to have their lights on in this daylight gloom – no people. He'd chosen the cabin well, half thinking the solitary location might interest Louise if she wanted to come back into his life, half realising that it would have its uses if she didn't. In the event there had been only one woman who'd passed through its doors, a magazine writer who'd flown from New York to write his profile, spent three days in his wake, oohed and aahed when he took her for a joyride in the Citation, then fallen straight into the king-size four-poster in the cabin for one long day and night of mindless, thoughtless fucking. He drove her back to Sea-Tac for the flight to the East Coast the next day and promptly forgot about her. When she called the following week, leaving a message on his voicemail, he didn't even recognise the name at first, and when he did he couldn't think of a single reason to call back.

And then he heard the news about Quinn, and Hal Jamieson's life, so secure, so safe, so insulated from the world, suddenly tottered on the edge of unreality. It was like living on the San Andreas fault: you never knew whether the quake was going to come or not. He hated that, hated it so much that when he thought about it the perpetual smile left Hal Jamieson's face and he suddenly felt old and ragged and edgy.

He scanned the road again then looked at the small clearing around the cabin. There was nothing there, nothing except Steve Baxter's Shogun (bought for cash, no links there, Jamieson had seen to that), a pile of logs for the wood stove, a small, rock garden area he had never got around to landscaping, and probably never would.

Hal Jamieson breathed deeply, got back in the car, turned the ignition key then stared out of the window. He hated the feeling of time ticking away at his back like this but sometimes you just didn't have a choice. He reversed out into the narrow blacktop lane, set off down the road and took the drive to the cabin, parking next to the giant Shogun. Then he breathed deeply, got out of the car, walked to the big wooden door, sorted out the two high-security keys needed to open it, and walked in.

Michael Quinn was hunched on the sofa, a set of expensive cans around his ears, rock music fizzing out of them. Baxter stood in front of him, warming his backside on the log flames coming out of the big stone fireplace, taking in what was going on. The music was so loud Jamieson could even recognise it from the door: Iron Butterfly, something from *In-A-Gadda-Da-Vida*. In his head the crackling sound from across the room turned into the original, played on the Barn's ancient hi-fi. The ease with which it all happened astonished him. He was amazed he could ever have listened to this shit – it was old even when he was young – amazed he could have been so indiscriminate in his tastes, and that, more than anything, somewhere in his head there lay the memory of the original, so accurate, so perfect, still intact after all these years, still waiting for some tiny trigger to reappear, fully formed, entire.

If Quinn had turned the whole fucking thing off right then Hal Jamieson could have played the rest of the track in his head, and the thought half scared him, made him wonder what else was still in there, inside his head, waiting to leap out, unbidden, unwanted.

Hal Jamieson realised that Baxter was looking at him with that slightly puzzled, slightly stupid expression that seemed to be the trademark of suited heavies everywhere. Quinn was lost in his own world, eyes closed. Jamieson motioned to Baxter and the big man walked over to join him.

'Let's talk in the kitchen, Steve,' Jamieson said quietly. 'We need to run through a few things before I start with this guy.'

It was a big, handsome room so full of polished pine it shone. The walls were pine, the floor and ceiling were pine, even the huge table, big enough to seat twelve, was a gleaming vast monument in wood. A long cooking range took up one side of the room. A wine rack with some of Washington and Sonoma's finest lined the wall opposite. At the far end was a door onto the small back garden. It was securely bolted, at the top and bottom, and the key that normally hung in the lock was gone. Baxter knew his business.

Hal Jamieson gave the bodyguard half a smile, didn't even begin to try to work out what was going on behind the angular, strong mask that Baxter wore as a face, and said, 'So how is he?'

The big man shrugged. He towered over Jamieson, almost a good foot taller.

'Beats me.'

'You elaborate on that a little, Steve?'

Baxter thought about it. He hated saying imprecise things. Hated anything that was fuzzy. It was a habit that came from the army. He didn't think it was the kind of thing you could lose easily.

'He's quiet. He understands the situation. I don't think he's going to do anything stupid.'

'Like trying to get out of here?'

'I don't think so.'

Jamieson thought about it. 'That's a start. What's he been asking you for?'

'The sort of things you'd expect. Can he have a woman? Can he have some dope? Not much else. I said it probably wouldn't be a problem but I didn't want to do something until you said yes. This morning, after we talk, he wants some wine, so I say, go pick one from the rack. This guy knows his stuff. Picks out a Quilceda Creek cab straight away, drinks the whole fucking bottle down in under an hour. Good eighty-dollar wine too. Amazing the things you pick up in the pen. That was OK? Me letting him have the wine?'

'That was OK. Michael's been picking up amazing stuff as long as I've known him.'

'And the other things? He's sure to ask.'

'You can handle it?'

Baxter didn't answer straight away.

'You want the honest truth?'

'Sure,' said Hal Jamieson and he could feel his wallet start to moan gently in the pocket of his jacket.

'You hire me for security work, Mr Jamieson. That's fine. No problem. This guy, dope, pimping for him, that's something else. That's not part of the contract.'

'You want more money, Steve? Would that make it part of the contract?'

'More money would help, Mr Jamieson.'

'I didn't say "help", Steve. You're normally a precise guy. I like that about you. I said, would it fix it?'

'I think so.'

'I give you more money, you can handle all this. *All* this?'

Baxter nodded. 'You give me more money, Mr Jamieson, I can handle most any damn thing you want. It's just a question of the rate for the job.'

'Same all over the world, Steve. Amazing the things money does.'

'Yeah,' the big man grunted happily. He sounded a little like a pig when he did that, Hal Jamieson thought to himself. 'Truly amazing.'

'OK. We'll sort something out. You take my word on that? Or you want to negotiate now?'

'Sure, Mr Jamieson. I take your word on that.'

'Good. So you go get him a woman. You go get him some dope. I don't mind about that. But you don't need me to tell you, Steve, don't do anything stupid. By which I mean don't do anything that brings other people here, except the ones you know about. And don't let *him* do anything stupid either. Yeah. And one more thing.'

Baxter liked the way Jamieson was staring at him now. All the happy hippy stuff had gone from his face. Now the guy looked like he really meant something. Now he could see why the guy got all this money in the first place.

'Yeah?'

'No fucking acid. You get me? Whatever he says, whatever he promises you. No. Fucking. Acid.'

Baxter nodded. 'I hear you.'

'I hear you too, Hal.'

The voice made Hal Jamieson's skin go cold and uncomfortable, even after all these years. Maybe because of all these years. Michael Quinn stood behind them in the doorway, leaning on the post, gaunt, almost skeletal. He was smiling, lips closed, sinking into his face, like an old man who'd worn dentures all his life. His skin was as smooth, as flawless as ever but it had the flat, dull look of old paper. His eyes – God, Hal Jamieson had forgotten about those eyes – seemed to gleam through a film, some transparent cataract that was somehow invisible but still there. He looked older but in a way that wasn't quite right. Not like a forty-year-old, more like an eighteen-year-old suddenly turned forty overnight. Yeah. And there was one more thing. One thing Hal Jamieson could hardly believe it seemed so odd. Michael Quinn's hair, that blond choirboy tussle, was now gone. His skull shone so brightly it might have been oiled, and Hal Jamieson remembered the face of a rock singer he'd seen on MTV, in a hotel suite in Tokyo once, singing about losing your religion, and looking like the angel of death. Michael Quinn's skull shone and it made him look like some-

143

thing you ought to keep hidden, something that deserved to be kept off the streets.

Jamieson put on his best face, the one he saved for analysts' meetings, grinned from ear to ear, walked over, shook his hand, felt his shoulders, gently, gingerly. Quinn didn't seem to react at all.

'Now you go leave us, Steve,' said Jamieson, still grinning. 'This guy's one old buddy of mine and we need to talk private. You pass us another bottle of that Quilceda Creek and you go make yourself scarce. Later you get someone you trust to replace you then you go get Michael here that stuff he was asking for. He's got a lot of making up to do.'

Baxter searched through the wine rack until he found the right bottle, placed it on the huge kitchen table, then left the room. Jamieson rifled through a drawer in the range and he found the corkscrew, started heaving at the bottle. Quinn pulled down two glasses from a huge cupboard, placed them on the table, sat down and said, 'Cut the fucking bullshit, Hal. You want me here as much as you want a hole in the fucking head.'

Hal Jamieson sat down and poured out the wine. It flowed into the glasses, rich and red and fragrant. Quinn could see its aroma the moment the cork popped out of the bottle. It bubbled out of the neck, in all sorts of colours.

'Wow, Michael. Now this is new. Realism. They really do teach you lots of things in the pen.'

'Twenty fucking years. You learn a lot of things in there, Hal. Things you couldn't even dream about.'

'I'll take your word on that, Michael. Believe me.'

'Oh, I do believe you, Hal. I really do.'

Quinn took a gulp of the wine. It was an ugly, animal gesture. Jamieson tried to remember if it had always been like that. It didn't seem possible. He would have remembered.

'So where are they? The musketeers? Maybe that's not the right term. The musketeers ran towards trouble, not away from it.'

Jamieson tried to figure out if he really meant it.

'You still bitter?'

Quinn hesitated for a moment then, 'No more than ever. No more than I was before.'

'Good, Michael. Because what happened is what happened. None of us had any choices. You know that just as well as I do. The only choice was you go down or we all go down. Some fucking choice. And the fact you're here now, the fact you're not out there on your own trying to dodge all those people who'd like to see you crucified shows something, doesn't it?'

'Sure,' Quinn said grinning. 'Shows you're scared shitless they might catch up with me.'

Jamieson tried the wine, only a little sip. He didn't want to drink much. He didn't want to relinquish an ounce, a proton, of control with Michael Quinn.

'That's in all our interests, Michael. All of us.'

Quinn nodded and it looked as if he half accepted that. 'And who exactly *is* "all of us" these days? I didn't get many letters when I was in Obispo keeping me up to date on things.'

'You got what we could get through to you. You got your stock. That's worth a real lot of money now.'

'The musketeers?'

'You, me. Louise you know about. Paul just stayed out there on the edge. He's still in the city. Runs some flea-bitten recording studio. Great. Don't ask me what he remembers because I don't know and I don't think he does either. He got hurt too. Remember? We got what news we could to you there in Obispo. You got to know. Things got a little fuzzy there towards the end.'

Quinn's face screwed up in something close to rage and spatters of wine leapt from his mouth as he spoke. 'Paul. The guy was so *straight*. Why the fuck was he *there*?'

'Like I said, Michael. What happened is what happened. There's no changing it.'

'Mouse?'

'Gone, man. Long gone. And don't ask me what happened to her 'cos I just got no idea.'

'So when it comes down to saving people's asses it's you, your little wife, the guitar player, that's all.'

'I think you forgot someone, Michael. You. You too.'

Quinn just glared at him with such fierceness it almost hurt. 'I got way past being saved a long time ago, Hal.'

'Maybe.'

'No. No maybes.'

More than half the bottle of wine was gone now and Jamieson realised he had hardly drunk a drop.

'You should go easy on that stuff, Michael. Seems a shame to spend twenty years in the pen then drink yourself to death the moment you get out.'

'Just winding down, Hal. Come tomorrow things will start to clear. You can get your baboon to fix me some dope – and no, I don't want no acid. I don't *need* acid. A woman though. That would be cool. But I'll be OK. I gotta be. You need me.'

'I need you to stay out of things. A long way out.'

'And then?'

'You know what these media creeps are like. They get real hot on a story for two weeks then, when nothing happens, they get bored, just fuck off to something else. They're like flies looking for horseshit – if one pile doesn't turn up they just drift off looking for the next one and where they were last week just goes straight out of their tiny heads. One month. Maybe two months. Everything will be clear here. We can get you out, fix you up with some new identity, a home. You tell me. Whatever you like. You got the money in your stock. There's income there, you could sell it if you want, though I'd appreciate it if you let us try to handle that inside the corporation first. And if that's not enough just tell me, I can come up with more. Maybe you'd like Europe. You got to start thinking about it, start right now. Need some real estate brochures we'll get them in for you. This is going to be a new life, Michael. God knows you deserve it. You start thinking. Things are really looking up.'

Quinn drained the last of the bottle. He looked more than a little drunk, even a little dangerous.

'Yeah,' he said, and there was a distinct slur to his voice.

'You know something, Hal?'

'What?'

'I just couldn't fucking believe it when I heard.'

'Heard what?'

'About you and Louise. I just couldn't fucking believe it. I mean some Boston Irish scumbag like you getting hitched to that supercilious society bitch. Specially after every one of us had fucked her already. That really killed me. Really it did.'

Jamieson put his glass of wine down on the table and tried not to listen, tried as hard as he could, knowing all the time it was like hoping to brush back the tide with a broom.

'You know what I think? What I think is, when I look back, when

I remember – and I remember everything, Hal, *everything*, even things you think I didn't even know about at the time – I *remember* fucking her and it's still there, everything, like the whole event, beginning to end, where I stuck it, what she did, the whole fucking thing. And I think that must be why you married her 'cos you see I know I fucked Mouse more than I ever fucked Louise, and for the life of me I don't remember a single time. So I guess you married her 'cos she's one great fuck. Not for the money. Not for the name. Not 'cos of the Barn or anything like that. You just married her 'cos your dick told you to. And you know, I *admire* that, Hal. I *admire* a man that lets a part of his body talk to him like that, doesn't just leave it to his brain, and you must have a real good brain, building up your business, building up *our* business, that way. And when it comes to matters of marriage you just let your brain go take a walk and ask your dick to do the thinking. What I remember of Louise that seems a real smart thing to do. Guess you must be glad things turned out that way, or you starting to find out that other guys get the same intuitions?'

Hal Jamieson was a man who just didn't lose his temper, it just didn't occur to him, but for a moment he thought that he could have killed Quinn right then. If there'd been a switch on the table, a button to press, a lever to pull, he could have done it. Just for a moment.

'I guess I owed you the right to that, Michael. I guess you got the right to want to get it out of your system.'

'Oh no,' said Quinn, and now his eyes were gleaming, no cataract there, they were just like they used to be, back in the days when Hal Jamieson used to feed him dope like it was candy. They were gleaming, just like his skull that was now positively iridescent, with sweat, the marks of his scalp, the spots, the blotches, so alive, so radiant in the airy interior of the cabin.

'No. You owe me more than that, Hal. Much, much more.'

EIGHT

Four Four, Thirteen Eight

For tribal man space was the uncontrollable mystery. For technological man it is time that occupies the same role.

MARSHALL MCLUHAN,
The Mechanical Bride

A composer is a guy who goes around forcing his will on unsuspecting air molecules, often with the assistance of unsuspecting musicians.   FRANK ZAPPA

'Genius.'

Frank Grayson's deep black voice seemed to come out of nowhere and it sounded angry.

'Huh?'

On the screen of the Mac, obscuring some complex jazz quintet score, was a still from a porn movie, pure porn, so red and livid Grayson felt a little queasy just looking at it.

'Jesus, Genius. You gonna sit there putting Mr Kleenex's kids through college the rest of your life or what? We got work to do, man.'

Frank was hugging his red Fender bass and staring at the fat kid like he could hit him.

Genius put on his Elmer Fudd act as fast as he could. 'What you saying, Unca Fwankie? I done my work. I gave you the notes.'

'You kill me, kid, you really do. Till I met you I always thought this sex and computers thing was a scam, they'd *never* get around to doing it until they invented some fucking Apple Mac you could use with just one hand. Man, I went into one of those Internet cafés off First last week just to try to get a handle on you and it sure beats the fuck outta me. All these kids look just like you an' got their face into a screen full of beaver and dirty talk and *they look like they're getting off on this stuff.* You walk into the john in these places an' you don't find a condom machine you find a fucking screenwipe dispenser. I always thought all this stuff about you could go blind staring at computers had something to do with the radiation, Genius. Didn't realise it was 'cos you guys were just sitting there burpin' the worm all night and day.'

'Don't catch AIDS in cyberspace, Uncle Frankie,' Genius said, looking a little hurt. 'Cybersex is safe sex.'

'That, Genius, is 'cos it ain't really sex at all,' Frank Grayson snapped back, looking really cross. 'Now can we get off the subject of your love affair with your fingers and talk work please? This is an ad for farm-fresh fucking milk. It is an ad for something ladies go down the supermarket to buy every day and buy without thinking. I go sending that agency some jingle that's written in thirteen eight they gonna be down here kicking my ass so hard I'll be wishing I'd spent Christmas Day drinking instead of working with some freaked-out bonehead like you. How many times I have to tell you? These are *jingles.* You write jingles in four four. People *hear* jingles in four four. You want to do the fancy stuff, you wait till the art museum are down here dickering for something for free. When people pay, we give them what they pay for.'

'Common time for the common people, you want my opinion,' Genius grunted and reached for the keyboard.

'Opinions are like information, Genius. The world's full of 'em and everybody just feels the width and says, "Wow, look how much opinion, look how much information we got here." Never ask to see the quality of what's running through their fingers.'

'I'll twy to wemember dat, Unca Fwankie.'

'Right, my boy,' Frank said, looking through the studio door into the grey exterior, seeing some shape cast a dark stain on the pebbled glass. 'And while you're there kindly close down that picture of the naked lady's private stuff. You don't know who's about to march straight in here. May be Mother Teresa herself.'

Then Joni Lascelles walked in, smiled at them and said, before either of them could get a word out, 'Lady alert.'

She seemed really thin today. Her jeans were narrow, angular down to the ankle. She wore a navy-blue jacket. The blonde curls bounced around her head, out of control. And the shades were gone. Her eyes, so bright, so blue, looked calm on the outside, looked ready for anything. But when Frank Grayson peered a little more closely (Genius didn't even try) he thought there was something beneath the surface, something working, thinking, something that might have given an older man, a more experienced man, pause for thought.

'Maybe not this time,' Genius mumbled to himself, left the picture on the screen just long enough for her to see a glimpse of it before the window zoomed back in on itself.

'He's in the studio,' Frank said, motioning to the door. 'You can walk in. See. No red light over the door. It's safe. Everything's safe here.'

'Safe as houses,' she said and walked into the little room.

Paul Dunsany was seated at the desk, listening to something through a big set of studio cans. He looked absorbed in whatever was playing there. She couldn't hear a note through the big soft wad of sound-deadening material around the ears. Joni Lascelles looked at the dials and sliders of the desk. They seemed old and worn, like the props from some seventies sci-fi series, things you pushed and pulled through uncertain amounts of pressure, never quite getting it right, never quite hitting the spot, full of inexactitude, not buttons you pressed and watched the lights flicker on and off.

After a minute or so he took off the headphones, put them on the desk, turned to her and said, 'Hi.'

'You knew I was there all along? I thought you were somewhere else.'

'You work in a studio for so long it gets like that. You can concentrate on something and still take note of what's going on some place else. Same as anything. The more you do it, the better you get.'

He was wearing a light shirt under a blue cotton mariner's sweater, newly faded jeans. She still couldn't shake off the impression that he wasn't a musician at all. That he was really some account executive at a middle-rung, trendy ad agency, someone who should have been carrying one of those big document cases from meeting to meeting, a little harassed, a mobile phone in the pocket of his Armani jacket. He looked so out of place in the dingy little studio, playing with the ancient switches and sliders. At least he did, until you saw the degree of absorption on his face when he came to concentrate on the music, the strict, intricate division and sub-division of time and voice and timbre that passed through the cans. When she thought about it she realised that it didn't matter to him what the music was, whether it was some kid's first demo or an ad for local radio. It was the notes that counted, and he liked to march them across the music safely, all together, all in time, like a lollipop lady back home marshalling children across the road and into school.

'Where are we going?'

'Out,' he said and reached behind the desk for his red Columbia mountain jacket.

'You mean the Zanzibar?'

'There are more varieties of "out" than the Zanzibar. Do I look as if I spend my entire life in either Pike Place Studios or the Zanzibar?'

She said nothing.

'OK. Don't answer that.'

They walked back into the office, he spoke a few quiet words to Frank and Genius, who were huddled over the Mac, pushing crotchets and quavers around the screen, and then they were out of the door, walking up flight after flight of stone steps, past the shops of Pike Place, past magic stores and women's bookshops, speciality kite shops, herb sellers, tea sellers, coffee shops and an Italian deli that had in its window a huge display of multi-coloured pasta in flavours (curry? boysenberry?) that would have caused riots in Milan. Past a whole line of restaurants offering everything from five-buck dim sum lunches and 'the best chilli in the world', up a sloping walkway, still under cover, still illuminated only by the cold steely grey light from the overhead lamps and the occasional ancient window. Then it got brighter, she could smell the odour of fish stained deep into the stonework. They walked past wooden stalls painted green and blue and white, a few people around, doing some maintenance, sorting things out, and then they were out in the fresh air, on the long walkway with the metal pillars at the front of the market, underneath the lighted sign you saw in the postcards. Was it three floors or four? She couldn't work it out. Before, she had gone down the side way, straight down the hill, straight down the alley going towards Post and found the studio door just staring at her, daring her to go in. But Dunsany had taken her out by the scenic route, even with every storefront closed in the market, and it was like being led through a maze that went in three dimensions, up, down, around, and all through the hoops again.

They stood on the cobbled road outside the market entrance and she said, 'You'd need a long piece of string.'

151

He looked puzzled. In the open air he seemed pale, younger somehow.

'Excuse me?'

'To find your way out again. Like the Minotaur's maze.'

'Oh.'

He looked like he didn't see the daylight very much, even the Seattle daylight. And he looked like he didn't understand what she said. There was something naive, something unfinished about Paul Dunsany, as if his growing up had been interrupted somewhere along the line and left him with the habits of a teenager. It intrigued, maybe even half attracted her.

'It's like I said. You keep doing it long enough, you just do it automatically.'

He started to walk up the hill towards First, watching the sporadic traffic, nodding, saying 'hi' to the people who walked past, people she half recognised from Pike Place, on their way for a quiet hour's work behind closed doors: the big man with the beard on the fish counter, who seemed so dextrous when it came to juggling king salmon, the little Italian from the deli, the woman farmer who stood so still, so silent behind a wooden table covered with dried fruit. There was a community here and Paul Dunsany was so much a part of it that just being with him seemed to make you a member too. What else could explain the curiosity, so open, so frank, they had towards her, the way they stared across the cobbled street and watched her, wondering?

'Do you do everything automatically?'

Paul Dunsany wondered about it for a moment, and tried to check his own mood, tried to work out what part of him was nervous, what part curious, what part hopeful.

'After a while don't we all?'

'I don't think so.'

They got to the top and looked right and left. The big avenue was deserted. He crossed over the road, heading towards the modern shopping centre a few hundred yards ahead.

'You know you're the second person in two days to have this kind of conversation with me. I *like* what I do. It's not glamorous. God knows, it doesn't pay very much. But I like it. A whole lot better than working in some office some place.'

She wondered where they were going. Wondered if he really knew.

'I don't think you'd ever have to work in an office, Paul. You're too good. You could do something with it.'

He looked at her and she wondered why he wasn't angry. Whether this was something Paul Dunsany just couldn't feel.

'I *do* do something with it. I help people make records. You listen to Little Feat? Some of the early Hornsby stuff? Read the liner notes. I was there. I played, I got paid, I left. What more can a man ask? I'm a player. Not a writer. Know what you're good at. That's what the books tell you. That's what I *do*.'

'But . . .'

And just then there *was* something close to fierceness in his eyes when he interrupted, though it didn't look quite right. 'But nothing. You know six, maybe seven years ago I had some kids come into the studio, cut a demo, go out as happy as pie. They used to play the clubs. Used to play the Zanzibar sometimes too. They made a little money. They were big stars in a little world. Everybody loved them. Then it all got bigger and bigger until one of them put a shotgun to his head. You know the name? Good. You go ask the people who really knew him about *making it*. You might find they've got a different perspective on things.'

He had stopped by an elevator built into the wall of the shopping centre, with a sign by the side of it saying 'monorail'.

'Oh, dear. First date and we're arguing already.'

He climbed into the car, she followed, and he turned round, grinning. Back to the smile of a teenager.

'Sorry. You hit my sensitive spot.'

And she wondered why, what made this sensitive, what complex mix of emotions lay inside him.

'You've got to be sensitive to play the Zanzibar,' he said and did a little 'don't mind me being a jerk' grin. 'It's in the rules.'

'The rules are OK by me,' Joni Lascelles replied and smiled back. When he looked at her, out here in the thin grey light of day, she didn't seem so young any more. And in a way that made her look prettier. Paul Dunsany didn't believe in perfection, didn't want perfect things around him. He was always afraid of breakages: him or them.

'This is real tourist stuff. You have to come here. That's in the rules too.'

'OK.'

They went up to a bleak, deserted platform and he bought a couple of tickets from the sullen-looking youth behind the desk.

'This is working?' she asked. 'It's Christmas Day, Paul.'

He leaned over the edge of the platform, tilted his head at the big steel rail, so worn, so shiny.

'Listen,' he said. 'That's all you have to do.'

So she followed what he did, and she could hear it too, the low hum of something vast and mechanical, moving rapidly down the line towards them.

'This is the stupidest form of transport known to man,' he said. 'I love it.'

The train pulled noisily into the station and she almost laughed. It was so bizarre. Like an illustration from a child's comic of the 1950s: What the Future Will Be Like. All rounded corners and streamlining, it must have seemed dated almost the moment it was built. They walked inside, sat behind the driver who was playing with controls that looked as if they came from a Disney film. Paul Dunsany caught the amusement on her face.

'See what I mean? Anywhere else they'd have pensioned this thing off years ago. Not here. Everyone in this city is crazy. The rain just penetrated our skulls or something.'

Then, with an electric rush that surprised her, the monorail pulled out of the station and they were floating above the city, floating along the humming, dun-coloured rail towards the outline of the Space Needle, like a concrete starship out of *Dan Dare* pointed skywards, fixed to the grey horizon in front of them.

'What's there to see?'

He shrugged his shoulders, a small, pleasant gesture.

'Nothing much. What'd you expect? They put this stuff up in '62 for the World's Fair. Someone got hold of a picture of a sputnik or something and tried to dream up what the world would be like. Maybe they were putting down some kind of a template. Maybe they thought that all this would be how things turned out, and the rest of the city would just start to grow like it over the years. I don't know. What we got is . . . I don't know. What do *you* think we've got.'

She looked at the Space Needle looming up ahead, the huddle of ugly buildings that showed their age, with peeling paint, ugly exteriors.

'A fixation with a past that never was,' she said, and didn't look at him.

The day wasn't turning out too bad. As they walked out of the station and stood in the shadow of the Needle the sky was a light grey, the visibility good under the cloud cover.

'You want to go up? Or are you scared of heights?'

'I'm not scared of heights,' she said.

'Not scared of anything?'

'I didn't say that.'

The elevator was small and rapid. It deposited them in the circular top of the building and they joined the handful of visitors wandering around the windows, looking at the mountains, the ocean, the huge, deserted, natural landscape spreading out on all sides. On a sunny day it would have been stunning. Even in the grey light that flattened everything and stole the colour from the scene, it was impressive, it gave her the sense that there might be more to the city, more to the place, than she could ever have suspected in her walks around the Pequod, her visit to Pioneer.

'And what's wrong with a fixation with the past anyway?' he asked. 'The people who did this, they could have been my parents. This is not history. This is part of us today. And they got it so wrong. They were looking forward to some great warm future in which life got better, the world got better, we built machines that freed us, instead of putting us into cages, putting us out of work. They built this thing in hope and maybe that's why it looks so stupid now. Maybe that's why I like it so much.'

He was staring out towards an inland splash of grey water, not focusing on anything in particular.

'See that?' he said, pointing. 'Lake Union. I live there.'

She followed the line of his arm, towards the oily pool of water. Lake Union looked like an afterthought, a sudden flood that had appeared in the centre of some grimy, urban city, as if the city came first and the lake followed. The margin ranged from industrial warehouses and boatyards to little seaplane bays, even a park that seemed to be made out of old machinery, deliberately turned rusty as some kind of statement: this is what I am, take it or leave it, but this is *all* I am. You might have made it a motto for the city.

'You *live* there?'

'Houseboat. Sounds *terribly* bohemian, huh? And see that?'

He pointed to a big, grey-green cabin on the water.

'Louie's. Best seafood around here. You hungry?'

'Starving. Is the sightseeing tour done?'

He smiled and said, 'I think so. You come here for the atmosphere, not for the sights. I guess you appreciate that already.'

Then they went back down in the elevator and found a solitary cab standing in the rank. It drove down to the west side of the lake then into the restaurant parking lot. 'Louie's on the Lake' was marked out in bright neon-green cursive handwriting on the roof of the cabin.

When they got out of the car, the air was different. It blew off the water straight into their faces, a weird mix of salt and spray and fuel oil. Seagulls and a handful of ducks skimmed the surface of the lake looking bored. The place seemed empty, dead, and when they walked into Louie's, that seemed empty and dead too.

'Happy Christmas,' said the bored, yawning waitress who led them to a table by the window. 'Can I get you a drink? Would you like to hear about the specials of the day?'

And this was America, Joni Lascelles thought. It just rolled on and on and on, always asking, always consuming, never letting go of the daily routine. Ever.

She ordered lightly – some king salmon, some asparagus, a glass of mineral water, just the kind of thing you eat on Christmas Day. And much to her surprise he did the same. No appetiser. No slab of meat. Paul Dunsany didn't fit her idea of the typical American man and, in some way she was still trying to work out, that was disturbing.

'So you got dumped,' he said, and there was a quick intelligence in his eyes that caught her by surprise.

'Pardon?'

'You come over here, a minute's notice. You don't know anyone. You don't even seem to know why you're doing it. You got dumped. That's it. I know. Men know these things. Particularly sensitive men.'

She put her napkin to her mouth as if it would hold in the laughter.

'Excuse me, Paul. But *men* know about very little. Very little indeed.'

He looked out of the window at the flat grey line of water.

'You don't want to talk about it. That's fine. Believe me. I'm not pressing. Really I'm not.'

'Paul. There is nothing to press. Why do you have to assume that just because a woman is on her own she must somehow have been abandoned or something? That somehow it's just not our natural state? What are we supposed to do? Carry a baby in one hand and a broom in the other? Which century are you inhabiting right now?'

156

He waved to the waitress and said, 'Shall we have a beer or something? It is Christmas, you know.'

'A beer,' she said and folded her arms in front of her chest, enjoying this, enjoying how it took her out of herself, stopped the little voice inside screaming. Stopped the faces.

'Two Redhooks,' he said loudly to the waitress across the empty dining room, and straight away the big cold amber glasses arrived.

'You see,' he said, 'you're right. It's not your natural state. Women are not naturally alone in the way men are. You're too ... conversational. And that's not a criticism. That's just an observation. A man can have a certain kind of stillness inside that women just don't know about. I'm not boasting about that. It's our curse. You're too sensible to want to be alone. You're just too goddamn clever.'

'That is the biggest heap of bullshit I have heard since...'

'Since the guy who dumped you,' he said and when he said it he was smiling in a way she couldn't help but like, a way that was not about victory, but about friendship. And recognition. There was, at that moment, something they recognised in each other, something that said hello, shook hands with itself behind the scenes, compared its separate likenesses and said yes to this and yes to that, nodded its head quite gravely then sat back in the wings and waited for whatever was going to happen to get on with the show. Right then, Joni Lascelles knew she could see Roscoe Sutter himself in the street and there would be no nightmares. Knew that all of those things that lay outside her head were somewhere else, painting someone else's horrors, not hers. Because there was something in Paul Dunsany they couldn't control, couldn't handle. Something simple and pure and genuine, something, and she hated the thought, very close to *goodness*.

She took a big swig of the beer and it tasted heavenly. Her cheeks were slightly flushed now. It made him realise something that had just stayed below the surface before, a thought he had unconsciously tried to ignore: how pale she was, how her skin seemed almost translucent, so you could see the veins, the blood beneath.

'You know,' she said. 'They told me a lot of things about you, your friends, most of them not directly. They told me you came from California.'

'College kid,' he said. 'Flunked out of Stanford so you're looking at someone who really knows how to flunk out of the best.'

'They told me lots of other things, too.'

'Only believe the good ones. The rest are vicious lies.'

'But they never told me you were that clever. Are you really that clever, Paul?'

He stared into the deep-red colour of the glass. It looked so familiar. Like a friend.

'If I was that clever would I be running a studio in Pike Place that turns over thirty thousand dollars a month on overheads of twenty-eight?'

'I didn't mean that.'

'No. I know.'

He looked at the glass. It was working its way towards empty. So was hers.

'You know,' he said, 'I'm not playing tonight. I'm not doing *anything* tonight. We could just sit here and drink beer and get maudlin drunk. Does that sound good to you?'

'You drink,' she said. 'I'll listen.'

But her glass was empty by the time the waitress came over.

'So he dumped you,' he said. 'He must have been really, really stupid.'

Joni Lascelles looked out of the window at the lazy grey sunlight and the boats bobbing on the greasy slick of water.

'You don't know that, Paul. You don't know me. You can't judge. I've been dumped, I've done the dumping. Both. Plenty of times. But that's back in the past. It's not why I'm here. Believe me.'

'Yeah,' he said.

He pointed across the water to a low-slung collection of wooden houseboats. More like houses than boats really, with front porches, trash cans around the sides, even a little garden here and there.

'You see that. Fifth from the right. Dark-red door, needs painting. That's mine.'

She stared across the water, screwing up her eyes as if she were a little short-sighted.

'I still can't believe you live on a *boat*.'

'Always have done. Ever since I came here twenty years ago. When I turned up, you could pick up one of those things for ten thousand dollars, maybe less if you were willing to argue. Today the real estate agents who keep banging on my door reckon it's worth two hundred thousand dollars for the site alone. Seems Tom Hanks did some film around the corner, since then the prices just keep going on up and up and up. Anybody who'd pay that kind of money for my kind of drains has got to be stupid, if you ask me, but that's what they say.'

'And you wouldn't think of selling now, would you?'

'Jesus, are you serious? Twenty years. Twenty years. Don't you know what the word "home" means?'

She laughed gently and, for the first time since he'd started jousting around the edges of her character, he felt uncomfortable, realised, and kicked himself for not seeing it before, that that was one thing that Joni Lascelles really didn't know a lot about at all.

'Home is where you keep your old guitars. Keep your old albums – I'm talking *albums* here, my girl, not little plastic disks that look like they come from some kid's arcade game, good old needles on plastic. Home is where you close your eyes and forget there ever was a world outside.'

'Home is where you're on your own.'

'Sometimes,' he said. 'Not always. I got through one and a half marriages in that old boat.'

She watched him, watched the way his eyes kept shining back at her. He was smiling, but he was serious too.

'You have half-marriages in America? How do you have a half-marriage?'

Paul Dunsany drank some more Redhook, wondered why it was always easier to talk, to think, to play too, when you had a beer there.

'Easy. Most marriages start off with both sides loving each other before they fall apart. A half-marriage is where only one side does the loving right from the very beginning. There are a lot of half-marriages in America. I've never been there, but I'd be willing to bet a considerable sum of money that you've got a good number of half-marriages back in England too if you knew where to look.'

'Oh.'

They could both feel the moment pivoting between them, both feel the tension running like an unspoken, humming wire through the air.

'If I invite you back to see my boat,' he said, 'will you view that as some kind of proposition?'

She looked at him, she didn't take her eyes off him, wanted to see what was happening there in his face. 'Should I?'

'No,' he said, and he looked as if he meant it. 'You don't know me well enough. And vice versa too.'

The waitress arrived with two plates, a bright pink salmon steak, some vegetables on each. He watched her eat, fast and enthusiastically.

'I didn't have breakfast,' she said.

'A person should always have breakfast. Breakfast is important.'

'Not when lunch is this big,' she said, then tidied up the plate and watched him pick his way through the fish and vegetables on his plate.

'It's not a proposition?'

'No. Really. Do I look the sort of guy . . .'

He liked the way she laughed with her eyes.

'No,' she said. 'You don't.'

'Thank you. I think that's a compliment.'

When the third pint of Redhook came she watched him drink half of it then put her hand over the top of the glass.

'I think we should go now. I think we should see your boat.'

They walked over, along the murky water wherever the path ran next to it, dodging the traffic on the big perimeter road when they had to, feeling themselves falling towards something, so easily, so slowly, so inevitably.

The boat was small, much smaller than it seemed from the outside. The interior was neat, tidy, but had that patina of neglect that men never seemed to notice. When she sat down, holding a big mug of coffee, she could feel it move slightly on the water, she could hear the gentle lapping on the hull outside. He put some music on the sound system, and it really was an album, guitar music she had never heard before, acoustic with a Mexican feel, mostly instrumental, mostly superb.

She watched him listening to the notes in silence, wondered at how enclosed the little cabin was, at the way it seemed to shut out the world and everything in it. You could sit inside this wooden cocoon and forget about all the badness out there, feel the silence, feel the warmth. And it came to her that Paul Dunsany would not, was unable to make the approach. Something inside him had frozen over the years and it was not the kind of thing she knew, had met before, not the fear of rejection, not weariness, or some fear of the idea of intimacy. There was a cause, a specific, discrete event, just as there was for her. And in this wooden cocoon there was some form of peace, some form of respite from its memory.

He would not move. He would sit listening to the music forever, however much he wanted to be with her. Joni Lascelles thought about this and, finally, said, 'Paul?'

He came back from the music, watched her from across the narrow cabin.

'Yes?'

'I'd like to stay. Just tonight. Call it company. Call it what you like. But I don't want to be alone. I thought I did. Now I know better. I don't want to be alone today.'

'Me neither,' he said, and smiled, not moving, so quiet, so childlike she could hardly believe it.

When they finally were in bed together, after she had gone into the bedroom, undressed and waited for him, underneath the big quilted eiderdown in a small cabin with wooden walls and porthole windows, the grey light flitting through them, the sound of gulls and lapping water outside, it seemed as natural as rain falling out of the sky.

It was late in the afternoon, with the light failing, when she thought about it, agreed with herself to dare.

She pulled herself out of his arms, leaned back on the pillow on one elbow and watched him in silence. He had that sleepy after-sex feeling that stopped you thinking straight, stopped you appreciating what was going on.

'Paul?'

'This is conversation time. I hear the signals.'

'Not really.'

And Joni Lascelles suddenly felt afraid. Not of what might happen if she trusted someone who could not be trusted. Not of anything that might threaten her. Afraid of the knowing, and having to face up to whatever it brought with it.

'You ever go back there. Palo Alto? You still have people there?'

He stared at the wooden ceiling, not liking the sound of these words, the way they echoed around the little bedroom.

'No. This is my life now. This is my home.'

She listened to the movement of the water on the wooden hull of the boat, the constant calling of the gulls, felt his breathing, the beating of his heart against her skin.

'You remember something from the papers there?' she said and saw her vision narrow, watched it turn into a slender tunnel of nothingness. 'Back in 1975? An abduction, a child getting killed?'

Paul Dunsany suddenly felt cold in the big, soft bed, felt the grey light coming into the room, sucking the heat out of his body.

'Sure I remember. It was on the TV, it was everywhere.'

161

'Still is. Do you still read the papers?'

'I read notes on sheets of music paper. And you won't find a TV on the boat. What's this about, Joni?'

And neither of them wanted to talk. Neither wanted to know, or say.

'It's about what happened then,' she said, in the end. 'It's about me finding someone, finding what happened. And you helping.'

He shook his head slowly and she watched his light-brown hair move slowly across his face.

'I'm a musician, Joni. I can't help you with something that's what, twenty-five years ago.'

'Twenty,' she said. 'Twenty to the day. The hour.'

'Oh, oh,' he said, and hated himself for the deception, for the pretence that this was just an ordinary thing, a thing that could be controlled and shaped and wiped away. 'This looks serious.'

She reached over, touched his hair, brushed it gently away from his cheek, looked at the scar there, the long, smooth line of flesh that seemed to be sinking into his face with age, touched it and felt the warmth, a little like electricity under the skin.

'It's serious,' she said. 'It's as serious as anything could be.'

NINE

Discoveries

If you believed they put a man on the moon, man on the moon.
If you believe there's nothing up my sleeve, then nothing is cool.

REM, 'Man on the Moon'

They are ill discoverers that think there is no land when they
see nothing but sea.   FRANCIS BACON,
The Advancement of Learning

'You did *what*?'

Louise Gostelow – this is a name to live through centuries, you don't throw it away on a whim or through the simple, forced momentum of necessity – stared across the drawing room and watched Hal Jamieson squirm deep in the mahogany leather armchair that looked too big for him, looked like the big wings might just fold together and smother him out of the world altogether.

It was four in the afternoon on Christmas Day. The light was failing on Mercer Island, the night coming down like a hazy curtain across the ragged line of pines, down across the waterline, where ducks squawked lazily and lone cormorants skimmed the moon-sparkled waves looking for some last sustenance before the waters turned to opaque blackness. The world was quiet, even if the people who inhabited it were not. Hal Jamieson listened to the hoot of an owl echoing around the pine forest, listened to the way it seemed to answer the squawking at the waterline, and wondered if there was some way he could measure the value of his world: in stone, in marble, in dollars? And if there was, some means he could weigh this value against some set, unchanging measure. Then realised he was dreaming. You didn't get joy per minute, you couldn't weigh love – or notlove – by the pound.

Somewhere else in the city Paul Dunsany and Joni Lascelles were

coupling for the second time that day, slowly, their breathing synco-
pated into a steady rhythm, their bodies closed in slow physical pleasure, not thinking about a climax, just happy to share in some dual
bliss, the one to the other, with no thoughts forming in their heads,
nothing but the dimly dancing colours and shapes that wheeled around
the carnal landscape of some inner, secret eye. Somewhere else, in a
cheap motel on the edge of the city, Tom Cordobes hunched over an
ancient monochrome Compaq LTE elite notebook computer, listened
to the modem clicking and hissing and chirruping down the RJ11
phone socket in the hotel bedroom, watched the screen surf across
the Net services, hunting, hunting, hunting, for something, anything,
to do with flying and some errant nerd whose Christmas Day might
be spent on-line.

'I thought this was over, Hal. I thought we could forget about it.
Now it's back. It's here on our doorstep. And you put it there.'

She was drinking, a single malt whisky in a tall glass, some ice, not
much in the way of water. He didn't like to see her drink, didn't like
the way her mouth sagged when she had too much.

'I didn't let Quinn out, Louise. That wasn't my decision.'

'You brought him here.'

'So what was I supposed to do? Leave him out there to go to the
papers, to go talk to the FBI again once he had nothing better to do?
Don't you see? He could bring us down. Everything. Dunsany maybe
doesn't remember what the fuck happened back then – *maybe* – but
I do, you do and so does Quinn. You want that running round the
papers? You want to walk into the Rainier Club and have all those
nice genteel city ladies turn round and look at you and say "Whoa, I
always knew there was something . . ."? I don't think so.'

She was drinking the Scotch too fast. Even she could tell. She put
the glass down on the fireplace – iron, an Adam reproduction that
probably cost more than the real thing – and tried to work out what
was going on. He watched her, waiting. It was rare for Louise to be
lost for words. It was rare for her to look like this: unsure, puzzled,
maybe even a little frightened.

Some place else in town Tom Cordobes started typing into the Net
chat area he'd found, watched the words appear on the screen, waited
for someone to start typing back in the great big buzzing void out
there somewhere.

Hi, AvNet, this is Barney Flyboy in Seattle, where the cloudbase is so low you couldn't commit aviation less'n you were flying one of Mr Boeing's wonders, and I'm just curious whether anyone on this festive day has found their way from the table to talk about the big blue yonder. Time to spare, go by air!

'What are you going to do, Hal?' she asked finally, then felt a small cold sensation firm up somewhere in her stomach when she looked into his face and saw the answer written there, behind the artificial confidence and his bullish exterior: search me.

He laughed coldly and the big leather armchair shook backwards and forwards on its huge wooden swivel base.

'He wants to see you. Can you believe that? And Paul too. Jesus, I think he'd even be asking to see Mouse if we knew where she was.'

'Stall him. That's something I can't face right now.'

'Don't worry. I told him. There are so many Chinese walls between him and us that no one could make a connection and I'm not going to go throwing all that away just because he wants to renew a few old acquaintances. I'll go there when I have to. No one else goes near.'

Afternoon, Barney Flyboy, this here is Jim R in Fort Lauderdale, sunny Florida. Sorry to hear about your weather, friend, and I hope I don't upset you when I say we spent this gorgeous holy day flying our forty-year-old Cub way down to Key West, taking lunch on Mallory, boy, do I like that Key lime pie, then back here as fast as that old bird could take us (which isn't very, but I guess you know that already). How you doing there? What we gonna chinwag about this fine day?

She tried to remember what Michael Quinn looked like. There was an image in her head but it was static, like an old photograph. Nothing moved. There was no flesh and blood there. Maybe there never had been.

'What's he like?'

Hal Jamieson shook his head. How do you answer that one?

'He's like he always was, only maybe more so. Crazy. Real, true, stone crazy. And sane at the same time. And bright. Michael's bright, which may be what eats him now. Knowing that of all of us he was the one who got caught. You know what he was like. You *remember* what he was like.'

And when she thought about it she could remember. There was something there that wanted to stop her thinking about it. Some sensible, rational lever in her head that said, no, you don't want to do this. But you could throw that lever really easily if you tried and the moment you did it all came flooding back. She wasn't like Paul Dunsany, she didn't have any excuses, any scars on her head that kept the lever in place. She remembered.

'He frightens me,' she said, and for a moment she was a different woman to the one he knew. For a moment.

Jim, I was kinda surfing here out of something to do – my loved one's in the kitchen right now cooking up something good for supper – but I was also hoping one of you real PC guys could help me out on something (I'm just sitting here with a real old machine, no sound, no CD-Rom, no *nothing*). You got that stuff? You got that new FAA registration database on CD-Rom I keep hearing about?

'What are you going to *do*?' she said, and it was the old Louise talking, the Louise who was always, always, in control. 'You can't keep him locked up in the forest forever.'

'I know that. He knows that too. Like I said. He's not stupid.'

'So?'

'First things first. We keep him out of the way. We keep him happy. We owe Michael. Don't forget that. What's more he has a substantial chunk of SCC stock. If he wanted to, he could cause us a lot of problems. I don't just mean bringing us down with the cops. He could bring us down in the business too. We need to keep him happy. We've *got* to.'

You bet, Barney, I'm running here one little sweetie, a Performa 5300 with the TV card, CD-Rom, you name it, all in a neat little box you could put in the front seat of the Cub and run off the 12 volt if you wanted, that's my guess. You looking for a PC I couldn't recommend it highly enough, got some deals going too, you shop around, and it being a Mac and all you don't end up giving nothing

*to that shithead Gates. Oh, oh. Seattle. He's not a friend of yours,
is he?*

'And then?'

*No friend at all. That sounds real good but what I was really
wondering was, that FAA database on CD-Rom. How good is that?
You find it reliable?*

'Then it's up to him. I told him today. He's got plenty of money
of his own. If he needs more, I'll see he gets it. Even if it hurts us.
We don't have a choice on this one, Louise. We've got to see it
through.'

Not used it much but for 50 bucks how can you go wrong?

She picked up the drink again, tried it, wrinkled her nose. The ice
had melted. It was too watery for her taste.
'I guess you're right. It's just that I didn't think he'd be so close. It
makes me uncomfortable.'

*You think we could maybe try it out? Look up one of my friend's
planes and see if it's in there? He's some guy. Flies a Citation.
N9925SW. You think he's in there?*

'Makes us all uncomfortable. Even Paul, if you want to know.'
'You spoke to him? How is he?'
He couldn't read the expression on her face.
'Some people just don't move on. Get stuck in some rut in their
lives, needle in the groove.'

*Gimme five there, Barney. I got to load this thing. A friend with a
Citation? Wow, that's *way* out of my league . . .*

'Meaning?'
'Meaning he hadn't even read the papers. Can you believe that? He
didn't even know Quinn was out.'
'So what does he do these days?'
She didn't know, Hal Jamieson said to himself. She genuinely didn't
know.

167

'Same as ever. Runs that little recording studio. Plays in a band somewhere.'

OK, Barney. I guess this is predictable but it looks like your buddy keeps that bird well behind the walls of his company. Guess I'd do the same with all that dough tied up in a hunk of flying metal. Says here the registered owner of Citation N9925SW is some outfit called SCC, 3214 Bellevue Avenue, Bellevue, WA. Aren't they those software guys or something? Sure my kid might have got one of their things on this Mac here. That sound right? Doesn't give any pilot's name, of course, but if your guy owns the company you could find it just by cross-checking the company records with the FAA licence database.

'We should see him some time.'
Hal Jamieson watched her searching for some reaction.
'Maybe. Maybe you should see him. We want to keep him in place, maybe that's going to be easier for you than it is for me.'
Louise smiled, that warm, rich, beautiful woman smile that still made him look at her and feel grateful, think: why me? Even for a moment.

That sounds like the guy. Lot of money in those PCs, Jim. Say, I hear the sound of dinner bells ringing in the kitchen. Guess it's time to hang up. You look after yourself and that old Cub, now.

'If that's what you want, Hal. If that's what you want.'

Sure thing, good buddy.

'Yeah,' said Hal Jamieson. 'You know, maybe I'll join you in that drink. You'd like me to fix you another one?'
She nodded. 'Plenty of ice.'
'Oh, yes,' he said, and inwardly thought to himself, plenty of ice, for Louise, always plenty of ice.
Halfway across town, in a houseboat moving to a slow rhythm on the grey, fetid waters of Lake Union, her head on Paul Dunsany's chest, gently rising with his breathing, Joni Lascelles fell into a deep, dark, dreamless sleep. But in this she was alone. Paul Dunsany lay awake, staring wide-eyed at the ceiling. Wondering why Hal Jamieson

hadn't called. Whether he really – *really?* – should be calling him.

After dusk, when the sun disappeared over the Pacific and left Mercer Island to the sound of cocktail parties, raccoons and the birds of the night, an old Buick drew up outside the gates of Desert Rose, checked out the Lexus still left in the drive, and Tom Cordobes wondered what to do next.

TEN

Tom Changes Tack

In all chaos there is a cosmos, in all disorder a secret order.

CARL JUNG,
Archetypes of the Collective Unconscious

'What you do next,' said Cy Langton, looking so red in the face he might be ill or something, 'what you do is you find out where the fuck the kid is.'

'He's not dead, Tom,' the Gourmet said quietly in the Captain's office, not wanting to boast, not wanting to make the point – and that made Cordobes madder than ever – that they'd been there before.

'Not that you know of,' said Cordobes.

The Gourmet smiled and Cy Langton said, 'Jesus, can we quit the bitching now? Please?'

'The hand you brought in for me to look at is definitely from a darker-skinned child. Maybe even Latino. And the Seymour child was white, pale white, from the photographs, from the descriptions. We know that. *You* know that.'

'Get that Sutter guy outta here, Tom. I don't want him seeing no lawyers advising him of his rights over things like wrongful arrest. Get one of the guys to take him some place where he can eat and drink and stay warm enough to keep his mouth shut till we got this one sorted. Last thing we need to be thinking about now is some bum who's pleaded to killing someone we don't even know is dead yet.'

'Sir.' Cordobes nodded, and hard as Cy Langton tried he couldn't detect any side to the way he said it.

'You're straight on the mother and father? No doubt about what happened there?'

Cordobes wondered about it, wondered whether it really was as pat as all that. This was one weird Christmas. A missing kid was one thing.

Some visiting VIP from England brained stone dead by his wife, who then goes straight crazy was something else. Something hard to credit.

'It's clear the Seymour woman attacked her husband and as a result of those injuries he died?' Langton asked. 'Right?'

Broadhead nodded vigorously. 'She must have been real mad at him though. He was one big guy. Heavy drinker from what I saw of the autopsy. Quite a lot of booze inside him at the time too. Seems pretty clear they had a fight. There's marks on her that can't be explained any other way.'

'This woman isn't talking,' Cordobes said. 'You got to understand that. From what the medics say it seems we shouldn't expect her to be talking for some time either. Catalepsy. Some such thing. So we just have to recreate as best we can. Started in the living room there. Judging by the blood, he was close to the stairs, close to the tree, and she attacked him. Big glass ashtray. Real clever thing to leave lying around the house for people who like to have arguments.'

'They did that a lot?' Langton asked.

'Neighbours said they'd heard them fighting before. Big fights. Lots of noise. What sounded like violence sometimes. Some of them had seen marks on the woman too. Like he hit her pretty hard.'

'Jesus,' Langton said. 'This guy was some real hot shot. Big professor type back in the UK. Who the fuck would have thought . . . ? You saw her, Tom. She a good-looking woman?'

'Sir?'

'You heard.'

'I heard. I just don't get the relevance, that's all.'

'Maybe there was somebody else involved. If she was good-looking, on her side. If she wasn't, on his.'

Cordobes closed his eyes for a moment and tried to tell himself he wasn't really hearing this.

'These domestic things are rarely as straightforward as that. Sir.'

'So just satisfy my curiosity.'

It was a question that hadn't even occurred to him.

'Yeah. I think she's good-looking, not glamorous, just kinda *wholesome*. What I could tell anyway. She'd been bawling her face out a good two hours before I saw her after the kid went missing. Her face was real puffed up so it was hard to tell. Now, she looks plain crazy, if you can get a good look at her face, when it isn't just buried in her hands. But yeah, I guess you'd say she's a good-looking woman.'

'So what do you think?'

Cordobes didn't know what he thought.

'I didn't meet this guy. I had someone else take care of it, see. From what I gather he was a fairly moody type. Big guy. Red-faced. Makes sense what you say, about him drinking. That came across too. Maybe . . . I dunno.'

'Maybe what?'

Could it really be that simple?

'When kids disappear, get hurt, whatever, their parents usually react by supporting each other. That's my experience, anyway. I was talking to one of the woman detectives though, and she said sometimes it wasn't as clear cut as that. Sometimes one side *blames* the other. Like it's his fault, or her fault, the kid went missing.'

'I can buy that,' said Broadhead. 'Sometimes people *need* someone to blame in these situations.'

'Yeah,' said Cordobes. 'But blaming someone's one hell of a long way from murder. That's a whole different level of thing.'

'You're sure that's what happened?' Langton asked Cordobes.

'Sure as anyone can be without her coming out and saying so, and I don't see that happening for a while. It was one hell of a mess in there. This was a local case, my guess is we'd be pressing for some kind of committal order. No way we're going to be able to put that woman on trial the way she is. God knows what we do with her being British and all.'

'And there was no warning?' Langton asked.

'Jesus. How are we supposed to know? This thing seems to have blown up out of nowhere. One minute they're alive and talking, arguing maybe, but talking all the same. Next he's dead, she's out of her head.'

'And the kid? What'd she say?'

Cordobes thought about the pale little child, who looked as if something in her had died too, she was so quiet, so drained of everything. 'Nothing. She says her pop sent her upstairs 'cos he wanted to talk to her mom. She didn't listen. She didn't hear a thing.'

'She must have heard something?'

'Yeah. Of course she did. But the kid's five. You expect her to give some good and cogent account of what went on there? Two things we do seem to know from her. First is there doesn't seem to be anybody else involved. No sign of that in the house. And she says no one else came in, not until we turned up after the neighbours called. Seems pretty certain on that.'

'And the second?' Langton asked.

Cordobes stared at Broadhead. This was his area. The Gruesome Gourmet might not like it, but it was his job.

'The doctors took a look at her,' Broadhead said, grimacing. 'It's not conclusive. Apparently it's very hard to be certain to the degree we'd want if this thing was to come to court. But it looks like she was interfered with.'

'*What?*' Langton's face was creased in disbelief.

Cordobes put it straight. 'It looks like her dad messed around with her. There's some bruising and when they talked to her she told 'em stories about games he played. This is not my field, you know. They find it hard to pin these things down, but it seems likely the guy stopped short of actual penetration, but maybe not a lot short.'

'Five years old,' Langton said. 'I coulda killed the bastard myself.'

'Yeah, well. Maybe that's what happened. Some argument started. One thing leads to another.'

'You think he messed with the boy too? You asked her that?'

'Yeah. She was vague. The poor kid's in shock. You can't expect much from her and if we're going to be safe on this one we've got to treat her with kid gloves. We can't use a word she says as evidence.'

'Evidence?' Langton asked, incredulous. 'Who the fuck needs evidence, Tom? The woman's too crazy to stand trial. Seems clear to me what happened to the boy. This English bastard's trying to fuck his five-year-old daughter, trying to mess around with his son, the boy runs away – that's the only *hard* thing we got. This isn't an abduction, it's a missing child case, you ask me.'

'Really, sir?'

'Yeah.'

'Then how'd we explain that kid's hand nailed to the tree? Whoever it belongs to, since Mr Broadhead here says it sure isn't Miles Seymour's.'

Langton glared across the desk and Tom Cordobes waited to see the miniature golf bag jump in the air again.

'Been a long day, Tom,' Langton muttered grimly. 'Guess I let things slip from my mind sometimes.'

'Happens to us all,' Cordobes said, and added mentally *but not usually when we've made Captain one way or another.*

Broadhead knew when to come in. Knew when the Captain needed rescuing.

'So what do you think, Tom? Where do we go from here?'

Cordobes shrugged. 'We assume that Mrs Seymour killed her husband, maybe because she thought she was protecting the girl somehow. We *have* to assume that someone out there has killed the kid whose hand we found in the woods. And we *have* to assume that Miles Seymour has either run away – and there are places you could hide around there, though I guess he'd be a mite hungry by now – or somehow been abducted, maybe by the person responsible for the other crime.'

'Action?' Langton grunted. 'There's no way you can *know* these two things are connected, Tom. No way at all. It may be that Seymour kid is just holed up somewhere in one of those patches of scrub off the rail track somewhere. Waiting for us to find him.'

'In which case Mr and Mrs Seymour seem to have had their little argument for no reason at all.'

'Yeah. Action?'

'We scour the woods again. We find out whether there are any kids from some of the itinerant families that are missing. Most of all, we go house to house trying to find Miles Seymour.'

'Door to door? This is Christmas, Tom. You really think we should be hammering on people's doors ruining their holidays like this?'

'We find the kid, frankly I don't give a flying fuck. Sir.'

'Yeah. But, Tom, house to house takes time. House to house takes resources. Every man you got trailing around Palo Alto and Menlo Park knocking on doors could be out there scouring the wasteland, looking in the real places, the remote places, where this kid is gonna be. He's not gonna be holed up in some nice timber four square off University Avenue. You know those people down there. They got eyes in their assholes. Anyone was looking after some strange kid we'd know about it already 'cos some nosy neighbour would've spotted the kid on the way in.'

'Maybe sir. But if this *is* an abduction it's one that's either been planned or else attracted an awful lot of luck. Why else haven't we got a clue what went on? Why else has nobody reported seeing the kid? He was dressed up as an angel, for chrissake. Somebody must have seen something, and if we go house to house we'll get it out of someone. There's hundreds of acres of waste ground out there we could scour, kicking over the shit for days on end. Shit don't talk. People do.'

'No.'

'Sir . . .'

'I said *no!*'

And this time the little golf bag really did jump up and down on the desk. Tom Cordobes sighed in disbelief. He may not have been half a human being. But he was a good cop. He knew that and he could *feel* his way into this one. Feel that house to house was the way to go, just staring at people until someone scratched around enough in their memory to come up with something that sent them after those little gold wings, after the little English kid who had *not* just wandered off like that, however much shit he was getting at home.

'You pour everything you got to searching the ground. Find where this kid has hightailed it to. You talk to those bums and find out what the fuck has been going on that one of their kids got his hand nailed to some tree there. Maybe these things are connected. Maybe they're not. But I'll be damned if I'm having half of Palo Alto on the phone whining about uniform cops banging on their door halfway through the holiday, and all for no real reason at all 'cos in my book that would just produce *zip*.'

Cordobes stared out of the window. The weather was changing. Puffy grey clouds, with dark undersides, were rolling in from the coast. It looked like rain was on the way. A ground search in the rain and mud. It sounded really wonderful.

'Sir,' he said, then closed the manila case notes folder on his lap.

'What about the girl?' Langton asked. 'The mother isn't going to be coming out of Trenton for a long time with what the doctors are saying. Who's going to look after the girl?'

This was one important family. He didn't want this new-found problem going down the county home, sitting alongside all the waifs and strays that had been picked up from the back streets of northern California. That could cause big shit later.

'We got her being cared for by one of the shrinks tonight. He's taking her home to stay with his family. She's got some relative flying out from England, the mother's brother. Sort out things with shipping back the husband when we're through, deal with whatever we have to do with her. Won't be here for two days. Some fucking Christmas for the poor kid.'

'Some fucking Christmas for us all,' said Cy Langton, then stared balefully at the golf pictures that festooned the walls of his office.

ELEVEN

Schrödinger's Cat (2)

Child of the pure unclouded brow
And dreaming eyes of wonder!
Though time be fleet, and I and thou
Are half a life asunder,
Thy loving smile will surely hail
The love-gift of a fairy-tale.

LEWIS CARROLL,
Through the Looking-Glass

No monster vibration, no snake universe hallucinations. Many tiny jeweled violet flowers along the path of a living brook that looked like Blake's illustration for a canal in grassy Eden: huge Pacific watery shore, Orlovsky dancing naked like Shiva long-haired before giant green waves, titanic cliffs that Wordsworth mentioned in his own Sublime, great yellow sun veiled with mist hanging over the planet's oceanic horizon.
No harm.

ALLEN GINSBERG,
letter published in *Paris Review*,
summer 1966, describing an LSD
experience in Big Sur, California

Michael Quinn switched off the TV, five minutes before the evening news bulletin, and turned to watch them. Desert Rose was here tonight. In the Barn. In the room. In their heads. He could tell that just by looking at them. They were different. They lived on some different plane. Not the same one he'd found, that just wasn't possible, but one that was far enough away from 'reality' for them to notice. It was like the big English guy had been saying in the lecture. There really *was* a multiverse and right now, thanks to Desert Rose – but not entirely, he knew that deep down somewhere – Hal and Louise and even Mouse, to some small extent, were each exploring a little portion of it. Mouse wasn't going to understand much but that didn't matter. Mouse didn't matter. Not at all. But both Hal and, to some extent he couldn't quite work out, Louise too, could get part of the way. They had to. This

177

went beyond turning people on. This was Castaneda with kicks and he wasn't going to give them a choice, any way back from the doors that led to his own particular version of perception.

And so Michael Quinn began to give the first and last lecture of his life, and gave it rather well, speaking with articulacy and feeling, spelling out complex ideas in simple, clear ways, explaining to them about the slit experiment and what it meant, two particles in different places simultaneously, and how from there you went on to other things, things with confusing names, like wave-particle duality and the uncertainty principle and those two big pillars of twentieth-century physics, relativity and the quantum theory, but when you got down to it – except there is no down, or up or sideways either – it all added up to the same thing. That we live in parallel with ourselves, in parallel with a million of ourselves, simultaneously lifting a left hand in one multiverse, a right hand in another, through all the possible multiplicities, chances, throws of the die, over and over again, awake, asleep, alive, dead, and through all the mid points in between.

In Michael Quinn's world, his current world, what Desert Rose did was bump the bones a little. Shake you from one part of the multiverse into another, just for a few hours at a time, just enough to let you see the light on the other side and leave you hoping you get to remember what it looks like when you land safely back home again. Just enough to make you realise that in the great big swing of things it just didn't matter. None of it. What they did. Whatever they did. There was no such thing as truth, since what was true in one part of the multiverse was a lie in the next. There was no such thing as morality: how can a particle – and we are all particles, we are nothing but particles – possess a property, a characteristic, that is only discernible to that jumble of particles we call man? Why not adopt the morality of ants? Or a grapefruit? It would be just as appropriate. In one world, Charlie Manson is a hero. In the next he is an outcast, the lowest of the low. All that gave things their moral state was the illusion of perspective and that had to be an illusion, the slit experiment proved it was an illusion, because perspective depended on, only made sense in, a single, finite, discrete universe, with fixed points: up, down, round, about. And what the slit experiment, what everything, from Einstein through to a whole flood of new work, including some by some new guy in England called Hawking, what it all told them, shouted at them – *everything* – was that there *were* no fixed points, could be no fixed points. Just the particles spinning and when you got around to naming them

three quarks for Muster Mark

you got so far off track you had to reach for some weird Irish poet to even try to pin down a tag that might stick.

Hal Jamieson listened, seeing the world spin in many colours in front of his head, and said, 'Rock and roll, Michael. Rock and roll's been saying that for years, my friend.'

Then fell to giggling, helplessly, watching the world fragment into eddying shapes of rainbow colours, watched, without being able to focus, Louise, in the chair next to him, sit, almost grim-faced, silent, hooked in concentration on something that was happening in a place only she could find.

'Schrödinger's cat,' Quinn said.

'Nice pussy,' Hal Jamieson giggled. 'What the fuck you talking about, man?'

So Michael Quinn started to tell them, tell them about Erwin Schrödinger, who was both believer and heretic, Erwin Schrödinger who, in 1926, developed a wave model of the atom that finally started to turn quantum theory into sense, since it explained why the dual nature of matter – as particle and wave – was possible.

And there was the problem, there in the proof. *Proving* something could happen was just stuff on paper. *Believing* it was something else, something that happened in your head, and that was where Schrödinger had the problem, something he just couldn't accept – apart from the Nobel Prize, Quinn thought, these guys always accept that – and this wasn't the theory it was the *idea*. He didn't like the *idea* that you could be in two places – *two million, two billion, two squillion* – at the same time.

'Commonsense kinda guy,' Hal Jamieson said, the smile almost breaking his face in two, then looked at Louise again, wondered where the fuck she was – no smile, no movement, but in her eyes some dark, intent intelligence moving among them. Looked at Mouse and just saw some semi-frightened kid with long, lank hair, wishing it was all over, wishing she could just get back to her joints and her Neil Young albums.

'Bullshit,' Quinn said, and said it with such vehemence Hal Jamieson felt the humour go out of him, saw its aura, a pink rosy whirl, like a tiny hurricane, disappear from the room.

And then Quinn was lecturing again, telling them how Schrödinger distilled his objections into an experiment, not one that anyone was supposed to carry out, just an enigma, an illustration, to summarise the problem. Schrödinger's cat.

'Poor pussy,' said Jamieson again, quietly, not laughing this time. 'So what the fuck you do, Michael?'

Quinn looked at him and wondered if he was ready, wondered if maybe he ought to just leave it. But if it didn't happen now, it didn't happen at all, not in this universe.

'You know about half-life?' Quinn asked and Hal Jamieson looked at him and felt the joke dry on his lips.

'We know what half-life is,' said Louise and it sounded like she was having to fight hard to control her voice.

'In Schrödinger's experiment, what you do is you put a cat in a box that contains a radioactive atom, a radiation detector and a phial of poison. You wire the detector so that if the atom decays, it smashes a hammer on the phial of poison.'

'Poor pussy,' Jamieson said again, not so loud, not so confident this time.

'The radioactive atom has a half-life of one minute so after one minute there is a fifty-fifty chance it will decay. A fifty-fifty chance the cat will be dead.'

'You can do that in Vegas, Michael,' Jamieson said. 'Don't need a cat, don't need quantum mechanics for that.'

'You're not thinking, Hal. This is a quantum process. After one minute, the atom is both decayed *and* undecayed. It has to be. It has no *choice*. And so . . .'

'So the cat is both dead *and* alive,' Louise said, and there was a light shining in her eyes.

'Exactly.'

Hal Jamieson shook his head and tried to clear some of the acid from it. This was the kind of heavy conversation he hated when he was tripping. You weren't careful it could catch your foot and send you head first into something you'd rather not chance upon. Either that or spin you straight out of the trip altogether, which would be an awful waste of money and good acid.

'So what you're saying,' he asked, 'is that it depends on when you open the box? You open it one second, the cat's alive, you open it another, the cat's dead?'

Quinn said nothing, just smiled in the half-light of the room.

'You can see why this Schrödinger guy had some problems with it, Michael. I mean. This is fucking great acid but even from here it looks like one huge amount of crap to me. Things can be alive one second and dead the next but far as I'm aware it's real hard to get things to work the other way round.'

'They don't. It is *either* alive or dead,' Quinn said. 'Can't you see that? If there is more than one universe, then in one we would see the cat alive, and in another the cat would be dead. There is *no* other possible explanation.'

'And what that means,' said Louise, 'is that at the moment the atom splits, it *creates* the second universe.'

Quinn's face was suffused with some cold triumph. He thought it would be Jamieson who got it, and maybe, in another universe he would, but he was wrong, and it didn't matter.

'This sure is good acid,' Jamieson grinned. 'Means I can sit here on Christmas Day, sit here listening to this loony tune stuff and *like* it. *Real* good acid.'

'The acid's what takes you there, Hal,' Quinn said, and this time he almost *was* disappointed. 'It's not what *there* is. Can't you *feel* that?'

Jamieson giggled again then said, 'Yeah, sure. We got any beer in here. Sure hope so 'cos there's *no* fucking chance of scoring some out there. Palo Alto on Christmas night is one big fucking *graveyard*, my friends.'

'Beer later,' Quinn said. 'First I got something to show you.'

He stood up, motioned for them to follow, and they walked out of the back door, Mouse following on behind, out towards the ramshackle collection of sheds at the back of the Barn, where once corn and fertiliser and other farm goods had been kept secure, behind lock and key.

'Surprises,' said Hal Jamieson into the darkness, but somehow his confidence, his cocksure self-possession was disappearing. It had been weird when he stood up. It seemed the acid that had started to slumber some place down within his being got kicked into life again, bounced back into his head and started doing the pyrotechnic shuffle there again. The darkness was alive with something, something like psychedelic fireflies, dancing in the black velvet interior, too small to

181

be real, yet so bright, so vivid, so alive. He caught Louise's eye: from what he saw there she felt the same way, halfway between fear and excitement, not quite knowing which was which.

Quinn took out a key, fumbled for the big padlock on the door to the old wooden grain store, found it, they heard metal click upon metal, the door opened and then they walked in. There was a light switch by the wall. Quinn pressed it. A small, weak bulb stumbled into life. Across the floor ran a thick, black power cable, ending at a dimly outlined rectangle patterned on the dust. Quinn walked over, bent down, pulled on an iron ring and lifted the trap door into some basement room, some subterranean cellar cut into the earth. Then he was moving down a rickety wooden ladder, and they did the same, unquestioning.

It was black, so black that even the acid fireflies didn't follow them in there. Hal Jamieson thought nothing would follow them in there because the place had a smell, a feeling about it that said *get out, go away, don't come back*. It was just the acid, he knew that, but that didn't make it any less real – was that what Michael was trying to say? – and didn't make it any less oppressive.

He felt something touch him, looked down, and it was too dark to see, but he knew what it was. Louise had locked her arm gently through his – *she's just finding her way through the dark, idiot* – and he could feel the closeness of her body, detect in the air, over the stench, some warm, expensive scent. Hal Jamieson closed his eyes and let some little dream – *of skin, of movement, of lovenotlove* – flit swiftly across the inside of his head.

And then Michael pulled down the light, a big inspection bulb on a cable, like car mechanics used, with enough candlepower to illumi-nate the Lincoln Memorial, and the room burst into golden brightness, their eyes blinked painfully against it for a moment, then adjusted, shapes took form – something moved, something made a sound – and, for a moment, it was hard to take your eyes off anything but Michael Quinn's face in the lamplight, so gaunt, so excited, so tense.

'What the fuck we doing here, Michael?' Jamieson said. 'We go back in the . . .'

Then the words just dried to dust in his throat.

On the far side of the room Miles Seymour squatted on the straw-covered ground. There was a chain around his neck, another chain around each ankle. The kid looked as if he was beyond fear. He looked as if he hardly knew they were there. Jamieson thought about it, dared to come a few paces closer, looked into his eyes. The pupils were huge, dark and pool-like, filling almost all the eye, and he wondered how long Quinn had been feeding him Desert Rose, how long a little kid like this would trip on a single tab.

'*Michael?*'

Mouse's voice was a thin reed of terror in the golden light of the lamp.

'*Shut up!*' he barked. '*This is not for you. You don't understand this. You just shut up and do as I fucking say.*'

Jamieson watched the poor, stupid girl sit down on her haunches on the floor, put her head between her knees, her arms across her eyes, go quiet. Crying maybe. Whatever it was it didn't seem to matter.

The kid was dressed in what looked like a grain sack, holes made in the corners for his arms, the end ripped out for his legs. Behind him something glinted: the remains of wings, golden, tinselled wings. This was where the smell was coming from. He'd been pissing and shitting where he was trapped. To Jamieson's growing horror, he saw, next to the kid, a wooden block, the kind you used to chop wood, and it was stained with something that looked dark and fresh. Looked like blood.

'Michael,' Jamieson said. 'This is serious.'

And then the most extraordinary thing happened. It was Quinn's turn to giggle. Like a child. In a way he'd never done before. His shoulders just chucked up and down and this thin, girlish sound came out of his mouth. Jamieson felt Louise unhook her arm from his, felt her attention shift from him, to Quinn, and felt her start to laugh too, not hard, not that deliberate, but enough to make it noticeable. Enough to draw the lines between them.

'Schrödinger's cat,' Quinn said and walked towards the boy, walked past him to the corner of the room, picked up something long and black and sinuous. A power cable. Gave one end to Louise and ordered her to find a mobile power socket hanging down from the trap door. She walked over, still laughing, walked past Mouse, head in hands, walked past Jamieson, struggling for words, wondering what he could do – *in this universe* – that might change things, make some difference.

Quinn pulled on a pair of gloves. Rubber power worker's gloves, picked up the end of the power cable – *which was now live, something, maybe their senses, their new senses, maybe Desert Rose, let them see the electrons fizzing down its wires* – and plugged it into some amateurish metal contraption that made no sense until he held it up and then they saw it for what it was: a helmet. A thin circlet around the head, two bands across the top, to the centre of the forehead and back, across to each ear. Something hummed. There was a box, some transformer, Hal Jamieson guessed, that would beef up the voltage – *why?* – to make it lethal of course, make sure the little bouncing electrons were up to the job, sparked by their own private Desert Rose.

The boy was spaced out. Not scared. Not that. Just too far away, too distanced, to move, even notice their presence much, even when Quinn leaned over him, greased the contacts to guarantee their conductivity, then placed the helmet carefully over his head, making sure the fit was a good one, a tight one, one that left no room for error or threatened the validity of the exercise.

There was some circular plate that linked the transformer to the helmet, wires snaking all over the floor, so many, so many, and Quinn knew them all, had made them all, laid them out, sorted them as they watched, talking all the time, and Jamieson didn't know, couldn't work out whether Quinn – *who was crazy, this wasn't just dope, he was crazy for sure* – was talking to them or talking to the wires, the electrons themselves.

Finally, Quinn stopped, looked satisfied, and said, 'You understand, Hal?'

Jamieson shook his head. 'This is crazy, Michael. You got to stop it.'

'Hah!' Quinn's eyes were iridescent with the dope now. 'Crazy? I *got* no radioactive atom, I *got* no radiation detector or poison. But you think you need them, you're missing the point. You're missing *everything*.'

'Maybe I'd be happier missing it, Michael.'

'No. You don't mean that. I'll *prove* you don't mean that. Here.'

Quinn picked up the circular thing. It was a piece of industrial switchgear with the CalTrain logo on the side, something Quinn had liberated from one of the trackside stations, and it looked like a sundial with a single hand in the centre, buttons around the edge that looked like contacts. Another wire led away from it to a hand switch, the kind you got on office tape recorders when people wanted to dictate: on, off, on, off. Quinn put the circular dial on a shelf built into the wall, passed Jamieson the hand switch. Then he went back to the transformer, turned some new control, they listened to the sound of it getting hotter, higher, crackling and fizzling like some robotic angry snake.

The hand on the sundial started to revolve, slowly at first, then faster and faster, until it set up a steady, fixed revolution, unchanging, constant, like a clock on speed.

'One revolution every two seconds. Always,' Quinn said. 'I timed it. Not that it matters. The contact studs are equidistant. That means it's fifty-fifty. You press the switch, the electromagnet in the hand pulls it down onto the dial. It hits the contact. It doesn't hit. Fifty-fifty.'

Jamieson almost dropped the switch straight away, then thought about it, held it lightly in his fingers, like it was poisoned.

'What does this prove, Michael? It's just like spinning a wheel at Vegas.'

'You think so? Watch.'

He pulled Louise to him and Jamieson hated the way she came so easily, hated the way she seemed to be amused by it all. Then he felt Quinn's hand around his back, pulling them all closer, three together, three as one.

Quinn took the switch, held it in his left hand, out in the centre of the space between them. Then he stretched out his right hand, took first Louise by the fingers, then Jamieson, so that they formed a warm, human tangle of hands that hovered, still over the switch.

'No,' said Jamieson, but everything was happening so fast, and it was kicking the Desert Rose up from the basement in his head and sent some real craziness soaring around his senses so he didn't know what was going on any more, didn't really care, because it really was like Michael had said it was, just particles driving through the dust and rain of the universe – *the one you happened to be in at the time* – and when you came down to it maybe it didn't fucking matter at all, not when you looked at the acid fireflies dancing there in the middle of space.

'Two universes out of one,' Quinn said. 'Close your eyes. And watch.'

And that was just what Hal Jamieson did. When he shut his eyes, the world went black, so black that he knew this really was true nothingness, no fireflies, no sparks of electrons in the dark, this really was the emptiness at the heart of everything that was there before the universe – *this particular one* – came into being. And he knew, too, that this was also what *they* saw, that the alkaloids were forging some gigantic neural link between the three of them, like cable TV through the cosmos, to let them see it all. Let them see what you weren't supposed to see, ever, ever, ever – *remember Frankenstein?* – and live to tell the tale: creation, substance from nothing, the sort of thing the smart guys left to the creeps in glasses in the philosophy department who looked like they never got off with girls for fear of losing their precious bodily substances.

Quinn's voice screamed through the darkness like a lost soul, '*NOW . . .*'

Their hands came down, no one pushing, no one forcing anything, a slow, conscious act of complicity that, one way or another, would stay with them for the rest of their lives.

Hal Jamieson never asked Quinn, never asked Louise, what they saw, he didn't want to know, in a way he didn't *dare* to know. Most of all, though, it was because you couldn't really explain it, there was nothing there that was so real you could talk about it and have people think you were sane, even people who'd shared the trip with you. Jamieson saw what he saw in those few seconds – *minutes? hours?* – that followed them pressing the switch together but it was too much like something you encountered in a dream, or in a trip. Intangible, only half remembered. Real but hidden behind some gauzy trick played by the brain so that you didn't hang on to all the details.

What Hal Jamieson saw, as the sweat poured down his forehead, as his hands swam in perspiration, was the kid's face in the darkness. He was calm, he wasn't scared. This time his pupils weren't so big. Maybe he wasn't even tripping – *wasn't everyone tripping?* – it was hard to tell.

The kid was still sitting on the floor but he was no longer shackled. He wore a neat white shift. There were wings, gold and silver, attached to his back and these were *real* wings. They moved with his body, there were veins in them, you could see the blood there, real and pumping. And the kid was smiling at him. No helmet this time. Nothing scared about him. This was the – *kidnotkid* – the same person and not the same person, the same place and not the same place. The light was different, more blue, as if sunlight was streaming in from a sky that couldn't exist.

Streaming on him and the kid – there was no one else there, no Quinn, no Louise, to save him – who just looked at him and smiled, peacefully, untroubled. Around his head, slowly arcing and fizzling, an inch or so from the flesh, a halo of bright, electric blue performed some demon dance, moving, shifting form, clinging to the child like a phantasmal parasite.

Cold with terror, Jamieson looked at him, reached his hand out towards his face. The blue halo arced and spat, shot at him, wounding him with a sharp, painful shock that ran along his arm right to his shoulder. He looked at his hand. Along three fingers a line of blue flame danced like ethereal jets from a gas fire. They felt icy cold and burning hot at the same time. Then he watched them join together, turn into a line of icy, fiery blue, skip through the air, consciously, deliberately, to rejoin the snapping, crackling circle around the kid's head. Going home.

A sleek, inhuman blackness now consumed the centre of his eyes, the pupils looked like deep, greasy pools that went on forever. Then they began to spread further, until there was nothing there but blackness, a void that was consuming him from within.

The kid was blind now but still tried to look at him, still did, his head held high and stiff, trying to look with those inhuman eyes, waiting for the end. His mouth was set in a fixed, taut smile, the lips just back from the white gleam of tiny teeth. A dark yellow flame appeared at the corner of his mouth, turned from something that was no more than the head of a lighted match into a fire, a real fire that was growing, fanning itself, feeding on something inside.

And then, finally, the kid began to scream, a quiet, despairing, unreal sound that rolled and echoed around the room, entered Jamieson's head, filled it, drew him to the enactment, the little play, made him watch more closely, made the world become nothing but this kid, dying, burning, in a world composed entirely of flames.

He could feel the heat, low and insistent, the fire beside him. There was a terrible smell, of grease, of smoke and charred flesh. As he watched, a line of calcined bone appeared near the child's jaw, spread, then made a rictus, smiled along the blackened teeth. Huge, oily flakes of soot started to hang in the air, and as Miles Seymour – *they* – screamed, the tongues of yellow spread from his mouth downwards, fast and heartless, scorching the skin of his neck into blackness, baring the sinews, burning, then snapping them. There was no scream now, only a death rattle, low and terrible.

A blue and yellow tongue of flame crawled from the centre of his midriff and wound around the stomach like a serpent. Jamieson wanted to throw up but something inside him was beyond nausea, something that told him this was real but this was not physical.

The flame settled around the child's torso, seemed to relax there, pulsed, *breathed*, then exploded. A vast column of fire engulfed his entire body.

Jamieson watched and listened, unable to move, listened to the sound of breaking bones, watched the corpse jump and dance as the flames consumed the flesh, snapped joints out of place, pushed and pulled sinews and muscle into new, extravagant shapes, turned Miles Seymour into a twisted, tortured pillar of carbon. Became solid. Became still. Then, in total silence, imploded, blackness turning in on itself, disappearing, disappearing, disappearing, and in its place, like tiny stars, a speckled band of lights.

Hal Jamieson opened his eyes.

The room seemed darker. The shadows had grown. In the corner, sobbing, Mouse had her arms around the child, comforting, daring them to come closer. The kid had his helmet off. He looked fine. He didn't look any different. He just looked doped up, ready to sleep, ready to dream. Quinn let her hug him, as if it meant more to Mouse than it possibly could to him.

'Two universes,' Michael Quinn said from nowhere. 'More. As many as you want. As many as you need.'

Hal Jamieson felt Louise's hand gripping his, looked into her face and saw the radiance, the joy, the bliss, there, saw it and felt like weeping.

Something in the storehouse, something in the air, told him the truth, something that couldn't lie, no matter how much he hoped and prayed it might. Hal Jamieson knew this was not the first time that Quinn had played Schrödinger's cat. The smell of death hung around the place like fetid fog. There was blood on the wooden block, blood on the ground. This was not the first time. It was merely the first that had brought forth a survivor.

RAIN TIME

ONE

Tailing Hal

It is vain to say human beings ought to be satisfied with tranquillity: they must have action; and they will make it if they cannot find it.   CHARLOTTE BRONTË,
Jane Eyre

Tom Cordobes watched the big grey Lexus pull off the bridge linking Mercer Island to the eastern shoreline, joining the steady line of traffic working its way through the highway, through the forest, north towards Bellevue. The winter day was warm and wet. The moisture sat on everything, the trees, the ground, the windshield of the car, looking like rain, except it had no movement, no momentum. It simply came out of the air and *was*.

He turned the key on the Buick. It started first time. He wasn't taking chances any more. Two days before, when he decided it was time to act, when he felt he couldn't keep on taking the English girl's money and failing to deliver anything but airy promises, he took the old car into a cheap mechanic's down in the city, got her checked over, new plugs, new distributor, new anything else the bug-eyed black mechanic wanted to throw underneath the hood. It cost $230 and Cordobes thought that maybe took care of his margin on this particular job. But he didn't really mind. Something was beginning to get to him about the whole affair and it wasn't just failing to deliver the dreaded value for money thing. Something about this job dredged up too many memories he wished had stayed buried, and trying to force events to some kind of conclusion was his way of paying it back.

Tom Cordobes now knew a lot, an awful lot, about Hal Jamieson but try as he might it was impossible to see where it led. The guy was a Stanford drop-out (which wasn't exactly unique in this world). He'd been around there in '75, but then so had thousands of others too.

And he'd got rich. Seriously rich. Cordobes had trawled through screen after screen of electronic cuttings, sitting in the Stock Motor Lodge, glued to the screen of his Compaq, and read most everything there was on-line about Jamieson and SCC – no pictures though, just words and words and words – and it seemed bizarre to him that this guy would have anything to do with a low-life like Quinn. There was no link, except Stanford, and if something had brought them together there, even the Seymour case, it didn't make a whole lot of sense that it could still be alive twenty years on. Even a sense of complicity couldn't last that long, not in Tom Cordobes' book. In his experience that lasted about six months in Obispo and by that time the guy inside was just screaming to tell all he knew about the ones outside just so's he could obtain a little light relief from getting fist-fucked in the shower block nightly. Just so he could get a few privileges.

Hal Jamieson had a beautiful business, a beautiful home and a beautiful, very beautiful, wife. Tom Cordobes had sat hidden in the trees outside Desert Rose the previous morning and watched Louise Gostelow drive out the gates in her open-top Mercedes, the roof up, even though the sky threatened rain. Cordobes didn't give much thought for women these days, just registered them while passing, like he did with the English girl, but Louise Gostelow was someone different. A real head-turner. The kind of woman you saw in the celebrity pages in the papers, sleek and dark and beautiful and oh-so-confident of where she's going. A little like the younger Liz Taylor, maybe, with the figure to match from what he could make out over the doorline of the Mercedes. Cordobes shook his head and couldn't figure it out: this Jamieson guy seemed to live in paradise, so why was he messing round with Quinn?

He spent two days just tailing the guy, even though after the first few hours he knew it was going nowhere. Jamieson just drove round a circuit, like a race car on the track. He went to the office. He went to the Rainier Club downtown and dined with all the other rich locals. Cordobes had followed him inside one time, talked quietly with the polite Chinese woman behind the desk, and marvelled at the polished wood, the deep leather armchairs, the smell of wealth and power inside, such a contrast with the streets beyond the door. The Rainier Club didn't quite match Jamieson somehow, he thought. This was something he did because it was expected of him.

Then another time he followed Jamieson to some house out in

Tacoma, a little estate home, where a blonde woman opened the door and the curtains upstairs closed soon after, and Tom Cordobes guessed that maybe being married to the young Liz Taylor wasn't necessarily the paradise the rest of us might think it should be, particularly when he saw how expressionless, how sour, Jamieson looked an hour and a half later when he left the house. Once, Jamieson drove to the airport, rolled the big Citation out onto the runway, took it out for a stroll up at thirty thousand feet, landed an hour and fifteen minutes later, having been nowhere in particular, on his own (Cordobes had watched from the perimeter fence, through an old pair of ex-army field glasses), then climbed back into the Lexus and drove straight home. Nice pastime for a bored moment, Cordobes thought, but at maybe ten thousand dollars an hour it wasn't the kind of thing that was going to catch on with the general public.

And then nothing. It wasn't that Jamieson thought he was being followed. He wasn't up to that. He wasn't even looking. It was just that he stuck to the same things all the time, and none of them led anywhere to Michael Quinn, or looked likely to. Cordobes, who seemed to have spent the best part of forty years tailing people, had an instinct for this kind of thing, and he knew when people were just doing the daily rounds. You could see it in the way they drove, running on semi-automatic all the time, not thinking about turning left or turning right, not wondering where the catch is on the door. If Jamieson had been getting anywhere near Quinn, Cordobes would have read it in his body language, in the way he handled the car. This man was not coming to him, Tom Cordobes told himself. He was unaware, he was outside of all this. And the only way to find out what he knew was to do the thing that people all his life had been telling him not to do, the thing that all his life had got him into trouble. The thing he had to do. So Tom Cordobes decided to act.

Bellevue was made for tailing people, made for getting in their way when you wanted. The four-lane highway was restricted to the big through routes. The rest of the time you were on pretty ordinary roads, except when you got into the big tangle around the shopping mall, and SCC's office was well away from that, in the northeast of town, where the streets were comparatively straight and narrow and old-fashioned, with lots of stop lights in between and plenty of space to play with. You could see for miles here.

It was around 10.30 in the morning, the rush-hour traffic had subsided into a steady stream of estate wagons coming back from the supermarket, cabs plying the spread-out network of hotels, and service vans looking to fix things, all the things that needed fixing in this bright clean wealthy outpost of Washington suburbia. Cordobes worked his way up until he was behind the Lexus, watched the way the lights were changing, overtook Jamieson as quickly as he could, then waited for the next red light. It happened to be the last before the SCC offices and he was lucky. As the car got closer the lights started to change. Cordobes slowed to a stop, watched the Lexus do the same behind him. There was no other vehicle in the queue. They had a moment or two alone and he wanted to make the most of it. Cordobes killed the engine on the Buick, got out and walked back to the shiny Japanese car behind.

This was Bellevue. This was that nice, quiet, ordered place you called suburbia, where the streets ran straight and spotless in every direction, every junction ninety degrees to the next, and every sidewalk clean and tidy. You didn't panic out here. Not if you had nothing to hide. If Cordobes tried this trick in parts of San Jose, parts of Palo Alto even, the guy behind would have been backing out at high speed the moment he saw someone come out of the car in front. Hal Jamieson just wound down the window – Cordobes could hear the little electric motor purring as it worked – put his head out and looked puzzled. It was the first time Cordobes had seen him close up. All he got at the airport was a short, distant glance. All he got from the on-line cuttings was words, no pictures. Cordobes looked at Hal Jamieson and smiled, wondered whether this recognition was mutual, wondered whether twenty years was just too long unless you were an ex-cop who liked to remember faces, liked to keep them filed away.

'Hi,' said Tom Cordobes. 'You help me? I was trying to track down an old friend. Acquaintance of yours. Name of Michael Quinn. Was thinking maybe you could help me out there.'

He watched as Jamieson went white, went real white and looked like he was about to die. This was not the kind of thing the king of Mercer Island wanted happening to him when he drove to work in his nice new shiny Japanese car and that made Cordobes feel good. Very good.

'What?' Jamieson stuttered.

'You heard, Mr Jamieson. This is no big deal. I got a client would like to talk to Mr Quinn. That's all. No media. No cops. Nothing you need worry about.'

There was a big station wagon stuck behind them now and Hal Jamieson could feel the driver staring at them, wondering what the hell was going on.

'If you like, sir, we could carry on this conversation in your office,' said Cordobes. 'No problem for me.'

Jamieson waved the station wagon on frantically. It pulled out, passed in a cloud of diesel fumes and from the passenger window a sulky-looking youth with shoulder-length hair extended a single finger at them both.

'Who the fuck are you?' Jamieson snapped. 'Stopping me like this.'

'I guessed you might prefer it that way, rather than I stop by your house or come to your company. Up to you. I don't mind. Like I say, this is a simple thing. I got a nice lady lawyer come all the way from England just to talk to this Quinn guy. Nothing criminal. Just a probate matter. He want to talk to her, that's fine. He don't, well, that's his choice. *His* choice, Mr Jamieson. We just want to give him that chance. You want to think about that. I give you my card, number of my motel's on the back. You just call me when you get the chance to talk it through with Mr Quinn. We're open to talk whenever, wherever he likes. Lady assures me it won't take long, won't hurt.'

Jamieson looked at the dog-eared card Cordobes had thrust through the open car window, the number of the Stock Motor Lodge, room 334 written on the back in blue ballpoint ink, committed it to memory, then threw the card on the ground.

'You got the wrong guy, Mr Cordobes,' Jamieson said and started reversing the Lexus to get himself some space to manoeuvre out into the road, Cordobes following him every foot of the way. 'This isn't California. This is a nice town. A town where they know me well. I think you should stop harassing people in the streets. I think you should stop wasting your time.'

The window went all the way up, Hal Jamieson turned the wheel and edged the Lexus slowly forward, towards Cordobes, pushing him out of the way. Cordobes was feeling good, so good, after this little exchange that he couldn't help it. Couldn't resist doing something. He balled up his big fist, grinned at Jamieson through the windshield, then banged as hard as he could on the roof of the car. The metal caved in nicely and Cordobes felt even better, felt his cousin Danny in Detroit would have been very proud of him.

There was a sudden shriek of tyres and Jamieson pulled around the ancient Buick, burst through the red light and was at the gates of the SCC offices before Cordobes could even get back behind the wheel. The old cop watched Jamieson get out of the car – you could see the dent in the roof even from here – and walk into the vast chromium and mirror-glass atrium entrance. He walked like a man who'd been shaken and couldn't quite get around to settling down all the individual pieces into something approaching stability, not quite yet.

'This was good,' Cordobes said. 'This was very good.'

And his smile grew even broader when he saw the next vehicle out of the SCC lot. It was a big silver Shogun, and behind the wheel was someone else, someone big and hulking, a shape that Tom Cordobes recognised. He turned the key on the Buick, the engine kicked and started sweetly first time. Then he went through the green countryside, the rows and rows of pine and fir trees stretching everywhere you could see, and settled into a nice distance from the Shogun. The big guy wasn't like Jamieson. He looked the sort of person who maybe would know he was being followed and Tom Cordobes wasn't taking any chances. Shaking Jamieson was good for the soul, shaking Jamieson had kicked the dust off some link that went back to the Seymour case that he didn't quite understand. But in the end it got him nowhere. Jamieson wasn't going to sort anything between him or anyone else and Quinn. Jamieson was so scared he might be changing his under-wear even now in his fancy executive bathroom at the top of the SCC building. Jamieson was a dead end unless you could shake him really well, and that was something Cordobes would rather not do now he had no badge to stand behind.

What he really needed was something direct. Something that took him straight to Quinn so they could talk this out man to man. Face to face. And who knows what might happen after that?

Tom Cordobes followed the flashing form of the big silver Shogun as it snaked its way out of Bellevue, out onto 90, out towards Snoqualmie, and thought he just might have it, thought to himself how nice it would be if all those people over all those years who kept telling him how Tom Cordobes was just plain dumb to take things into his own hands like that, if all of them could just turn up for a reunion real soon. You act, things happen, Tom Cordobes said to himself. It was as simple and as straightforward as that.

TWO

Miles and Flora

There's night and day, brother, both sweet things; sun, moon,
and stars, brother, all sweet things; there's likewise a wind on
the heath. Life is very sweet, brother; who would wish to die?

GEORGE BORROW,
Lavengro

Miles Seymour walked out of the subterranean transit train at Sea-Tac,
straight off the United flight from JFK, and tried to get his bearings
in the main terminal. It was his first time to Seattle. Being a Wall
Street forex broker didn't bring you out to these places. Only a summons brought you to these places and Joni Lascelles, who had issued
the summons, now stood a good three hundred yards away, at the
wrong baggage area, confused by the airport signs, its foreignness, the
commotion and crowds.

Twenty years separated them, yet she recognised him instantly. He
was wearing a serious grey business suit, neatly pressed, in spite of the
flight. A white shirt, a red tie, doubtless silk. He was tall, not big like
his father, there was little of his father there, she said that very firmly
to herself, and striking. And he was as lost as she was. Waiting for his
bags. Not knowing where to look. Not knowing what to do to bridge
this twenty-year hiatus between them: who she was, what she looked
like, where they went from here.

She fought her way through the crowds, down towards him, watching his shape, his personality, grow more certain, more distinct, as she
approached. He seemed older, more mature than she expected. More
thirty than twenty-five. And what little resemblance there had been
when they were children was now gone altogether. Miles Seymour had
dark hair cut short then brushed back tightly against the skull so that
his forehead gleamed under the sharp fluorescent lights of the airport,
gleamed as if he was sweating, out of exertion, maybe out of nervous-

ness. His face was open, honest, with an angularity that could pass as handsome. He wore gold-rimmed glasses through which intelligent eyes peered, forever darting around him. He was tall but not hulking. No rugby player, more a marathon runner. And he looked fit too. Fit. Confident. Capable.

This was what her brother had become in the intervening years, and what route, what adventures, had taken him there she could not guess at, could only recite to herself the old litany that seemed to underpin everything on this side of the Atlantic, the circular refrain, 'In America everyone starts equal, everyone has a chance, to take or leave as you please.'

Until then, she had never believed it.

Then his head bobbed beneath the flood of faces that crowded around him, disappeared altogether, and Joni was filled with a sense of dread that peeled away the years, flooded her with fear and guilt and longing. From somewhere overhead she thought she heard the rustling of wings – *gold and silver* – turned to stare, saw nothing but the ceiling lights blinking fuzzily back at her.

She looked again at the baggage reclaim and he was there again, a tan leather overnight case in his hand. And this time he was smiling, straight at her, *recognising* her, through the faces, through the crowd. Unbidden, tears began to form over her eyes, she wiped them with her hand, blinked, blinked again, saw the world become clear, saw Miles Seymour walk up to her, felt his arms grip her shoulders.

She looks into his face, a kind face, not a face that remembers too much, and hears, for the first time, her brother's adult voice. It is a grown-up, even, rational voice, a voice that makes all her fears disappear, fills her with wonder and gratitude, thanks that all the work, all the toil and heartache, finally bring their reward, and then the voice says, 'Flora.'

She is almost as tall as him, barely needs to stretch when she reaches forward, sinks her face into his neck, feels the softness of his skin, the grey silk fabric of his suit, holds him and lets the tears flow warm and salty onto him, feels the dampness between them, and in this public place Joni Lascelles – *or Flora Seymour, she is unsure which* – finds herself made complete, in some mysterious, holistic way that she has never known before, so full, so overflowing with benevolence.

He says her name and she listens to the voice again, a serious, almost flat voice, with an accent that is wholly East Coast, middle class, sane and courteous and forgiving, and the voice says only one word, over and over, '*Flora, Flora, Flora, Flora, Flora, Flora, Flora, Flora* . . .'

Until she thinks the world will burst with those two syllables, spoken with so much love, such happiness at their reunion.

'*Flora, Flora, Flora, Flora, Flora, Flora, Flora, Flora* . . .'

She opens her eyes, pulls back her head to look at him, lifts a hand to his face, and gently places it on his lips.

The crowd has dispersed quickly. They seem to be almost alone and, without noticing, they have walked the few yards to the little coffee stand close to the gate. A young man, in a white nylon jacket, stands behind the metal counter and smiles anonymously at them.

'What do I say to you?'

He has a broad, warm smile, good, even teeth, perfect whiteness, he is a handsome man, and he says, 'Say my name, Flora. Say my name.'

'*Miles, Miles, Miles, Miles, Miles* . . .'

Her voice sounds disjointed, unreal.

He turns to the man behind the counter and orders coffee – *two skinny lattes with a double shot, two skinny lattes with a double shot* – and the words come out so quickly, like a chant, the sound of a tape machine being fast-forwarded, that for a moment she finds it impossible to catch them, to translate them, to wonder why he never asked, just ordered, then waited, until the paper cups appear, almost instantly, on the metal counter top that now shines so brightly under the arcing lights of the airport.

His smile is so wide. He is so happy. Nothing in the world can do more for her than this: to see Miles happy, to *see* Miles happy.

'Miles,' she says, and still the voice has some strange, foreign distance in it. 'Look at me, Miles. Tell me. What do you see?'

Miles Seymour looks at his sister, with love and wonderment and excitement, and at that moment she believes that there can be nothing better in her life than this, that no other single experience in her future existence, not the birth of children, the discovery of love, or death itself, can hope to compete with this instant of mystic wonder, when the circle, broken for so long, is made complete.

Miles Seymour looks at her, smiles, laughs almost, and says, in the perfect voice of a five-year-old child, 'Things sparkling, Florrie. I see things sparkling.'

On the collar of his grey suit there dances now a flickering blue flame. It is part of him. Part of this Miles Seymour's being and as she sees it, feels she recognises it, Joni Lascelles – *not Flora, not Florrie* – knows this cannot be, wants to stop up her ears with her fists to drown out the sound of his voice, but her arms are locked around him, locked to the smooth, cold fabric, and the flesh, which is also cold.

There is nothing she can do but listen as Miles' face comes closer and closer to hers and he whispers, the breath so fetid on her now, very quietly into the delicate pink skin of her ear, 'Will you tell, Florrie? Will you tell? Will you tell on the little Angel Gabriel and send me back forever?'

Roughly, he pushes her away, her arms fall to her sides, paralysed. She feels as if she has no control over her body: she feels as if she is about to wet herself. She can see the man at the coffee stand laughing at her, half hidden in a cloud of steam from the machine.

'*Will you tell? Will you tell, you fucking bitch?*'

Miles Seymour's voice is that of an adult now and it is roaring. The noise drowns out everything else in the universe. There is nothing she can do but listen, waiting for the piss to turn damp and sticky and sore on her skin.

'No,' she says weakly. 'I won't tell, Miles. I promise not to tell.'

And she feels her arm obey, finally. She holds it out in front of her. His face is so huge, it seems as large as his chest, and it is taut and grinning.

'*No, you will not fucking tell,*' shouts the roaring voice and she watches as his hands rise up into the air, pounce upon her wrist, and start to turn, turn, turn, twisting the skin, so hard, so fast, until it feels as if she is on fire – *there is a blue flame flicking across her wrist, she can see it* – and the fabric of her flesh will explode.

There is a moment when all of this is a dream, unreal, something which she can hope to observe from some safe, guarded distance, but that moment disappears when the pain strikes hard, like a red-hot iron spike through the cerebellum, and she screams, so loud that this world shatters into a million pieces in front of her, Miles Seymour disappears in a cloud of colours, and there is nothing outside this sudden, breathtaking universe of pain.

Joni Lascelles jerks upright and stares – *in this real world* – at her arm. She is naked and her skin is chill with sweat. There is a wasp, the biggest wasp she has ever seen, crawling over her naked wrist. She

201

can see its body, black and yellow, the colours of danger, the colours of death, arching as it pumps the poison into her, raising livid red weals on the flesh and she remembers, the recollection comes back from nowhere: *only the females have stings, and they can use them over and over and over again.*

Without thinking, she reaches down, pinches its chitinous head between her thumb and forefinger, feels the creature's shell give way, brushes it from her skin onto the floor.

There is half-light in the bedroom, she looks for the porthole windows, looks for Paul Dunsany, does not understand the emptiness there until the walls become more distinct, she realises there is no gently rhythmic motion to this place, no distant sound of music on the air. No one there but herself. She is back in her little room in the Pequod Hotel and she wishes she could hear the lapping of the grey, oily water on the thin wooden hull of the houseboat.

Joni Lascelles draws her arm and its agony to her, closes her eyes and starts to cry quietly, for herself and her lost brother and maybe, in some way she does not understand, for Paul Dunsany too.

There is a damp feeling in her groin. She can feel the onset of her period, blood, the same blood, and the distant pain of cramp singing faintly through the roar of the wasp sting.

Finally, she curses the voices for their return, for the way they turn the screw – *but you knew they would come, Florrie, you called them –* and heaves herself, covered in sweat, softly bleeding, out of bed.

THREE

California Rain

He maketh his sun to rise on the evil and on the good, and
sendeth rain on the just and on the unjust.

Matthew 5:45

When the rain comes, we run and hide our heads.

LENNON AND MCCARTNEY, 'Rain'

It didn't rain like this in northern California. It just wasn't supposed
to happen. After that first downpour on Christmas Day some strange,
unforeseen shift seemed to affect the character of the skies. Roll upon
roll of big black clouds just kept on coming in from the city and
dumping sheets of rain down on the town. The roads were a mess.
The water ran down University Avenue, blocking the gutters, sending
greasy swathes of filth and garbage onto the sidewalks. Each morning
the storekeepers came out and swept it back into the drain. Each
afternoon, the rain came back and deposited the filth on their doorsteps
again. The Christmas decorations, hung across the avenue on wires
tagged to the streetlamps and the trees, looked sad and bedraggled.
Festive green had turned to a miserable, rain-soaked grey. The red
robes of the huge Santa straddling the avenue were now close to black,
with the cardboard peeling off around the edges. The reindeer had
lost antlers, lost limbs. The holiday season was dying in a downpour
so heavy, so insistent, that it drove into your consciousness, made you
wish for anything that would take the rain away, anything that would
let you walk to the car without feeling you'd stumbled into a bog.
Beyond the avenue, towards the Gresham Woods, the scrubland had
turned into a quagmire of mud and worse, making Tom Cordobes'
men livid with fury every time Cy Langton sent them back out there
to comb it for evidence, just one more time, just one more time.

Cy Langton had been briefly thrown by the arrival of Rosamund

203

Seymour's brother from England. Even in the circumstances, Langton found it hard to summon up any sympathy for the man. He was some big-shot doctor from Harley Street, money written all over him, little sign of much in the way of human feeling. He was one of those doctors you were supposed to call 'Mr', which Cy Langton never did understand. *Mr* Lascelles took the girl under his wing, booked into the best suite of the Stanford Park Hotel, announced he'd be there for two days at the most 'making arrangements', then promptly hit the roof when Langton told him there was no way the body was getting shipped out of the morgue this side of February, no way Rosamund Seymour was coming out of the sanatorium until all the paperwork was done.

Rules is rules, Langton kept saying, over and over again and it was like talking to a solid wall. An English solid wall that looked like it had a steel rod for a spine and talked back to you in a voice like Ronald Colman trying his hardest to get right up your nose. Cy Langton had grown so used to the rain, so used to the way the case just refused to shift and how that made the TV crews wonder even harder about what to rant and rave about next, that in the end he didn't even think about his golf clubs, or what it felt like to be walking across springy green turf with a caddy behind your back and not a fucking telephone in miles. All he thought about was what manner, what degree of shit might land on his lap next.

And then the rain came down really hard and this time it flushed out something that changed it all, changed it all for good.

Afterwards, Cordobes made out he'd been thinking about this before, that he'd wondered whether they shouldn't be looking through the drainage system. That maybe he'd even mentioned it if someone had been listening. Langton heard out the big, walnut-skinned man with the Zapata moustache patiently, didn't call him an asshole to his face, gave him the benefit of the doubt, nodded and said, yes, Tom, no, Tom, maybe we'll look at procedures later and think about how we can improve them *after* we get somewhere with this case, after Ronald fucking Colman gets off my back, takes his little five-year-old semi-orphan back to England with him, and two caskets, one in the hold, one strapped to some seat in economy too, with something half alive inside it, if only that were possible. But that was just for public consumption. Given what happened afterwards, Tom Cordobes would have been lucky to have kept his job in any case. It didn't matter.

When Cordobes made those noises about checking the drains, some meter just silently registered overload in Cy Langton's head and he made a mental note (and he was a man who only needed mental notes, didn't even need a scorecard on the course except to prove things to his opponent) that Cordobes was finished. When it all died down, when no one could point the finger and say that dread word that finished a captain in the eyes of his men, the word 'scapegoat'. And truly, Langton said to himself, Cordobes wouldn't be a scapegoat. He'd be gone because he deserved to be gone, and that wasn't a judgement Cy Langton, alone, had reached.

Cordobes' outburst, the one that would have eventually cost him his job in any case, only later, when the Seymour case was starting to fade into history, had come a day earlier, in the afternoon of December 26, after the recovery team normally used for ocean work finally donned aqualungs and disappeared into the big main drain that ran from the San Jacinto creek directly under University Avenue and into a culvert by the CalTrain station. That morning the cops had got a call from a CalTrain employee who had smelled something, caught a glimpse of something he didn't like near one of the drain covers. Something that might have been a dead animal or worse. The furious police switchboard had asked the caller whether he thought, by any fucking chance, they had stopped investigating murders, like the TV reports kept telling them to, and started clearing the drains every time some dead dog got stuck in the outlets. To which the CalTrain man had said no, he hadn't thought that, and this was most definitely the first dog, or, more accurately, part of dog, he thought he'd seen that wore what looked like a kid's T-shirt and had fingers. Fifteen minutes later the blue and white plastic ribbon was going up and round the main drain outlets that ran beneath the track at Palo Alto station and Tom Cordobes, who could see what the train company man was talking about, some six feet down beneath the grating, looking like it might be swept away by the flood of swirling grey water, was standing in the pouring rain wondering what the fuck to do about it.

It didn't rain like this in northern California. It just wasn't supposed to happen.

Three hours later the recovery team arrived from San Francisco, looked at the Palo Alto guys like they were country hicks way out of their class, put on their gear, and disappeared down the hole. Cordobes had people who could swim real well, who could handle the sub-aqua stuff too, up to a point. But there was something about the force of the water down there that told him he didn't want to make any widows from his own men, and anyway these big guys from the city were always going on about how they trained and trained and trained, so why not give them the chance to show it?

They were down there the best part of the afternoon, until the grey rainy light started to fade. By the end of it, they'd been back to the surface twice with something they'd recovered, each time with it stashed in a dark-green underwater bag: an entire arm, severed at the shoulder; an upper torso still wearing part of a black T-shirt. Whatever else might have been there was now gone, floating through the underground web of sewers that wound its way to the cold, grey ocean.

On the light-grey cement of the station forecourt, the lead diver had gently opened up the bag and showed both finds as they came in, laughing a little to himself after the second, when, out of the corner of his eye, he watched two of Cordobes' men walk over to the sodden grass verge and heave their guts out onto the damp, mud-stained lawn.

'Shoulda been with us last week,' the man said quietly to Cordobes. 'Took out an entire carload of teenagers, four of 'em, near Half Moon Bay, dead in the water for a week, still sitting in the Ford, cans of beer floating around the inside. Man, that was something else. Sure beats the Monterey aquarium. Guess you guys get a quiet life out here.'

'Yeah,' Cordobes grunted. 'Mostly we just deal with old ladies committing parking violations, apart from the odd weirdo dismembering kids, and a captain with shit between the ears just to help us all along.'

The city guy stared at him. You just didn't talk like that. Not if you wanted to hold down your job. The remark came back to Cy Langton, too, of course, and that really set the seal on Tom Cordobes' police career.

The Gruesome Gourmet had, in the unwitting words of Langton himself, made a real meal of the remains. By midnight that night he'd proved pretty conclusively that they matched the hand found in the Gresham Woods. And that they didn't belong to the missing Miles Seymour. The skin pigmentation, once you had that much to work on, was clearly too dark. Probably Hispanic. And there was a small tattoo on the kid's upper arm, a red and blue rose, that was, most definitely, not the kind of thing fine upstanding English families put on their offspring.

Langton blinked hard when he heard this. What kind of people went around tattooing their kids?

Hippies, came the answer, straight away, from almost everyone in the room. Didn't Cy Langton know about hippies? The truth was, only as far as their dope habits went. Everything else was a mystery.

The following morning, they'd held a press conference and put out a request for information: they were looking for someone who knew a Hispanic child, with a rose tattoo on his left shoulder, aged five to six, last seen wearing a black Mickey Mouse T-shirt. Two hours later, a spaced-out woman calling herself Sunflower Harris had walked into the station, eyes like dinner plates, asked about her son. She was so doped up it took an hour before anyone believed her and even then the picture was hazy. Sunflower lived rough with whoever happened to be around, whoever had some smack, in Menlo Park most of the time, had lost the kid, Zak, some time on Christmas Eve during the day, kept thinking he'd turn up. He always did turn up. Before. She'd seen the news item in the hostel in Palo Alto where she'd been staying since the rains began and, so Tom Cordobes thought, had actually *forgotten* about him until she heard the mention on the TV. And then she came running, running and screaming all the way through the station until they took her to the morgue and showed her, as tastefully as possible, the tattoo on the arm, and then Sunflower Harris just went wild, disappeared off to some planet where no one was going to commune with her for a very, very long time. Tom Cordobes sent her off to one of the detox units with the most sympathetic woman police officer he could think of. But something inside had warned him already: this woman was seriously astray. What she'd told them already was what she knew. The kid went walkabout and stumbled into something worse than any bad trip his mother had ever encountered, and if he screamed 'Mommy' at any time when someone was ripping him apart with a knife – and an axe too, said the Gourmet, when he'd looked at the new parts, there was definitely an axe there too – then she wouldn't have heard even if she'd been in the next room.

And Tom Cordobes was right, of course, Cy Langton appreciated that. He was right too when he pointed out how the kid's body had got where it was. How the San Jacinto creek dribbled into the drainage system just at the edge of the Gresham Woods and you didn't have to travel far from knowing *that* to realising that the hand nailed to the tree was just some kind of joke, maybe some effort to lead them into the dark, into the trees, where you'd expect to find the bad stuff, where you'd think it ought to be lurking, when all the time it was behind you. All the bits neatly stuffed into the big open mouth of the culvert half a mile from University Avenue, left there to rot.

The irony was, said Cordobes, that if there hadn't been the rain, they might have taken much longer to find the Harris kid's remains. You could stick them up the tunnel, which was a good four feet high for its first two hundred yards, and just leave them there to decompose, to get eaten by the stray dogs and anything else that scavenged through the drainage system, and run a damned good chance that no one would know any better provided the stuff was far enough along the pipe to keep the smell away from the joggers puffing and panting their way around the wood's periphery. Without the flood, they might never have come to light at all, said Cordobes, and said it in that smartass way Cy Langton was rapidly coming to hate.

'So where do we go from here, Tom?' Langton had asked, unable to keep the side tone out of his voice. 'Any ideas?'

'House to house,' said Tom Cordobes. 'Like we should've . . .'

'Shut up, Tom, for chrissake,' Langton snapped. 'I had a bellyful of this. I had a bellyful of you.'

Cordobes just sat there and said nothing. It was hard. It was very hard when you didn't just know you were right, you had all the signs, all the evidence, all the bodies in the world to prove it for you too.

Langton puffed and wheezed, then said, 'You just get out there and do it. And mark you come back with something, you hear? If you're gonna go ruining the domestic peace of this town, you do it good and proper. These people gonna give me hell for this anyway so you just do what it takes.'

'Sir,' said Cordobes, then smiled, not too hard, not too obviously, just enough so's Langton could see. And after that, he looked at the rain still pouring down outside for a moment, then went away and called a team briefing for 3 pm.

Ten minutes after Tom Cordobes had left, Rosamund Seymour's brother was back in Langton's office and the Captain was starting to find his patience wearing very thin.

'I want my sister and brother-in-law home, Captain,' the English guy said, in that same strangled voice. He had a long, pale face that looked as if it had been stretched on some kind of rack, and, to Langton, seemed to favour the same kind of black, shiny crew cut

Gene Pitney used to wear until someone plucked up the courage to tell him he looked like a jerk. 'I want them home and that is that.'

Langton spread his arms out over the desk and tried – though not very hard – to look conciliatory.

'I told you, Mr, er . . .'

'Lascelles.'

'Yeah. That French or something?'

'Norman.'

'You don't say? Well, I told you, sir, you can take the little girl home any time you like but until we conclude this case the body and your sister have to remain here. We'll keep you in touch on how things are going with the boy, of course, not that I got anything more to say right now.'

'Good God, man,' Lascelles barked, and with the volume his voice started to crack. 'Flora's no problem. The girl can go straight into prep school. Presumably she would anyway even if this damned thing hadn't happened. That's simplicity itself. It's Rosamund and Daniel I'm talking about. I want her home. I want him buried.'

'When the time is right, sir. When the time is right. See, we think we know how he died . . .'

'Ridiculous idea. They *adored* each other.'

'I don't think so, sir. Plain as anything that your sister, she killed Mr Seymour. No other explanation. Pretty plain she isn't going to be explaining it herself either. Not as far as any of the doctors can see. That means we've got to wait for the coroner. Soon as the coroner agrees what's happened, soon as it's neat and tied, you get the body. Likelihood is you get your sister too since the probability is we'll see this as a mental case and I'm willing to be flexible there. No point in paying state taxes to keep her in jail or a sanatorium here. But there are procedures to go through. Once they're done, you get them. Not before.'

'And when is that likely to be?'

'Five, maybe six weeks. You should just go right on back to England. Take the little girl with you. There's nothing you can do here. We'll keep you in touch. Let you know when the body gets released.'

'And when you've blackened our reputations. With this nonsense about murder. This utter *crap* about Daniel and . . .'

He let the sentence drift off into space. Langton watched the English guy squirm and tried, with little success, to feel sorry for him.

'And what?'

'You know exactly what I mean.'

Cy Langton was getting tired of walking down the same footpath, ignoring the same 'keep off the grass' signs while everybody else ran riot on the turf.

'You mean the abuse, sir. The evidence of abuse.'

Lascelles leaned over to look at him, leaned and spread his palm on the desk. It was a delicate, pale hand. Not the sort you found on cops. Not the sort that did dirty, manual work.

'I *know* my brother-in-law. I *know* my sister. I *know* that cannot have happened.'

'Really,' said Cy Langton. 'You know, sir, someone once told me that the greatest thing you learn through being a cop is that nobody ever really knows anybody else. Wives and husbands. Fathers and daughters. I believe that's true. I'm not a smart man but I've turned up to too many nice little homes and seen a puddle of blood on the floor, blood that's almost always spilt by someone who says they couldn't have done it, 'cos of they love that person, they love them more than anything else in the world. In this case, I got one long and detailed medical report from someone who's a very respected expert in these cases. And he's got no doubts. That little girl got messed for sure by someone or other and I'm damned if we can find anybody to put in the frame except her father. That woman, your sister, she got beat up too and as far as that's concerned I *can* prove it, I got witnesses from the next-door house who heard it, one occasion they even saw it. So let's not fuck around here, sir. You know something, I know something. But what I got can go before the coroner and stand as evidence whereas all you got is wind and piss and family loyalty. Now family loyalty's a good thing, but like I keep trying to explain to you, rules is rules, the law is law.'

Lascelles took a long, deep breath and, for the first time since he met the man, Cy Langton sniffed victory.

'Do you *know* what this is going to do to us, Captain? Have you any idea?'

'Sir, your sister's crazy, your little nephew's missing, and for all I know the only person who can say where he is happens to be lying in that morgue down there with half his brain gone. This has happened. You can't walk away from it.'

'You don't really think Daniel had something to do with the boy's disappearance, do you? There's this other case I heard about on the television. Horrible.'

'Nothing to link them, sir, nothing whatever. We *do* know that your sister killed her husband. And that he was messing with the girl at least, and from what we think we know, with the boy too. I don't *know*. Frankly, I don't know if we'll *ever* know.'

Lascelles stared at the desk. For a moment – only a moment – Cy Langton felt sorry for him. This was one big pile of shit for anyone to deal with.

'Captain. It's precisely because this *is* a tragedy that I hate the idea of this abuse idea coming out too. Even if it's true, and I don't believe that, can't you see, it just makes things worse?'

'Ah,' said Cy Langton, after a moment's thought. 'You know what the word "dicker" means? 'Cos I think you may be dickering with me, sir.'

'I am thinking of the family. I am thinking they have suffered enough.'

Langton wondered how far he could push it, judged quite a lot.

'Fine. You dicker well. For an English guy. I tell you what. You get the fuck out of here, you go catch a plane back home, take that poor little kid with you, you get the fuck out of my hair and wait till we say the casket's ready, you do all that and I see what I can do. I'll ask the coroner if we can't leave this abuse thing out of the public hearing, get your sister home as soon as possible once we've got some paperwork from you to say she won't be running loose as long as she's in the state she's in. That good enough?'

'You guarantee it?'

'I'm a cop. I got all hell on my hands out there. I can't even guarantee I'll be in a job come this time tomorrow. It's the best offer you're gonna get, Mr, er . . .'

'Lascelles.'

'Yeah. The best offer you're ever gonna get.'

The English guy took a Du Maurier cigarette out of a silver case, lit it, watched the grey sky out of the office window, wondered how soon he could be out of this, how quickly he could be back in a place where he felt, if not happy, at least at home.

Four hours later, Simon Lascelles was in the front row of British

Airways' first-class section on the evening flight to London. In the seat next to him, Flora Seymour sat in silence, waiting to wake up from this long, long dream that seemed to go on forever.

FOUR

Syncopation

Life is what happens while you are making other plans.
JOHN LENNON, 'Beautiful Boy'

Ben Rawlins looked through the glass panel and watched the two figures seated at the mixing desk. Paul Dunsany and Joni Lascelles were talking quietly in an intense, animated way that left him troubled, against his better nature.

'That nice English lady a permanent fixture you think, Frank?'

Grayson looked up from a sheet of notes on the desk and shrugged.

'You know what women are like around musicians. Couple a weeks it looks real good, it looks real glamorous. Then they get to know the routine. They get used to the late nights and the late mornings and all of a sudden they get bored with sitting there, listening to the same thing over and over again. Jesus, it bores me. So they don't come so often and what *do* you know? Suddenly there's some other nice chick smiling up at you from the tables. We all been there, Ben. Fool to expect anything else.'

'Not Paul,' said Ben Rawlins. 'He's not been there for a long time.'

Genius looked up from the Mac. 'You ask me, the best thing that woman can do is fuck off back to England right now. Just leave us alone. Quit coming in here like this, interrupting the work flow.'

Grayson and Ben Rawlins stared at each other, uncomprehending.

'What work flow might that be, Genius?' Grayson asked eventually.

'We don't *do* nothing most of the time. Don't that strike you when it comes down to paying the bills? We didn't have that gig in the Zanzibar we'd be panhandling Pioneer Square right now along with all the other bums.'

'Yeah,' the kid grunted. 'All the same, I just wish she was gone from here. She messes things up.'

'Poor boy,' said Ben Rawlins. 'Poor sad little boy.'

Then watched the conversation behind the glass for a moment, picked up some sheet music and sat in the corner to read.

She was wearing a cream-coloured polo neck sweater and dark slacks and there was something about her today, some excitement, some trepidation that made Paul Dunsany feel cold inside. It was the third day they had been together and, for both of them, it seemed much longer. She still left him alone. She still kept the room at the Pequod, which he had never seen, and went there, even spent the previous night there, after they had made love, slowly, imaginatively, on the floor of his boat, then watched the light disappear out of the sky and the grey, greasy waters of Lake Union turn into a shiny film of black, lit by the reflections of the street lamps. But there was a bond already, unspoken, and one that came from different directions, different needs, and they were both aware of these facts.

She had arrived at the studio fifteen minutes before, gone straight in to talk to him. He didn't argue. There was nothing pressing. There rarely was these days, as the growing frequency of phone calls from the bank testified. But there were times when he wished he could take his mind off her, times when he wanted to be diverted into thinking about something else.

'You heard from him?' he asked her. 'The detective guy?'

'Yes.' She looked fragile. For all her exterior hardness, there was something there he felt needed protection, maybe as much from herself as anything else, because behind the fragility was some kind of desperation, some kind of need, that pushed her too far sometimes. Maybe made her do things she didn't really mean.

'And?'

She waited, weighed her words, tried not to think too fast, to let the words just spill out of her.

'You were there, Paul.'

He thought he might choke on the sudden halt in his breath.

'Excuse me?'

Her face was so pale, so intense.

'You lived there. You must remember. You must know why I feel like this.'

There were some things he could remember – two small figures, wearing wings, seen through the window of Moore's Music Store, old man Moore letting him go early, go to the Barn, to Louise – and some he couldn't, not in any real, tangible detail, no matter how much he fingered that pale, smooth scar on his face, thought about the old motorbike and Louise and that dark, hazy time that changed his life forever.

'Paul?'

There was something about her desperation, something about her need, that could begin to frighten him, could wrap them in a choking, stifling shroud of craziness if he couldn't bring her out of it, back into the light.

'This is America. We do Murder of the Week. Haven't you noticed that? Sure, I remember the story. I remember OJ too. Where's it get you? When do you leave it go?'

'You don't,' she said firmly, with such certainty that he knew this came from the real her, not from the need, not from the desperation. '*It* leaves you. When it decides. When it feels like it. I don't have any choice in the matter.'

'That's crap, Joni. You have all the choice in the world. We've all got things we hate about ourselves, things we've done, things we regret. You can't just let the past keep eating you up like this.'

She stared at the control desk, wishing you could touch these buttons, these sliders, and apply them to yourself, just run down the emotion button here, tone down the guilt, the memories there.

'You think there's a choice in this? A way to stop it?'

'Sure,' he said, and half believed himself. 'You say, it's gone, it's behind me. You call off this detective. You quit looking. You accept that what's happened is done and get on with your life. You've got to do that, Joni. It stands between us now. It stands between you and whatever you want to do with your life.'

She smiled and she said, 'I know that, Paul. That's exactly why I have to face it. *Because* it stands between me and what I really am.'

'Then just cut the rope. Let it go.'

'Do you think, for one moment, I wouldn't do that if I could?'

The way she looked at him, almost pleading, he knew it was true. If a way of cutting the rope existed, she'd take it. And he couldn't help wonder what would remain there afterwards. If this would be the same person. If she would run to the same feelings, the same rules.

'The reason I'm doing this is not revenge. It's not knowledge. It's not anything as simple as that. It's guilt. Can you understand that?'

'No,' he said, and the fierceness in his voice took her aback. 'You

215

have *nothing* to feel guilty about. You did not *do* these things, Joni.'

'I didn't do them, Paul. But I started them. You can never know that because I won't ever tell you. You just have to take my word. Everything. I started it. And I remember how. Exactly.'

He pushed the ancient, worn sliders up and down the deck absent-mindedly, wondered if this was how it happened, how your world fell apart, piece by piece, day by day.

'So what do you do? If you find this man?'

'I don't know,' she said. 'That is the truth. I honestly don't know.'

'Hadn't you better think about it?'

'No. I don't need to think about it. What will happen *will* happen. Maybe *nothing* happens. Maybe things become clearer. It doesn't mat-ter. I just want to see him. I just want to *hear*. Once that's over, it's over. It's like believing in magic. I don't need to understand how it works. I don't even need to see the tricks happen. You just need to know there is magic there, and that it can work, sometimes it can work. Do you see what I mean? Or am I just crazy?'

'I don't know,' he said. 'I like the idea of magic. I *know* you're crazy, else why would you be here. And afterwards?'

'Afterwards,' she said leaning over, and kissing him on the cheek, her skin so soft and fragrant, 'we think about what comes next.'

'Yeah,' he said, and watched as she picked up her bag, opened the glass door, smiled at him, said goodbye to the crew in the office, and left. He tried to hope. Maybe the desperation had cooled down a little. Maybe the need, the hunger, wasn't so loud. She looked a little less crazy, a little less obsessed, than when she'd walked in, and he knew that he was the reason, though the knowledge gave him no pleasure.

Paul Dunsany wished you could bury the dead forever, wished they would just stay down, under the ground, where they belonged. He hated this rotting corpse that seemed to have sprung out of the earth and back into his life. Not for threatening him, but for what it meant to her. He couldn't remember everything, but he remembered how the poison had crept into his – *their* – life that Christmas and how it now seemed as if it might never leave them.

Dunsany walked back into the office and Genius said, in a resigned voice, 'Lady alert. *Again*.'

In the corner, looking like she'd been there a long time, looking much as she had twenty years before, maybe even more beautiful, sat Louise Gostelow, smiling, smiling, smiling.

'She's very pretty, Paul,' Louise said. 'Sounds English too. Lucky man.'

'Looking for hippies,' Genius grumbled. 'Comes all this way just looking for hippies.'

And Paul Dunsany was trapped in the brightness of Louise Gostelow's eyes, felt himself floundering there, lost for words, gasping for air as the rain came down steadily outside, in thick grey lines visible beyond the glass door.

FIVE

Complicities

Guilt always hurries towards its complement, punishment; only
there does its satisfaction lie.   LAWRENCE DURRELL,
Justine

When Hal Jamieson came down off the trip, some time during the
early hours of the morning of December 26, he sat in the darkness of
the main room of the Barn and tried to think straight. It was the
last time Hal would ever take acid, though the flashbacks still came,
occasionally, and something about that knowledge, that decision,
gave him a little strength to start thinking about what to do, which
way to go.

When they finally came out of the storeroom, Quinn and Louise
and Mouse had smoked some more dope. Mouse was as silent as ever
but there was something about her, something in the way she wouldn't
look them in the eye, that made Jamieson wonder, made him think.
Then Quinn and Louise went to bed and Hal Jamieson listened, tried
not to, couldn't help it, listened to the sound of the iron frame creaking
in the next room, the sound of Louise screaming and screaming when
she came, that hot panting noise that was so loud it drowned out all
his thoughts until it fell away into gasps, then silence, and left him in
this cold black miserable place with nothing to do but think. For
himself. For all of them. For both of them.

And try as he might, that night, the next day, and through the next
night again, when Hal Jamieson hardly slept, there was no way around
it. No way he could come to any other conclusion.

Quinn had been feeding the boy. Sometimes he did it himself.
Sometimes he sent Mouse out to do it, and more and more it became
a new job for her, a new piece of shit to wipe off the floor. The kid
seemed to be in another world and hardly noticed they were there,

though when there was food – ham, sausage, beans, bread – he ate it quickly enough. And he noticed too that on the few times he went in *after* Quinn, something radical had changed. The kid was tripping, or something else. He had those black pool-like eyes Jamieson had seen that first, terrible night and when he went like that he seemed to stay the same way for hours on end.

'We could all trip like that, at his age,' Quinn had said, half in wonder. And Hal Jamieson realised that that was true, and the idea scared him so much that he was glad he'd forsworn Desert Rose and all her companions, and landed in the arms of friendlier narcotics, like Bud and Sierra Nevada and good old Jim Beam.

What worried him most, what nearly *killed* him with worry, was their complicity. Any way he thought about it, Hal Jamieson couldn't get away from the fact that they were tied into the thing together: he and Louise and Mouse were all in there with Quinn even though they hadn't done a damned thing, not a damned thing – *and you could see the look of amusement, of merriment, on the pigs' faces when they told them that* – except let the fucking lunatic open the door, let him show them a little of Desert Rose's dark side and wave them on in.

Life didn't work like that. It didn't let you go call the cops, say, 'Look what my friend did here while I was out of my skull some place,' then walk away untouched. Whatever way out of this there was, it had to be a way that exculpated them all. If it didn't, they fell together. And Hal Jamieson didn't want to fall. Back in Boston Hal Jamieson had a lawyer for a father who had worked his tail off to put his son through Stanford and he couldn't even dare to think about what the old guy might say if someone turned round and said, 'No, sorry, Hal's flunked this one, James, seems he got mixed up in some murder and kidnapping stuff and that just *isn't* compatible with our mores in Stanford, not compatible at all.'

It also didn't fit in with Jamieson's plans on another front. For all his looks, for the earring, the hair that curled down to his shoulders, the T-shirt with the picture of Che on it, Hal Jamieson had plans. He had plans to be rich (and dealing the dope was just one way of finding out about supply and demand, judging the markets, building up a little capital, nothing else, nothing more) and this again was not compatible with hanging around with kidnappers and murderers.

Unless . . .

That Saturday afternoon, two days after Michael had taken them into the storeroom for the first time, while Louise was God knows where and Mouse was working, Hal Jamieson sat down in the main room, on the old, threadbare sofa, sat down next to Quinn, who seemed as sober, as sane, as he was ever likely to be. Sat down, tried to look into those big clear blue eyes and catch some sense there. It wasn't easy.

'Michael,' Jamieson said. 'We got to talk. I got to know. What we do with the kid. You gonna kill him? What?'

Quinn peered at him through those ice-blue eyes and Jamieson knew that inside he was laughing.

'You kidding, Hal? *Kill* him?'

'Yeah.'

Hal Jamieson thought he could get tired of these games pretty quickly. Thought there could come a point when Michael Quinn fucked him over so much that it might just be worth walking down to see the cops and lighten up their imagination a little.

'Michael. You don't watch TV enough. This morning they started pulling bits of some Latino kid out of the sewer system off of University. Bits that had been cut up. Matched that hand they found in the woods. Beats me why we ain't seen them at the door already. Beats me why you put the fucking hand there at all.'

'We hadn't had that rain they would *never* have found the kid.'

'Except for the hand. Why put the fucking hand there in the first place?'

'You don't get it. You won't *ever* get it. You got to show things. Sometimes things don't get real unless they're *seen*. I owed the kid that. He went one way down there when I pulled the lever, one bad way. I owed him that.'

Hal nodded and wondered whether Michael Quinn's head would ever really straighten up again.

'This kid's alive, Michael. He could put us all in jail.'

'Yeah.'

'So what happens? You gonna get rid of him or what? What do you plan on doing? We got a right to know.'

Quinn looked at him as if he didn't get the question.

'You kill me, Hal. You were *there*. We rolled the dice. The kid *won* when we rolled 'em. Can't you get that through your thick fucking skull? He *won*.'

'So what you're saying is that saves him. The other little bastard, he gets burned, you go to work on him with a kitchen knife. This kid, we turn the wheel, he lives. You don't kill him.'

Michael Quinn smiled, a really crazy smile. 'That would be murder, Hal. Don't you get it?'

Jamieson wasn't used to feeling his temper run away with him but it felt like it would right then, felt like he could just drift off into some red impetuous universe of hate and blood – which Michael Quinn knew well – if he didn't just hang on to things.

'Michael. Cops don't think about Schrödinger's cat. They just think about guilty people. And in their book we're all guilty. *All.* You understand me? In their book, that kid could put *all* of us away. I don't want him dead. But I don't want to go to jail either.'

Quinn picked up a packet of cigarette papers, a tobacco tin with a fold of dope in it. Then watched amazed as Jamieson took it away from him, put it back on the stained little coffee table in front of them.

'No,' said Jamieson, and he could feel the tension in the room, could feel the subtle little shifts of power switching backwards and forwards between them.

'Not now, Michael. When we talk this through, you can smoke. But not before. You got us into this place. I want to know how you plan to get us out of it.'

Quinn stared at him and something, some distant shred of sanity inside, told him to back down. That time. That one time.

'OK,' he said. 'We just take him somewhere. We let him go. Put him in the car and get him outta here. No problem.'

Jamieson shook his head. He'd been through this, a million, a trillion times, and it just didn't add up.

'Can't do that, Michael. Where do we put him? In the desert? Might as well kill the kid now, wouldn't live five hours out there. Outside some orphanage some place? Fine. The kid starts talking and they say, "Hey, you're English, what's your name, aren't you the kid from Palo Alto?" Bang, he's back here, walking through the woods, straight back to the Barn, and they're fitting us out for the arrow jackets quicker'n you can say Richard Nixon. I don't want that, Michael. I don't *want* to go to jail.'

Quinn thought about it.

'OK. We kill him. No choice.'

'Boy, that took a long time, Michael. Real good job you never went in for philosophy. Coulda been the shortest course in history.'

'No pleasing you today. When?'

He would have done it there and then, Jamieson said to himself. Like treading on a roach.

'You know that storeroom, Michael. You think it's secure? You think there's any way he can get out, someone can hear him?'

'Kid's tied real good. He won't be going anywhere and those walls are solid dirt. Besides, he's on good acid most the time. Where you think he'd be going?'

Jamieson nodded. He could feel some organisation thing, some shadow of a plan, building there somewhere at the back of his skull.

'You got money, Michael? I mean *real* money?'

'Not much. The folks tie things up till you're older. Don't yours? If you're thinking of running away I won't be paying for it if that's what you're thinking.'

'No,' said Jamieson. 'I wasn't thinking of that. Not just that. This kid's folks, they come from one big family in England. Old money. And there's no money like old money. Seems to me that maybe there's some way we can help spread a little bit of that around *and* get rid of our problem at the same time.'

'Whoa,' Quinn grinned. 'Now you *do* surprise me sometimes, Hal. There I was just thinking you was some kind of jumped-up dope dealer when deep down inside there's a *real* criminal waiting to get out there.'

'Yeah,' Jamieson said, and there was ice in his voice. 'You think so? Well, you just remember something, Michael. Anyone gets us out of this it's *me*. You won't do it. You *can't* do it. And no one else will.'

And Hal Jamieson waited, waited for the objection, and it didn't come. Quinn just looked at him, grinning, and Hal Jamieson felt the weight fall on his shoulders, wondered if it would ever lift.

'That means you do what *I* say from now on, Michael. That means when I say move, we move. No questions. No arguments. This is not a democracy. This is survival. Understood?'

Quinn did a little salute, smiled so those big yellow teeth shone in the dim interior of the room. Then reached for the dope tin. Jamieson beat him to it, picked the tobacco tin up, and held on to it tight.

'What I want you to do, Michael, is I want you to go round this house, pick up every piece of dope and acid you can find, stash it into one big bag then drop it down the hole with the kid. And I want you to do that now. Right now. You watched TV more you'd know what the fuck was going on in the world. Right now I know those cops are starting to do house-to-house visits round here and my guess is anyone living in the woods is going to be high up on their list.'

There was so much dope there it took them an hour to clean up every little stash, and even then they weren't sure they had it all. When the last piece they could find was safely thrown down into the underground storeroom, they went back into the house, opened some beer and watched some TV. Quinn was bored after fifteen minutes, wondered how long it might be before the women came back, went to his room and started to read.

At six in the evening, there was a knock on the door. Hal Jamieson opened and stared into the stony, walnut-brown face of Tom Cordobes, smiled and said, as pleasantly as he could, 'How can I help you, officer?'

They'd cleaned up well. Ten minutes later, Cordobes and his sidekick turned down the offer of a beer and left. And there was only one thing about this encounter that registered anything unusual in Tom Cordobes' head. It was the wonderment he felt then, and rediscovered twenty years later, that a kid who looked such a good-for-nothing hippy bum could be so polite, so normal and so helpful.

SIX

Louise in the Studio

One's past is what one is. It is the only way by which people
should be judged.   OSCAR WILDE,
An Ideal Husband

She sat in the control room, playing with the sliders, like a little girl
who'd found a new toy, smiling, smiling, and Paul Dunsany couldn't
take his eyes off her. Twenty years on, she looked the same, looked
better even and it made him almost sick with fear, with the shadows
of recollections he didn't want inside his head.

'You look good, Paul,' she said, and only her voice had changed,
become deeper, throatier. She reached forward, touched his cheek, felt
the smooth line of the scar.

'Dead skin,' he said flatly, letting the warmth of her hand roar
through him, stir some small storm of craziness deep inside his head.
Then he reached up and forced her fingers away from him. There
were things rolling around in his head right then, great dark shapes
that made no sense, that looked like nothing he could recognise,
nothing he could understand.

'Just dead skin.'

'Really?' she asked, then took a long silver case out of her bag and
lit a cigarette, watching him all the time. 'Felt warm to me, Paul.
Older. But everything gets older. You, me, the world. Don't kid yourself
otherwise. Michael's back. You know that, don't you? You know what
it could mean to us?'

Dunsany wondered, not for the first time: what *could* it mean? And
she watched him thinking.

'You really *don't* remember that much, do you? Hal thought it was
some kind of act. Always did. But he was wrong, wasn't he? It really
isn't there, is it?'

There was concern in her voice. But for what? And who for?

'Some things. It was a long time ago. Some things come back.'

'There were some good things too. You remember those?'

Soft shapes in a white bedroom, the warmth of her skin, the heat of her breath against his neck. There were things he could remember, strange shards of detail lost in the dense, impenetrable fog of the past.

'They all seem mixed up together, good and bad. You understand?'

Louise Gostelow took a deep suck of the cigarette and shook her head. 'People fuck each other all the time, Paul. You take too much on yourself to think it means anything. It means a few minutes when you can share your skin. That's all. You're fooling yourself if you think it means something else.'

'I remember,' he said, and wondered if he should say this, realised he no longer cared about the consequences. 'I remember that I did something for you, something I didn't understand. I remember the night, getting hurt. Not much more.'

She smiled in a way he couldn't interpret and he realised that he really never knew Louise, not even when there was more, much more between them. She smiled at him, with what looked like some real warmth, and said, 'Maybe you don't remember it but we do. *I* do.'

'And Quinn?' Paul Dunsany tried to summon up an image, a memory of Michael Quinn from wherever it might be kept in his head. He had a picture of a thin, gaunt, grinning face, a shock of blond hair, the face of an angel, and that stirred something there too, something that was about more than Michael Quinn, more than Louise.

'Michael could kill us, Paul. He could just say the word and all that stuff from twenty years ago would blow apart in our faces. You, me, Hal, we'd all be in jail. Or worse. They got the death penalty in California now. I'm not a lawyer but you ask me to take a bet on it and I'd bet pretty heavily on the idea that it's retrospective, too. You know what that means? It means they caught us back then, we'd get life. They catch us now, they kill us.'

She was still smiling when she said it, and there was something in her face so hard, so resolute, that he hated being so close to her, hated having to share the same air in the cramped, ancient studio.

'You don't seem so scared, Louise,' he said and something rose inside his memory, it came to the surface, rolled, like the white underbelly of a fish, fell back into the depths. The remembrance of flying through the dark on his old Triumph, with her screaming at him to go faster, faster, faster: Louise *never* was scared.

'No time to be scared. We got to think this through, make sure nothing *does* happen. Hal's good at these things. Always was, though maybe you don't remember that either. Hal can keep Michael out of sight until everything dies down, until we can find some place he can live out of harm's way. He *has* to. No choice in the matter.'

'Good,' said Paul. 'I just run a two-bit recording studio and play in a band of an evening. That's *what I do*. Nothing else. Don't *ask* me for anything else.'

She seemed to be weighing every word he said.

'Are you scared, Paul?'

He thought about it and shook his head. 'No. I'm not scared. I'm not *involved*. You say Quinn can do this to me, do this to us, fine, I believe you. You say, keep quiet, don't talk to people. That's fine. No problem. But whether Quinn does or not, it's out of my control, Louise. I do not *own* people like Quinn. I do not *own* anyone. You and Hal you just go ahead and do whatever you big people do to fix things and let me get on with my life. I don't want to know, I don't want to hear. I am not a part of you. I wasn't twenty years ago, I'm not today. Clear?'

It was if she was laughing at him and, for the first time, Paul Dunsany felt hatred towards her and was ashamed of the fact. Hating people didn't come naturally to him. Hating people seemed such a waste of precious time.

'You were a part of us. You may *say* you don't remember, Paul. But I remember. I remember Telegraph Hill. I remember us riding that old bike faster than you ever wanted, all the way, from the Barn, back to my house. I remember that. What happened to us. It doesn't fade.'

'That is enough,' he said. 'That is all history. Dead. Buried. And I remember enough to know it was like that even when it was happening. I got this thing missing from my head, Louise, but it doesn't mean I'm stupid.'

She did not fit in this place. She came from somewhere else. She was foreign, and he hated her presence there, hated the way she sat there, smiling at him, knowing that there was nothing he could do or say that would make her go.

'No. You were never stupid. Good. Honest. And maybe that's the same thing.'

'You done?' he said. 'It's only a little thing but I have some money to earn.'

She stubbed out her cigarette, brushed a little ash from the sleeve of her silk blouse, looked at him, looked right into him, and it was like seeing the same person, twenty years ago, on a dark San Francisco night, foghorns booming in from the ocean.

'I got lots of time, Paul. Hal leaves me lots of time these days.'

'So?'

And he didn't want to hear it, he really didn't want to hear it.

'We could meet. We could start again. No ties. No promises. Nothing that matters outside the sheets. You remember what it was like? I'm not good at many things, Paul. But that, I'm good at. You remember.'

And he did, he could see her olive skin under the moonlight, he could see the darkness of her thighs and hear her moan just like it was last night – *but last night it was Joni and she is different, she is different* – and he could taste her salt, her fluid in his mouth.

'I got older,' he said. 'I realised after a while that without those ties, without those promises, it just doesn't mean anything, Louise. I may be lousy at doing anything about it, but I know they matter. That's the difference between us.'

'I could make you forget that,' she said, and he believed her, he believed she could. For a while.

He didn't want to say it but sometimes words come out unbidden, sometimes they just happen and it's only afterwards you feel their impact, realise the weight they carry.

'The idea ... the thought of touching you, Louise. You know, I think it makes my skin crawl.'

And briefly, only for a second, her mask dropped, there was ugliness there, something dark and fierce and primeval that lurked beneath the bright, beautiful shell that the world saw as Louise Gostelow.

'You know what you did for us, Paul?'

And he almost put his hands over his ears.

'I don't know. I don't *want* to know.'

'You saved us. All of us. The fact we're here now, the fact we're doing what we're doing, we owe all of that to you, without you we couldn't have got this far, without you, this couldn't have happened. You're *responsible*.'

227

And she judged that well. He felt hurt, in some interior, mysterious way. He felt ashamed. It would live with him that knowledge, harden, get bigger and bigger.

Louise Gostelow stood up, with the pose, the decorum, the posture of a catwalk model, all feline, all composed, and walked out of the room. And the thing that astonished him most was the transformation. In twenty years she had gone from being, briefly, a lover to a distant, cherished memory, kept hidden somewhere in the darkness of his past. And in a few minutes she had been transformed again, was something he barely recognised, something he had barely met in his life. Louise Gostelow was now an enemy.

SEVEN

A Reacquaintance

Nobody stopped thinking about those psychedelic experiences.
Once you've been to some of those places, you think, 'How
can I get back there again but make it a little easier on myself?'

JERRY GARCIA,
Rolling Stone interview, New York, 30 November 1989

And the crazy thing about 'freedom' was how tight, how restrictive it
seemed. In Obispo you got up each day and you didn't know what
the world was going to bring. Maybe some dope. Maybe something
interesting in the library. Maybe getting fistfucked in the shower by
some goon who didn't understand the meaning of the word 'no'. None
of this fitted into the normal definition of the word 'pleasant' but for
Michael Quinn that didn't matter. It all fitted into the way he saw the
world: the blur of flying electrons that surrounded him, made him
part of it all, worked like this. Rapid, random, without 'meaning'.
Whatever that was.

In the cabin, Quinn felt trapped into some straitjacket of normality
that just didn't match his measurements. It was oppressive. It was
restrictive. It was suffocating. And it stayed that way whatever Baxter
brought in from the outside world, fur, feather or fowl. This was a
real prison and you couldn't hide the bars with flowers. No way.

Quinn guessed Baxter had pretty much been given *carte blanche* by
Jamieson. When he asked for things, he got them. That first day Baxter
had brought in some lookalike goon to take his place for a few hours,
then come back with a neat, Mexican-looking whore in a tight red
satin dress, a basketful of dope – no acid – and some hard liquor.
Brought them back, plunked them down in the room like he was some
kind of Santa Claus from the underworld, grinned half-heartedly and
said take your pick.

It just didn't work.

He'd taken the whore into the bedroom, got the clothes off her, thought about things, got nowhere. She was no fool. She'd worked the rough side of Pioneer night and day for three good years since coming north from Guadalajara and she knew when someone looked sick. Knew how to recognise that skinny, haunted look and lay down the rules. You wear a condom. No sucking, no fluids exchanged, you stay away from the butt. It was like trying to fuck a nurse through her uniform and all the time he could see her eyes watching him, making sure nothing got too close, no particle of his being could leap from his living, infected body and start to poison her. It just didn't work. He just couldn't make it. He couldn't get hard, worse than that he couldn't get his mind around the thought of doing it with a woman. The shape seemed wrong after all these years and he couldn't get this image of her out of his head, this picture of her in a white uniform, a red cross on her hat, looking like she was about to perform an enema.

In the end she jerked him off, then rushed to the basin and carefully washed off every trace of his come, washed her hands with antiseptic, walked out of the room without saying a word, collected her money and was gone. Baxter didn't tell him she'd made it clear when she picked up the cash that whatever happened, whatever money there was on offer, she wasn't coming back. He didn't need to. It was written all over her face. Even whores got careful these days. That was a new concept to Michael Quinn and one he didn't quite understand, but when he thought about it, he couldn't really get worked up about the idea. The truth, and he quickly came to realise, to accept it, was that fucking didn't matter any more. It was just a bodily thing like pissing and shitting, except that it was optional. You could choose, one way or the other, and the more Michael Quinn thought about it, the more he realised there were bigger things to occupy his time than this sudden clash of hot flesh, this rush of stuff from inside.

He gave in on the acid after a day. In Obispo you just didn't get acid. You got most anything else – from hash to smack to crack cocaine – and you got as much of it as you could pay for, in whatever way you chose. But acid was out somehow. Maybe people didn't want to take the risk of having someone go that kind of crazy inside there. Other kinds they had to take. Other kinds they had no choice. But the acid kind, that was something that scared them. He didn't know why. He didn't even think to find out. Prison was like a microcosm of some primitive, tightly regulated society. Like being in Nazi Germany when things were getting rough. You knew what the rules were. You knew that being Jewish got you fucked over. You knew what was on offer and what was not. And you just went with it. Trying to change the rules was like trying to tell the sun to start moving west to east each day: pointless.

But after the session with the whore Michael Quinn relented, told Steve Baxter he wanted some acid. Right then. And wanted some Desert Rose. And so Baxter made a phone call to Hal Jamieson, who agreed, once he was sure the big guy could handle things the way he wanted, and two hours later someone was at the door with a little box. Quinn nearly hit the roof when he saw the little pieces of blotting paper there, with their blue dragon symbols, like tattoos, neatly imprinted on the surface. This didn't look like Desert Rose. Acid didn't *look* like this. And then Baxter invited the kid with the box in and he and Quinn argued pharmacology for a good thirty minutes, the kid filling Quinn in on what you could and couldn't get these days, what was good for slow, shallow tripping, what was nice for colours, what you only took when you really wanted to go to the edge and peer right down into the grey slimy stuff you find at the bottom of the world.

Blue Dragon, the stuff he'd brought, was kind of the Grayline bus tour of the nineties acid world: it took you to all of the places most people wanted to go and usually avoided all the weirder spots in town. Quinn told the kid to fuck off and bring back something harder. It took another two hours, it took another hundred and fifty dollars of Baxter's wad of bills, but finally he was back, complaining about the long drive back into the city, which Michael Quinn noted, and how hard it was to get the stuff. Blotting paper again: a picture of a green mystic eye, like the one you found on dollar bills on top of the pyramid.

When Quinn asked again, the hope fading lightly inside him, the kid just looked dumb. Whatever dope ran around the streets these days, it didn't go under the name Desert Rose or anything like it. And even when Quinn started to outline what he understood of the recipe – how you mixed the synthetic LSD with natural alkaloids – it was like he was talking Martian. These days you got good acid and you got bad acid. You didn't get connoisseur acid, or even, it seemed, anyone who knew what it meant.

So Michael Quinn took the acid they gave him and didn't ask what

231

it was called because it no longer mattered. Things were moving inside him, things that seemed to get bounced by the air up here, by the pine particles, the ozone, the icy sharpness of it all. In the sluggish, sweaty atmosphere of the pen they stayed silent, they stayed calm, and he knew where they were. But all that was changing. He could feel the virus getting restless, thinking about *growing* and while that was exciting in a way it also alarmed him. He also knew that he had to get out of the cabin, he had to escape, get back to the sweat and the fug where he could keep it under control, because if he didn't it would all go too far, there'd be no turning back, and it would be this 'freedom', this escape, that set the demon loose inside his blood and tore his life apart.

The place this acid took you to was like no place he'd ever been with Desert Rose. It was like the times: cold and dark and serious. You didn't see the colours any more, you didn't watch the wavicles dance. Just sat in some living darkness and listened to the world breathing, wondering, wondering, wondering. Maybe it was age. Maybe it was the chemical composition of the drug. Maybe it was just that this was 1995, not 1975, and there was something in the make-up of the time, the universe he lived in, that altered with the years and said, like the mesmeric Don Henley song he'd listened to for hours on end in Obispo, that you didn't look back, just didn't look back.

And you thought. This acid made you think, not big, wordless thoughts like the old quantum stuff, but logical things, things that had names that you could mouth and hear them dance on the air. Things about surviving. Things about escape.

The cabin was big: one main living room, three bedrooms off, the big pine kitchen, a guest bathroom, then a huge main bathroom, with a jacuzzi in the corner. Jamieson had frosted glass covering the outer part of the wall near the bath, the WC pedestal and the bidet – bidets in Washington, God help us, Michael Quinn thought – and then had plain, wall-to-floor plate glass installed over the jacuzzi. It meant you could have a shit without letting the woodchucks and raccoons get sight of you squatting, but when it came to relaxing in the jacuzzi, you could do what the fuck you liked and stare right out of the window, right into the green, green woods

the field glasses glint half a mile off in the undergrowth

232

and do whatever you did in a jacuzzi. Fucked some secretary out of marketing till she screamed in Jamieson's case, probably. Quinn could see him doing that. It just fitted him so neatly, fitted his personality like a glove.

The plate glass was so thick Quinn thought it could probably survive an atomic blast. The windows were sliding ones, with expensive-looking metal runners top and bottom, and they had on them the biggest window lock he'd ever seen. The sort they'd have had in Obispo if someone told them bars were out.

He wasn't even sure Baxter had the key. Michael Quinn knew nothing about locks. Obispo was so tight, so hermetic, there was just no point in even thinking about getting out. He looked at the big chunk of silver metal that melted into the sliding glass door and didn't even think about trying to open it, knew he might as well try to fly a space rocket. Knew he was lost, without a key.

But at least Baxter didn't follow him in there. It was like the goon had some kind of reservation about being in the crapper alongside someone else. Better hope he never makes it to the pen, Quinn thought, and laughed a little. He didn't want to push this. He didn't want Baxter to think there was something going on in there that he ought to be taking an interest in. So Quinn spent most of his time out of bed either in the living room or in the kitchen (where he was watched like a hawk every minute). But gradually, when he'd dropped some stuff, when Baxter got to recognising that dreamy look in his eyes and thinking he was way past anything bad, he got into the habit of locking himself inside the big bathroom, leaving Baxter outside the door, turning on the jacuzzi, turning *every* fucking thing on. Letting the water flow, lying down fully-clothed in the long raffia lounger next to the tub, and tripping. Going to that big dark place where he could think. Could even look out of the plain plate-glass window at the woods if he wanted, turn on the internal stereo system that was built into a floor-to-ceiling pine cabinet along one side of the wall, think, without the goon staring malevolently at him every waking second of his existence. And that was important. Because Michael Quinn needed to think, needed to work out how he was going to get out of this place, how he was going to survive.

It was getting well into the afternoon and the acid was working slowly. He could hear the blood churning around his head. He could feel the world slipping slowly into a distinct, limited set of colours that defined everything, *everything* it contained. It was interesting. Like watching good TV. But it wasn't the stuff you got excited about, and it didn't give him a clue about how to get the fuck out of there.

And then something made Michael Quinn look up from the swirling, raging waters of the jacuzzi, look up at the plate glass window, and the leaden sky, the dull green forest outside.

He blinked hard twice because this kind of thing, this *hallucination*, there could be no other explanation, did not normally happen to him, whatever the dope that was racing through his veins.

At the window, plain as day, looking just as big, but somewhat older, was the cop from twenty years ago. The one with the walnut skin and the Zapata moustache. The one that smiled when he wasn't happy, got too loose with his fists and didn't really care what happened afterwards. The one that put Michael Quinn inside for life and laughed in the courthouse when they took him away, laughed a lot but kept on looking 'cos he knew he was only getting half the answer, he knew he was only boxing half the problem.

And the old cop was tapping lightly on the glass. No. Something different. He was tapping lightly at the lock on the door, the big single metal lock fused into the glass, the one that seemed so impregnable – but you're a con, not a cop, Michael said to himself and started to laugh – the one that now clicked and clucked like a happy kid's toy.

The radio station was playing Blue Oyster Cult – *don't fear the reaper* – and way up here in the Cascades the reception got pretty strange sometimes, wavered in, wavered out, so Quinn couldn't really make out the words, like the singer was mumbling them.

The kid's toy on the window clicked and clucked again, it sounded like something snapped, and he watched as the big old cop looked at him, grinned really wide, pushed something on the door, took hold of the glass and pulled it open. The air rushed in from outside, cold and damp and stinking of pine – Michael could feel the thing inside his blood sniff it, get excited, start hunting – and he tried not to breathe it but there wasn't much choice. It just came right in and at him, just like the old cop, and you could feel the triumph in both of them

this is bad acid, michael, this is bad acid and you should start thinking about eating the twinkie bars right now, eating and eating them until your gut just runs over with the sugar and you come

right down out of this place, you drink some wine, you watch
some tv, maybe even eat some real food till the next time

as it washed over the room.

The old cop bent over the raffia lounger, looked into the big iridescent pools of his eyes and smiled.

'You're not fucking real, man,' Michael Quinn said, and half believed himself.

The old cop, his avatar, whatever the fuck this was, reared up over him, still grinning, and said, 'No?'

Then he walked over – was he happy, was he just mad? – to the controls on the stereo, turned the sound way up loud. Blue Oyster Cult were still playing. Michael Quinn shook his head. He didn't think the track lasted that long. He thought he knew every damned second of it and he was *sure* it didn't last that long.

The old cop came over, picked him up by the collar of his denim shirt, pulled him up to his face – you could smell his false teeth there, all chemical and age, and when you do that you begin to wonder: this real or this bad acid? – and whispered loudly into his ear, over the sound of the music.

'Got people want to talk to you, Michael. People need to know things you should've been telling us a long time ago. Things you *would* have been telling us if they'd given me the chance to talk to you alone a little while back then. Like we are now. You get me?'

Quinn closed one eye, tried to grin at the guy then wondered what the point was in grinning at a ghost.

'You just fuck off outta this trip, old man,' Quinn said, and even as the words came out he could hear how they rambled, he could hear how little real control he had over the words. 'All I got to do is eat some Snickers and you just disappear. *Pooouuffff!!!*'

He tried to snap his fingers but it didn't work, the skin didn't hit together in the right place, the noise never came.

'Cold turkey time,' said the ghost, then grabbed Michael Quinn real hard around the neck – *this ghost hurts!* – and dragged him over to the bubbling jacuzzi. Quinn stared into the swirling, milky-blue waters and felt the heat rising up from there. It looked like something out of a lab experiment that was getting right into his face.

'Cold turkey,' the ghost said again, then pushed Quinn's head hard, right beneath the water, and, as if someone had snapped a lever somewhere, some automatic thing that said, this happens, do that, Michael Quinn started to scream and the water came into his mouth, his ears, his throat, his eyes, the world started to burn and choke him all at the same time, and there was no air there, nothing but this milky ozone blueness, bubbling and churning and roaring in his ears, and the lights, the bright-blue lights that filled this fish tank world, so bright they hurt you, got louder, got brighter then, as the pain got worse, got harder, got dimmer, somehow, almost by the second as the water filled his lungs, filled his head, and somewhere, deep within him, the acid kept on laughing, kept on taunting him – *can you die in two universes at once?* – till he felt sick, till something came up from his guts, voided itself into the milky blueness, and all the lights started to go out real fast.

Tom Cordobes picked his moment, had learned this moment in an underground chamber in Saigon in another lifetime, and jerked Quinn out of the jacuzzi just as he started to throw up. He held him by the collar, watched the yellow stuff drip down his chin, shook him once or twice, and said, 'Real enough, Michael?'

And that was the moment that Michael Quinn gave up acid for good. When he just pushed it way back inside and realised that survival didn't come from a tab of alkaloid, it came from somewhere within.

He didn't move his head, not an inch, he just watched the old guy and waited. You wait, he thought. You get the advantage. Because one thing he knew, one thing he could recognise from all those years with those animals in the pen, was the moment that someone lost control.

'Fuck you,' Michael Quinn said, then felt himself hurled through the air, across the room, towards the bath, the cabinets there, glass-fronted, a maze of mirrors, line upon line of aerosols and deodorants and all the other shit you got to find in these places, and all the time he was breathing hard, waiting, waiting, and waiting.

When there was enough air there, just before he hit the great big shiny thing in front of him, he yelled, so hard he thought his lungs would burst, so hard he thought it would bring down the walls.

'*BAXTER!!!*'

And then Michael Quinn flew head first into the mirrored cabinets, his skull shattered the glass, there was blood in his eye, phlegm and vomit rose up in his throat, and the world splintered into a million sharp and deadly pieces.

Tom Cordobes watched him slump to the floor in a sea of broken glass, looked at the door, heard the banging, saw the big iron key, almost as long as his fist, solid there, the lock scarcely even moving under the barrage from the other side of the big hunk of pine.

'You acted again, Tom,' he said to himself dryly. 'There you go doing it all over again.'

He walked over to Quinn's slumped figure, heard the banging on the door increase in volume. The body didn't move. There was blood matted in the golden hair. It ran down Quinn's face in a thick, greasy line, left a smear at the edge of his throat. His eyes were open and they still looked alive. Still had that steely-blue intelligence that had made him get so mad twenty years ago when Michael Quinn could have told him everything, could have opened up all the doors, and instead just laughed at them, laughed himself all the way into Obispo as if he didn't even care.

Tom Cordobes crouched down and looked at the unmoving, bloody head and said, with some genuine remorse, for himself, not for Quinn.

'Fuck it.'

Looked amazed as a single eye winked back at him.

And in that single microsecond Tom Cordobes suddenly realised that when you get old you forget stuff, you forget something from all those years of training in 'Nam. You get unlucky and you pay the price. You forget something about not believing your eyes until you'd made damned sure you *could* believe them.

With a tired, almost resigned feeling in his gut, he turned his head slowly to the source of the sound, the sound of atoms whistling through the air, faster than you could *ever* imagine, faster than light, faster than death.

Michael Quinn's right hand was wrapped in a bloody towel. Inside, the point gleaming upwards, was a sliver of glass the size of a dinner knife: long and sharp and lustrous. It rose like a gleaming crescent and the last thing Tom Cordobes heard was the screaming, Quinn screaming in triumph, in glory, as the point went into the old cop's throat, in as far as he could push it, turn it, twist it, move it any way he could, listening to the sudden gushing there, feeling the sinews and guts and muscle slicing under the blade.

Tom Cordobes looked like he'd just put on a new crimson neckerchief, one that stretched almost from ear to ear, one that moved and grew and ran. He staggered backwards, holding both hands to his neck, trying to pretend that if he held it there long enough he could keep the life inside him. But it just leaked through his fingers, leaked, then poured, in a great black-red bloody rush through his hands, pumped Tom Cordobes' life out onto the tiled floor of the bathroom in great warm gouts.

The old cop fell to his knees, his head rolled forward until it touched, gently, on the tiles, his hands let go, he crouched, his temples on the cold stone tiles, and then a red tide flooded out in front of him.

Michael Quinn got up, still holding the bloody glass dagger in his hand, walked over to Cordobes. The banging on the door had stopped. Baxter had got smart. Baxter was racing round the outside of the cabin and planning to come in through the open glass doors.

No exit, Michael Quinn thought. Not this time. Baxter was no fat old stupid old cop. Baxter could swat him away with one finger.

Still, as someone – *something* – had once said to him long ago: *What the fuck?*

Michael Quinn wiped away the blood that was running down from his head, bent down over Tom Cordobes and started sawing. By the time Baxter was through the glass doors, he had removed the best part of the fatty flesh and skin of the dead man's right hand and was starting to work hard on the bracelet of sinews there, panting, panting, panting, all the time.

EIGHT

Ransom

When Black Friday comes I'll stand down by the door
And catch all the grey men as they dive from the fourteenth
    floor.
When Black Friday comes I'll collect everything I'm owed,
And before my friends find out I'll be on the road.
                                        STEELY DAN, 'Black Friday'

'Jesus,' Hal Jamieson groaned, and looked at the mess on the floor.
Tom Cordobes was still hunched over, his forehead on the tiles, the
blood now a dark, sticky puddle around the body. Quinn had managed
to remove his right hand. He held it up for Jamieson to see and said,
'Like I told you a long time ago, Hal, it's real important, you've got
to have something to *show*.'

Baxter hadn't objected. He thought it would occupy Quinn while
Jamieson drove all the long way out from Mercer Island. He thought
it would keep the crazy fuck busy while he got round to fixing the
window, fixing what he could of the room, fixing in his head how
much he was going to be charging for sweeping up after this, provided
Jamieson didn't fire him on the spot for screwing up. Not that this
was a likelihood. Jamieson wasn't dumb. You didn't call in rent-a-maid
to clear up after this one, it wasn't some late-night Mercer Island coke
party that got out of hand and messed up the furnishings a little. Hal
Jamieson had all of a sudden found himself in the middle of the *real*
thing, and not many people to turn to when he wanted to leave the
shit behind and sniff the air. Baxter didn't like clearing this kind of
mess up but it was amazing how money could help you get round to
doing things you'd ordinarily hate.

'You know the guy?' Baxter asked.

Jamieson looked at Tom Cordobes. The walnut colour had drained
from his skin. It now looked like old parchment: the sheen was gone,
it was dull and lifeless. The big Zapata moustache, half grey now,

239

though he'd never noticed it earlier, when Cordobes had stopped him in the street, was soaked in blood and mucus that had dripped down steadily in twin streams from the nostrils and settled, caked solid, in the facial hair. He wore the same old faded cotton suit he'd had on when he played the trick with the car outside SCC's office and Hal Jamieson couldn't help wondering whether, at some time during those last moments, Cordobes didn't blame him for this, didn't think this was some sort of set-up to get him out of the way. But Tom Cordobes knew Michael Quinn, who was now gently shredding the flesh from the bones of his hand in one corner of the bathroom. He knew what to expect. He must have decided to take that risk.

And Hal Jamieson's eyes are bright and shiny and sober when he looks at Michael Quinn, in the half-light of the Barn, and says the single word, 'Ransom.' The steel-blue eyes stare back at him in amazement, amusement and Quinn starts laughing, a little high-pitched, a little soaked through with dope, then drops the laughter, goes mock-serious, says, 'How much?'

'Yeah,' Jamieson grunted. 'I knew the guy.'

'Bad news.' Baxter didn't put it like a question. 'This could be real bad news, sir.'

He bent down, rolled Cordobes over. The body was stiffening. Baxter could feel its resistance, feel the way the muscles were hardening, as if something still alive was shouting the orders, tighten, tighten, tighten.

'Got to be two hundred thousand, Michael. These are big people. You read about it in the papers, you'd know that. They got stakes in all the big things, sugar and banking and transportation. And they got people in politics too. These are big people and they can get the money. They have to get the money 'cos if they don't what will the rest of the world think: maybe they don't have it or something?'

Baxter started to go through Cordobes' pockets, slowly, methodically, turning each one inside out, emptying the contents onto a section of the floor that hadn't been stained with the dead man's blood, making a little pile: notes, coins, keys, a packet of breath fresheners, some receipts for parking lots.

'You done this before?' Hal Jamieson asked.

'You sound like you done this before, Hal?' Quinn grinned at him like some big crazy death's-head.

Hal Jamieson felt cold. 'No, Michael. I run dope. I go to college. I done nothing like this before. But you don't leave me with much choice.' And this was the moment Hal Jamieson first got that feeling, the idea that somehow his life was going to be spent clearing up, sorting, organising, getting people out of shit that wasn't of his own making. 'You just don't leave me with a choice.'

'You want to know that?' Baxter asked, and Jamieson could feel the aggression there, feel how the big man resented being asked. 'You know how this could go? *Sir?* You know what would happen if the cops walked right through that door right now? The less you know about me, the less I know about you, the better. Shouldn't even have asked if you knew this guy. Don't give a fuck either way. This wasn't supposed to be *my* business but I guess it just ain't turned out that way.'

Jamieson watched the little pile of objects grow. Now there was a wallet, a little credit card case, a small notebook, an address book.

'I'll write you a cheque for twenty-five now, Steve. You're earning it.'

The big man stopped and looked at him.

'Twenty-five? Man, I'm looking at jail here. I'm maybe looking at life. And you want to throw me the kind of money your wife would spend landscaping the parking lot?'

'Ransom's not a pretty thing, Michael. I post this note we get in deep.'

'Make it a million,' the death's-head said. 'Make it two.'

And Jamieson had thought about that. They had the money. But they didn't have the opportunity. And he didn't have the time.

'No.'

'Why the fuck not, man? What the fuck?'

'Because I want them to pay it. This isn't some game, Michael. We need them to pay it and these people aren't local, they're in England, it's going to take time, they need to telegraph money, they need to go through the practicalities. Also we need cash that we can carry. They turn up with a truck, what the fuck do we do with it? This is like a deal' (and Hal Jamieson was cutting his first deal with the *same kind of ease and skill that would serve him so well later, in the real world)* 'and the point about the deal, all the books say, is that it's got to be practical. You got to ask a price they can pay. And we need to be outta here real quick so that means it's got to be a price they can meet, real quick. Get me?'

And Hal Jamieson finally knew what it was like to be on the wrong end of a deal like this, couldn't help wondering where this big man would stop (at this cheque, at the next?), couldn't help wondering if that great Jamieson gift for improvisation would really win through this time round.

'I'll write you out a cheque for a hundred thousand, Steve. And that's *everything*. You get me? Then when it's all over, when things are nice and neat and tidy, I write you out another one, give you a plane ticket to the East Coast. We got offices there. We got work. If you want it. If you need it.'

Baxter nodded, started sifting through the last side pockets of Cordobes' jacket, said, 'Yeah. You write those cheques, Mr Jamieson, you *will* write them but you bear in mind two things.'

Jamieson waited.

'I got that money, *sir*, I don't need your fucking work.'

Quinn thought about it and shook his head. 'What you mean?'
And that really worried Hal, really made him wonder how he kept this whole thing in some kind of equilibrium. 'What I mean, Michael, is that whatever happens, whatever, our life here is over. We get lucky, we don't go to jail. We get lucky, we get the money, we just go, just be like all those other kids who flunk Stanford, flunk the parental thing, drop out, turn on, call it any fucking damn thing we like, we just fall through the holes in the floor of this great nation for a few years, fall through and come up some place else, a few years later, new lives, new people. You get it?'

Hal Jamieson nodded and said, 'And number two?'

'So you see why the money's so important? No money, no life. Plain and simple as that, Michael.'
Quinn thought about it and grinned. 'Born to organise, Hal. Born to organise,' he said. 'Seems to me you'd best go post that note.'

Steve Baxter picked up the address book, threw it over to him. Jamieson caught it in a single, swift movement, felt the blood sticking to the cheap plastic cover. Then Baxter did the same with the notebook. He didn't look in either.

'That's for you,' the big man said. 'Whatever's in there is *no* business of mine.'

He looked out of the window. The day was starting to fade away, the greyness beginning to turn into deep, limitless black.

'Number two, *sir*? Number two is I ain't digging this fucker's grave on my own.'

DISAPPEARANCES

ONE

1996

I believe every man is born with his quantum, and he cannot
give to one without robbing another. I very well know to whom
I would give the first place in my friendship, but they are not
in the way, I am condemned to another scene, and therefore
I distribute it in pennyworths to those about me, and who
displease me least, and should do the same to my fellow pris-
oners if I were condemned to a jail.   JONATHAN SWIFT

I wish not to be given a title or an appointed position. I can
and will do more good if I were made a Federal Agent at
Large, and I will help best by doing it my way through my
communications with people of all ages. First and Foremost I
am an entertainer but all I need is the Federal Credentials.

ELVIS PRESLEY,
letter, 19 December 1970, to Richard Nixon, offering Presley's services
as a Federal agent to work to curb drug abuse by young people

Nothing changes. She had known this all along, seen it happen every
year, from those early, half-remembered days when there was a 'family',
before the change, and she had seen it later, in the grim, dead halls of
prep schools, boarding schools, in England, in France, in Switzerland,
during that strange period when those with homes went to them, and
those without stayed, watched the resentful skeleton holiday staff go
through the motions of entertaining the odd ones, wondering all the
time why both of them were there.

Nothing changes. At midnight, when the clock sweeps through the
hour, when the hugging and the shouting and the singing begin there
is no molecular shift in the air, no lightning bolt from God to rend
the sky, place a marker in the world that says, 'From here on forward
... no pain, no guilt, no poverty, no cruelty, there will be no cancer,
no AIDS, no Alzheimer's, madmen shall not hijack planes or kidnap
small children, buses shall not crash, Jews shall love Arabs, a change

in the laws of science will render all nuclear devices as harmless as a domestic waste disposal unit by outlawing the rules of fission and fusion that make them work, all these things *shall* happen . . .'

And Miles Seymour, Gabriel, will walk from heaven with gilded wings. In the first minute of the new year the world will rise anew.

She sat alone at the table, littered with empty beer glasses, and listened to the Zanzibar crowd singing the same old anthem, the one they always paraded just after midnight, watched them hugging each other, some tears, some laughter, some thinking this just might be their lucky night. And already she was beginning to feel like a guitar widow, beginning to understand how, in the end, this life could tear you apart if you let it. *If you let it.*

Paul Dunsany was on the stage, in a sense, he is always on the stage, trying to lead the drunken maul through the tune, played a little like a Mexican dance number, and already she can feel the gloss wearing off the show. Already she recognises the numbers the band plays, the intonation of his voice, the weariness that lurks beneath the surface, that no amount of artistry, no degree of commitment (which she did not doubt) could, in the end, hide from someone who sat and listened without participation night after night after night. At the heart of the musician's life, she thought, was dissatisfaction and boredom: the challenges went and what you became was your own past, someone who played what the audience wanted, the old songs, the old songs, not what you forced them to hear. And it was this familiar boredom that could drive you crazy, make you write something about the smell of teen spirit one moment, then bite the bullet the next, when you've played it one million times too many, or played worse, like this, much worse.

She could recall one New Year's Eve in a château boarding school outside Geneva – 1985? 1987? so far away, so near? – when the tedium grew so bad that she spent the first few hours after midnight looking up every word of the stupid song in a battered edition of the Oxford English Dictionary, wondering at the banality of it all, that such encoded drivel could hold the world – but not the Muslims, not the Hindus, not the Taoists and Confucians and Buddhists – together like some vast global glue. She recalled looking up the word 'syne' and finding three meanings that were not simply distinct but also, in part, contradictory: that the stupid little word could mean both before and after and next, all at the same time. And something within her tried to say that it was right that you could tie yourself together, in this clinging midnight mass, wrapped around such inanities. It was right because it was some kind of defence against the world, one that made no sense, but one that worked, was magic, and, like everything magic, you didn't need to know why, you only needed to know that it happened.

It was at that moment, as she recalled her previous self, that Joni Lascelles knew she could give up the quest and go home, to the grey, shabby streets of Hackney, the real London, drab, neurotic, always watching the street corners each night, back to the life of conveyancing over-priced crumbling houses from one debt-laden owner to the next, checking the planning laws and the deeds of covenant, looking for liens and torts and bills of exchange, shuffling electronic money from one account to another and raking a thin little margin off the top to pay for her small, single-bedroom flat with the walls so thin you could hear the rap music and the couple next door fucking, the sound of their creaking bed, their panting, late into the night. She could go home and, each weekend, take the tube to Finchley and put flowers on her mother's memorial. She could go home and let these bright-red lights of fear and guilt and anger wink out under the grey and everyday pressures of 'normal' life. She could become like the rest, forget the pain, forget the need, forget the desperation. What had happened, when her mother died, was the worst sudden flame of despair, the one that threatened her the most. But it was also the last throw of the game. This was the demon trying its utmost before it gave up the ghost. This was the only chance it had to win because from this point forward it could do nothing but recede into the catacombs of her memory, a distant ache, a scar that no longer burned, and the reason came not from Paul, not from Seattle, not even from Michael Quinn if she found him. The reason was within herself. There was a struggle going on inside her and what she thought of as the dull, the sane, the ordinary part of herself was starting to win.

The band stopped playing and the sound of the crowd, so many people in the club that night, so many it seemed you couldn't get the air to breathe, drowned out everything. Then music again, taped this time, something she recognised but couldn't name. The crowd parted and they were back with her: Ben Rawlins, covered in sweat, looking ecstatic, Roseanne Fitzgerald, tired, very tired, Grayson, the tall rangy black man as aloof, as distant as ever, and Paul, last, as always, looking worn out, exhausted. It struck her that of all the members of the band only Ben didn't rely on music to earn a living; and only Ben seemed to continue to get the inspiration, didn't see it as just another day, just another gig.

The big drummer walked over to her, embraced her gently, kissed her on the cheek, all so soft, so finely gestured, that it didn't fit correctly with his size, whispered in her ear, 'Happy New Year.'

Then beamed at her. This inner, relentless drive of his to make anyone, any stranger passing through, regard this space as 'home' was so huge, so *gross* it was astonishing. It was like being washed over by a warm, laughing tide that didn't discriminate about who it overwhelmed, where it went.

Even Roseanne seemed changed tonight. Even she seemed to accept her presence, gave her some kind of complicit acceptance into the club – *did she want this?* – with a shrug and a smile and another kiss, all of which said: *we know, we know, but this is what it's like, so why fight it?*

Roseanne stared at the stony, sweating face of Frank Grayson and said, 'You ever smile, Frank? Not even on New Year's Eve?'

Grayson shook his head. 'You should know, Roseanne, I'm a Muslim. We got our own calendar. We don't recognise New Year's Eve.'

Roseanne looked at the two dark brimming glasses of Redhook in front of him, queueing like brown-coated soldiers in a line, and said, 'Frank. Muslims don't drink. Don't you know that?'

Grayson tipped a wink, grinned, big white teeth that Joni Lascelles thought rarely saw the light of day, and said, 'That's *orthodox* Muslims, my girl. The ordinary kind.'

And it just went on. This was the way they lived, slowly, bantering, running through this lazy, endless bickering. Nothing changes, Joni Lascelles said to herself. Nothing changes, and that was part of their secret, part of their stillness. The world had shrunk for them, retreated into this defined, familiar parcel that they could recognise without worrying about where the road in front of them led, or how long it ran into the distance. She watched Paul Dunsany finally get to the table, after seeming to shake the hand of everyone in the club, letting the girls place big sweaty kisses on his cheek, flirting with them in that quiet, understated way, watched him sit down, push the big glass of beer in front of him halfway into the table, wave his arms and say, 'We're done.'

Rawlins' big furry brows met together in the middle.

'What you mean, we're done? Another two, three hours to go by my watch.'

'We're done.'

'Am I to take it,' asked Ben Rawlins, 'that my arrangement of the dreaded "Auld Lang Syne" toon in the manner of a Mexican mariachi number played by the venerable Monsignor Cooder did not meet with your approval?'

'Nope,' said Dunsany. 'I doubt anyone could have done it better, Ben. Really I do.'

'That a back-handed compliment or what?' Rawlins asked, and for a moment something not too far distant from anger flashed across his face.

'It's a real compliment. A *real* one. But we're done. For God's sake, you think they're going to know the difference between us and the DJ?'

The band looked at the dance floor and fell silent.

Finally, Ben Rawlins said, 'You don't think that would be kind of cheating on them?'

'*Cheating?*'

Paul Dunsany looked as if he couldn't believe he was hearing this. 'Ben, these people listen to us five nights a week for most of their lives. We're *cheating* them?'

Frank Grayson asked, 'You sure we get paid if we don't play no more?'

'I have a dispensation from the management. Worry not. This is 1996. For a few brief hours, men, we are free. You too Roseanne. If you feel like it.'

'I thought maybe I'd stay on here,' she said, then lifted her glass. 'What the hell else is there to do?'

'Me too,' said Rawlins, and the rest of them nodded, as if in a conspiracy.

'Yeah, well,' Dunsany said and looked at Joni, so quiet, always watching him, always thinking. Wondered about this gap between him and the band, and whether it was growing, getting so big he ought to think about it. 'I got tobacco smoke and beer fumes coming out of my ears. We're going?'

Joni stood up, smiled at them and said, 'Happy New Year.'

Then, as they worked their way through the crowd to the door, felt their puzzlement behind her, felt no resentment, just something that queried the way he was acting, queried this arrival of something new in his routine.

Outside the air was cool and damp, you could see the atmosphere, thick and grey, hanging round the circular street lights as it wafted in from Puget Sound. Music seemed to be oozing out of every pore of Pioneer, coming right out of the cracks in the walls, a little tinny, but always there, a live thing behind the bricks, making a noise like hip bees buzzing in a hive. It was as if everybody was inside, listening to the noise, partying so hard that maybe they thought it was a race, that you could go at it long enough, hard enough, so the music never stopped, the buzzing just carried on forever.

She shuffled her jacket around her, caught up with him, linked her arm through his, wondered about these changes happening inside her, and what they might mean.

'They think I'm stealing you.'

'They do?'

The idea seemed genuinely strange to him.

'Yes.'

'They're wrong. I don't get stolen any more. Just give myself away real cheap.'

They walked down a narrow street, half lit by old iron lamps, tall, brick buildings either side, so high they seemed to reach to the sky.

He stopped, leaned against the wall, reached for her, felt her warmth, and said, 'I'm sorry. I sound really down. Like everything's bad.'

Then checked himself straight away, looked at her, so pale, so striking. Louise Gostelow was beautiful in the way women in magazines were beautiful, beautiful in a way you could tick off in points. But Joni *shone* from something, some strange, radiant thing, inside her and he could lose himself there, in her person, in her being, any time he felt like it and wander for hours without knowing the words to say what kept him, what fascinated him.

'And it's not. Not bad at all,' he said, still amazed at these feelings that just came out of nowhere and took him over, *ruled* him. Then, changing the subject so quickly, asked, 'You heard from him yet? The detective guy?'

Joni thought about Tom Cordobes, their meeting in the room at the Pequod, how suspicious, how tense, the old guy had been. Wondered what had happened to him. Wondered if it really was as simple as she thought: that he had just taken the money and run back home. Maybe via Tahoe. Whatever. There was no one there on his answerphone in Milpitas. There was nothing to show for the money she gave him, money she could barely afford. And, most of all, she wondered why none of this bothered her. Why, in the days since she and Paul had found themselves swamping each other, she had, in the moments she had thought about Cordobes, *dreaded* the idea that he might call.

'Nothing since he left a message at the hotel saying things were going OK.'

'When was that?'

She thought about it. Today was Monday. She had heard nothing since the previous Wednesday.

'A while,' she said, and could feel the blame in her own voice.

He walked over to an iron bench and she joined him there. Beneath the arches of an office block she could see the bums moving, watching them from the dark

rassenfrassenrassenfrassenrassenfrassenrassenfrassen

wondering whether to try to ask for money. Something kept them away.

'You know the worst thing?' he said, and there was something in his voice she hadn't heard before, something strange and foreign. 'The worst thing about getting old? You discover worrying. When I was young, I never worried. No matter what happened, however bad things got, I didn't worry. I just did my best to make things better, and if it didn't work then that was that. And you think the rest of your life you'll be like that. You'll be the same. Always the same. Then one day you wake up and that nasty little letter from the bank all of a sudden looks *real*. You feel it and that's *real* paper. One day you start to think about passive smoking and drinking-related diseases. Too much salt on your food. Too much cholesterol in your eggs. One day you start to think about what happens when you get old, when you get slow, when you can't work, and there's no one there to push you round. One day you see kids playing with a kite in a park and wonder why *you* never get to play with any kids. You just worry about things. You get to worrying about yourself. You get to worrying about you. And where the hell this is all going.'

'I don't know where this is going, Paul,' she said straight away. 'I don't know. That's the honest answer.'

'And that's a fine answer. That's the answer I gave when I was twenty-five, thirty, whatever. But you push the other side of forty and suddenly it all starts to sound kind of hollow. And it's not because you hear things ticking away behind your back. It's because you *change*. It's because something *happens*.'

They watched a little drunken gang, four men, four women, no more than twenty, twenty-two, stagger along the road, arm in arm, oblivious of the world, so happy happy happy.

'I got lost in you, Paul,' she said. 'I forgot why I came. And I *know* I don't want to remember. I *know* I want to be rid of it. But it's not gone yet. Not altogether.'

Paul Dunsany took a deep breath of the night air. It was clearer than anything you got inside the Zanzibar. It didn't taste too bad: a little diesel on the back of the salt. It could be worse.

'I know,' he said, and recognised the point, recognised that this was somewhere that his life could divide, one way or another, good or bad, up or down, heaven or hell.

'What if finding out tore you apart, Joni? What if there was something you didn't expect there? Something that was so bad it made things *worse*? Worse than not knowing?'

She didn't even need to think about it and that, more than anything, was what decided him.

'You give me a choice? Nothing's worse than not knowing, Paul,' she said, and wondered if she really meant it. '*Nothing.*'

'I see,' he said. And he really did.

Paul Dunsany stood up and, for only the second time in his life, felt truly afraid.

He reached forward, touched her cheek, felt the softness of her hair, golden and curling in the night. And somewhere deep inside of him he could hear John Lee Hooker's voice, a huge ebony voice the size of the sky growling deep down low ... *change, change, change.*

'Tell me, Joni,' he said, 'is it big enough? This big black thing that's rolling between us, is it big enough to keep us apart? Or is what's between us bigger than *it*? Do you think that's a possibility? Do you think *we* can make it go away without ever having to face it? Do you think it could happen if we want it to?'

And his eyes were blazing at her in the moonlight, there was something inside Paul Dunsany now that she had never seen before, some fire, some heat. He looked so sober, so serious, so *grown up* that she felt he could almost be someone else.

'I don't know,' she said, without thinking, without having to face the question.

'Joni,' he said, and took her hand, felt the skin, warm and real in the night, and walked with her out of the street lights, into the dark pool cast by the shadow of a foursquare brick building, led her to an empty iron bench that was barely visible in the blackness.

'We could make this all *not be* if we wanted to,' he said. '*We* can do this. You know that. You've *got* to know that.'

'I do,' she said, and felt his hands move slowly inside her jacket, felt the way they reached inside her shirt, held themselves against her skin, brushed lightly against her navel, then lower, so gently, so knowing, felt for the top of her skirt.

They reached an iron street lamp, and he kissed her, let her body fall gently back against the upright frame, reached down, felt between her legs, everything happening so fast she could not think, so fast there seemed no stopping.

He was strong. That too was new to her. There was so much inside him that she did not understand, so much that remained hidden until it surfaced, made itself known, then left her wondering where she was. He was strong, and when he was ready he lifted her with both arms, felt her legs clasp around him, took the strain so that she could hardly feel the lamp at her back. He held her there, waited until the moment appeared, let her fall gently, slide onto him, and her legs clamped tight around his back, a movement so sure and smooth and fluid that it was like fitting two parts of a puzzle together, fitting them and seeing no light make its way through the join. And they hardly moved. What brought them, shivering, mindless, to the end, and there was no way either could say how long this took, was something that happened in their heads, something that passed between them, turned some giant interior trigger and let the world explode, so warm and fluid between them.

'We can do it ourselves,' he said, when his breath had returned. She looked at his face. There might have been tears there. It might have been sweat.

'I know,' she said. And she had cried. She could feel it stinging in her eyes and she didn't mind.

Three hours later daylight broke through the leaden cloud scudding across the Seattle skyline for the first time in 1996. She was asleep beside him, her hair a golden field of curls on the pillow, her face so pale, so calm, so serene. Something new, he said to himself. This *was* something new. This could happen. If everything else worked out, maybe you could love someone out of this nightmare. *If . . .*

Paul Dunsany watched Joni Lascelles sleeping and wondered what it would be like never to see her again, wondered how far on this earth you could run and hope that the picture of her, so bright, so real inside his head, might some day start to fade.

TWO

Tom's Deal

The last temptation is the greatest treason:
To do the right deed for the wrong reason.

T. S. ELIOT,
'Murder in the Cathedral'

I'm reading last year's papers, although I don't know why
Assassins, cons and rapers might as well die

STEELY DAN,
'King of the World'

They just didn't get this kind of case in Palo Alto. And what had Cy Langton worried most was the notion that, having dumped itself on his doorstep, the whole thing would, just as quickly, get away from them. That it would make that gentle little transition from being a local matter into becoming a Federal one. And then the big guys with shades and dark suits, the sort of people Cy Langton *hated*, would be crawling all over him, sneering through their Ray-Bans, taking credit where credit wasn't due.

That wasn't going to happen. Not if he could help it. That delicate line between local and Federal responsibility had not yet been crossed. If he was lucky it would *never* be crossed. And they could wrap the whole thing up, give a press conference, parade some bodies around, look real good.

Langton gazed across his desk, over the head of the little golf bag, and grinned at Tom Cordobes. Things had moved on now. Things had moved into the arena where Tom turned from being a liability into being maybe the best guy he could possibly have around. The delicate days, the days when you trod so lightly people couldn't even feel you on their toes, were done now. This was all nice and straightforward. This was a kidnapping and a murder. They had the demand.

257

They had the wheels in motion. This was the kind of thing Tom Cordobes could handle with his eyes closed.

'Forensic get anything from the note?' Cordobes asked half-heartedly, as if he knew the answer already.

Langton threw a plastic evidence wallet across the desk and Cordobes peered at the pale piece of paper inside it.

'Posted in University Avenue yesterday afternoon. Nothing much they can tell us at the moment. Beyond the obvious, these guys love the obvious.'

Cordobes looked at the typed text, the small Polaroid photograph of Miles Seymour, staring blankly into the camera lens. The picture was taken with flash. The background was a nondescript brown. Maybe old wallpaper. Maybe plain wood. Maybe even earth. It was hard to tell. Cordobes stared hard at the child trying to make out what was going on there. Trying to figure if there was something to read in his face. You just couldn't tell. He didn't look scared, he didn't look happy. He didn't look anything. They'd had a picture of him from the parents. He looked much the same here. Dirty. More tired. What else could you expect?

'What you think?' Langton asked.

Cordobes shrugged. 'If the kid was older, driving a pickup with that goddamn rock music blaring out everywhere, I'd take one look at those eyes and say he was on dope.'

'Yeah. Me too,' Langton lied, transparently.

'Five years old. Maybe they're feeding him to keep quiet.'

'You believe the stuff these guys would do?'

'They killed one kid already. We'd better believe it.'

'Maybe we should be asking round the dope scene. They doing that to the kid maybe they're into it in some way. You got the grasses onto this, Tom?'

'Yeah,' Cordobes said, and for once kept his mouth shut. The way things were going in the world saying a case was, in that wonderful phrase, 'drugs-related' was a little like pointing out it was probably committed by a human being. When you got down to it, most crime had some drugs side in there somewhere. It was so common, so pervasive, it didn't really help a damn to know about it.

Tom Cordobes looked at the text.

Tell these people we want $200,000 cash, mixed bills, nothing new, all 50s and 20s. We want it on Tuesday. We know they got it so you tell them they don't fuck with us or they get to pick the kid up in pieces all over town. We don't wanna hear from you. You get the one chance. We tell you where, we tell you when, later. The money's there, the kid goes. Plain as that. No negotiations. No phone calls. Either they do it or they don't. Their decision.

'Well, I'll be damned,' Cordobes said.

'Huh?'

'A ransom note that's got no spelling mistakes and apostrophes too. And they say the education system is just a crock of shit these days.'

Langton watched Cordobes thinking. He was one smart cop. Maybe the smartest in the whole department except when it came to simple things: like talking to people as if they had the right to breathe the same air. If Cordobes had that gift he'd probably be sitting in Cy Langton's chair this very day (no little golf bag penholder on the desk then) but that didn't happen, wouldn't happen, because when you got down to it Tom Cordobes couldn't keep the lid on himself, and however bright, however smart he got, that would always puncture a hole in him sooner or later.

'Well?'

'They got the typewriter yet?'

'Olympia. Probably a portable.'

'Cheap?'

'Yeah.'

'Ah,' Cordobes said, scratched his chin, massaged his neck which felt a little sore. Cy Langton watched the walnut skin get pummelled in the man's big fist, then looked at the calendar.

'January the sixth. Tuesday's January the sixth. If you were a religious man, Tom, you'd know that. Epiphany. The day they showed the baby Jesus to the Three Wise Men. You get saddled with all this church stuff like me, you'd remember that. You get to change the colours of all the robes and things. Marks the end of Christmas.'

'One hell of a fucking Christmas,' Cordobes muttered.

'You bet,' said Langton. 'And it ain't over yet, Tom. So what you think?'

Cordobes looked non-committal. 'Olympia portable's an amateur's typewriter. You don't find that kind of thing in offices. Reporters. Writers. Students. Those kind of people.'

259

'People who know about spelling and apostrophes.'

'Yeah,' said Cordobes. 'You know that's so kind of obvious, you wonder if it isn't just deliberate. You really do.'

'I never go for these clever ideas, Tom. Even clever people don't do things like that. They just stumble along making a few less mistakes than the rest of us. Still make mistakes, though, and that's when we got 'em.'

Cordobes nodded. What Langton said was right.

'So this uncle guy's gonna play? These people are right when they say the family's loaded?'

'Weird thing is, when I spoke to the guy it was as if he didn't really care that much about the kid at all. Just cared about what people would think if he didn't stump up the cash. What it might do for him in his club back home, I guess. We don't get any problems there.'

'He know the kid's likely to wind up dead, if he ain't that way already?'

'Like I said. That didn't seem the main thing.'

'You try to get him to hold out? See if we can negotiate?'

'Would you with this?'

'I guess not.'

Langton didn't like the way he said that.

'You think it looks bad?'

Cordobes stared at Langton and wondered how much he really wanted to hear.

'Maybe you ought to think about getting the Feds in, sir.'

The blood burst into Langton's cheeks and the desktop went bang again.

'Damned if I will, Tom. Not unless someone makes me.'

'See, we win out on this one and everyone's a hero, then that's all fine. But you got to weigh up the odds. These people are being truly fucking smart, smarter than your average scumbag. They say they won't phone. They say they won't give us *anything* else in the way of proof the kid's still alive. All we gonna get is some instructions on where to leave the money and as for the rest we just *trust* them.'

'So we got the one chance. Unless your people come up with something on the streets.'

'That's right. And that really puts us against the wall. See usually in these cases you get them through the contact process. They talk to us, we talk to them, we pick up something along the way. No contact, that whole avenue's closed to us. And for all we know the kid could be dead already. Probably is, you ask my opinion.'

'We could put it out through the TV guys that unless they give us some proof the deal don't wash.'

'We could. But from what they say that don't matter. They don't get money, they kill the kid. Take it or leave it.'

'You think that's right? Maybe we just don't pay and see if they talk to us.'

'You want to take that risk? They killed one kid already. Not that we got any way of proving that. And that bugs me too. They're being smart in that note. They could have thrown the other kid in, add some ballast. But they didn't. They're holding open options. The way this thing is it's like the money is only *part* of it. Like they decided if they can get some money out of it, fine, they'd like that, but if not, what the hell, they get their kicks killing him anyway. Hell of a corner to fight from. What I'm saying is, the way things are, strikes me the chances of getting this kid out alive are pretty minimal either way. Someone's gonna catch it for him getting dead and maybe the Feds ought to be the ones.'

'No,' said Langton. 'Those bastards are not coming in here.'

'Then you may need a broad back come Tuesday. Sir.'

Langton stared out of the window. The rain had finally stopped. It was a pleasant winter day. Cool, thin sun through high, thin stratus.

'I'm not as smart as you, Tom. You know that. No. Don't say nothing. I *know* you know that. But I get there, you know. I got where you are now pretty damn quickly before we even spoke this morning. Point is, you're right, we'll be damned lucky if we get this kid out alive. This Lascelles guy is going to pay the money anyway so in a sense it don't mean a damn thing either. It's gonna happen or it's not. But they're dumb if they think we're gonna play by their rules. They're dumb if they think we're gonna play by any rules at all.'

There was something sly, something almost sinister, in Cy Langton's face.

'You don't forget, Tom, I got your file here. I *know* what you were doing before you joined the cops. I *know* if I say to you, I'm gonna walk out this room, let you do what you want, never ask you afterwards how you did it, what you did, I *know* that come the end of this you're gonna have more bodies to show for it all than that poor kid in the picture. Am I right?'

Tom Cordobes didn't even blink, didn't say a word.

'And you see, Tom, that's all that matters. These things, whether you're a hero, whether you're a jerk, that all gets decided in the sixty seconds of TV that people watch in a bar. They see this kid dead, no one in the can for it, we're the scum of the earth. They see this kid dead, see the bodies of the people we say did it, we won the championship. They gonna be printing the T-shirts.'

'What you're saying . . .'

Langton waved him into silence.

'I'm not saying *anything*. Not hearing anything. Not asking anything. You're a smart guy, Tom. You know the way things are blowing in this place and you know they ain't blowing your way. You go away, you do what you have to, things could change real rapid. For you. For me, yeah. Why not?'

Cy Langton closed the folder on his desk, brought the meeting to an end.

'I guess you got some work to be doing, Tom. Don't want to hold you up any more than I have already.'

'Sir.'

Tom Cordobes got up, walked out of the door, thought about it, not deeply, not for a long time. He just thought about it and the more he did the more he thought: *what the fuck?*

THREE

Louise Makes a Call

When I hold you in my arms
And I feel my finger on your trigger
I know no one can do me no harm
Because happiness is a warm gun.

LENNON AND McCARTNEY,
'Happiness Is a Warm Gun'

There's a man all over for you, blaming on his boots the fault
of his feet.

SAMUEL BECKETT,
Waiting for Godot

'You think we're safe?'

She was standing over the big marble fireplace, a glass of whisky in
one hand, a long thin Marlboro in the other. The day was bright and
hazy. It came through the window the colour of old straw. A layer of
condensation stood outside the glass, making the lake and the forest a
swirl of grey and green that had little in the way of form. It was hard for
him to tell whether Louise was more angry than she was scared. Both
emotions made her face look the same way: a little hard, a little ugly.

'Been the best part of four days now. No one's called. Not a murmur.
Way it looks from the papers seems nobody is taking responsibility
for the guy in any case. There's not a word there.'

She took a big gulp of the drink and stared at him.

'So?'

'So it seems like he didn't communicate whatever he knew to whoever he was supposed to. Why else would we be sitting here? Somebody'd be on the phone. The cops. The newspapers. The TV people.
Whoever it was set him onto Quinn in the first place.'

Louise Gostelow came and sat opposite him on the pale calfskin
sofa.

'That doesn't mean a thing. Does it? We just don't know. He had
time. From when he stopped you outside SCC. He had time between

then and when he found Michael to do what the hell he liked.'

'Yeah,' said Jamieson, and he felt like getting a little angry himself now. 'He had time to go to the moon and back if you find the right transportation, Louise, but what the hell does that tell us? We don't *know* who he was working for. All we know is since Quinn carved the guy up we heard *nothing* from nobody. And that's that.'

'Really wonderful, Hal. Really wonderful that makes you feel secure.'

'Jesus, Louise. I run a corporation. I run a software business. I am not a criminal. I do not *excel* at these things. I just want them all to go away. That's all. Don't expect me to go around behaving like Don fucking Corleone 'cos that isn't what I do. It wasn't what I did back then, it sure as hell isn't what I do now.'

And that was the truth, Hal Jamieson said to himself. What he did was he coped. While everybody else around was busy fucking things up, then running to him, pointing at the mess on the carpet, and saying, 'Look!', he was busy thinking of some way he could sweep it all up, maybe make a little profit on the side.

'So what you're saying is we just wait. Wait till someone knocks on the door and says, "Hi, we thought we just wanted to maybe talk about some murder and kidnapping twenty years ago, Mr and Mrs Jamieson, but maybe we could throw in some old cop getting his throat cut last week too"? We just wait for them to come through the door and say hello, do not pass go, do not collect your two hundred dollars, just go straight to jail, thank you kindly.'

'If you like. If that's the way you want to put it. We make sure we're keeping the lid on things ourselves. You make sure Dunsany isn't getting restless. We wait.'

She didn't say anything.

'You're worried about Paul,' he said. 'You think there's something we've got to worry about there.'

'I . . .' She wondered how to put it. Not to lessen the effect on Jamieson's feelings. More in the interest of accuracy. 'I can't do that with him any more. He doesn't jump and beg. He got smart to that one. Guess you can't blame him.'

Although she did.

'That's a shame,' Jamieson said, and he meant it. He didn't like losing control points. They were often what won you the battle in the end. 'You think we need worry about that?'

She shook her head, then wondered. 'I don't know. I don't *know*

Paul any more. He's got some little hippy chick in tow, real pretty thing too. And young.'

Louise Gostelow missed being young. Wished there was just something you could buy somewhere to give you back all those years that just drifted by on the wind and never seemed so precious as when they were out of reach.

'If we have problems with Paul, I'm telling you now, Hal, I lost the magic.'

'Yeah,' he replied and thought of the old cop's body on the floor of the bathroom, crouched over, head on the tiles, blood going black and sticky all around. The older you got, the more simple, the more brutal the solutions seemed. When you couldn't wind people round your fingers with love, all that was left was hate and something inside Hal Jamieson was still revolted by that idea, even after all these years. Still found it intensely, insanely *wrong*.

She was watching him, wondering what made his face cloud over like that. Hal Jamieson was a man who could liven up most occasions, smiling, joking, laughing. He was a man who *performed,* however bad things really were. It was one of the things, one of the few things these days, she really liked about him. But that was disappearing too. Hal was starting to look old. There was the hardness, that resignation you saw in his face that marked the transition from the time when the future held possibilities to the time when it spelled decline and decay. Between both of them, unspoken, only dimly recognised, was the feeling that things really were going to change, really were going to need new solutions. Nineties solutions. Not the kind of half-assed ideas you cobbled together twenty years ago.

'You know that if it comes to it, Hal, you could get indicted over that old cop?'

This wasn't the conversation he wanted, wasn't what he wanted to hear.

'If it comes to it, Louise, I can be indicted on everything from stock fraud to tax evasion and beating up the planning laws. What are you trying to tell me that is new?'

And that was the point when she knew she'd won. When she knew he had been facing the same set of crossroads, waiting to be pushed down the only road that was going to save them.

'What's new, Hal, is this. Twenty years ago, when Michael pushed us all into this, I knew you. I knew what you were trying to do. Get us out of this. Get us something that could start some new kind of life. And do it cleanly.'

Hal Jamieson wondered about it and knew that it was true. Knew that that was then and this is now.

'What's new,' she said, and he wanted to clamp his hands over his ears and wanted her to say every word, wanted both these things simultaneously, 'what's new is you. You *know*, Hal, that we are not going to get out of this without killing people. You know you're going to have it done. And I think all that's stopping you, all that's preventing you asking Steve Baxter to go get Michael right now is some kind of hope that it won't be necessary. Some kind of hope that the good fairy will walk through the door, wave some magic wand, make it all right again. That won't happen, Hal. It *won't*.'

'No,' he said, and wondered whether you couldn't just do it again, take the money, there was lots more money this time, and run, all the way to somewhere else where they couldn't get you, where you could just rewind the clock and start your life anew. And the absurdity of it almost made him laugh. When you were twenty, you could do these things. When you were forty, you lost the places to hide. People knew you. There were stock options to trade and annuities to think about. There were things like extradition treaties with countries you couldn't *believe*. The world was older and smaller and utterly lacking in dark, safe, comfortable little corners where money could buy peace and happiness and anything else you might want to pay for. Hal Jamieson could feel his old self, the kid of twenty, with those long ringlets that had not a trace of grey, the pocketful of dope, bought with a little danger, sold for a lot of profit, feel this kid looking at him over the years, shaking his head and saying, 'Why me? Hal, why me?'

And that made him feel cold and hard and grim inside.

'Yeah,' he said.

'I'll be with you. You know that, don't you?'

And at that he could have cried. Because with this kind of thing, with *just* this kind of thing, he could have relied on Louise to the ends of the earth and beyond.

'I know,' he nodded.

She picked up the little notebook from the coffee table, the one Baxter had picked out of the dead cop's jacket.

'I can't believe Baxter or one of his people didn't dig up *anything* about this Cordobes guy. He seems half-smart.'

'Baxter's just a bodyguard when you get down to it. And this Cordobes guy was just one big loner. We know he was a cop. I could've told them that myself. Not a face you're likely to forget. Then he got busted. Worked as a private detective after that. Out of Milpitas. No relatives they can find. No money from what it looks like. I got them to take a pass at where he lives, look inside. Once they made sure no one was around. No records there of what he was working on. Who he'd talked to recently.'

She flicked through the book. All California numbers. All just the kind of thing you'd expect. Police departments. State organisations. A couple of bars. A restaurant.

Hal Jamieson reached over and took the book from her.

'My guess is there's only one recent thing he wrote in here. The pen's different. Here.'

She looked at the writing on the page.

Joni L, Pequod

Somewhere across the back of her head an image flickered: a tall thin girl in black, an English accent, floating through Pike Place Studios like the breeze. *Joni?* Did she really hear that?

'Baxter tried to track something down but there's nothing here. Nobody in Seattle they could find called Joni L. Pequod, or anybody else in the national phone books either. Could be anything. Some hooker even.'

She looked at the page again. The old cop's handwriting was bad, but not that bad.

'It's not a full stop,' she said. 'It's a comma. Look.'

Hal Jamieson looked again, shrugged his shoulders. Maybe she was right.

'So?'

Louise Gostelow thought for a moment, thought about what kind of thing she would write as 'Joni L, Pequod', then reached for the local phone book. The Pequod Hotel just had an ordinary listing. No bold type. Not even bigger letters than the Perpetual Pumpkin restaurant over in Denny Regrade that made up the next number in the list.

She dialled the number, waited for a bored receptionist to answer, then said, 'Hi, is Joni there? I got a call from Paul Dunsany on hold, she may want to take it.'

The receptionist went off-line for a few moments, it got so long that Louise wondered whether maybe she had been cut off. Then she came back and said, 'That's Miss Lascelles, ma'am?'

'That's right,' she answered, and just the name, just hearing the name made the world go a little cold on her, made the light fade just a little for a moment.

'Putting you through.'

The phone rang five or six times then an English voice answered, said, 'Hello?'

'Miss Lascelles, I have a collect call from Mr Paul Dunsany, says he needs to talk to you urgently. Will you accept the charge to your room?'

'Yes,' she said, and the sound of her voice was all you really needed, all that was required to damn her, damn them. 'Of course.'

Louise Gostelow said nothing, quickly clicked the receiver once, hung on.

'Paul? Paul? Are you there?'

Then Louise put down the phone and watched Hal Jamieson squirm and sweat on the sofa.

'Time to grow up, my love,' she said. 'Life is just about to turn nasty. I'll call Steve Baxter. I can trust him. I'll call you after that.'

Hal Jamieson looked at her, wondered how much he'd ever really bent her will over the years, how easy Quinn was compared to her. 'This is my business, Louise. My solutions. Where are you going?'

And he really didn't want to know the answer.

'Hunting,' Louise said, then drained the rest of her glass, got up and left, without looking at him. Hal Jamieson could feel things slipping away, in some new fashion he didn't really understand. He poured himself a whisky, sat by the long bay window and stared out over the plush green lawn, over to the lake, stared at this perfect view, this perfect place, and thought about the price he'd paid to be a tiny, distant figure in this flawless, verdant landscape.

FOUR

Miles, Mouse and Michael

Heaven lies about us in our infancy!
Shades of the prison-house begin to close
Upon the growing boy.

WILLIAM WORDSWORTH,
'Intimations of Immortality'

Childhood is the kingdom where nobody dies.
Nobody that matters, that is.

EDNA ST VINCENT MILLAY,
'Childhood Is the Kingdom Where
Nobody Dies'

Margaret Zalinski, who would answer to the name of Mouse for only a few days more in her life, sat in the cellar of the storeroom, under the mealy yellow aura of a single electric light, sponged Miles Seymour's face gently, washing off the dirt, watching his skin, so white, so unmarked, come through from under the grime. He'd told her he was five but there was something about Miles that seemed younger. There had been no other child in the trailer park home outside LA where Margaret Zalinski had grown up. Only her mother and whatever man happened to be sharing the big rusting metal can at the time. And there had been nothing there of childhood. For Margaret Zalinski, the life of being a child meant the learning of survival. How to pacify the big people who wanted to hit you for things you didn't know you'd done. How to get food for yourself out of the refrigerator. When to recognise the smell of cheap whisky on the air and keep well out of the way. When to say yes (or more truthfully, when not to say no) and how to keep your mouth shut, however much you hurt, afterwards.

She had been on the road since she was thirteen, working diners, working bars, working anywhere that gave her a wage. Not hooking. Not once. And Margaret Zalinski was proud of that. There was some hard, simple, moral spine inside her that said that smoking dope was

269

OK, fucking, or rather getting fucked by men you'd rather stay away from in an ideal world, that was OK too, just. But hooking was just plain wrong. And all those drugs that did more than just make you feel warm and sleepy and good, they were plain wrong too. And what she had got herself into with Quinn and Jamieson and the girl from the city, the rich girl who looked like she should be modelling, not toking in some scruffy Menlo Park dive, that was wrong. Even before she started talking to Miles she knew that. And when she did start talking to him, taking some responsibility for seeing him through the day, keeping him alive, it began to dawn on her that here was something she had to do just because that was how it was, because she was drawn to it like a pin to a magnet. Here was something she had no choice about. She had to wait. She had to judge the moment. And she had to save him. It was like a little closed loop in her head: a three-stage argument that went relentlessly from one point to the other, closed itself, was done. Margaret Zalinski had fears, strong fears, particularly about Quinn and Louise Gostelow. But she didn't have doubts. She was an economical person. She had learned to be. There was no room inside her for thoughts, emotions, that occupied floor space without bringing any practical return.

What surprised her, what disappointed her in a way, was that none of them minded. Not Hal or Quinn or Louise. They'd let her know her position, then let her go about it. Knowing the chains they put on her with just a few words, they let her stay down there with Miles for hours, talking to him about England, about families, about Christmas, and they didn't care. They didn't even register it. And this rankled inside. Margaret Zalinski knew that it seemed to be her place in life to get taken for granted but she thought it was impolite to advertise it quite so much. They thought that she was not just dumb, but that she was tame too. Like a slave. Or an animal. Something less than human. And inside her, some inner voice said that was wrong somehow. And maybe one day soon they'd find that out.

She wiped the child's head, felt something wild swoop through her mind when he smiled, so nicely, so sweetly, back at her, then gave him some food: some pizza, some fries. She kept the dope Quinn had given her in her pocket. Those little tabs, those little sheets of paper, were getting to be a big pile now and real soon she ought to think of some way of getting rid of them. But that wasn't easy. You couldn't flush them away for fear that they might just come back, float back, into the pan. You couldn't put them in the trash because they might look. And then someone else would be looking after Miles. Someone who would have other ideas.

His eyes had lost that big glassy look. He was straight. He was normal. In a way he wasn't even afraid, and that was because of her, because he knew she was on his side, trusted her.

'Tell me about England, Miles,' Margaret Zalinski said, then sat with her back to the cold, damp earth wall to listen. It was her favourite conversation and she knew almost every variation there was for it. She thought she could listen to Miles talk for hours, just babbling on in his high-pitched babyish voice, a real talker, never lost for words, never lost for connections that meant one story would lead on to the next. And if they got confused sometimes, repeated themselves in some twirling web of narratives inside his head, inside her head, none of it mattered. There was something inside the child that hadn't entered into her life very much over the years, some kind of simple, naive, unsullied goodness, and the truth was she could just sit and bathe in its light forever and never get bored.

'England,' Miles Seymour said very seriously, 'is a green and pleasant land. Daddy told me that.'

She thought about his parents, the news story she'd seen on TV when she was upstairs getting food. Wondered what the boy would make of it when – *if?* – he found out.

'Tell me about your daddy, Miles? What's he like? I didn't know my daddy.'

'You didn't?'

'He went away when I was a baby.'

'Oh. My daddy is *big* and he plays cricket. He writes books and he gets his name on them in big letters on the outside.'

'You read some of his books?'

'Too hard. He says "when I'm older".'

'He a nice daddy?'

'*Yes!*' said Miles Seymour, a little too loud. She looked at the trap door, made sure there was no chink of light there, saw it was sealed, hushed his lips with her finger.

'Not so loud, Miles. You wouldn't want them to get cross now, would you?'

And he looked so worried, so frightened.

'It's OK. Just quieter. That's all.'

Miles Seymour swallowed, you could see his little Adam's apple bob up and down in his throat.

'My daddy gets cross,' he said. 'Sometimes.'

'Sometimes all daddies get cross,' she said, and tried to believe it.

'And my sister too. She *hates* it when I call her Florrie,' and he grinned at the little picture that came into his head.

'You gonna see them *real* soon,' she said, and tried to believe that too.

He looked at her, a little too knowing.

'I didn't cry, did I? Not much, anyway. You won't tell Florrie I cried at all, will you? She *teases*.'

'I don't recall you crying *ever*.'

'No. I did. A bit. Before you came. I think.'

Miles Seymour peered into nothingness, trying to remember.

'Sometimes, Margie, they give me things. They make me feel poorly. And then I don't know really. I don't know.'

'They don't give you things any more, Miles. Don't you worry. Real soon, *real* soon, we get you out of here. You and me. Both.'

'You'll come to England with us?'

'Yeah,' she said, and wished it could be true: green, green, green. To imagine a world that was nothing but green was like imagining heaven for Margaret Zalinski, pure, green heaven. There was a line from the Woodstock song that went round and round her head sometimes, saying over and over again how we've got to get ourselves back to the garden. And Margaret Zalinski knew what that garden was. Knew what it held, what it promised. And what it looked like. Green, green, green.

'That *would* be nice,' Miles said. 'But I don't think you'll like the cricket. Girls don't like cricket.'

She felt his hair. It was so dirty, so caked in grease. She wished she could wash it and there was no way to do that. But she could imagine what it would be like, to get the bowl of warm water, to care for him. To give him whatever she could and not expect a damn thing back. Margaret Zalinski closed her eyes and prayed, not to some god, not to anything in particular, just let her prayers go up through the earth, through the air, hoping for some way in which she could get him out, some opportunity for escape. And still nothing came. Nothing except walking straight out of the house down to see the police, leading them back there, showing them the storeroom, saying, *there, there, there.*

And hoping she would be in time, that the deadly seconds would not run out on them. Hoping that they wouldn't notice her disappearance, and Quinn, grinning, grinning, grinning all the time, would do just what he said he would do if she took off out of the house. Would climb down into the cellar and do to Miles just what he did to the other kid, stupid experiment or no stupid experiment. So she was chained to him with invisible shackles, which in truth she did not mind, and what ate her away from inside was the way she just couldn't think of some release, some means of tunnelling through the compacted brown earth that enclosed them until they felt the warmth of the sunlight in the outside world, the *real* world.

'I could learn to like cricket, Miles,' she said. 'I could learn to like anything.'

And she held him in her arms, that small warm human bundle, and made sure he didn't see her crying, made sure he didn't see that, though both of them knew what was happening, and both of them tacitly agreed to ignore the fact. Margaret Zalinski held Miles so tightly she could feel his breathing, those little laboured pants you get when the tears come, kissed his dirty, matted hair and cursed herself for being so fucking stupid, so fucking dumb that nothing inside her head could come up with some way out of this thing.

There was a sound above them, light peeped through the cracks of the trap door. Their responses were automatic, electric. Their bodies shot apart, she wiped the tears from her face with the sleeve of her cotton Afghan smock, and then waited in silence, expressionless, waited for the footsteps on the stepladder.

Slowly, with a gait that meant he was drunk or worse, Michael Quinn clambered down into the cellar. It was hard to make out his face in the light of the single bulb, dangling from a power cord extension nailed into the trap-door frame. She didn't want to look too hard. She didn't want to know. Then he lurched forward into the light, his face loomed out at them like a yellow mask, grinning, and she smelled the fumes: cheap whisky, it billowed out from him like it was part of his body, a big cloying cloud of chemical fug.

He waved a half-pint bottle at her and the smell made her feel sick.

'I brought you something. I thought maybe you were getting bored. Jesus, who wouldn't get fucking bored stuck down here with *that?*'

He seemed more drunk than she'd ever seen. His voice was slurred. His eyes just looked focusless.

273

She shook her head and wondered at the changes going on inside her. A week ago she just wouldn't have done this. Wouldn't have turned him down.

'You could get really fucking bored down here, Mouse. I mean *really* fucking bored staring at this goddamn kid all the time. Why don't you come upstairs and we get to have some fun?'

'The kid needs looking after, Michael. He's been sick. Someone's got to do it.'

He had hold of her arm.

'I was thinking of some fun,' he said coldly.

And she just stared him out. Just looked him in the eye, grabbed his hand off her, and said, 'You are hurting me. You understand me, Michael. Those days are over.'

It could have stayed just like that. She was praying for something and maybe this was what it was. That he backed off. That he felt the reward was worth less than the effort. Then Miles – *sweet Miles, who knew a bully when he saw one* – just couldn't help himself, couldn't stop himself saying it, stop himself bunching up his little face until it turned all ugly and yelled, '*You stop that! You don't hurt her, you . . .*'

Michael Quinn strode over to the child, clenched his fist and punched him hard in the face. His head shot back, the pale, soft face contorted with shock and anger and pain, and you could see the redness there, even under the pale-yellow light, see the cheek starting to flush straight away. He didn't cry. He gasped for air. He didn't cry, though he was fighting it back as hard as he could.

Quinn pulled back his arm a second time and she was on him, kicking, scratching, screaming, all thought gone now, not trying to work out where this went, just letting the fury come out from inside her. And if she could have thought about it, if there were words for what was running through her head, they would have been simple words, words like kill and rip and maim and wound. Words that didn't really belong inside Margaret Zalinski and never would again.

But she was small and she was weak and Michael Quinn had no difficulty in pushing her away, no difficulty in holding her off, like a kicking, biting cat, pulling back his arm, throwing a single punch, hard as he could, straight at her mouth, watching it pucker, watching her head jerk back as it struck, letting her body fall away, strike the cold earth wall, slump to the ground.

She was sobbing, so hard, so mindless, that it didn't even occur to her what was happening. Not until she heard him whistling, that strange, low, monotone noise.

Quinn looked at the boy in the corner, looked at the boy now so bright-eyed and alive in the gloom, waiting silently, waiting expectant.

'You see this woman, Miles,' Quinn said, and the slur had gone from his voice now, the adrenaline in his blood had chased the alcohol, and everything else, every other foreign particle, back into the dusty, hidden corners of his being.

'This is a *bad* woman, Miles. A *bad* woman.'

He reached down and for a moment she thought he was reaching for her smock, would take her right now, in front of the boy, and she thought that then she really *could* kill him, she really could just tear the eyes out of his face.

Instead he reached down, swept the floor by her skirt, by the pocket, now leaking its contents guiltily into the earth, red and white and blue, tab and cap and paper, a little pharmacological rainbow that had built up over the days in the cotton fluff and fuzz, a little army of bad dreams going sour in the dark.

'You know, Miles,' Quinn said, and those big teeth shone in the yellow light, 'a *good* mommy *always* gives her baby boy his medicine. A good boy *always* takes it too. So what you think?'

He had a whole handful of the stuff now, not everything, not the whole rainbow, just a half or more of it, and it shone, it glittered in his hand, a little mountain of alkaloids in need of a bloodstream.

Quinn smiled down on the boy, tried to look like some friendly doctor come to call.

'So what you think, Miles? We get your naughty mommy off the hook here? You take your medicine like a good boy, maybe we forget about all this *bad behaviour*. Maybe the social people don't come along waving pieces of paper at you, take you away to some home some-where, some place they got no mommies or daddies at all, just bad kids and bad people who come in the night and poke you in places you don't want to be poked, poke things in your ass and pull your little dick till it cries. You want that? Huh? You want that?'

'No, Michael,' she said, and she was alarmed at how calm, and rational her voice sounded. How she wasn't screaming, clawing at him to stop. 'You'll kill him. Don't kill him. *Please* don't kill him.'

Michael Quinn turned to look at her, some theatrical expression of puzzlement on his face.

275

'Don't follow you there, mousegirl. We *all* got to die. Just a question of where. And when. Ain't that so, Miles?'

The child was silent. Somewhere inside of him he could hear a clock ticking away and he was hoping that it wasn't his life, hoping that it might be something else, just slowing down in the dark.

'Take your medicine, boy,' Quinn grunted, then walked over, pushed the entire handful of red and blue and white and yellow poison into Miles Seymour's open mouth, laughed once, an abrupt, humourless little sound, then turned to meet Margaret Zalinski who was now rising at him from across the room with murder in her eyes.

Michael Quinn lifted his leg back behind him, kicked forward, kicked her full in the face as she came off the floor, the sole and heel of his leather Cuban boot connecting straight with her face, and the world, for Margaret Zalinski, turned red and black and ugly.

'*Margie!*' Miles Seymour screamed, and the last thing she remembered was so vivid, so vivid. It was Miles, his mouth stretched like it was on a frame, so wide, so open, so red, and in it the little rainbow of pills there, jumping up and down in the spittle as he tried to cough them out, tried to gag them out from inside, some sticking there in the saliva, some trickling down his chin.

She was falling and falling and still she could see it happen, still she could watch Quinn reach down, close Miles's mouth with a single violent sweep of one hand, hold the boy's nose, pinch so hard between finger and thumb with the other, so hard that a thin line of blood from his nostrils seeped through Quinn's knuckles. She watched Miles go redder and redder and redder until it looked as if he might explode.

Then, finally, Miles Seymour swallowed. And Margaret Zalinski fell into some world of darkness that rose up to engulf her, consume everything there was to her life, so fast that her thoughts, her fears, her screams just died into nothing.

FIVE

Pike Place Again

All happy families resemble one another, but each unhappy
family is unhappy in its own way.   LEO TOLSTOY,
                                          Anna Karenina

Joni Lascelles watched the man on the fish stall, well over six feet tall,
dressed in galoshes, jeans and a white apron stained with water and
salmon guts, watched him pick up a silver corpse from the counter,
send it flashing through the air. This was the show. It just seemed to
go on and on and on and when you asked someone, as she had in
the early days, why they did it, they just shrugged and said: why not?
This is Pike Place. This is trade and commerce, food and drink, lots
of different shapes and sizes and brands and kinds of people all jumbled
up together in a ragtag of stone floors and corridors that smell of old
salmon and lavender, the musk of freshly dug potatoes, the lilting,
foreign pungency of patchouli. And bad drains too, let's not forget
the drains. This is Pike Place and asking why is, when you come down
to it, plain stupid.

It came to her, out of nowhere at all, that this was Paul Dunsany
too. The one matched the other and she could see why he didn't leave,
couldn't leave. It would be like casting off your favourite coat and
standing naked, shivering in the wind. This jumble of people and
things and voices, this big stew of individuals pushing and shoving
each other all to get nowhere in particular, then laughing at the very
idea of it all, added up to something he found familiar, maybe in some
unspoken way even loved. It was messy, sometimes it was precarious.
But so was life, and at least this way you got to sharing it all.

The fish guy was a real people watcher. Like everyone in the market,
he knew what went on, he knew who was making it with whom, and
who would like to. He grinned at her and she smiled back. It was

ridiculous but Pike Place *was* ridiculous and the only thing you could do was shake your head at the stupidity of it all, laugh, then walk away.

She set off down the long slope of the first-floor corridor, walked past the magic store, the man who made pasta, the place with some weird little trinkets. She walked past the stand with the dried berries, blueberry, cranberry, things she didn't recognise, stopped to take a look.

'You can try,' said the woman behind the wooden stand, a slight, middle-aged, blonde woman with that severe, unflattering spiky hair that seemed so popular in Seattle. She stepped forward, and picked at the blueberries, tasted them, so sweet but sour too, and bought a packet, not even thinking what you did with them, what they were for.

'You're Paul's friend,' the woman said, quietly, as if she didn't quite want her to hear, as she handed over the change.

Joni Lascelles nodded.

'That's nice. That's real nice.'

'Thanks,' she said, and it was all done so quietly, so neatly, it was impossible to take offence. If they knew, if they *all* knew (no, the little voice inside her said, they *do* all know) then she didn't mind. It was a family and no family got away without talking about each other in the quiet spaces of their lives.

Then she walked down the next floor, turned two corners to the left, one to the right (she was getting to know this now), found the opaque glass door, walked in, blinked a little at the brightness of the lights, watched Genius, head down in the Mac, not even bothering to look up, so engrossed, so full of concentration that a bomb could have gone off outside and he wouldn't have noticed. There was the sound of mariachi coming out of a tape somewhere in the back of the studio. On the radio by the reception desk Tom Petty sang something about the losers, and how they got lucky sometimes.

'He's not here,' Genius grunted without looking up from the screen.

'Where . . . ?'

'Dunno.'

There came a time, Joni Lascelles said to herself, when you just had to face it. She stepped around the counter, walked over to the kid, put a hand on his shoulder, stared furiously into his face and said, 'Genius, have I offended you in some way?'

278

The kid jumped as if he'd just been hit by an electric shock, then stared at the four slim fingers touching him through the grubby fabric of the Pearl Jam T-shirt. The mariachi music came to an end, leaving nothing in the air except the thin reedy wail of Petty's voice.

'No fights please,' boomed Ben Rawlins's voice from the door. 'We have delicate electronic equipment on these premises and a lamentable lack of insurance.'

Then watched her, so puzzled she could feel it from across the room.

She took her hand off Genius and stared the kid out. There was some sad little craziness, not far from fear, in his eyes, and she had to steel herself, she had to say no-no-no-no-no over again to the stupid, ridiculous analogy lodging somewhere inside her skull. Why'd you pick on him, Joni? the voice said inside. He's just a kid . . .

'He's just a kid,' Ben said, his voice echoing somewhere outside the space in her head. 'He doesn't mean it.'

She smiled, as sincerely as she could manage, held out her hand. Genius took it, with a worried look on his face. His skin felt warm and damp and pudgy, so young, so untouched by everything in the world.

'Sorry,' she said. 'Can we be friends?'

The kid went red, bright red, from ear to ear.

'Yeah,' he said, and there was something that could pass for a smile there, maybe the best she was going to get. 'I know I'm a pain in the butt sometimes.'

'Are you?'

'Sure, I am. You just talk to the guys.'

'You're just a little . . . unformed, Genius. I think I have to learn to take that into consideration.'

His eyes narrowed.

'Unformed?'

'Waiting to be finished. If you want to know the truth, we're all waiting to be finished. We're all a pain . . .'

'In the butt.'

'Where else?' asked Ben Rawlins from across the room, and she watched the fascination in his eyes. There was something so sharp, so acute about the man that she almost feared him, feared the way he might see inside her.

She looked at the criss-cross patterns of notes on the screen.

'What are you working on?'

Genius shrugged his big, fleshy shoulders and said, as if it was just one of those things, 'A string quartet. They want something classy for some promotional video for some software stuff. You want to hear?'

Rawlins rolled his eyes in the doorway and said, 'Sure, Genius, we really want to hear. *Really* we do.'

'Yeah,' the kid said, turned down the radio, moved the mouse and clicked some buttons on the screen. The music poured out of the stereo speakers either side of the Mac, and it wasn't what she expected, it wasn't the thin, reedy sound of computerised music at all. They'd done something to it. What was happening was too real, it was using real sounds, real voices, real instruments, taking them out of some other place and making them sound so authentic it was scary. If the notes hadn't been so precise, so predictable in their inflection, you could have imagined that somewhere deep down in the bowels of the kid's Mac a miniature string quartet was scratching away there – what was it, two violins, a viola and a cello? – bowing into life a complex web of melodies that walked in and out of their respective orbits with an ease, a fluidity she didn't even want to follow.

'That's amazing,' she said. 'You wrote *that*?'

Genius smiled, it was a real smile this time, and there was something she found so pleasing in it, the way he was smiling *at* her, not at the wallpaper or the computer, at *her*.

'Joni,' he said, and it was the first time he had ever used her name. 'That was *Haydn*.'

'Oops,' she laughed. It sounded so English, so strange to them. There was so much inside the kid's head that perhaps it crowded out all of the things other people thought so important: what she thought of as the essential but pointless rounded parts of life, the words, the gestures that took off the harsh, sharp corners of people bumping into each other over the years, made the impact less painful, less of a strain.

'It sounds lovely anyway.'

'Lovely,' he echoed, another word that was from a different part of the world, so foreign, so distant. 'It's my arrangement. So thanks.'

Ben Rawlins came up and looked at the sea of notes on the screen.

'How you hold all that together in your head sure beats me,' he said, and there was genuine admiration in his voice, and maybe genuine pity there too. Unformed, she had said, and, he thought, she had been so right. Genius *was* unformed and there was precious little you could do about it until the kid realised that for himself too.

'Lunch time,' Ben Rawlins said, in a tone that brooked no argument. It was scarcely 11.30. 'Do I have two takers for some of the finest Chinese food this side of Hong Kong?'

'Gotta work, Unca Ben,' Genius said, and he was back there straight away, back inside the screen, pushing crotchets and quavers and rests and bars and humming to himself, listening to the new sound they made, not needing to hit the keys to hear it from the machine.

'Paul's not here?' She didn't want to be distracted. She needed to talk to him.

'Not been here all morning,' Ben said, and there was a note in his voice she didn't quite like. 'If he shows, Genius knows where to send him.'

'Yeah,' the kid said. 'You go eat.'

And without him, she realised, there really was nothing to do but wait. 'That would be nice.'

'Nice,' Genius echoed, and there was a pleasant tone in his voice, it was still with her when she walked out of the door.

They went up one flight of stairs, out onto the street, then back into the market by some side entrance, into a restaurant that hung on the side of the hill, with big bay windows that looked out across the Sound. The Chinese woman behind the counter beamed when they walked in, looked at him and said, 'Ben. You've not been here in *years*.'

'Weeks, Annie. Please don't exaggerate. We get to sit by the window today. My guest's come all the way from England and I think she'll appreciate the view.'

'England?' She made it sound as if it was the other side of the universe. 'Sure, you come with me.'

They went through one room, then into another that opened out onto a big panorama across the waterfront. It was a fine, clear day. You could see all the way across the Sound to the Olympic Mountains, snow-topped and huge in the distance. Annie cleared a table made to take six until there were just two settings on it.

'You want to choose, Ben? Or just leave it to me?'

'Anything you don't like?' he asked.

'Nothing.'

'Good – we'll bow to your better judgement, Annie. Couple of Redhooks would go down fine too.'

She scurried off, returned in a flash with two big brown glasses, condensation dripping down the sides.

'*Salud*,' Ben said, then took a long drink. 'I thought you'd spooked my boy there. I really did. Sometimes I think you're spooking all of us. Do you think that yourself?'

Two bowls of hot and sour soup arrived on the table. The steam drifted up into their faces.

She stared out of the window, watched the traffic on the Sound, the boats moving so slowly, white trails in their wake. This was not her place, everything inside shouted that at her. This was not her place, and it was wrong to think, to even *begin* to think, that it could be, that there was some magic wand that you could wave and turn it into home.

'I'll be gone soon, Ben,' she said. 'I have a job. I have a home back in London.'

'Paul know that?' he asked, looking at her with a direction, a force, that she couldn't turn from.

'That's our business,' she replied, and watched the food assembling on the table, looking so good: chicken, pork, fish, rice, noodles, such strong colours, such strong aromas. There was nothing pale here, she thought. There was nothing hidden about this place. It all came into the surface, stared you in the face and said, 'Yes?'

Ben Rawlins shovelled a whole spoonful of chicken swimming in red sauce into his mouth, thought about it for a good minute, and said, 'You're right. I'm sorry. I shouldn't have tried to intrude.'

There was some basic, integral kind of solidity about him she could only warm to. Ben Rawlins was a rock. They fixed their lives around him. He was constant. He was always there. Maybe Ben was even a little jealous of her, the way Paul had detached himself, now swam in her orbit.

'There's change in the air, Joni,' he said, his face now warm, friendly, but so serious too. 'And we're people who are getting old, we're people who aren't used to change. There's something going on here, something with Paul, with you, maybe things that none of us understand either. I get protective, that's all. Paul's a guy who goes through life getting hurt. Has been as long as I've known him. It's inside what he is. If I was being cruel, I'd say he brings it on himself. The rest of us grew up somewhere along the way, but – and don't ask me how – something happened to Paul that froze him, left him locked up inside some kind of kid's view of the world, years ago, years before I ever came across him. It's one of the things we all love in him, that and him being one of the most decent people you're ever going to meet in your life. But it's something that harms him too. Maybe even harms those of us around him. You know what I'm talking about?'

She could hear her mother's voice just then, hear it coming across the years, saying, 'All you're looking for is goodness, thinking that goodness is all you need to heal you. But it's not like that. And the line between goodness and weakness is so narrow, so fine, so grey, you might never know the difference until it's too late.'

She pushed the food to one side. It was wonderful, but she wasn't hungry any more, and she didn't want to look at the view, didn't want to feel herself getting sucked into this place.

'Ben, he's lucky to have you as a friend,' she said. 'Anybody would be lucky to have you as a friend. But what's between us is between *us*.'

'I don't want him hurt.'

What was it about Paul, she wondered, that made them all want to protect him?

'And I don't want to hurt him. Don't you believe me?'

'Of course I believe you, Joni. But there's things . . . Jesus.'

For once he looked lost for words. It was something that plainly made him unhappy.

'I don't know what's going down here,' he said. 'I don't understand these changes. Hell, I don't even know where he is. And that just isn't Paul. That just *isn't* him.'

'He's not been in the studio today?'

'Not a sign. Have you seen him?'

'Not since last night. I stayed at the hotel. We're not married, Ben. I'm not *responsible* for him.'

'Well, who the hell is then?' Ben Rawlins asked. There was the harsh red glare of anger in his eyes, and it shocked him just as much as it did her.

SIX

Miles in the Darkness

This is a puzzling world, and Old Hal's got a finger in it.
GEORGE ELIOT,
The Mill on the Floss

To live outside the law, you must be honest.
BOB DYLAN, 'Absolutely Sweet Marie'

'He might die,' Hal Jamieson said. 'That's real smart, Michael. You just might have killed him.'

Miles Seymour was slumped on the floor, breathing heavily, unconscious. A trickle of vomit was drying on his front. It ran down from the corner of his mouth, onto the sack shift he had worn since he was taken into the cellar more than a week before. Beneath the grime, beneath the caked yellow bile, his face was pale, the colour of moonlight.

'Mouse.' Hal Jamieson looked at the figure crouched in the corner. Two eyes, bright eyes now, stared back at him and he wondered what changes were going on there, wondered if there were changes happening inside all of them just like this.

She looked at the three of them, Hal so close, Louise and Quinn distant, by the ladder, then shuffled over on her knees to Hal. The entire right side of her face was one livid bright bruise, red and purple and swollen. It looked like something might be broken there. He didn't even want to think what it felt like. What pain – pain frightened Jamieson, pain was the worst thing in the world – she was feeling.

He put a hand, very slowly, on her shoulder and she didn't seem to object. Hal was always the best of them, the guitarist kid apart, but he never came, not since they'd taken the kid, and maybe that was his good luck because she knew, she *knew*, that Paul would have had nothing to do with this, Paul would have stopped it from the very beginning, whatever the cost.

'Mouse, just tell me what you need. For him and for you. I'll go down the drug store and get it. Anything.'

'Jesus,' Quinn spat in the corner of the cellar. 'The kid's dead anyway, Hal. It *doesn't matter.*'

And Louise walked over, felt Hal Jamieson's hand, her touch so warm, so real, and said, 'He's right, Hal. Maybe it doesn't matter.'

Mouse was staring at him so hard, in a way the others couldn't see, and he wondered how she, alone, knew, how she could tell – *I do not want this kid's death on my conscience, I did not come here to kill* – and then he said, 'We agreed that I run this. You know that's best, Michael. And that means what I say *goes.* We don't *know* what's going to happen from now on. We don't *know* what kind of hand we got to play once this thing starts to happen. Letting the kid die would be like going into a poker game and throwing all the best cards under the table even before we sat down to play.'

'But we told the cops . . .' Quinn said, and Hal Jamieson heard it for the first time then, the whine, the teenage whine in his voice, and understood it had always been there, that what was different was his *hearing* it. And how this separated them, made him more responsible than before.

'I know what we told the cops, Michael,' he interrupted. 'And I know what we're gonna do. Conversation *terminated.*'

'He needs a doctor,' Mouse said, and he wished she wouldn't look at him, in this new way, so directly, talking straight into his eyes. 'Hal, *he needs a doctor.*'

Hal Jamieson shook his head. 'Can't do that, Mouse. You've got to see I can't do that.'

'Jesus,' Quinn grumbled, then set about climbing up the trap-door ladder. Louise followed him, but not without pausing, looking Hal Jamieson in the eye in a way that gave him some hope, made him think that maybe she was coming round, back into the real world, and seeing he was there already.

'Get me some water. Lots of good water,' she said. 'The kid's been throwing up so much he must've lost a lot of water. I got to make him drink. Make him keep the water down.'

'Yeah.'

Jamieson looked at the boy. He might have been sleeping, one long deep sleep.

'What else?'

'For chrissake, Hal, I don't know,' she said, and he thought for a moment she would start to cry. Then something happened inside her, some door opened, some strength came out from nowhere, and Hal Jamieson wondered again what he really knew about people, how he'd ever come to regard Mouse, quiet little complacent Mouse who'd turn a fuck just out of pure boredom if you just looked at her right, come to see her as some sub-species in the corner just waiting to be tagged and classified and told what to do.

'And you?' He looked at the bruises on her face, big purple weals that looked so painful, so huge, he didn't even want to think about what had happened to the bone and the sinew underneath.

'Just some aspirin. That's all,' she said. 'And plenty of water. A bowl.'

Margaret Zalinski felt she could go on washing and washing and washing herself, slowly sponging down the boy's still body, until the end of the world and still they'd be dirty, still they'd be tainted.

'Sure,' he said. 'Kids are strong, you know. My guess is he'll wake up from that, maybe trip a little, whatever, be fine in the morning. You wait.'

And wished he hadn't said it, wished he couldn't see the recrimination in her eyes.

'You think I'm stupid, Hal,' she said. 'And you're right. I'm not smart. Not like you and Michael and that girl are smart. Doesn't make you *superior* though, does it? Doesn't make you God. Over me. Over him. You don't own our lives. None of you. Not yours to take away.'

Hal Jamieson felt sick inside and said, 'I'm just trying to cope, Mouse. That's all. I do my best, we *all* get out of this alive. I mean *all.* But don't you let Michael think that, not for one moment. Louise will be OK. Trust me on that. But if Michael finds out, then there's a whole new world of badness coming your way and you know what that world is already. Michael's world. And you don't want that, you *know* you don't want that.'

'You just keep us alive, Hal,' she said grimly. 'We didn't *ask* for this.'

And you think I did? Hal Jamieson asked himself. You think I asked for any of this?

'I'll get some water. I got some aspirin in the Barn. Some towels too. I'll bring them down. Anything you want. But you talk to me from now on. You just keep quiet and out of Michael's way. You stay down here, that's the truth, you hear me? Michael finds he *can't* find you and you know what he's going to do to the boy. And I can't stop that. What I can do goes as far as being able to pull us all out of this. Once Michael thinks I've screwed up on that – and you go walking out of here and that's exactly what he *will* think – then I'm just like you. No use. And he's gonna do what he likes. You understand that?'

She nodded, her ugly bruised face going up and down in the blotchy yellow light.

'We can *all* get out of here if we just keep our heads straight, so don't let go,' he said.

And then he grunted his way up the stepladder, disappeared for thirty minutes, returned with the water, the bathroom things he promised, a bottle of aspirin, some food, a cheese sandwich, some packets of potato snacks, put them down on the earth floor beside her, watched her holding the boy's head. The dark, matted hair didn't move but he was breathing, a little shallow, a little strange, but breathing.

'Don't let them kill us,' she said, quietly, without turning away from the child to look at him. 'Please, Hal.'

She hadn't wanted to see his eyes when he said softly behind her, 'No.'

In a sense, she thought, it didn't matter. In a sense, their fate was already decided. Whatever happened, Margaret Zalinski knew that from that moment on she would be staying with Miles. Would share whatever he had to face. Would always be with him, always be there, because something told her Miles would need her. And that was something new. No one before had needed Margaret Zalinski as anything except a piece of flesh that was expected to mould itself into the right shapes, make the right noises, do the right things. And Miles's need came into a different, special category. Miles's need was to do with love, something that had stayed hidden deep inside her like a slumbering beast, something Margaret Zalinski didn't even think she recognised until it came out and tapped her on the shoulder and she found it had an English accent, troubled, dreamy eyes and the need, a huge, sponge-like need, that could soak up everything she could give it.

She washed the boy clean, wiped the caked stuff away from his mouth, around his neck, wondered about taking off the shift, cleaning him all over, decided it was too risky, the cellar was cool and damp. He could catch something, catch a cold. Along with everything else.

Then she set about cleaning herself up as best she could, feeling her way around the bruises with the sponge, feeling the dirt come painfully away from her face, feeling the cool, clean touch of the water.

She had no watch. There was no time down here any more. It could be the middle of the night. It could be the middle of the day. And even the sub-divisions of time seemed uncertain. When she tried, she could no more gauge that a minute had passed than an hour. All she could do was listen to his breathing and wait. For him. For Hal. Maybe even for Michael. And this *was* all she could do. Margaret Zalinski had figured it out carefully in her head, more carefully than anything in her entire life. She had counted the possibilities like beads on some stone necklace, one by one, scratching little marks in the earth to make sure she missed nothing, to make sure she couldn't return to one possibility just because it got lost somewhere in the jumble. She wasn't smart, she said to herself, but she wasn't stupid either. And that counted. That meant she knew the *only* possibility was to wait. To hope that Hal would get his way. To listen for the sound of the trap door. To wait until they saw the light again, then see what happened. See when the chance came to pick him up – *but he's heavy, Margie, you know that* – and run and run and run.

And then – *and then they take him back to England, Margie, no more kind voices in the night, no love, no need, no tenderness in your life* – you found out what the real world was like and hoped it wasn't as cruel as the one you just left. Somewhere deep inside, with thoughts that didn't form enough to have names or even feelings attached to them, Margaret Zalinski played out a little scene in which she tried to talk her way through court arguing that a diner waitress who smoked dope and slept around was not, was *not* less suited to take care of a child than some smartass social worker with a college degree, that what it all came down to was love and faith and grit, that what mattered was not the books you read but the thoughts you shared, and the way you never, never, never let the boy go until his wings got ready. And somewhere deep inside she could hear them laughing, too, a chilling, cruel laughter Margaret Zalinski thought she'd heard following her everywhere through the twenty years of her life.

She closed her eyes and held him, held his warm body, trembling a little now, sweating too, hot underneath the harsh sack shift, something happening there, something changing, that would reshape her life one way or another, good or bad, short or long. Then she wrapped herself around him so they were pressed together like one warm bundle in the dark and fell asleep under the dusky yellow light of the bulb, fell into some place where there were no minutes or hours, nothing but the half-darkness and the gentle human moisture of his breath on her neck.

There was no knowing how long they slept like that, one out of exhaustion, one out of the chemical shock that coursed and raged through his blood, sent fire and ice and madness through his head, a million tiny neurons a second racing, racing, racing through the cerebellum and the cortex, through thalamus and hypothalamus, pituitary and amygdala, roaring, roaring, roaring all the time, dispatching the chemical fire like napalm in the jungle and not waiting to see what remained after the blaze, the brightly coloured blaze, died inside.

When finally she awoke, the boy was stiff in her arms, staring upwards, his eyes unfocused, glassy, dark pools once again, and his arms, his legs were rigid, unmoving, locked. His breath was rhythmic but shallow, like that of a machine.

'Miles,' she said, and there was nothing there, not the recognition of anything she said or whispered, quietly, anxiously in his ear.

Margaret Zalinski did not know words like 'catatonic' and could only feel her way through the next few hours, feel her way around his body and its changing state, admit some gratitude into her worried mind when his limbs relaxed a little, lost that rigidity, lost it enough to let his bladder and bowel vent themselves slowly through the sackcloth shift, so that she could move his small body as she wiped him clean, could call his name, whisper gently, gently in his ear, 'Tell me about England, Miles, tell me about cricket and how it's green, tell me, tell me, tell me . . .'

And Margaret Zalinski knew nothing about dissociative disorders and the way psychotropic drugs could, under unknown circumstances, disrupt, *alter* the consciousness, the identity, even the memory of a person. She knew nothing about psychogenic fugue, that invisible demon that might change a person completely so that there was no memory of what went before, of who you were, who you loved, where you belonged.

These were big ideas with long names and Margaret Zalinski could never, would never, understand them. All she knew, as Miles Seymour slowly turned, writhing, sweating in her arms, as he pissed himself slowly, unknowingly, through the long, long night, was that the child was being reborn, remade, as she held him. And that there was nothing she could do to help keep alive the narrow thread that linked him to the world and the black space beyond, except bury her face in the dank, sweet roughness of his hair.

SEVEN

Making Arrangements

Money doesn't talk, it swears.

BOB DYLAN, 'It's Alright Ma
(I'm Only Bleeding)'

All things are sold: the very light of Heaven is venal.

PERCY BYSSHE SHELLEY, 'Queen Mab'

Tom Cordobes felt the weight of the gunbelt stiff inside his jacket. It was a time since he'd worn a .45, a time since he'd stood in the police firing range and let the big thing blare noisily away at a cardboard target on the far wall, watched the holes punch themselves in the figure, felt the kick of the recoil send the gun flying skywards every time he pulled the trigger, jumping away against gravity like it had smelled something awful. It sat beneath the jacket and felt warm, long after he came off the range, warm against the smooth no-iron nylon of his shirt.

He could close his eyes and remember that shape from another time, when the world was green and damp and humid, when there was the sound of foreign tongues on the air, and it was Eden for the special people, an Eden where you just did what you wanted, no fear of reprisals – this was before My Lai – no fear that the clerks and the accountants and the pen-pushing people who worked in offices everywhere, from the Pentagon to Saigon, might come in one day, shake their heads, and say, 'No. You do things *this* way.'

It was a time when you just *improvised* and Tom Cordobes liked, no, *loved*, the idea that it might come again. Even if it was just briefly. When he thought about it, and he didn't like to think about it too much because that surely was a way of getting good and mad, there was an awful lot of stuff to get back on out there. From Berkeley to Ohio State, from the Weathermen to the Symbionese Liberation Army, there was a whole litany of things that made that .45 feel warm in his hand: Tom Hayden, the Rolling Stones, Huey Newton, Bobby Seale, psilocybin, Eldridge Cleaver, Haight-Ashbury, Jerry Brown, anyone who lived in Watts, Abbie Hoffman, Patty Fucking Hearst, the Russians and the Chinese, the Jews and the Arabs. And the list grew longer day by day.

Even when they sat in Cy Langton's office, with a cheery winter sun now flooding through the window, a light wind rippling the maple leaves outside the door, New Year shoppers wandering down the street looking for sales bargains, even then that gun felt warm, its heat made it hard to think about what the stuck-up English guy was saying, hard to wonder why they even bothered with this, why they didn't just set it up and get on with the job, let Tom do what the Captain wanted him to and hang loose a little.

After all, the kid was dead anyway, he was sure of that now, and as the certainty hardened inside him like indigestion, he came to wondering what the English guy was really thinking, wondering why he wore that stuffy pinstripe suit and pressed white shirt, skinny blue silk tie with the pattern on, here in California, where you could feel the heat starting to get friendly on the afternoon breeze coming in through the half-open office window.

'You think he's dead already, I assume?' the English guy said, and Tom Cordobes came out of his little reverie with a start.

'No, sir,' Cordobes lied, pretty convincingly he thought.

'Why?'

'These are clever people, sir. If they're gonna kill the kid my guess is they'll kill him once they got the money. Once they're sure they're away with this thing. Otherwise they're just throwing away some life insurance. Got no reason to do that.'

'Really,' Simon Lascelles said with a degree of resignation Tom Cordobes swore had a fair swash of boredom rolling around there with it. 'Well, at least it gets poor Daniel off the hook. I presume I'll hear no more of that nonsense.'

The phrase 'cold fish' came into Cordobes' head out of nowhere and when he looked at Lascelles he guessed he finally knew what it meant.

'You don't get kidnappings in the UK so much, I guess,' Cy Langton said, only half trying to be polite, and skipping over the issue of the dead brother-in-law altogether. 'We got too many for our own good.

Lieutenant Cordobes here says what he thinks happened; my guess, sir, is that is pretty much what *has* happened.'

'I hope so,' Lascelles said. 'I'm giving you two hundred thousand dollars precisely because I *do* hope so.'

'Your decision,' Langton snapped. 'You know our advice, sir. We don't believe you *should* negotiate with kidnappers. They get away with this one, they'll be ruining somebody else's life once the money runs out. You give in, you legitimise it, you give in . . .'

The English guy screwed up his long thin face and said, 'Oh, for God's sake, man, spare me the lectures. I had enough of those from Daniel.'

'We got a duty to uphold the law, sir, but that also means we got a duty to advise people how they can help us uphold it. That means you don't give the criminals a break. You don't give in.'

'Very good. Very good. Very *noble*, I'm sure. Well, I have a duty too, Captain. I have a duty to the family, a duty to stop the bloody gutter press hounding us from pillar to post asking when we'll come up with the money to free poor Miles. As if *we're* responsible. It's bad enough having to smuggle Rosamund back home without too much fuss. I really don't want this descending into some squalid Italian farce with half the world's paparazzi permanently on our heels. If it costs two hundred thousand dollars then I imagine it's worth it.'

'And I guess you can afford it too. Sir,' Langton said without a smile.

'Actually,' Lascelles answered brightly, 'you would be wrong there. A common misconception. We're old money, Captain. Probably not a term you're familiar with in California but never mind. It means we once had lots and lots. But the more life goes on, the less we've got, it seems. You don't have the Labour Party here. You *are* lucky. These people timed things well as it happens. Had they waited a year or so, they could have seen off Rosamund's father and I have to tell you that once that happens the death duties will doubtless take care of the rest. Once that happens we become like *you*. The only money we have is the money we earn. Strange idea. I imagine we will have to get used to it. Quite where Rosamund's hospital bills or the girl's school fees are supposed to come from then I have no idea.'

'You can't afford it, that's all the more reason not to pay,' Langton said.

The English guy smiled in a way that made them think he was

293

genuinely sorry for them, genuinely upset they couldn't understand.

'Oh dear. This is hard. It is precisely because we cannot afford it that we *must* pay, Captain. If you have only two pennies in your pocket, you really have to rattle them together as loudly as you can. Do you follow?'

Langton nodded, barely moving, wanting this man out of his office as soon as he could, and said, 'I guess so.'

'Our goal,' said Tom Cordobes, and he noticed how he was slipping back into the military terminology already, 'what we want to achieve, sir, is to get both back. Your money and the boy.'

Lascelles smiled. 'That *would* be nice. Or even just one? It would be a tragedy to lose both.'

'He looks a nice kid, from the pictures,' Cy Langton said, and Tom Cordobes wondered whether, for a moment, the old guy had been contemplating taking a pop at Lascelles across the desk.

'Miles?' The thin face was non-committal. 'Pleasant enough, I imagine. Frankly, Captain, children aren't my *field*. God knows what I'm supposed to do with Flora during the holidays. I can't really send her to stay with her mother now, can I? And these boarding schools want an arm and a leg for keeping them out of term time.'

Nice phrasing in the circumstances, Cordobes thought, looked across at Langton and saw the same idea floating around his head too.

'We'll get someone to pick up the money, sign for it from your bank when the details of the handover come in,' Cordobes said. 'Mrs Seymour is free to go once we have the court papers signed for her transferral to the British authorities. Then they can take care of her, get her home and all that stuff. We don't need nothing else from you.'

'No,' said Simon Lascelles, and congratulated himself on holding back some remark about the quaintness of the double negative. 'Then I shall sit in my hotel and read, gentlemen.'

They watched him go out of the door, the pinstripe suit a little shiny for its own good.

'You think we'd be doing the kid a favour, sending him back to be with that fucking English shit?' Langton said. 'I got my doubts.'

Tom Cordobes shrugged, felt the warm gun sticking to the nylon shirt like sweat. He wasn't thinking about the kid much any more. Simon Lascelles didn't figure much in his head right then, though he felt sorry for the woman, and the years she was going to spend in some British mental home, felt sorry for the girl and the long, black future that seemed to spread out in front of her. But these were little things. What he was really thinking about right then was Bobby Seale and Patty Fucking Hearst, and trying to remember what it sounded like when the slug hit hard, that low, flat *paff* noise of soft lead piercing even softer flesh.

EIGHT

Joni and Louise

So far as we are human, what we do must be either evil or good: so far as we do evil or good, we are human: and it is better, in a paradoxical way, to do evil than to do nothing: at least we exist.   T. S. ELIOT, 'Introduction',
The Intimate Journals of Charles Baudelaire

Cruising around the lower streets downtown in the big silver and grey Shogun, Steve Baxter almost smiling in the driver's seat, Louise Gostelow couldn't help but wonder how long it had been since she had done this, looked at the city, looked at the dull stone streets, the people flitting between Bon Marché and Starbucks, looking bored, lost, travelling without direction, trying not to notice the bums panhandling every corner. When she shopped, she shopped in New York or San Francisco, Paris or London. This wasn't Fifth Avenue or Union Square, this was no Left Bank, no Bond Street. Downtown Seattle looked like some place frozen in time, something out of the thirties or earlier. Even the monorail and the distant slender outline of the Space Needle looked so dated, like an illustration out of some ancient sci-fi comic that might sell for a hundred dollars over the counter of a speciality store. It was drab and this drabness pervaded everything, the architecture, the atmosphere, the clothes the people wore on the streets. The thin channel of water that separated Mercer Island from the city might as well have been an ocean as far as she was concerned. This was not a place you visited out of choice. It was not part of her world, not elegant or desirable, with no obvious dividing lines between rich and poor, those making it, those throwing it away. It was the old template for a city, a mixed, polymorphous community, people living cheek by jowl in buildings that should have been pulled down, or at the very least *refurbished*, a millennium ago, living on top of each other, hands in everyone's pockets, sharing the same air and water through the same communal lungs and throats. For Louise Gostelow this was a template that had failed, a blueprint that deserved to be stuck in the drawer and left there for a thousand years. She preferred the new city, the Bellevue model, where you erected barriers at the border, big economic barriers that were more effective than anything you could build with barbed wire, barriers that said, 'You pay the entrance fee, you come in. You don't, you sweep the floors, you mow the lawns, you fix the plumbing, then you go away at night, back across the border, back to wherever, and the place doesn't really matter, you choose. *If you're lucky.*'

Louise Gostelow didn't want to know who her neighbours were. She didn't even want to *see* them from any part of her green and perfectly manicured estate, with the landscaped terraces, the boat jetty that strutted out into the clean, fresh water with not a hint of an oil rainbow besmirching the surface. The blueprint for the new city dictated that you had space and you created that space by keeping people out, by setting some economic limit – and calling it conservation – that defined who lived there and who didn't. And you had to be careful. You had to watch what that limit was, accept that it changed with the times. That when the city grew more prosperous, as it was doing now, you kept on raising the barrier so that the intake stayed the same, and the border was maintained. So you could keep on planting fir and pine, in neatly equidistant rows, between the offices and the malls and the business centres, and call the city green. Louise Gostelow had, in her landscaped terraces running down to the waterside, a twenty-foot totem, carved on the Suquamish reservation, and underneath, in big straight angular letters, some words of Chief Seattle: 'There is no quiet place in the white man's cities. No place to hear the unfurling of leaves in spring, or the rustle of an insect's wings. But perhaps it is because I am a savage and do not understand. The clatter only seems to insult the ears.'

And visitors to Desert Rose, who made their way down to the waterside, would read it, look at the view, so quiet, so natural, so clean, and listen bright-eyed to her talking about Chief Seattle and his letter to President Franklin Pierce and some of the other aphorisms it contained. Louise knew it was all a myth. That Chief Seattle's little hunks of folk wisdom were mainly the work of some TV scriptwriter putting together a junk historical epic, but it didn't matter. She had a blueprint that made sense to her and if it excluded people like those walking through the streets of the city then that was OK. This was America. You got a choice.

'Where to, ma'am?'

Baxter wore a dark wool suit, his hair was cropped close to his gleaming skull. He didn't talk. Just waited to be told and then acted. In her world, he was one of the people who served the new city, knowing he would never make it across the border except for the day, but glad to be let in all the same, glad to be paid to serve, willing to do it without bearing a grudge, letting the money trickle down just enough to take him out of the old ways, get him somewhere into the suburbs, Renton or some place, and move into some nice little home that was a cut-down version of the new city, with fewer trees, less space between the boxes you inhabited, but just the same spiritual distance, the same spiritual divide between the people who lived there. You maybe needed to wear blinkers a little more but it was better than the alternative. He was someone you could use when you needed it. And the nice thing about little people with aspirations was just this: they were *so* dependable.

She sat in the back and surveyed First Street: shoppers aimlessly wandering down to Pike Place and Post, to buy, to lunch, bums leaning on street corners staring sullenly at anyone who walked past them.

'Let's try the hotel again, Steve.' She smiled into the driver's mirror.

It was the second time in two hours but there was nothing for it except this: to travel the endless triangle, Pike Place, Paul's boat, and the Pequod, until she turned up at one or the other. And then ... Louise smiled. She remembered what it had been like twenty years ago in California. She remembered the excitement, the buzz, a fire inside that was better than the best sex, better than anything else in the world. She remembered letting go, and letting go was what really turned Louise Gostelow on, letting go, until you didn't know who you were, what you were doing, until you didn't even *care*. Letting go was what took her into her real world. Where you didn't think, where things didn't have names. Where you just *did*, then stood back, breathless, waiting to see the consequences.

The Shogun cruised slowly through grey, faceless streets then pulled up outside the meagre blue-and-white awning over the front door of the Pequod. No one stepped out to help her get out of the car. Even in the downtown, where you could pick up a bellboy for the price of a good daily lunch, this was unusual, this showed the kind of place it

298

was. She walked into reception, a cramped, narrow room with a wooden desk, an old phone switchboard behind it, the same thin man from earlier, in a wrinkled grey suit, wire-rimmed glasses. He looked bored, he looked as if he didn't care. He didn't even remember.

'Miss Lascelles,' she said.

'Oh yeah,' he answered in a flat Seattle accent, then picked up the phone. He looked eighteen trying to pretend he was forty.

'I have a visitor for you,' he said, after a few seconds. 'In reception. Yeah.'

He handed the phone over the counter without a word.

'Hello?'

She sounded so young, so English.

'Miss Lascelles, you don't know me. I'm an associate of Tom's. He asked me to come and collect you. He's found something. Says he's sorry he didn't contact you before but he's sure you'll understand. We got a car outside right now.'

And in the small, grey bedroom Joni Lascelles felt her heart skip a beat, wondered if she really wanted this, if she hadn't already talked – *fooled* – herself into thinking, wishing, this would not happen.

'I'll be with you in a minute,' she said and put the phone down. Joni Lascelles walked to the mirror, looked at her pale, thin face, no make-up, no beauty here, just the mask that had stared back from the glass all her life, wondering, asking, challenging. She picked up the phone and dialled the number. She knew it by heart already. Genius picked up the phone.

'Yeah? Pike Place Studios?' The thin little voice sounded so aggressive.

'Genius. Is Paul back? Have you heard from him?'

Genius hesitated, then said, softly, a note of concern in his voice, 'No, Joni. Ben's gone looking for him, see if he's gone on a drunk or something. Not done that in a long time though. You two argue or something?'

'No,' she said, puzzled.

'You want me to give him a message when he does turn up?'

'Yes. Tell him Tom Cordobes called. He says he's found something. Sent someone to pick me up. Tell him I'll phone him, at the studio, at home, wherever. I wish I knew where he was.'

'We all do,' Genius said. 'We all do.'

She put down the phone, feeling uncomfortable, unhappy, with the conversation, and walked to the door. Then cursed herself, couldn't believe she had become so detached, so distracted. Went back to the bed, pulled out the suitcase from underneath, threw it open. The little handgun looked old now, even after these few days, and she wondered whether it really worked, whether this was anything but a talisman, some piece of magic she hoped would cast some sparkling spell over the world. And just holding it, feeling the heavy dull metal in her hand, the smell of the mineral oil seeping into her skin, made her feel a little sick, a little ashamed that she had once, not long ago, thought that cures came with guns and hate and violence, that blood healed blood, that there was some other ache that she needed to resolve than the simple, most basic one, of knowledge. She put the gun back in the suitcase, tipped it onto the floor, pushed it back under the bed and went downstairs.

Louise Gostelow looked like a businesswoman, well dressed, affluent, assured, not the kind of person she associated with Tom Cordobes. She thought she'd seen her somewhere before briefly but her mind was somewhere else, it just didn't come.

'Hi,' said Louise, and thrust out a tanned hand, the nails polished carmine. She had a perfect white smile, perfect skin, perfect hair. The more Joni thought about it, the odder she found it that this woman should have anything whatsoever to do with Cordobes.

'Tom said you wanted a meeting. Well, I'm here to tell you it's on. We got the car outside. We can go now.'

'Who with?' she asked. And there was something else about the woman too. Something about the way she looked at her. Like an examination. Like being given marks, compared, judged, assessed. It was strange.

'I just do the organisation. I don't know the details. Tom said to pass on the message. Pick you up. That's all. You want to go, we take you.'

'Can I phone him? You have a number?'

Louise shrugged.

'It's a private address. I'm sorry. I don't know.'

'I see.'

Louise Gostelow pushed open the narrow door of the Pequod. The day was turning sunny. The cloud over Puget Sound was breaking up quickly into puffy cumulus, behind it bright-blue sky. In the distance she could see mountains.

'Are you coming?' the woman said and it was Joni's reluctance that made her say yes, it was the knowledge that, having come this far, something inside told her to stop, to let the door close, to take the quiet, the easy path. And she remembered the dreams, she remembered the voices and knew this was not possible, that there was some kind of catharsis that her life required in order to be fully whole, to allow her to grow, to move on, to breathe.

She walked outside and stepped into the Shogun, sat down on the shiny leather of the back seat, with its musky, polished smell, noticed how the driver didn't even turn to look, just inspected her in the mirror.

Louise Gostelow walked around the other side of the vehicle, climbed in, sat next to her, and smiled.

'You'd better handle the locks, Steve,' she said, and the driver reached down, popped a button on the central console. Some mechanism in the skin of the vehicle clunked hard and solid and metallic all around them.

'You can never be too careful in the city,' Louise said, still smiling. 'Really.'

And then the Shogun started the slow crawl out of the city, across the floating bridge, past the cormorants skimming inches above the still, glassy waters of Lake Washington, out onto the long, winding road that snaked its way through the low-slung suburbs and out into the Cascades, so big, so empty, there in the distance.

NINE

A Change of Heart

Well, she was an American girl,
Raised on promises
She couldn't help thinking that there was a little more to life
Somewhere else
After all it was a great big world
With lots of places to run to
And if she had to die
Tryin', she
Had one little promise she was gonna keep

TOM PETTY AND THE HEARTBREAKERS,
'American Girl'

Paul Dunsany grimaced. 'Bohemian Rhapsody' was coming out of the music store sound system and there was nothing more he hated right at that time than the sound of Freddy Mercury pretending to sing opera, the pretentious arrangement, the ridiculous words and the thought that 1975 almost gave up the ghost on the world with this at number one in the charts.

'Scaramouche, Scaramouche, will you do the fandango?' the speakers bellowed and the thing that annoyed him most was the way the sound, just a few notes, put that picture of the video, all that gothic crap, with the heads, and the heavy posing, straight into your head.

'Sweet Jesus,' Paul Dunsany said quietly to himself, measured the week ahead, all that empty time left before college began again, and wondered if he really could spend it listening to Freddy yelling away in Moore's Music Store. It was 4 pm on a slow Saturday afternoon. Davie Fraser, the long-haired kid who played bass and worked part time too, was near the record deck, doing air guitar movements to the music. Paul Dunsany tried to guess how easy it might be to get him away from the vinyl and put on some Little Feat instead, and then the thought went right out of his head. Louise Gostelow walked through the door, walked up to him, and she was different, she looked smaller, almost more human somehow. There were rings underneath her eyes, some darkness in her face. She looked like something had come out of the world and marked her.

'Hi,' he said, and tried to measure his own feelings, to work out what they were.

'We've got to talk, Paul,' she said, and he nodded, it was automatic, what she wanted was what he did and something inside tried to rebel, tried to get him to hate himself for that.

'Sure,' he said and looked over at Davie Fraser, who was grinning, making obscene little gestures with his free hand, playing with the cord of the headsets with the other, bopping and moving to the music. Dunsany mouthed at him. The kid took off the headset, gawped stupidly.

'You can close up, Davie. No business needing me around.'

'OK,' the kid yelled. 'You do the same for me some time?'

'Sure,' he said, and then went behind the counter, picked up his cheap cotton casual jacket, and they walked out into the street. The winter seemed to be going away fast. It was sunny and this was real sun, not the washed-out watercolour impostor you usually got in January. It seemed low in the sky, so low you could feel the warmth, feel things starting to move, to grow again. He looked at Louise Gostelow and wished she wasn't that beautiful, wished the sun didn't make her skin so golden and tanned, wished he could look at her and stop the thoughts rising to the surface, unbidden, unmasked. These were things that were beyond his control, as much as he fought them.

And she *was* different. It was somehow more obvious out in the daylight. That hardness, that arrogance that had surfaced more than once now seemed gone. She looked what she was: twenty and lovely. Her face had some simple, classical beauty you found in a painting, something he had never expected to see outside a book, never experienced, never dreamed could even touch him in his life, in the circles he'd grown up, struggled through over the years. She even dressed differently, a simple, plainly embroidered cotton shirt, light slacks. This wasn't the society princess, this was someone else.

They walked to the Good Earth Café, bought two coffees, a couple of pieces of carrot cake and sat down by the big windows, watched the afternoon crowds mooching down University Avenue, gazing into the stores, wondering what post-Christmas bargains there might be out there.

'You must think I'm a real bitch, Paul,' she said.

And as soon as he started to say something, she waved him into silence. 'No. Don't answer that. You don't need to. I owe you an apology. I owe you a lot. So take it. I'm sorry. Real sorry.'

And he wondered: where were the words when you needed them? Paul Dunsany was not prepared for this. He did not know what to say. He did not know what to do with these feelings.

'You look . . .' he said, and tried to quell this feeling that this was *wrong*. Something here was so wrong – *but hope can cure everything* – that he really ought to know it.

'Are you OK, Louise?'

She was watching him. Judging him. And she seemed so real, so *new*, that there was nothing he could do except listen.

'I am not used to nice people, Paul. Can you understand that? I am not used to the idea of trusting someone. It doesn't happen like that in my world. I'm not used to the idea that there is anything more between two people than . . .'

She swore quietly under her breath.

'I'm really screwing this up, aren't I?'

'I don't know,' he said. 'I don't know what you're trying to say.'

'I am trying to say that I am not used to the idea that someone might love me.'

He stared at her, trying to believe this. 'Are you serious?'

'Yes, I'm serious,' she said, and he couldn't stop looking into her eyes, they were so bright, so intense, you just couldn't avoid them. 'You think that sounds so crazy? There is a difference. Even I know that. I know I'm attractive. And you know what that means? Can you guess what it's like to find that every man you meet just wants to get laid? After a while, Paul, that is *it*. There is nothing more. And it becomes a question of yes or no. You get treated like a piece of meat, that's how you treat people back. It's hard, Paul. It makes you hard too.'

'I didn't see you like that, Louise.'

'I know that. But what you did see me as frightens me. That person, I don't know if it's me, Paul. I don't know if I can be that kind of person. This is real life. It's not *The Partridge Family*. In real life people do what suits them. In real life things just *happen* and you don't know why, you don't think them through. I didn't think through what we did. I didn't think through what I said to you then. They were bad things. I owe you an apology. I didn't mean them and anyway half that stuff wasn't true either.'

'It's OK,' he shrugged.

'Shit, Paul. It's *not* OK,' she said a little too loudly, and the couple at the next table started to stare none too discreetly. 'If we're going to go on with this thing you can't just sit back naively and let me act like that. You've got to say something. You can't be scared of me.'

'You want to go on?' he asked, amazed.

Louise Gostelow shook her head and it almost looked as if she was going to cry. 'I've been doing a lot of thinking, Paul, and I don't want to carry on like this. You're the one good thing that's been through my life recently. I want to leave all that shit behind and do my best to start over. I got myself into all kinds of things you don't want to know about and I just want to wipe it all clean, start again and get some sanity back into my life. And I don't think I can do it on my own.'

He tried the coffee. It was cold. And Paul Dunsany looked out of the window and thought about her, dared to think about whether this thing could really work, could really grow.

'If you tell me to I'll just walk out of here, Paul. I couldn't blame you.'

'Don't walk,' he said, and the world was reeling.

'I can't promise anything. I can't promise this will last. I can't promise I haven't got myself all wrong. That I'm not that person, Paul. The person you saw. You've got to understand that. I can't make promises because I just don't know if I can keep them.'

'I don't want promises,' he said, and thought inside: all I want is to stand in your presence, to look at you, to talk to you, to listen. 'I don't want anything except to be with you. You don't have to rush anything, Louise. If this thing's important, you don't need to rush it.'

She laughed, and there was so much intense physical beauty in her face, so close to him, that it took his breath away. She recognised this, she leaned over the table, closed her eyes, kissed him on the mouth, not caring what anyone saw, not caring what anyone thought. Louise Gostelow put her hand to his cheek and felt the roughness of the bristle, stroked his face, let her tongue roam into his mouth, and kissed him hard. And all the thoughts, all the doubts, all the shapes and emotions inside his head lost their names, ran together into some fusion of pleasure, of promise, of desire.

Eventually she pulled away and his head still was spinning, it was as if there was no one else in the room, no one else in the world.

'Paul, I may want to change but I'm not changing everything. My folks are away for the entire week. Telegraph Hill is empty. You don't come back with me there tonight, stay as long as you like, I think this thing's going to have a very rocky start indeed.'

And he held her arms across the table, felt the strength there, the determination, the humanity of her and it was the best thing, the best thing in his life, some pivotal moment never to be forgotten.

They rode the bike down the highway, as fast as he dared, the wind pummelling their faces, their hair streaming behind them, rode into the city, through the streets that shone in the late-afternoon sun, *shone*, so alive, so bright, so full of life. She bought them dinner in some place off Washington Square, a fancy Italian restaurant where the waiters looked at his jeans, his hair, and screwed up their noses, so much tomato, so much garlic, so much wine, she paid with her credit card, and the evening just went, time just compressed itself somehow, the hours turned into minutes, everything flew past them like a clock-work toy with a spring gone wrong, flew past them in the restaurant, slowed down when they reached the house, reached the bedroom.

She had wanted him and she was strong, this was her decision, and her way. She straddled his body in the humid night, with the foghorn booming way off in the distance, even the occasional clanging of a cable car carried on the wind, and she moved so slowly, with such intense strength, that it felt as if he could explode, as if the physical pleasure in his body, so powerful, so hard, would just build into something that would consume them both. And when it happened and it was like a nova bursting into life, so bright, so vivid that the borderline between pain and ecstasy seemed impossible to discern, when it happened it was not sex, it was not love, it was some strange crazy catharsis that took this physical form, and painted wild colours in their heads, painted their bodies in sweat and semen, inside and out, conjoined into a single soft mass of flesh. He felt his liquid race inside her, felt the acknowledgement that came from her body, so tender, so sweet, and held her gently over him, held her breast, the nipple hard and taut under his grasp.

She stayed over him, head tilted back, eyes closed, feeling his presence inside her grow soft, sit in the liquid there, feeling this damp link between them, waiting for it to wake again, waiting for it to feel

306

the hunger. And when this was finally finished, when there was no more energy, no more sap to share, she lay in his arms, face half in shadow from the full moon outside, opened her eyes, so bright, so sharp, so intelligent, and said, 'I need you to save me, Paul. Can you save me?'

He saw her waiting for an answer, still only half believing that this was true, that this was the real world.

'I can try,' he said, in the end. Then stayed awake, watched her smile, felt her head find its place on his chest, watched her go quietly, peacefully to sleep. These next two days Paul Dunsany walked in paradise and felt, *knew*, it would last forever.

TEN

Escape

Freedom's just another word for nothing left to lose.

KRIS KRISTOFFERSON (WITH FRED FOSTER),
'Me and Bobby McGee'

Louise Gostelow's Shogun was thirteen miles from Snoqualmie when Michael Quinn made his move, and it was a thing of such simplicity that, when he found out, Baxter kicked himself almost straight away, almost straight away *knew* that it had to happen like this. After Quinn had killed Tom Cordobes, after Baxter had taken the body out of the bathroom, buried it in the forest, in a deep grave dug with the help of Hal Jamieson, he had quietly, slowly begun to clean up the room, scrubbing the blood from the tiles, the walls, the furnishings, carefully picking up every piece of shattered glass, every broken piece of porcelain.

Quinn had watched him for a while, grinning, said, 'Like to help you there, Steve, but I get squeamish with these things. Sounds strange, I guess. But it's true.'

And Baxter had looked at him in a way that even Quinn couldn't stand, so he walked off into the kitchen, opened a bottle of 150-dollar claret, got quickly drunk and listened to the radio turned up loud, listened to the FM rock stations that just about reached out there from the city, though they crackled and they were mono and no one who thought anything about music would have put up with that quality.

It was like having a caretaker that packed a pistol, Quinn thought. The guy even mended a couple of broken shelves himself, finding the holes in the wall, nailing up the new brackets, hanging them real carefully to make sure they were straight and level. Then three heavies had turned up from the city with a whole heap of hardware and ironmongery in a wooden fruit case, piled them on the kitchen table and set to work about the house, two of them working, one of them watching the drive, the woods, some other kind of hardware none too discreetly hidden under a tartan check Columbia sportswear jacket with the Microsoft logo embroidered on the right breast.

Quinn looked at the guy and said, 'Give my regards to Bill. Tell him that Dreamworks deal is a real good one. Microsoft in Hollywood. Movies that crash. One *cool* concept.'

The goon just stared back with some kind of mixture of menace and stupidity over his face.

Baxter went round and wrapped that cabin in a whole new level of security: locks and chains and bolts just everywhere. From the outside the place was now impregnable. From the inside, you could manage something, but it would take some time, more time than anyone was likely to get. Quinn watched him take a long look at the big panoramic windows in the bathroom, where Cordobes had worked his way in so easily. The big man fitted one huge new lock then got out a welder, fixed in iron bars top to bottom, temporary, Mr Jamieson, you understand, once this thing is over we just take them out and no one will notice. Then, when the cabin felt more like San Quentin than San Quentin itself, they sat and waited. The way Baxter saw it, and the way Jamieson did too, they just had to wait and see what happened when Cordobes didn't go home. Wait and see if he'd told someone where he was, and if he had, whether they would show up, and if so with what.

It worried him. It didn't worry Hal Jamieson quite so much. He'd seen Cordobes in action once before (and he didn't count the little meeting in the car outside the SCC offices in that calculation). He knew exactly what kind of guy Cordobes was: a crazy guy. Go in there first, tell everyone afterwards, when you'd won, that was the way people like Cordobes worked. And that was why he wasn't surprised that no one came. Wasn't surprised that the only way they could find out who was employing the crazy old cop in the first place was to track her down themselves. And that way they got to relax. That way they got to let Quinn wander where he liked inside the cabin, leave him on his own with whoever was doing the babysitting again, just let him get drunk, get stupid, get invisible. And they did.

Baxter was out hunting the streets of the city with Louise Gostelow and in his place was Mr Microsoft, who was a big guy, a regular guy, not talking much, not thinking much, the way Quinn saw it. When

Mr Microsoft ate his meal – microwave pizza, microwave popcorn, microwave freezer dinners, the man would be *glowing* by the time he hit forty, Quinn thought to himself – he sat at the big kitchen table, placed both big elbows on the pale polished wood, and just sat there, filling his face, slowly, relentlessly, always in silence, never taking his eyes off Quinn. Then, when he was done, he went to the little single WC, the one with a pretty pink hand basin, just inside the door. He was a regular man. He could stay in there a good ten minutes or more, always with his Microsoft jacket, the keys safely inside, and from time to time you got to hear little grunts, and when he came out there was always that stiff, metallic whiff of shit just creeping out of the inch or so space between floor and door. You could time your watch by it, the way he finished the last piece of food, wiped his hands and his mouth with the napkin, stared Quinn in the face as if to say, 'No', then went in there to lighten his bodily load a little. And, thought Michael Quinn, regular men create their own problems. They wear out jackets in the same places because they roll their elbows on the bar in the selfsame way every night. Regular men do things like that because they can't be bothered to *think* of anything else. And that is a sign of laziness and a lack of mental agility.

When Mr Microsoft sat down to eat the meal – a big stoneground pizza groaning with cheese and pepperoni and onions – Quinn drained the remains of a goblet of wine, went to the rack, pulled out another bottle, poured some more and made like he was drinking it. Made like he was drunk. He'd eaten that day, more than usual, not an hour before, and this was a trick you learned in the pen, this was a trick you could use as many times as you wanted until they wised up to you. Not with 150-dollar claret in Obispo but the principle stayed the same.

Mr Microsoft got down to the last slice and Quinn looked at him from across the table and belched, mumbled, 'Shit.'

The big man looked at him disgusted and said nothing. He didn't need to.

'Feel like shit,' Quinn slurred. 'Feel like fucking shit.'

Then belched again, waited till the last slice was going into the big guy's mouth and ran for the WC. Quinn got inside the little room, locked the door, worked hard on his guts, put his fingers in his mouth, worked harder and harder until his guts began to churn, felt the bile rising down below, tautened his stomach as hard as he dared, then threw up anywhere, everywhere, anywhere. The red stuff coated the walls, the floor, the porcelain, and the smell was rank. It even made Quinn feel bad so he washed out his mouth in the hand basin, spat over the WC pedestal, wiped his face with one wet hand, breathed deeply, got himself back in shape, got himself back to normal, put the grin back on his face, and opened the door.

Mr Microsoft was standing there, a regular man, and he looked at the red sea of bile, looked at Quinn's smiling face, and held onto his belt like a man whose body was telling him he needed to go bad but his head was having second thoughts.

He glared right into Quinn's face, but not so near that he could smell him, and said, 'When I get through I'm gonna come back and make you clean up every drop of that. I'm gonna watch you.'

'Not me,' Quinn grinned. 'Don't do menial labour no more.'

And wondered for a moment if he'd gone too far.

Mr Microsoft turned his back on him, walked across the room, pulled open the door of the main bathroom, and Quinn followed him, you could catch a smell of the jacuzzi even as he opened the door.

'Man who shits with his jacket on,' Quinn muttered to himself, 'that's what I *call* a gentleman.'

Then the big guy closed the door, Quinn listened as he went across the room, listened as the little grunts started, and he reached into his pocket, took out the big iron key that normally lived on the other side of the door, put it in the lock, turned it, left it there, screwed halfway round in the hole so no one on the other side could push it out and insert a duplicate.

'All a question of logic,' Quinn said to himself. 'No one can get in, then no one can get out either.'

It was a good five minutes before Mr Microsoft had finished taking his shit, walked to the door, found it locked, realised what had happened, and realised how he was now prisoner of his own cage. But by that time Quinn had recovered the screwdriver he'd stolen from a toolbox when all the work was being done, and was attacking every interior screw on the main section of the room-length lounge window cage, was soon ready to kick the entire glass out of the frame. He tried to get the angle right, thought twice about it, went back over to the coffee table, picked up a massive antique side chair and threw it straight through the pane. It took a couple more throws before the hole was big enough to climb through safely, and Quinn still managed to cut

311

himself quite badly on the left hand on the way out. But then he was through, out into the fading afternoon daylight, out on the strange forest floor, with the giant pines staring silently down at him, and the clean mountain air pouring into his lungs like some overpowering cloud.

He walked round to the side of the house, looked through the long bathroom window. Mr Microsoft was throwing himself at the huge pine door and getting nowhere in a hurry. Quinn tapped lightly on the glass, gave the big guy a smile and wished he hadn't. He gauged Mr Microsoft was a man who knew how to control himself, knew when to do what, when to be silent. But right then, Quinn thought, the big hood would have happily torn him apart and eaten the pieces. And he'd have done it for the TV cameras too, if they'd been watching.

'Ciao,' Michael Quinn said quietly, listened for a moment, thought he heard the sound of a distant car, then walked into the forest, not thinking which way he was going, just heading, in a straight line, along what looked most like a path between the giant trunks that leapt to the sky around him.

Quinn was a good four hundred yards away when the Shogun pulled into the drive. Baxter, sensing there was something wrong, ushered the two women under the porch, unlocked the bathroom door, glared at Mr Microsoft, went back to the women, made small talk, didn't let on that something was wrong, though Louise seemed to know it, just through her eyes. Then he told Mr Microsoft to get the hell out of the place, watched him go, then left the two women drinking coffee and making uncomfortable small talk in the kitchen.

Baxter went back to the front door, stared into the lazy light of the afternoon, wondered if it was worth the effort, whether it might not just be best to leave Quinn to the forest and whatever was out there. The nearest cabin was twelve miles away. Quinn's chances of finding it in the sea of pine were nil. You needed to know how to handle the forest, how to look at the sun and know the direction you were walking. You needed to have confidence. You needed to have a plan. You couldn't just blunder in there, get your head down, walk on and on and on, and hope to meet Mr Park Ranger, all ready and waiting with a picnic basket under his arm, smiling, ready to wave you on into the great wide open that spread out just beyond the tree line, just beyond the point where the mountain gave way to scrub, then pasture, and fell all the way down to the city by the sea.

Baxter sighed, looked at the carpet of needles at his feet, and started to walk.

It didn't take long. Michael Quinn had found out for himself that the forest was not a place to be alone. The air, that pine scent that seemed so hard you could almost touch it, made him feel more ill than he ever remembered in his life, made the blood inside of him – *and the notblood inside of that* – boil and scream and fight to get free. After fifty yards his nose was pouring red and snotty down his face, and already he was getting disoriented. In twenty years, this was the most of the outside world Michael Quinn had ever seen and it was so huge and so strange it overwhelmed him, it left him lost for a plan of action, wishing for some small place to hide until his thoughts came back and shuffled in a nice orderly fashion inside his head. And in what seemed an astonishingly short time Quinn was lost, absolutely lost, did not know north from south, up from down, had no idea whether he was walking towards the cabin or walking away from it, was getting dizzy trying to look at the huge, threatening pillars of pine that stood over him, hemmed him in. There were animals here too. They made sounds that could drive you crazy, sounds that had you turning your head, looking for the source, and seeing nothing, sounds that left you wondering whether you were being bugged by a squirrel or a raccoon, or whether it might be something worse. Something with teeth and claws. Something so big it could take a chunk out of you or just squeeze you into juice between its huge, furry arms.

He tried to think. He tried to place markers: this tree, that tree. But they all looked the same. They all *were* the same in this grey half-light. He leaned back on one of the trunks, hating the feel of it, the bulk of it through his back, worked out what he had to do. And that was to go back, back to the cabin. Think things out from there. Maybe make peace with the big guy if he could. If he had to.

Michael Quinn thought that made sense, walked round the trunk, back towards the fading light in the sky, then wondered why it wasn't there, wondered what the big black shape obscuring it could be. The gun caught him round the side of the head, took a big scarlet chunk out of his scalp, sent his mind, his thoughts reeling, and it wasn't about pain, it wasn't about safety, it was about pride. Even in Obispo, you got to see first before they hit you and this just came out of nowhere, and it hurt, it made him bleed, he could feel its warmth,

313

the redness running slowly down the side of his head as he slumped back against the tree.

Baxter's big angular face peered down into his and then something huge and black and metallic came between them, hung steady in the air, the barrel pointed straight at his face.

'Pretty soon,' said Steve Baxter, 'your friend Mr Jamieson is gonna pay me to blow your fuckin' head clean off your shoulders. But you know something, *Mr* Quinn?'

He was grinning and it looked strange. Quinn had never seen the big guy grin before.

'Right now I'm minded to just do it for free.'

And then the world exploded outside Quinn's head, so loud, so loud, and there was heat, an acrid, choking smell in the air. Something damp and sticky, something with an odour like cough sweets, began to drip down on him from the tree. He felt it fall on his face: resin. Looked up, saw the scar, the white scar, with black smoky borders, cut into the flesh of the pine.

When the smoke cleared, Baxter was leering out of the half-light. Then the big guy's foot came back, kicked him hard in the leg.

'Get your fuckin' ass moving,' he said. 'You got some cleaning up to do. And some people to meet.'

EPIPHANY

ONE

Preparations

A Fisher once took his bagpipes to the bank of a river and
played upon them with the hope of making the fish rise, but
not one fish put its nose out of the water. So he cast his net
into the river and soon drew it forth filled with fish. Then he
took his bagpipes again, and, as he played, the caught fish leapt
up in the net. 'Ah, you dance now when I play,' said he. 'Yes,'
said an old Fish: 'When you are in a person's power you must
do as they bid.'
Aesop's Fables, 'The Fisher'

Even this close to the end there was a moment when Hal Jamieson
thought there might be another way, that maybe he could just dump
all that stuff that he and Louise had been working on, practising what
would happen, what *might* happen, in their heads for hours on end.
Thought that maybe the world, a sane world, ought to hold some
alternative. That you just called the cops, said look, this was a *misunder-
standing. OK?* We got just the one crazy here and you can have him.
Frankly you're fucking *welcome* to him. This guy deserves locking up,
deserves whatever you feel like throwing at him, no one's going to
object. But *we* don't. All we did was drop some acid at the wrong
time and – he could see Miles Seymour burning in front of his eyes
still – get a little lost, get a little caught up. We're just college kids.
We don't think straight. We deserve a break. We deserve some credit
for being stupid because that's what kids of our age are: people
undergoing some slippery, fumbling metamorphosis, feeling their way
from the world of childhood into the big grown-up one that you
inhabit, that you rule. And by the way, let's not fool ourselves, officer,
you got some pretty stupid people out there too. Matter of fact, you
got people out there who make us look pretty bright. That Manson
guy was no spring chicken. And all those people who screwed up in
Vietnam, who lied and then lied again, and then when everything else

317

failed just waved the flag and dared you to call them traitor, they were old people, they should've known better. Maybe I don't want to push this point too much, sir, but there is the question of role models here. And what kind do you think *they* make? Precisely . . .

The trouble was the more he thought about it the more improbable the idea seemed. There was a time when he could have done it. That first morning. When the world looked different and dreadful, he could have plucked up the courage, walked into Palo Alto, just told them, led them there. Got the kid out alive too probably. They would have given him some credit for that, surely. But he waited, and he knew, from the beginning, why he waited too. He waited for her. He waited to see her come round, come down from the big dope dream, think straight, think about the kind of mess they were getting in, and how the shit was piling higher and higher by the hour. He waited for Louise to recognise what was happening and help him out a little there, maybe (and he could still hope) *join* him. And her indecision, all those hours she spent in the bedroom with Quinn smoking dope, just letting loose, getting stupid, they just ticked away and made the chance of escape fade in front of his eyes. It was bad enough that he couldn't save her. What he certainly couldn't live with was the idea that he would be the one condemning her instead. What a trial that would be. Hal Jamieson pointing the finger across the courtroom and saying, yes, I slept with her, yes, I loved her and, yes, she did all those things, yes, we both watched Quinn playing with the kid's life and afterwards, when we came down it was a while before Louise came to, before she gave up on the game. That would be his fifteen minutes of fame and after that you might as well just pour a long cold shot of whisky and a deep, warm bath, jump right in with some nice sharp razor blades. You could just see it splashed across all the papers and wouldn't life be fine thereafter? Wouldn't that make a great start to a lucrative career in stockbroking in the better circles of Boston? Wouldn't it just?

And even when she did come down, the truth was the longer it went on, the more the complicity grew, enfolded them, trapped them in its little intricacies, its dark and delicious nooks and crannies. It grew until, in truth, he now felt as much, maybe even more, a part of it than Quinn even. Michael had merely set the ball rolling, in this terrible way that Hal Jamieson still failed fully to comprehend. It had been left to him to turn the chaos into something that made sense, something that could be salvaged, polished, fine-tuned, given shape, then used to save them, for good, forever. *And with one bound . . .*

Yeah, Hal Jamieson thought. Maybe. Maybe he could keep it all together, keep *them* all together, and hold the wire up long enough to get them all through free. And maybe not. The point was, and even then Hal Jamieson was starting to show a sense for organisation, a talent for sorting the wheat from the chaff, the point was to keep a sense of priority. To realise that you were now negotiating, on more than one level too. Negotiating with the cops for the money. And with each other for your mutual cooperation. In negotiation you didn't really expect to win everything you wanted. The smart thing was to make sure that what you did lose was what you *planned* to lose. The smart thing was to have plans and priorities and something up your sleeve.

And what delighted him, what made him crazy with anticipation, was that the waiting wasn't long. That what he wanted to happen really did happen, so quickly once she got bored with the taste of dope in her mouth, realised what was staring out at them from the world, the pure physical threat of it all, and how only he could keep her clear of it. Even before Quinn had really screwed the kid up with all that dope, Louise came down from outer space, sat down with him, made her peace, almost said sorry in her own way. It was as if something just opened her eyes one minute to what it all meant, the planning, the thinking ahead, and then she came round so quickly. She was with him before 1975 died and the new year slipped in, for them hardly noticed, and that gave them days to think, days and days, while Quinn slipped slowly into the background, living off dope and booze as he did so. And it was here that their relationship began for real, here that the bond that finally turned into respect, affection, even, for a while, fidelity, and eventually led them along the downhill lazy path to marriage – but not St Peter and St Paul, he couldn't face California right then, he couldn't face anything but an anonymous civil ceremony in Seattle, whatever her parents thought – started to grow. And they found themselves falling, just rolling with it, just like everyone else. What the hell else was there to do?

'Whoa. Behold. Lady Macbeth,' Michael said one day, with a sudden shocking lucidity through the dope, as he watched her leading him on, walking through things, helping him go through the planning, both of them so fired up, so close.

And that remark shook him. He had forgotten how perceptive

Michael could be, and in a way Quinn had faded into the background, become a minor character in the endgame they were now playing. That shook him because it rang so true and he didn't even want to think about what it might really mean, deep down.

She smiled when she heard it, threw her mind back to those classics periods in the finishing school in New England, looked at Hal and said, mock theatrically, ' "But screw your courage to the sticking-place and we'll not fail." '

Then kissed him, just as theatrically too, and as he tasted her mouth, he watched Quinn laughing out of the corner of his eye.

'I don't want you sleeping with him any more,' he said after that. 'You get me?'

And she smiled back, looked so happy, so certain, so sure of herself, and said, 'I don't want it either.'

Which said it all. From then on, it was all a question of time, it was all a question of planning and working and thinking, and that all came, just naturally, as something they did together. And Louise Gostelow, who would never need money in her life, finally found something that fired her, that gave her existence some shape, some reality. Finally understood that planning and scheming and working out where the cracks in the wall were likely to appear, these were her gifts, these were what made her whole.

When they started thinking about the last day, trying to work out what finally happened then, the first thing he said was, 'This is not *Dirty Harry*, Louise. This is real life. We can't play those games. We can't play cops and robbers because we're *not* robbers. We're not crooks. We don't have guns. I don't *want* guns.'

'You need something, Hal,' she said, and she meant it. 'We've got guns, back in Telegraph Hill. You need something.'

'I don't know how to use a gun. I don't *want* to know.'

'You don't need to know. But *I* want to. I need to. You just leave this to me.'

And the way she said it, there was no refusing, however much he hated the idea.

'OK. But you don't let that get anywhere near Michael, you understand? You don't even let Michael know you have a gun.'

She nodded. 'That makes sense.'

And said nothing for a while.

'Hal?'

He was poring over a map of Chinatown, trying to bring it all to life in his head. Trying to have alternatives, options, the flexibility to change things if he needed to, trying to work out what resources there were at his disposal. And when he looked at her, something in his heart turned, missed a beat.

'What happens to Michael?' she said, smiling, looking so lovely, so *perfect*. 'What *will* happen to Michael?'

This was not something for a discussion, not something he was prepared to argue, in part because he feared it would be hard to win.

'Things go right, we look after him. Plain and simple as that. Michael's crazy but he's not stupid. He knows that one of us goes, one of us talks, we all fall. Hell, Louise, we *all* know that. They catch me somehow, I put up my hand for *everything*. Except killing the first kid and they can't pin that on anyone anyway, can't even pin it on Michael if he keeps shaking his head and saying no. Same goes for you. Remember the Three Musketeers? All for one, one for all. It's the only way.'

'You can't look after someone for their entire life, Hal. It doesn't make sense.'

'None of this makes sense. We've just got to try to cope. You think about it. We abandon Michael, any of us abandons the others, we've got someone in the hands of the cops with a grudge. What do you think's gonna happen then? The FBI . . . everybody's looking for us. One of us gets caught, that's a different thing. You got a reason to stay quiet. But you get betrayed, you betray the people you think put you there.'

'Yes,' she said, and nothing more, though he could tell from her eyes, from her face, that something was going on there, something he'd maybe hear about later. And he had to say it.

'Louise,' Hal Jamieson said. 'I am not a criminal. I do not hurt people. I do not kill them. Killing people – all this shit we've got ourselves into – it's wrong. We *have* to remember that. We have to get out of this in a way that means we don't just go round the loop and wind up back here again some other day.'

She smiled, and he knew right then she could make him do almost anything she wanted. *Almost.*

'I know,' she said.

'And all these decisions about who goes where, these are for later. We've got to think about the day. On the day we play smart. That's the only thing we've got over them, Louise. The *only* thing and if we don't use it we're dead. We play like this is *Dirty Harry*, we're dead. Only way we win this is by being what we are. Smart college kids. Thinking our way through and then getting on with the job. And that's going to be hard. Because there just aren't enough of us.'

She didn't like the look in his face. For the first time, the first time she could remember, Hal Jamieson looked as if he might have doubts.

'You got me. You got Michael.'

'You're going nowhere near this pick-up, Louise. That's not just me being chivalrous. I need you to look after Mouse and the kid, see what they're doing. And Michael . . . yeah, I got him. What do you think that's worth at the moment? It's not enough.'

So then they sat down again, for hour upon hour, looking at maps and timetables, checking out routes and journey times, thinking about how much two hundred thousand dollars was going to weigh, how long it would take to get the hell out of California by the safest (in other words the most circuitous) route. What vehicles they could legally and safely use to flee the area. And who would do what. Most of all, in the end, who would do what.

They had agreed where they would run to first and that was Oregon, so big, so empty, so easy to disappear into. And, after that, maybe further north. Vancouver looked good, at least you had some kind of law system barrier there that might give you some breathing space if things turned bad. Seattle looked good too and deep down, in some part of them that only lodged notice of the fact, never formalised it, Seattle took root, grew into some distant image of what they might become. Not that they knew the place. But they had some picture in their heads of somewhere that was kind of like San Francisco, kind of like the life they knew now, but older, greyer, more sober, more serious. A place where it rained more often (and Hal Jamieson still had the sweatshirt he brought back there from his one brief stop in Sea-Tac, between flights, the one with the legend 'Seattle Rain Festival, January 1st to December 31st' on the front). A place where life had a different pitch, a different intensity. A place where you could grow older without looking behind your back all the time. Because Hal Jamieson realised one thing above all others. He really wasn't bullshitting Louise: he really *didn't* feel cut out to be a crook. If you could get some seed money that way, no problem. Just the once. But where his future lay was some place else, legitimate and safe and prosperous through his, through their, efforts. And he promised himself that when he had that place, when he was founding that prosperity too, he would give them, give Louise and Michael, a share in it too. Because that was what they deserved. That was what was right. He owed them that and Hal Jamieson was never one who liked having debts around his neck.

So the plans they made were immediate ones, plans that took them up to the big day, the sixth of January, and on into the murky few days afterwards. What lay beyond that was merely the foetus of an idea, the foetus of an ambition, but it grew, steadily, inside them.

And these were good plans. These were college kid plans. These were very good indeed, with lots of hooks and options and alternatives you could throw in if things changed a little. You'd have to be stupid to even think about throwing them in the trashcan and walking up to the cops and saying, 'Sorry.'

Good plans except for one thing, one thing that he and Louise had seen so quickly. And that was what he came to think of as 'the resource problem'. The lack of that most basic of commodities: people. His heart sank when she told him how she could fix it. He struggled for some other way, struggled with it for the best part of a day. But when it all came down to it, Louise was right. Louise knew what she was doing too. This was one problem Louise could fix really well, and if it added to the baggage that he had to carry afterwards, in more ways than she could ever begin to guess, then that was something he would just have to face.

When he said yes, when he told her she could do it, she kissed him, she looked so delighted, so in love with something, not him, it couldn't be him, that he just reached forward and held her, held her warm body close to his, and stared over her shoulder into the emptiness of the Barn, wondering what kind of life they were shaping for themselves in this particular furnace, in this particular universe.

TWO

Michael Hears the Roar

Death is the king of this world: 'tis his park
Where he breeds life to feed him.

GEORGE ELIOT, 'The Spanish Gypsy'

Maybe it was the way the big guy hit him, or maybe it was the stinking shit that kept coming out of the trees. Maybe it was anything. Listening to Tom Petty singing 'Don't Come Around Here No More' on the radio, a random quark that had just passed through his gall bladder via Mars and Schenectady, New York. It didn't matter. What mattered was that it had begun. Michael Quinn lay back on his bed in the cabin, half of him listening to the voices outside the door, the low voices that sounded like they were on the other side of the world, and the other half just hearing the roaring, the roaring inside his blood. It had begun, the thing had woken up inside him and it was on the march, cell by cell, hot and murderous. And Quinn discovered something new about himself, something that had never occurred to him over the years – the *what the fuck?* years – and that was the simplest thing. He was afraid. He knew the sound, the dull, relentless murmur of fear, of mortality, at the back of his head, and its total absence from his life, from his consciousness, until now, made it all the more real, all the more terrifying. Listening to the virus roaring through his blood, Michael Quinn was briefly in touch with something human in himself, something that breathed in deeply, shrieked and reached out for help. Reached out into nothingness.

There was a sound at the door and he turned to look. The big pine slab swung back. There was Louise Gostelow and Michael Quinn found it hard to believe this was really happening. He could have been somewhere else, in a wooden building twenty years ago, he could have been looking at her then. The clothes were different, more elegant, more expensive. There was more make-up, maybe a few more lines in the face, a little heaviness in the lower body. But this was unmistakably Louise, with her shining eyes, with her gleaming black hair, and the smile. The smile that didn't mean anything, ever.

'Lady Macbeth,' Michael Quinn said and tried not to notice the look in her own face, the look of surprise, maybe shock, at seeing him. Ordinarily this wouldn't have bothered him. You grew older, you looked like shit. But it was different with Louise. With Louise you somehow always wanted to look your best, always wanted to make an impression. And Michael Quinn knew exactly what that gleaming shock of skull, the emaciated gauntness of his face did to people. Maybe she could hear the roaring in his blood too, maybe that was another of Louise's talents.

He looked like shit and crazy shit at that. And this was one of those rare times it seemed to bother him.

'Michael, Michael,' she said in a dreamy, detached kind of way that didn't fool him for a moment. 'All these years. All that wasted time. What *are* we going to do with you?'

'You'll think of something, Louise. You *always* think of something,' he said, and wished he hadn't.

'And we got someone dead already, Michael. That's fast work. Even for you. Not much more than a week out, and we're cleaning up behind you. Some things never change.'

'Accidents happen.' He shrugged, wishing he couldn't hear this roaring inside, so loud, so gushing, that it was impossible to believe, absolutely impossible, that she couldn't hear it herself.

'Around you, Michael, accidents happen all the time,' she said, then watched him, waiting for the moment, feeling the air.

'Tell me,' she said eventually, and her face was so radiant that even Quinn, who now knew that he would no longer have any interest in sex, in something that physical, not because of what was in his blood but because that was just how things were, just couldn't take his eyes away. It was so beautiful it *shone*. It had simple stark ecstasy written there, the sublime ecstasy of seeing, knowing the world as it is, and being able to control what was there, every last element of it. And, for Michael Quinn, that was a shocking realisation. To know that Desert Rose had saved its greatest gift for someone else and given this mastery of the world and the people in it to Louise.

'Tell me, Michael. Where were you going to run to?'

Some questions you answer, some you don't. How do you explain to someone like Louise, someone who feels a different godhead roaring inside her blood, that sometimes you don't run *to* things, you run *from* them. You don't even try.

'Malibu,' he said. 'I got an itch to become a surfer.'

And they both laughed, neither feeling the slightest humour inside them.

'There's someone to meet you,' she said. 'Someone to meet all of us.'

'That why the big guy was so keen to get me in here without you seeing?'

She smiled at him. 'He thought that maybe you'd like to clean up. You look . . .'

The words just hung in the air, then Louise Gostelow turned and he got up, followed her through the main room; she opened the door into the kitchen with the gleaming pine table. Hal Jamieson was there, he sat at one end, in the master chair, a big mug of coffee in front of him. Baxter hung in the background, huge and silent, and Quinn could feel the big guy's eyes staring into him. It made the wound on the side of his head start hurting again, so that he was aware that it was starting to weep, the corpuscles coming to the surface and blinking at the daylight. And the woman. This young, thin, pale woman, with such bright, piercing eyes, and the radiant blonde hair, so full of light it almost hurt your eyes, and she was just staring at him, watching the blood drain from his face, staring at him as if she wished she could be anywhere else in the world but here right now.

He sat down opposite her, tried to smile, and she seemed both frightened and fascinated, she couldn't take her eyes off him much as she wanted to.

His blood wasn't just roaring now, it was booming, booming in big waves that pumped and raced with every beat of his heart, and they had to be able to hear that, they just *had* to. He swallowed. His throat was dry. There was the taste of blood in his mouth. Michael Quinn realised, for the first time, that he was actually starting to feel ill. That this was how it began. The long trip down the hill. And you couldn't see what was at the bottom, or how long the street ran because at the foot there was just some big dark cloud, like a thunderstorm that had got its polarity switched and was coming up from the earth instead of down from the sky.

326

The thin pale woman was still staring at him and she said, in a voice that sounded so strained, so foreign, 'I am Miles Seymour's sister.'

The words just hung in the air of the room like bubbles from some strip cartoon suddenly made real, weighing down on them, ready to fall to the floor with a thud.

Quinn smiled, to his surprise he really did manage it. Then, like a school teacher pondering a question, he pointed one finger towards the ceiling, and said, 'Ah.'

Waited, and asked, 'Anyone going to offer me a drink around here?'

THREE

Mr Cat

Duties are not performed for duty's sake, but because their
neglect would make the man uncomfortable. A man performs
but one duty – the duty of contenting his spirit, the duty of
making himself agreeable to himself.

MARK TWAIN, 'What is Man?'

We're on a road to nowhere
Come on inside

TALKING HEADS,
'Road to Nowhere'

Tom Cordobes knew, deep inside himself, this was going to be the
last time he ever looked at Cy Langton and didn't say what he was
thinking. Didn't say, no, this is crazy, this is wrong, this just won't
work. Whichever way the day worked out, he'd earned the right for a
little frankness, one way or the other.

Later, he tried to tell himself he said nothing because there was no
point. The old man was just so set on things, so set on this being
something that stayed within the department, didn't bring in the Feds
or the city people, didn't go outside his own, well-defined territory,
that it was impossible to get him even to think outside the box. We
handle it and we *finish* it, was what Langton said, and there was no
question of debate.

Tom Cordobes wanted to tell himself he said nothing just for that
reason alone, and not because some little voice inside kept on intoning
that maybe he really was still a little scared, scared for his job, scared
for his future. Scared this thing might get out of hand and all the little
messes along the way, from Roscoe Sutter's confession to the crazy
decision not to go house to house until it was so late, until the kid
could be just *anywhere*, all these things were going to come down on
their heads. No. His head. Cy Langton was a gruff old cop with an

328

inborn talent for getting out from under. Maybe he was going to need it this time. But if Langton was going to walk the plank, you could bet he'd be pushing a lot of men overboard in front of him first.

'You see what I'm doing with this one, Tom. We contain him. We shrink the net. We move. And you're there first. You do what you judge is right. That's your decision. I just *know* you'll make the right one.'

Cordobes picked up the transparent plastic folder on the desk and read the second note.

> This is the final communication. The kid's alive right now but 11 am tomorrow we kill him unless the money's in our hands. You don't show, we kill him. You don't do exactly what we say, we kill him. You got to believe this because this is TRUE. One cop. Wears a grey suit. Carries one yellow bag with the money in. No guns. We'll be checking. 10 am by the slip road, main football field, Thoreau Park, tomorrow. Nice and open there. You stake it out, you put cop cars around, we get to see and the whole thing's off. You know what happens next. You do this right, the kid's yours. That's the deal. Take it or leave it.
> Mr Cat.

'Same typewriter,' Cordobes said. 'Same people. Genuine.'

'Yeah,' Cy Langton nodded. And didn't say, didn't want to get into an argument just now in the proceedings – that could wait – that it was all they had. That Cordobes and his men had turned over the underside of half of east Palo Alto, the drug dives, the whoreshops, the pimps and the thieves of most of the area, and come up with nothing. Not a single thing except that look of outraged innocence: *sure, we move smack, sure, we got women, but you think we'd do something like this?*

'Thoreau Park,' Cordobes said, mainly to himself. 'What the fuck would some east-side hood know about Thoreau Park? Where in God's name is all this coming from? Mr Cat? How the fuck did he come up with a crazy name like that?'

Langton folded his arms and did his best to look like a captain, like he knew things other cops didn't have access to. 'They get these names outta their books, Tom. You mark my word. There's some subversive junk out there, maybe from those Black Panther guys, and it's got Mr Cat in it. You bet. As for the park, maybe it's convenient. Think about it. It *is* convenient. For them.'

329

Thoreau Park was an average-sized sports field just off the university campus, one side running along El Camino, criss-crossed by a couple of dirt slip roads for the park people who kept the grass half green the majority of the time. Most days you could see people playing football, sometimes soccer, there. It was on the opposite side of the busy highway to the Gresham Woods and would one day form part of the valuable real estate that was sold to become the great Gresham Mall. But right now it was just flat open grass, so open you could see who was moving there for a good mile in every direction. And there was no way you could park on the slip roads, that was too obvious. Or on El Camino, since parking was banned there and anyone who tried it was likely to have some irate accountant from Hewlett-Packard yelling through the window and calling the cops the moment you came to a halt in the constant traffic.

'It's a smart place to try for it,' said Langton again. 'Either he goes for somewhere with lots of people or hardly any people at all. Makes sense.'

'Yeah,' Cordobes said. But it was nagging him. 'Lot of guys from the east side gonna know about Thoreau Park? Sure. Where else they spend their days? Couple of hours in the Stanford library then a game of *soccer* before they shift some dope?'

He shook his head. 'There is something so . . . *odd* about this.'

'Yeah,' Langton grunted, and he really didn't want to think about *oddness* right now, he really wanted Cordobes to get on with the job. 'Well, we can think about all that stuff later. All we need worry about now is how we make sure these guys don't run away with us. We get close enough to trip them up. You get in there. You get the kid out . . .'

Tom Cordobes just looked at him and didn't need to say anything. He could feel his career slipping away by the second.

'. . . or you do just what you got to do. That's the score.'

'What do I get authorised to carry?'

'What do you want?'

'What I took out already. The .45. I been working with it. One of those new radios too. The small ones. What kind of range they give?'

'Six, eight miles. So the salesmen say.'

'One of those.'

'Fine. Anything else?'

'Not that *I* can think of.'

'Me neither, Tom. We got the cover arranged. Some guys will be

330

playing a practice game on one of the fields, they should be able to keep a good eye on you. Also we got some others around the edge. Nothing too obvious. Nothing he can pick up.'

'He's picked them up already. He *knows* we're gonna do that.'

'That case there's no reason we should disappoint him now, is there? We got vehicles close by too. You can interrogate the guy there. Do pretty much what you like. No one else is gonna be around.'

'That simple?'

'Jesus, Tom. You know how these cases run. I been through the files, the stats. Kidnapping is a low-grade offence. The people do this kind of thing are *stupid*. Sure, they get to kill people from time to time but they get *caught*. They get caught 'cos they're stupid. Plain and simple. This guy's gonna have a plan, for sure. Maybe he's gonna run you around a little. There's a public phone in the park. I got that checked out. We'll put a tap on there. Maybe it rings, maybe you answer it, he tells you to go some place else. What the fuck? Sooner or later you're gonna have to do something with the money, you're gonna have to give it him. This is a nice town, mostly, full of honest people, but I don't see him letting you put the bag down in the street and walk away. Do you? Sooner or later you have to *hand it over*. And maybe he will run you around, send you some place else. But the guy's got his own deadline. Says right here on paper. He don't have the money in his hands by eleven in the morning the kid's dead. This is gonna happen real fast, real quickly, whether it's in Thoreau Park or some place else, and when it does . . .'

'That's *his* deadline,' Cordobes said. 'That's what *he* says.'

'This guy isn't half as clever as you think, Tom. Like I said. Look at the files. Look at the stats. Losers do kidnappings. It's a dumb crime perpetrated by dumb people. You just wait. Some point tomorrow this creep is gonna come out and ask you for that bag. Then you got your moment.'

'Then . . . ?'

Langton breathed a big deep sigh.

'You want it spelling out?'

'That would be nice.'

'You know I can't do that, Tom. You know I can't write you a letter on that stuff.'

And it was good to watch the old man squirm. Good to be in *that* position for a change.

'I'd like to hear it. Really I would. Just between the two of us.'

Langton's mouth went entirely horizontal. There was no blood in the two flat lines of his lips. No blood in the grey face, with its early traces of bristle already starting to appear.

'What I want,' he said, after a while, 'is for you to take this guy, when you finally get hold of him, and you get out of him where the rest of them are. The address. When you get that, you radio it to us and we got a whole SWAT team ready to go in. Get the kid out alive, if he still *is* alive. And meantime, what happens between you and your guy is up to you, Tom. *Whatever.* Like I said, we got two bodies or more on the ground after this one, we get to win. We got just one, and that's the kid's, and we got a whole lot of trouble on our hands. I'm relying on you there, Tom. And I *know* you can do it. Plain as that.'

Plain as that, Tom Cordobes thought to himself. How Cy Langton loved that phrase. How he loved the idea of a simple, predictable world, where everything was black and white and you didn't need to worry about any shades of grey in between that might send you down to hell if you just happened to step on the cracks.

'That's the plan?'

'That's the plan.'

Tom Cordobes nodded. You met people like Cy Langton in the military. They got their desks. They got their medals. They even got their MBAs from Harvard. And when things got rough, when things weren't about logistics or manpower or personnel, they just went running, found the nearest *real* soldier and said, 'You fix it. You know how. We're turning our backs right now and really we don't want to even *know* how you do what you do. But when we turn right round again, we want it done. We want to be able to walk out there and let the cameras roll and say, "Pat me on the back because I just came through with the goods again." '

Yeah, Cordobes thought to himself. Sometimes the military and the cops looked much like the same thing. Sometimes, when you were a foot soldier, the only difference was the clothes you wore and the place you happened to be fighting.

FOUR

Michael Peers Beneath the Surface

Valour is of no service, chance rules all, and the bravest often
fall by the hands of cowards.   TACITUS,
                                                The Histories

He stared into the glass of Cabernet Sauvignon and thought how much
it looked like blood, how it had the same dark, viscous redness about
it, how even though there was no way you could see beyond the
surface, the opaque meniscus, see what lay beneath there, what moved
and shifted in the thick liquid hidden underneath, you could still sense
the movement, the complex structure that ran right down to the
molecules, the convoluted soup that made it what it was. It tasted like
blackberries that had sat for too long in a vat, and he gulped it
down, not liking the taste, knowing that this was something that was
disappearing from him too, knowing that one of the changes in his
body would lie in its ability to assimilate these chemicals, these *poisons*,
that once seemed so familiar, so essential.

'You are very brave, Miles Seymour's sister,' Quinn said, in a voice
he tried to make mock noble, mock English, and returned her stare.
She was striking, not beautiful. The golden shock of her hair stood
around her head like a halo. She was thin and pale. He couldn't read
her expression, couldn't read the shifting mix of emotions there. It
could be hatred, it could be pity, it could be anything in between.
And Joni Lascelles gave him no clues. She did this quite deliberately.
When she knew, when she was sure, that there was something wrong
here – and that had happened in the car, though she refused to
recognise it – she had felt some kind of relief, some sort of satisfaction
that events, finally, had started to pick up their own momentum. That
the endgame, whatever it was, now seemed to be in place, and was
taking her with it, to wherever it felt like going. Joni Lascelles was

333

not daunted by this and, somewhat to her surprise, she was not frightened. She did not regret her decision to leave the gun behind in the case in the Pequod. She did not fear these people, what they might do, or even what they stood for in the jumble of emotions and events and tragedies that made up her past and formed her present.

She stared back at Michael Quinn and decided to take him – to take *them* – for what they were. Another generation, worn down by the same sadness that afflicted her, looking for some way to shake it from their bones.

'These are serious people,' Quinn said, smiling, looking at her in a way that spoke of complicity. 'My friends here. They really deserve to be left alone.'

'I didn't invite myself here,' she said, and there was some steel to her voice that they all noticed. 'I was brought.'

Quinn grinned at her. She could smell the miasma from his throat, from his yellow, tombstone teeth.

'But you was *looking*, girl,' he said, in an accent that was meant to sound black and southern, it was so corny, so forced. 'You was *looking*!'

'Where is Mr Cordobes?' she asked. 'I was told he would be here.'

'Ah . . .' Quinn said, back to his normal, somewhat vapid voice, then stared at the shiny surface of the table and said nothing for a while.

'Mr Cordobes, the famous Mr Cordobes. They told you that? *Louise* told you that?'

She looked at Louise, at Jamieson. The woman stared back at her, half smiling, refusing to speak. The man seemed lost for words, seemed as if all the sadness and guilt in the world had just descended on his head.

'Where is he?'

'We met once before,' Michael Quinn said. 'I think I came out best this time.'

And she watched them around the table, trying to work out what was happening, not to her, but between them. Trying to work out the balance here, between Quinn, who looked half crazy, the long-haired man she'd heard called Hal, and the woman, Louise, the woman that, the more she thought about it, the more she disliked. This was not simple. These relationships did not make themselves plain. Not even to those they entwined.

'Cordobes is dead,' Quinn said flatly. '*Dead.* Mark the word. It's gonna be applying to you and me real soon. Right, Louise?'

And it was Hal who answered, Hal who looked at her, and there was something in him that spoke of so much pain, something she recognised.

'It was an accident,' he said. 'A mistake. Your man just broke in here, there was a fight. He was killed. I wasn't here. If I was, I could have stopped it. That does *not* mean . . .'

Quinn was grinning, skull gleaming, yellow teeth bright in the big room. And Hal Jamieson was close to losing his temper.

'Michael,' he said very slowly, very deliberately. 'Michael, it seems like I have spent most of my life either cleaning up after you or waiting for the next pile of crap to come in right after the last one. Those days are over. Those solutions are over. We grew up while you were in the pen. We got old. We got serious. We got weights on our shoulders and they help keep us in place. We did not want to behave like that then. We *would* not if you had given us a choice. Now, those days are over.'

And it sounded nice, it *was* nice, except she couldn't read the expression on Louise's face. More than that, Hal, who surely was this woman's husband, you could sense, could feel this much between them, couldn't read it either. That worried him, she thought, and if he was worried, maybe they all should be worried too.

Joni Lascelles said, 'I didn't come here to find out about Cordobes.' And realised how hard it sounded, realised it was the kind of thing they could have said. That she didn't really own, or mean the words, that they just came out that way because that was what was expected of her, that was what they wanted her to say.

'No,' Jamieson said, looking directly into her face, and she could tell right then that he was a good salesman, he had the voice, the looks, the poise, the conviction. 'The Cordobes guy is a different issue. He was breaking in here, for chrissake, and that is not a smart thing to do. You're here because of what happened all those years ago and that *was* a tragedy. There's no denying it. You don't want to know the details. You just got to take my word on it. Michael here is sick. He should never have been allowed to do what he did. But what we got to do now is set things right as much as we can. I know that's never going to be enough but it's the best we can do. And we'll do it. You're owed that.'

'I just want to know what happened to him,' she said, and the words tasted dry in her mouth. 'If he's alive. If he's dead, where. It's . . .'

And there really was no point in trying to explain. It made no sense to her, believing that there would be some comfort in burying a set of dry white bones. It could make no sense to them. The dividing line between yesterday and today, which once seemed so vague, so mutable, was now starting to become obvious, to stand out in the sand.

'I just need to know,' she said. 'I feel responsible.'

The word just floated in the air between them, all of them, and they let it hang there for a good half-minute before Hal Jamieson spoke.

'You weren't responsible. We were. It was entirely our doing. Everyone in this room, bar Mr Baxter there. We did it. You have nobody to blame but us.'

Louise smiled and said quietly, 'And one more. One more to come.'

Joni Lascelles heard, but she didn't need to get side-tracked. She said, 'Is he dead?'

But Hal Jamieson wasn't thinking about that. He was thinking about the tone in Louise's voice, and that certainty that something was going on here. That there was something in the air he didn't like. Didn't like at all.

FIVE

An Act of Trust

A wonderful thing to reflect upon, that every human creature
is constituted to be that profound secret and mystery to each
other.   CHARLES DICKENS,
A Tale of Two Cities

Some are born to sweet delight,
Some are born to endless night.
                        WILLIAM BLAKE,
                    Auguries of Innocence

This was the position she liked best, she said. They sat facing each other on the bed and he moved gently inside her. This was the position where no one ruled, where no one was dominant, there was no force, only the warm damp softness of their skin, meeting, remeeting, and the totality of their fucking. This was fucking for the mind, she said, this was the second stage of fucking, the first being the purely physical thing, the red roar in your head, the lostness and the rage. This was the second stage, where you fucked somewhere else, somewhere your body took you to and kept you there, somewhere behind your eyes, where all that shapelessness took form, where she could move so slowly, waiting, fading, then rising, feel him softening almost imperceptibly within her, then, with a gesture, her lips on his nipple, the warm hard ivory of her teeth on his neck, bring him back to hardness, so hard she could pivot her body forward, pivot herself on him, bring his strength to bear on this strange, hot focal point that was part of her body, but part of something else too, let the world burst red and hot and wild inside her mind, then rest, with him still there, his presence, gently moving, waiting, locked together, waiting.

And they could talk too, they could fuck and talk, and this was new to him, this *all* was new. Louise could say things to him, in the big white bed in the big and empty timbered house on Telegraph Hill, things that told him the world was like this and would be always, that told him some corner in his life had been rounded, turning what he thought was a dirt track into some great, broad highway stretching out forever into the distance. He lost count of the hours they spent on the big white bed, he lost count of the times they coupled there, how many times, with what ingenuity, what curiosity, they explored their bodies, probing, tasting, testing the damp flesh, the dark salty mats of hair, whispering, listening to each other's breath, the laboured panting, the rhythm of sex, rolling, entwined, like a single creature, sinews, skin, sweat interwoven in joy, in an ecstasy he couldn't begin to give a name.

'What does it feel like?' she would ask. 'When you come?'

And he would try to describe something that was so elusive, so beyond plain words that you could find in a dictionary. Then ask her too and she would say, 'Like something opening, opening a jar of something sweet that comes from inside you.'

Sometimes she would make him fuck her so physically, with such force, at such speed, that it shocked him, made some darkness come down in his head that came close to frightening him. Sometimes it would be the opposite. So slow that time stopped and he wondered whether they would ever reach the end, and she would wait, wait until he was falling, slipping away from her, then tighten her grip, talk to him, kiss him, bite him, take control of his body. For her, they both knew, this was the best way, and this was the way too that took the most from him. That drained him. The truth was, whatever the position, whatever the way their bodies interlocked, it left him in her power, and they both knew it.

The light was fading outside and this was not just the end of the afternoon. The weather was on the change. After days of sun, the sea fogs were starting to gather out in the ocean, gather like grey amorphous ghosts in the distance, wondering discursively when to move, when to come in from the passive salty waters and swamp the land. She held the nape of his head in her hand, feeling the sweat there, listening to the sex noises, the soft liquid sound of their groins coming together, and stared out of the window, judging his movements inside her, wondering, when she contracted herself around him, how much he could feel, wondering whether it could be this easy to manipulate his physical being, to think about her own muscles, the tightness of herself, to flow along his strength, teasing the life out of him, teasing until he could not hold back. Paul Dunsany arched, his body out of control, the breath breaking from his lungs, felt himself stiffening, jerking, as if from an electric shock, and then the warmth came inside her, coated the mysterious inner self that Louise Gostelow thought of as *her*. And she smiled out of the window. Smiled at the change.

She felt nothing, or almost nothing. Louise knew those secrets, she knew about the first stage of fucking, and she knew about the second. But she also knew, with a rookie mathematician's eye, that there was a thing called the S-curve. What that meant, what that would always mean, was that there was a third stage too. After the physicality, after the higher place, the place where the physicality took you on tiptoes and let you almost touch the sky, there was a third stage, back down in the physical region. Where what happened turned into the humping and grinding of bodies, the passing of fluids. Procreation and child-rearing. Counting the times, fucking by rote. An act of familiarity among friends, with no passion, and no panting. And, most of all, no shapeless imaginary creatures dancing in the dark, the depthless dark, of your head. It was an S-curve and the only thing that was different, from lover to lover, was the unit of measurement you used in the x-axis, whether you went through stages one to three in days, weeks, months or maybe – and for Louise Gostelow this was pushing things – in years. It was all a question of timing.

She let him come down from whatever place he'd reached – Paul was in the second stage, would always be in the second stage – then gently pulled herself away from him, rolled back on the bed, wiped the sweat from her face, reached to the floor, pulled on a cream silk shirt. After the heat of their sex, the room felt cool. She lay back on the pillow and looked at him, her olive skin radiant underneath the unbuttoned shirt. He couldn't take his eyes off the intense excitement in her face, the paleness of her breasts, the dark, full triangle of hair. The room smelled of sex, smelled of semen and the undercurrent of fucking, something like ozone, something like the smell you got when a power cable snapped, then whipped around fizzing, crackling, look-ing for release.

She reached for a cigarette and said, quite suddenly, quite seriously, 'We ought to get away, Paul. We ought to be free of all this. *All* this.'

It happened so swiftly he wondered whether he really heard right. He looked around the room, the big white room, out of the window, at the view out to the ocean. The fog had joined together now, joined

339

into a band of opaque greyness that was moving in slowly across the water. You could almost feel the cold push of air that was rolling in front of it. A foghorn boomed on the stillness.

'Who'd want to leave all this, Louise?' he said, staring into nothing. 'Who would ever want to leave all this?'

'Paul?'

He looked at her and wished she wasn't going to say this thing, wished he couldn't feel it all winding down.

'Paul. They're coming back. This week. I have things to do. You have to go. They can't know you've been here.'

'I know,' he said. 'But some time, Louise. Some time.'

And she just shook her head and said, 'Paul. You don't know my family. We're bloodstock. There's a line to perpetuate. That's not my way of thinking, that's *theirs*. But I can't change that. It's how it is.'

'Yeah,' he said, and looked around the room for his clothes, looked at the furnishings and the paintings, the embroidered quilt that now lay on the floor, the *money*.

'Yeah,' he said. And wondered where the hell it would all lead, wondered if he really wanted to find out.

She came over to him on the bed and her face was shining, *shining*, she wouldn't let him look away.

'How much do you want me, Paul?'

The greyness outside the window seemed to become a whole degree more palpable, a whole degree more real.

'You need me to answer that?'

'I need you to say it. I *need* you to. It's important to me.'

And you didn't grow up where Paul Dunsany did and learn the kinds of words he wanted to use. They didn't come easily, they didn't shape in his head.

'I don't know *how* to say it, Louise,' he said eventually. 'I don't have that kind of ability. I love you. I feel things when I'm with you, not just in bed, but *with* you, things that make me feel real. That make me feel the world's a real place and I don't want to be anywhere in it without you.'

You didn't ask for a return serve on that one, he said to himself. You didn't want to find out.

'We could be free of this, Paul,' she said, and her eyes wouldn't leave his, her eyes wouldn't let him escape. 'All of this. Having to rely on *them*. I run away with you now, Paul, and I'm out of *everything*.

They just cut me off and I don't have a thing. You believe that, because it's true. That's what they're like. But we get the money, we could be free of them, we could go do what we like. Build a life. Be together. We might have to go away. But I don't care. So long as it's with you, I don't care.'

He blinked and the greyness outside was almost painful, there was something so bright behind the dead lead sheet that had fallen across the sky that it seemed to fill the room with its wan, sick light.

'I don't understand,' he said.

'There are things going on, with Hal, with Michael, things you don't need to know about, Paul. Things you can forget. But there's money coming through there and we could get some of it. We could get a lot of it. We could get enough to get away. Be together.'

He didn't want to hear this, he didn't want to feel himself even thinking about it, weighing the thing in some set of scales inside his head.

'Louise,' he said, and wished she wasn't watching him so closely, so intently, 'I smoke a little dope if it's there, but I'm not involved in this thing. I don't want to get involved in dope. I don't want *you* to get involved. That's not a moral thing. I just don't want trouble with the law. That's not going to help us.'

Then she kneeled upright on the bed, came to him, put her arms around his neck, stared him in the face, as if she was trying to give him something, trying to offer him strength.

'This is a one-shot deal, Paul. You go with them, you fetch something, you carry. They need you, Paul. They can't do it on their own. And *I* need you. Because once you do that, we're out of here. We're out of this life. We can start again and we can do it together. It doesn't mean we *ever* have to do this again. We just get free.'

'Free,' he said, and listened to the sound of the word bounce around the big white room.

'I've been thinking about this ever since we came here, Paul, ever since I left the Barn. I've been thinking about nothing else. I love you. I want you. I want us to be together. But if we wait, if we hesitate, then they will have me, Paul. They will wheel in some goddamned society jerk and *have me*. I break loose or they make me part of all *this*. If I stay, I don't get the choice. You believe me, don't you?'

He said yes, it just happened automatically. Choices. It all came down to choices.

'I need you to save me, Paul,' she said. 'We do this just the once. Then we get out of here, out of this life, forever. We get out and we're together.'

She leaned forward, looked into his eyes, kissed him hard, held his face tightly, so tightly he didn't think he could move from this place, move from the power, the strength of her embrace.

'We do this all tomorrow,' she said. 'We start at eight. Come midday, we're free. You and me.'

Through the open window came the low, distant rumble of thunder, some massive knot of blue fire and writhing energy hidden from view in the rolling grey cloud that was starting to sweep the city, the real, the living world, that had disappeared from his view, disappeared from his thoughts the moment they had rolled under the great soft white coverlet in the bedroom of the mansion on Telegraph Hill.

SIX

Miles Reborn

Monty this seems strange to me.
The movies had that movie thing,
but nonsense has a welcome ring
and heroes don't come easy.

REM, 'Monty Got a Raw Deal'

He was awake now, and he could speak, slowly, incoherently, but you could understand the words most of the time, even if they didn't always make sense. Miles could speak, and Margie could listen, keep on listening, forever, waiting until there was a time when she could talk back to him and hear something that was like recognition, something that meant he was starting to heal.

The cellar was so fetid. It stank of them, their excrement, their sweat. She had spent so long under the yellow light – *how long? how long?* – that she had no idea what day it was any more. But there was something in the way Hal spoke that told her change was on the way. And you could feel it in the atmosphere too, the cloying high pressure that found its way into this little dirt hole and told them this present state, this present arrangement of affairs, would not last long.

And when it came, she found herself wishing it would take longer, wishing she could stay there another hour, another day. Whatever the four dirt walls were, they were also security. They felt safe, and outside had nothing in it but doubt. Margaret Zalinski, who no longer thought of herself as Mouse, would scarcely even recognise the name, feared what was to come. Feared the outcome. Feared the decisions more.

Hal Jamieson came down the stairs, undid the chains on the child, held the ladder while they climbed out into the stuffy, humid night. She blinked. It seemed too bright. The sky was a velvet cloak of blue marked by the scattered yellow points of stars, a hint of haze high up. This was the Bay area and this was the Bay area weather. In the city, twenty miles away on the coast, it was already deep, thick fog, a vast grey blanket that swirled through everywhere, found every corner of the street, of people's lives. But out here, close to the rumbling traffic of El Camino, close to the passing metal thunder of the CalTrain line, the sky stayed clear. You could have warm sun in one, cold, bone-chilling cloud right down to the ground in the other. Two sides of the same mirror.

Under the light, Hal's face looked older, there was a tautness, an adulthood there she hadn't really recognised before. He looked at them, asked how the kid was doing. She shrugged.

'He needs a doctor, Hal. I can look after him. I can keep him whole. Whatever went through his head, it ain't killed him. Just done something to his brain, that's all. Like he went simple or something. He needs a doctor. You gotta fix that.'

'Yeah,' Hal Jamieson said, and knew it was true, just looking at the kid's dark-eyed, fascinated stare, looking at the way he gazed at the stars like they were something he'd never seen before in his life, he knew it was all true.

'First things first, huh, Mouse. You stay close to me. You do what I say. I will see you safe. But you have to trust me.'

And she didn't want to correct him. She didn't want to tell him her real name. Not right then. But there would come a time. There would come a time when they all knew she was Margaret Zalinski, not someone called Mouse. A person, not a piece of human shit to be kicked around any which way you felt like.

'I got some hot water in the house. Some clean clothes. Tonight, we get out of here, we get away from this place and we start finding something new. I promise that.'

'And Michael?' she said, feeling cold just at the sound of his name.

'You keep out of his way, now. You hear me? You keep out of his way, keep the kid out of his way too, and everything will be all right.'

'Yeah, Hal,' she said, and she could almost believe it. She could almost think this was true. She looked at the stars so Hal Jamieson couldn't see her weeping. This was the moment, she thought. This was the moment when maybe they could've escaped. They could've got outside and just run for it, if he could run, just let their legs take them all the way through the wood, all the way past the bums and the big green playing field where the college kids played football, past the railroad line, down on into University Avenue, yelling and shouting and screaming all the time, and that way they'd be free – *but they'd take him away, Margie, you know they'd take him away* – and as for what happened after that, well, you just waited and waited, and hoped that somewhere there was a God in the world, someone who could put the grey people, the social workers and the cops and all the other people who used to look at her when she was a kid, shake their heads and say, 'Well, what *do* we do?', who could put them straight on a few things.

'Yeah, Hal,' she said, looked at Miles, so still, so rapt, looking at the stars, and wondered what he would say, what he would do if she took his hand and tried to tell him, tried to make him race off with her into the night. Miles, so beautiful, so trusting. So damaged, in ways she could only begin to guess at. 'Yeah,' she said, took his hand, and they walked back into the Barn.

It looked so strange to her now. So cold. So without life. So meagre. And Margaret Zalinski promised herself something right then, promised herself that one day, if she got out of all this alive, they'd live somewhere better than this. One day they'd do more than sit around watching the flies shit on the wallpaper, waiting for their lives to flicker out like candle flames in the night breeze.

Quinn grinned at her from the threadbare old armchair by the window. He looked seriously doped up. He looked crazy. She wondered what gap in her own life had ever led her to think there was something right in letting this creature use her body like it belonged to him.

One day . . .

She looked at the pile of faded dresses and the kid's jeans and T-shirts Hal had pointed out, wondered where he'd got them from, picked out a few, stuffed the rest in a plastic carrier bag – you never knew – and then took Miles into the bathroom and started running the water. It flooded out in a rush, two continuous shooting streams icy cold, burning hot, but that didn't matter, because this was water, so pure, so clear, it could wash away anything, and she couldn't wait to get him in there, in with this fast-flowing stream that seemed to promise so much.

'You need to take your clothes off . . .' she said to him, and Margaret Zalinski wondered what was happening in her head, wondered why it was working overtime like this, whether it was the dope, the fucking stupid dope, that Quinn had forced on her, getting some vicious kind of revenge, all these long days afterwards.

'Yeah,' he said, and for the first time she heard the softening – *harshening?* – of his accent, for the first time he didn't sound like one of the kids out of *Mary Poppins*. For the first time he said 'yeah' and not 'yes' and she watched him trying to struggle out of the filthy sack, helped him, held it over his head, didn't want to think about the thing, threw it into the corner, forgot about it, told herself to forget about it forever.

'We ain't got a lot of time,' she said. 'Maybe the best thing is we get in the tub together. You don't mind that. You used to do that back home.'

'Don't mind,' he said, and slowly, like an old man, climbed over the edge of the open-sided bath, stood upright in the water.

'Hot.'

She felt the water. It was way too hot. She cursed herself for not checking it. Not thinking about it. You don't know about these things, she said to herself. You don't *know*.

'Know how to love him,' she muttered. 'Knowing how to take care of him's something you learn out of that.'

Then helped him out, poured some cold into the tub, tested it with one hand, pulled her clothes off with the other. He didn't even look at her. Just kept his hand in the water, seeming amazed at the changing sensation of the fall in temperature.

'OK,' she said, then helped him in, holding his hand, holding his arm until he'd seated himself on the ceramic base, and she remembered how scratched, how old it was, how it felt like you were sitting on sand, and wondered if this could harm him, hurt him somehow.

'Got time to wash your hair, no time to dry it,' she said, trying to put some form to these concerns, sort the real ones from the crazy ones that kept popping into her head. 'That don't matter. It's warm out there. It'll dry soon enough.'

It seemed to take so long, to wash out the filth, to sponge him down, to get the grime, the dirt that seemed to lie in every pore, out of him, so long she looked at the door, took the risk, poured away the first tubful, got him out, poured another, and this stayed cleaner, this just went milky white with the scum from the soap, so she climbed in herself, and they sat opposite each other while she rubbed him down, washed off the suds, watched his face, watched how he enjoyed it. Enjoyed the care. Enjoyed the love. Enjoyed the closeness, this thing that they both found so new, so rare, so wonderful.

'You do this before?' she asked. 'Back home?'

And you could see he just didn't know how to answer. There was no answer there, it was all hidden so deep, buried inside him, that maybe nothing would bring it to the surface, ever, and even if it did appear, he wouldn't know what to make of it, wouldn't recognise the shape, the sound, the smell, the feel of that old life.

Before the Barn. Before Margaret Zalinski.

'Home,' he said, and it was just a statement, it was just a word floating in the steamy air.

'You remember that?' she said. 'You do?'

She felt breathless. It wasn't just the heat. It wasn't just the tub.

He thought about it, slowly shook his head, and smiled, the same smile, nothing changed about the smile. Smiled at the way she was washing his hair, rubbing the soap over his shoulders, smiled at her nakedness and the way it seemed so natural, so familiar.

She leaned over to him, kissed his forehead, and he smiled again. Then she reached down, cupped her hand, let the milky water fill there, lifted it up over his head, let it run down his dark, shining scalp, held her hands out over his brows to make sure it didn't get near his eyes, to make sure nothing was going to hurt him, nothing would *ever* hurt him.

'I'm gonna call you Joe,' she said, and told herself, *swore* to herself that this was not a sin, that God didn't punish you for doing things out of kindness, even if there was something wrong that started it all in the first place. 'You hear that? You're gonna be my Joe. And we're gonna get the hell out of here and go live some place nice. You hear me? Joe?'

He closed his eyes, smiled and pointed to his head. She picked up the milky water in both hands, held it over his head, let it go and it ran down in big, splashing streams, down his face, down his cheeks, over his laughing mouth until so much of it got in there he started to taste it, and spat it out, laughing still. And when she was there, in the tub with him, it was so gorgeous, so delicious, Margaret Zalinski thought that maybe this would be the best moment of their life, the simplest, purest moment they would ever experience. She held him close to her, felt the damp, naked warmth of his skin, stared over his shoulders into nothingness and waited for the tears to go away, waited until he wouldn't be able to see them there, until he'd think it was just the water, running hot and a little thick down his back.

When they'd finished, when they were clean and dressed in these faded new clothes that felt strange to their skin, when they felt all new, all ready for the night, she held him tight to her again, held his face up with her hand, looked at him, tried to make him understand.

'We stay together, Joe,' she said. 'Now on, we're always together.'

'Yeah,' he said, and, listening to his voice, his new voice, if she hadn't known, she'd have said he came from New England, not some other country.

She was still staring at him, so serious, so intense, when the knock came on the door. Then she kissed him again, on the forehead, where he liked it best, and they went out to meet the world.

Hal Jamieson was there, looking so old, so solemn. And outside a VW camper, a pale colour, with a stripe down each side that might be blue in the night light. Hal opened up the back of the camper and they climbed in. There were no windows. Just two bench seats down either side. The darkness, the confinement, which he thought he'd left behind for good, frightened him afresh. She could feel it. He didn't need to say anything. So she held him and he felt her warmth through his new clothes, and then the engine came to life, lights began to wink on the dashboard, Quinn, who was up front in the passenger seat, turned on the radio without looking at them, stared out of the front window without even acknowledging they were there.

The camper pulled out of the drive and away from the Barn, pulled out into El Camino, the evening flow of traffic, people feeling slow and sad and stupid in the hot, fume-laden air.

It took forty-five minutes to get into the city, along the straight flat highway that ran past the airport, by the waterline, a piece of road so familiar to them, and one they could already feel slipping into the past. Change, some big, magical, fundamental change, hung in the air and made it impossible for them to talk sensibly about anything at all.

When they arrived, when they drove up the steep hill at the end of Filbert and parked outside the house on Telegraph Hill, the fog was so dense that you could see nothing for more than a few yards in front. Even the floodlighting around Coit Tower was no more than a faded silver corona somewhere up the hill.

Margaret Zalinski walked into the mansion, looked at its size, its

348

opulence, and knew that whatever was going to happen would happen. That there was now no turning back, no running, no opportunity to do anything but wait and pray.

SEVEN

Crossroads

Got a feeling I've been here before
Watching as you cross the killing floor
You know you'll have to pay it all
You'll pay today or pay tomorrow

STEELY DAN,
'Your Gold Teeth'

When he finally returned to the studio, after so much walking, thinking, deciding that led him to parts of the city he didn't even know
existed, it took ten minutes to discover it was all in vain. Ten minutes
before he got the phone call from Louise, her voice so controlled, so
full of quiet delight. Then, when the call was over, he just walked out
of the studio, took the long flights of steps down to the waterfront,
stood there watching the grey water shifting in slow motion out in
front of him, watched the tourists meandering into the aquarium,
through the lines of souvenir shops, the bars, the restaurants, mooching, mooching. There was something in the situation that made him
hate himself all the more. To reach a crossroads, to decide which road
to choose, that was a big thing for Paul Dunsany, that was something
he usually avoided. And then to find, when you got that far, when
the decision was almost upon you, that someone had made it for you
already. That was like being cheated. That was immoral. That changed
things, for good or bad, in a way that couldn't be undone.

And once you did get that far it was like being on one of the ferries
crossing the Sound. You committed yourself the moment you got on.
There was no turning back, no getting off until you reached the other
end, even if you found you'd got on the wrong one. Even if it scared
the hell out of you. The choice went out of the window. You were
moving, travelling towards wherever the destination just happened to
be, and all you could do was sit and wait until you arrived, then deal
with whatever happened to be waiting there to greet you.

He stood at one of the restaurant counters, bought a bowl of clam chowder, thick and creamy, ate it slowly, turning over the possibilities in his mind, trying to work out how you might shift some of the generalities down into things you could feel and touch, and never asking himself the trust question, never, ever asking himself that, because trust was a thing you couldn't put in words. He'd learned that once before and it seemed to mark him badly, it still, twenty years on, put pictures in his head of damp skin and soft, animal moans, white sheets, white rooms, and he knew now there were some things you couldn't say. That trust was something that lived in the air, in the electric space between people. It was like the real name of God. You couldn't write it down, you couldn't say it because the moment you did, it fell to earth, it disappeared.

It was just after 2 pm. A couple of hours before, three hundred yards away, unknown to him, Ben Rawlins and Joni Lascelles had looked out at the Sound from the bay window of a Chinese restaurant, and wondered what happened next. Now Joni and Louise were together, how he didn't quite understand, and it all seemed to be taking its own course. Paul Dunsany finished the chowder. It felt warm and solid and good inside him. And the odd thing was, in spite of everything, he felt good too. He hadn't been drinking so much since Joni came into his life. The music was good. The studio was a mess. The studio always would be a mess. But for the first time in as long as he could remember there were fine things in his existence, things that moved him, things that he could look forward to and not just deal with, process, in tray, out tray, like some penpusher in some big accountants' office downtown.

Something made him wonder if this wasn't nature's way of forcing a naturally indecisive person to do something. To act. Maybe it was nature's way of saying, 'OK, you're scared, you don't know what to do, you're worried you might lose *everything*. But the bottom line is, they screwed you. They cheated you. They took something away that was yours, not theirs. And that was your right to act, maybe do the wrong thing, who knows, but *your* thing. They took away your right to screw up, and you *deserve* to get mad, you *deserve* to get angry, however badly that sits inside your head.'

He bought a bottle of Redhook, drank from the icy neck, watched the ferries and a big white cruise ship slowly making their way across the horizon. There were mountains in the distance, snow on their peaks, and it was pretty clear just then, clear enough to see the beauty there, the stature, the power of the place. And if the colours were a little faded, if they'd somehow been leeched out of your vision over the years, that was just because you were getting old, the world was getting old. It wasn't a comment, it wasn't a criticism. It was just a little cosmic fatigue, the fabric of everything spinning down a little, yawning, and getting tired.

He finished the bottle, threw it carefully into a trash can so as not to annoy any passing members of the litter police, then walked back up the steps, feeling well, feeling healthy, not getting out of breath, not worrying about his heart, his head, his liver these days. Not exactly feeling young either, but knowing where he stood in the world, and finding that, at least, was something new.

Paul Dunsany walked around the market, looked at the flying fish, talked to people, talked to the right people, talked things through, grew more and more certain. Then went back to the studio, watched Ben Rawlins working with Genius on some new jazz score for a free theatre show, listened to them catching fire as they tapped themes into the Mac, liked what he heard, felt good about it.

Grayson was in the recording room playing Mingus noises on a new fretless electric bass.

'I guess Charlie would kill me he heard that, man,' he said. 'Mingus on an *electric* bass. That heresy or what?'

Paul Dunsany came straight to the point.

'You want *what?*'

Frank Grayson played a violent little run on the bass then stared at him like he was out of his mind.

'Paul. Two objections there. First, even if I *did* find you a gun, you'd probably wind up shooting yourself with it. Second, what makes you think I *know* the kind of people who mess with that stuff?'

He thought about it. 'I shoot myself, Frank, that's my business. And you and Genius and Ben are the only three people I *know* well enough to ask this. You want I should ask *them?*'

Grayson looked through the big glass window at the two of them, heads stuffed down the Mac, grunted and said, 'That's flattery, I guess. Of a kind. But the answer's still no. Definitely *no*. And what the fuck you want with a gun anyway?'

It took around five minutes and he kept it clean and straight and economical with the facts.

When he was done, Grayson looked miserable and said, 'Oh shit. Oh holy fucking shit, Paul.'

Then went into the office and made a call.

EIGHT

Walkie Talkie

It is an odd thing, but everyone who disappears is said to be seen at San Francisco. It must be a delightful city, and possess all the attractions of the next world.

OSCAR WILDE,
The Picture of Dorian Gray

The morning of January 6th was hot and steamy in Palo Alto. On the coast, the storms continued to rumble inside the dense, cloaking fog, a busy time for the weathermen on the local TV stations who had to grin through it all, with their neon jackets and perfect white smiles, and then shrug their shoulders and say, weather like this, who the fuck knows? All that high pressure off the coast just stirred things up into a witches' brew of trouble, and those little black devil thunderstorms could wander in pretty much anywhere they liked, from Monterey all the way up to Fort Bragg, and then have their fun. This was 1975, before people got to thinking about chaos theories and whether the flap of a butterfly's wing in the Amazon rain forest might be the root cause of a prolonged bout of smog in Vladivostok, but if you lived around these parts you knew the idea already, it just sat there in your bones and said: Why worry? What's going to happen is going to happen and there is not a damned thing anyone anywhere can do about it.

Tom Cordobes was drenched inside his light-grey polyester suit by 8.15 that morning, when the briefing finished, when they'd run over all the possibilities in the station briefing room, when he'd cast his eye across the other men and women in the party and thought to himself, it could be worse, Langton could have picked a less worthy bunch to tail him. Some of the guys were in sports outfits already and they looked the part if you didn't examine them too closely. They weren't young enough, really, and if you looked into their faces there was that dull, almost stupid look of mute aggression that marked out someone who had taken this noble profession on as a career, then found out, too late, it was really a straitjacket. One you didn't escape. A couple of the guys were wearing park workers' uniform: pale brown, caps with the city badge, that big pine tree, on them. The women, three of them, were in civilian clothes. Dog-walkers. You just got them strolling past. All stuff straight out of the book. Cy Langton loved the book, and all Cordobes could keep thinking was, this isn't someone who's working to the same manual. This isn't someone who follows the rules.

When the briefing was done they broke for coffee, weak and milky, the routine cop station stuff, made the usual stupid small talk that happens before these things get started, then sat around, watching the crowd slowly disappear, watching the park people and the pedestrians, the ball players, the back-up drivers all go out, take up their positions, try to act natural. Finally, it was just Langton and Cordobes, and the Captain said he'd drive him over there. So they went to Langton's office, took the money, all old bills, all carefully counted, and put them into a yellow Adidas sports bag. It was a tight fit. Then they went downstairs and climbed into the big, unmarked police cruiser, and Langton turned on the air conditioning straight away.

'Shit weather,' the old man said. 'I wanted weather like this I would've got a job in LA.'

The streets were empty. Palo Alto looked pretty normal. Not the place for this kind of crime, thought Tom Cordobes. Not the place at all.

'You got the measure of this one, Tom,' Langton said. 'I know that. I know you're gonna do what's right out there. End of today, this is gonna be big news one way or another. I know I can rely on you to make sure it works out our way.'

'Yeah,' Cordobes said. 'What's the weatherman say?'

'Real unsettled on the coast. We got this shit all day long, probably. Real hot. Real sticky. Guess you're used to that kind of thing, huh? In your previous line of work?'

And Tom Cordobes thought there was no way you could explain it to this old cop, who'd never got further east than a couple of golf courses in Scotland in his entire life, who just couldn't get a handle on the idea that there was a difference between jungle heat, all sweat and flies, that big flat wave of air that knocks the breath out of you, and this California cloud of smog and oxygen. One was foreign, one was a part of your home. It wasn't just a matter of temperature.

'You happy with the situation?'

Cordobes felt the weight of the .45 in his shoulder holster. Felt the smaller .38 pistol clinging to his right leg where it was taped, just right, so as not to spoil the line of the suit, the baggy suit, they'd bought specially down the men's tailors in University Avenue the day before. The big gun was so obvious he just had to see it. Had to ask him to get rid of it (if he had the time). And even if he did have the time, then maybe he wouldn't be careful enough to spot the little pistol taped inside his leg. If he got close enough that Tom Cordobes was being frisked, the thinking went, then they were close enough for Tom to be doing his stuff. And the word in the station was that he didn't *need* a gun for that. The word in the station was that Tom knew how to kill you in several very messy ways just with his bare hands. Nobody doubted this much. Nobody really wanted to find out.

'Happy as I'll ever be,' Cordobes said quietly and stared out of the window.

Then the car pulled up on El Camino, opposite Thoreau Park. Langton left the engine running, said, in a perfunctory manner, 'Good luck, Tom. I know you can do it. I know you'll do us all proud.'

Tom Cordobes picked up the yellow sports bag and was out of the car, so glad to be away from the pompous prick, even if it meant he'd just walked into some cut-down version of a sauna with the fumes of El Camino thrown in as an added blessing. He watched Langton drive off and wondered where the guy might be right then. Where he would have stationed himself to watch the little drama play itself out. They'd been right in a way. There were a lot of places you could hide – in the Gresham Woods, among the strollers in the park itself, in the little nest of shops that had been built close to where the highway ran over the rocky bed of the San Jacinto creek. But they weren't ideal. Langton already had a team quietly sweeping through, looking at the people there, seeing if anyone might be dumb enough to be using a pair of binoculars. Nobody had squawked a word on the radio to say they'd found something interesting. Somehow, Tom Cordobes thought it likely they wouldn't.

He wiped his forehead with his sleeve, wondered whether that counted as committing damage to police property, then looked at his watch. It was five to ten, time to take up position. Not that he knew precisely what that position might be. Mr Cat had not been specific. They guessed it was a good idea to be near the single public phone in the park. But it was just a guess, and Cordobes couldn't help but think that if Mr Cat had really wanted him there, he would have said so. This was not a person who left things to chance. It really didn't matter where he was in the park, except close to the big playing field. Mr Cat was going to find him.

Cordobes walked to the phone, feeling the heavy weight of the sports bag at each step. Money *was* heavy, he thought. Money weighed you down. He hoped he didn't have to do much running on this one. It was too hot for that. And his running wasn't that good any more. Nothing like as good as his aim. So he just leaned against the open phone booth, waiting, only half in hope, for it to ring, and let the minutes pass by. It had got to five past when a long yellow San Francisco cab pulled up the dirt service road and started to drive towards him. Tom Cordobes peered into the cab. Just one guy, medium size, black, behind the wheel, and he could see the people on the team watching the car, see them getting tense, and he just hoped, just really hoped, they didn't blow it too quickly, didn't scare the guy away.

It seemed to take forever to negotiate the bumps and potholes of the dirt track and something about that depressed him. The idea that you picked up two hundred thousand dollars and looked after your suspension at the same time struck him as almost funny. Then the car did a little roll down the last two craters in the dry, dusty earth, came to a stop a couple of yards away from him, and a thin black face poked out of the window.

'I knew this was agricultural work, mister, I'da given you a surcharge there,' the cab driver said. 'You any *idea* what it costs to change the underneath on these goddamned things?'

Cordobes gently took out the .45, more because he felt like it than for any other reason, and waved it slowly in the cab driver's face.

'Aw, shit, man.' He looked angry more than anything else. 'I got fifteen dollars on me right now. We gonna go through all this for *fifteen dollars?*'

Cordobes reached into his jacket pocket with his spare hand and pulled out the badge.

'Oh,' said the cab driver. 'You Palo Alto people sure don't like us guys from the city working your turf, huh?'

Cordobes had been watching the guy's hands. They hadn't even moved. He doubted there was much inside the car except a tyre lever stuffed under the seat just in case some drunk got a little mad late at night.

'Why don't you just put your hands on the door there, friend,' Cordobes said. 'You do that and tell me what you're doing here. You're right in the middle of a major felony, I got to tell you that, and I'm gonna need some persuading to stop me reading you your rights real soon. So you get persuasive.'

The cab driver leaned on the open window and winced, showing a smile that ran like an ancient picket fence, full of black gaps and snaggles.

'Shit, man. All I did was get sent out on some fucking fare by the cab company. Pick up some parcel, deliver it, pick up some guy, take him somewhere. Where's the felony in that, huh?'

'What guy?'

'Some guy in a grey suit. And only person fits that description right now is you. So you tell me, you expecting something from a Mr Cat or what?'

'I'm expecting . . .'

'Good,' said the cab driver, and faster than Cordobes expected, faster than he could handle, the guy reached down under the dash-board, picked something up, placed a red and white carrier bag on the door. It bore the name of some ex-military hardware store in the city.

'Parcel from Mr Cat,' the cab driver said. 'Now will you quit waving that fucking thing at me? I come out here on these jobs 'cos you Stanford people are supposed to be nice. Downright rude to go waving those things in my face.'

Cordobes thought about it, then stashed the pistol. Then he picked up the bag carefully, looked inside and pulled out a grey-green hunk of iron that brought back so many memories he couldn't cram them into his head all at once.

'Say,' the cab driver's eyes were wide open just looking at it. 'We used that stuff in the army. Some kinda mark something or other transceiver or something.'

'Yeah,' Cordobes said, knowing exactly what he had in his hands, knowing the feel of it, knowing what every switch and dial was for. 'Mark something or other.'

'You know, you'd give your ass for one of those things out in 'Nam,' the driver went on. 'Now you just buy 'em down Radio Shack. Who'da thought it?'

It was like yesterday. Cordobes popped on the switch, pulled out the long metal telescopic aerial. The set was pre-tuned, the scrambler was on. He was trying to remember the range. Fifteen, twenty-five miles? Illegal for civilian use, of course, but just 'cos you sold something didn't mean people were going to use it now, did it? In Tom's world they'd keep this stuff out of the hands of anybody but the chosen few, but this wasn't Tom's world and he knew it.

He listened on the channel, heard nothing, then pressed the PTT button and said, 'Got it.'

There was a blast of static and then a voice, a male voice, not a Californian accent he thought, but it was hard to guess through the static fuzz and the degradation that scrambling seemed to inject into every RT conversation he'd ever had, said, 'My, that was a long time. You really cut things close. Name?'

He's not here, Cordobes thought straight away. It wasn't just the static. Something else *told* him the guy wasn't here. They'd wasted the entire team on setting up for something that wasn't going to happen.

'Lieutenant Cordobes.'

'First name, Lieutenant. We have a lot of work to do over the next few minutes. We need to build some trust here.'

'Tom.'

'You fit, Tom?'

'Fit enough.'

The static crackled. It was as if the guy didn't like the answer.

'We'll find out. Tell the guy to take you to Nolan, close to the San Jacinto rail stop. You know it?'

'I know it.'

'Good. You need to be there in five minutes. And I don't want to see anyone following you.'

You don't *see* anything, Cordobes said to himself, then threw the yellow bag of money into the back seat and jumped in the cab.

'I heard that,' the driver said. 'You gonna be there in three. Sure thing.'

Cordobes got on the police walkie-talkie, passed on the movement, told them to keep back as much as they could, to reposition in Nolan, leave him clear, leave him alone for the pickup.

'I get paid for this?' the driver asked. 'You make sure of that, huh?'

Cordobes reached down, opened the yellow bag, threw him a fifty. He could hear a long, low whistle from the front seat.

'I like working Palo Alto,' the guy said. 'People shove guns in your face, then throw you fifty-dollar bills. I *like* this place.'

And then they were there, and Cordobes' heart sank. Nolan was a wide, open street on the edges of suburbia: low wood-fronted houses with white-painted picket fences and nicely manicured lawns. Two blocks away was a commercial development. Opposite was the commuter stop for the slow CalTrain service into the city. During the rush hour, the San Jacinto stop almost approached being busy, as the accountants and lawyers and PR people who liked to live 'up country' rolled up, parked their big station wagons, then sat and grumbled together on the 45-minute journey to work. Same again on the way back in the evening. But in the day the train stopped just once an hour or so, and even that was a waste of time, since hardly anyone got on, hardly anyone wanted to take the ride, since all you had to do was drive a mile and a half further down the track, park at Palo Alto, and catch a fast service that left every twenty minutes.

Cordobes got out of the car, looked around, thinking as fast as he could, wondering where the guy could be, 'cos he was here, he *had* to be here. But there was no one in the street and you couldn't go through all the houses, you just couldn't do that. Not without breaking the rules. *His* rules. And you start doing that he'd just hop out the back door and be gone. For good.

'You stay here,' he said to the cab driver. 'There's people gonna be along real soon will want to talk to you.'

'There goes this day's earnings,' the guy said, popped the meter off, leaned back in the driver's seat and closed his eyes.

It seemed even hotter here than in the park. There was nothing green to soak up the sun. It just bounced off the pale dusty ground and came right back at you. Tom Cordobes weighed the bag once with his right arm, felt the cash there, let it fall to the ground. He was just coming around to the conclusion – the right conclusion, as Hal Jamieson could have confirmed, from the rooftop of the low-rise Bay area bank building two blocks away to the east, a pair of powerful ex-military field glasses in his hands – that the guy must be on a roof somewhere, maybe over near the commercial buildings, when the radio barked.

'You got a gun in your jacket pocket. You got a walkie-talkie too. Give 'em to the driver, man. You won't be needing them.'

It was closer, the voice was closer. You heard more of it, Cordobes thought. It was closer and it sounded different. It sounded *young*.

He pulled out the big .45, threw it onto the passenger seat, watched the cab driver jump a little at its bulk, then threw the police walkie-talkie down there too.

Cordobes glanced at his watch and pressed the PTT switch on the transceiver. 'We need to be doing this now, Mr *Cat*. You got your 11 am deadline, we need to be giving you this money, *now*.'

And on the roof of the bank building Hal Jamieson felt cold, felt the hatred, the violence there in his voice and wished there was some other way out.

Then he said, 'Deadlines change, Tom. A man's got to be flexible in life. Don't you know that?'

And it was Tom Cordobes' turn to worry.

'I see 'em coming, Tom. Where I am, I see *everything*. You didn't do like I told you. You brought your friends.'

'Get smart, kid,' Cordobes barked, so loud the cab driver jerked in his seat. 'We're fucking cops. We're fucking grown-ups. This thing's all gonna come down around your ears if you don't smarten up right now.'

And then he just stood there, feeling too hot, feeling like he could kill someone.

Eventually, the radio barked again.

'My. That's one bad temper you got there, Tom. I think you should keep a handle on that, I really do. There's some five-year-old kid who's counting on you and right now I just don't know how he ought to feel. Do you?'

Cordobes squinted hard, looked at the rooftops. The kid *had* to be up there somewhere.

'You ready to ride, Tom?'

He punched the PTT button hard. 'What?'

'You heard. Look down the track. That's the 10.32 to San Francisco coming in bang on time just for a change. You know these CalTrain schedules, they drive you crazy. More complex than a Chinese puzzle. Most times these trains stop every single goddamned station so nobody ever turns up and uses 'em. *Most* times.'

Cordobes peered down the long straight track. Over the top of the

361

wall he could just make out the roof of the big engine coming down, very slowly, just hear the squeal of its brakes.

'But the 10.32 is just plain weird, Tom. It just makes two stops. You know what they are? Think your guys know too? Who knows? There's no one on the station, Tom. No one waiting to get on board. That makes it real easy for me to make sure you're on your own because I know that only one person *is* gonna get on board and that is you.'

It was pulling in now, he could hear the big iron wheels screeching to a halt behind the tall cement wall. The backup guys were way back down the street, still gingerly walking their way into position. They probably never even saw it, probably didn't even know it was there. He could hear the automatic doors opening and, somewhere in his head, could feel the driver wondering how quickly he could hop this dead stop, whether you really needed to let the big train slow right down to nothing, like the book said, or whether you just let her roll until she was just leaning forward on the brakes, just about to get still, then pumped in the power again, like common sense told you to.

'I got a better view'n you,' the radio said. 'He's gonna go, Tom. You'd better run.'

And the big cop picked up the bag and went for it, legs pumping, soaking the grey suit even more, raced past the empty ticket kiosk, found the platform, punched the automatic door back open with his fist just as it was starting to shut, leapt on board the train, stared inside the carriage, wondering how long it would take him to get the little pistol out from behind his leg, how long it would take him to beat the truth out of some snotty kid.

'Well done,' said the voice over the radio. 'That was real good.'

The 10.32 pulled out of San Jacinto bang on time, just as the backup team was getting into place, getting its act together, started moving in behind him, and then wondering where the hell Tom Cordobes had disappeared to so fast, wondering what the hell was so interesting inside the station, whether he just ran in there, ran out again. Wondering why the fuck he didn't call them.

It took them fifteen minutes before they realised what had happened. And by that stage Tom Cordobes was seated on his own in a carriage rattling towards the city, and he knew what the game was. Knew that this was one he was going to have to play on his own.

NINE

Schrödinger's Cat (3)

The Goddess Fortune is the devil's servant, ready to kiss any
one's arse.   WILLIAM BLAKE

Joni Lascelles looked into Quinn's eyes and wished the two of them
weren't sitting like this, facing each other across the shining pine table.
It made it seem as if the encounter was personal, involved no one
else, and that was not true. This was about more than Michael Quinn
and it was an illusion to pretend otherwise.

'What are you saying?' she asked Jamieson, her eyes still fixed on
Quinn, locked on his gleaming skull.

'I'm saying that I will do whatever I can. I'll pay for people to track
Margaret Zalinski down. To find out what happened. To put you in
touch with them. I can start right now. We can settle this now. It can
be done in days.'

She stared at her hands, tried to see some light in all this, tried to
think about the woman, what it was that bothered her.

'And Mr Cordobes?'

'Nobody's going to know about Cordobes,' Jamieson said, and she
wasn't wrong, there really was some regret in his voice. 'People disappear in this country all the time and he's just going to be one more
who doesn't get missed. No relatives, no employees. I'm not proud
saying this, believe me. I wish it hadn't happened. I wish he hadn't
broken in here. That we could have done this in some other way. But
there's no point in even thinking about that. We can't turn back the
clock. It's done and the point is, it can't be brought out into the public
without involving us. Without bringing this whole thing down around
our heads. I don't expect you to do us any favours. I don't expect you
to give a damn about us. But think about yourself. Think about what

363

you want. You need me to get that for you. I can do it. But I can't if I'm sitting in jail some place.'

Quinn laughed, his big yellow teeth opened wide, and it came to her straight off: there was real craziness here, a kind of craziness she'd never met before.

'Hal fixes things, you see,' Quinn said. 'He fixes things real good. Always has. Always will. There's a real talent there.'

She couldn't help but notice that Louise wasn't laughing with him, Louise just sat there, stony-faced, listening to the talk, looking slightly impatient with it all.

Finally, Joni said, 'So. I have a choice in this matter?'

And Hal Jamieson couldn't help thinking how feminine, how much like a woman, that answer was. Nothing about the questions, nothing about the practicalities. Just that sullen dull complaint about not getting a choice.

'Welcome to the club,' he said straight away. 'Some of us have been going through life wondering all the way what the word "choice" meant. Choices are for people with lots of time on their hands and nothing much in the way of decisions. All the big things in life don't come with choice attached. You either say yes or no, you either go up or you go down. Sure, you got a choice. You get sort of happy, and we stay sort of happy, or you get sad for sure and we all join you there. Either way you get to regret something in the end, most likely. The question is: which one are you likely to regret most?'

She looked at Quinn, who was listening hard. The yellow teeth moved again and he said, 'That's pretty good for a beginner, Hal.'

Then Joni watched Louise Gostelow, watched her reach down below the line of the table, into what seemed to be her bag, watched her pull out a big grey pistol, so big it looked like some kind of stage prop, and say, 'We don't have any choice either, Hal. You thought about that, you'd know.'

Jamieson looked down the table, watched her place the gun there on the shining surface, and wondered if he really knew this Louise, this new Louise, at all. She looked so poised and ready, looked as if she could take control of the situation just by saying the right words. And it baffled him. He couldn't work it out.

'Put the gun away, Louise,' he said, and heard the tension in his own voice. 'We don't solve things with guns. We never did before. We're not starting now.'

She smiled at him, the sort of smile you'd give a bank clerk, and said, 'Jesus, Hal, you really slay me. You really do. We've got two people here who could put us in jail for the rest of our lives, maybe even get us *killed*, and you're sitting there trying to reason your way out of this. Like it's some deal. Some contract. We're not talking stock options here, we're not talking rights issues. This is our lives, Hal. And I'm not having mine disappear from under me just because you have some kind of principles . . .'

'Not killing people isn't anything to do with principles,' Jamieson interrupted, and kept wondering why she was doing this, what she was trying to prove. It all seemed so pointless. 'Not killing people is the place you start off from, Louise, not some point out in space you just happen to float to one day.'

She lit a cigarette. She was so calm. It came to Jamieson: she was prepared. Whatever she was doing, this was something she was ready for.

'Wise up, Hal. This is the 1990s, not the 1960s. All that peace and love crap's gone. We're talking survival and these two people are *threatening* us.'

He looked at his hands, tried to keep calm, and said, 'Put the gun away, Louise. Put it away now. We can talk about what happens to *us* later but right now I'm telling you that this *crap*, this nonsense is not an option, that we're going to talk this through, agree it between us, do the right thing. So put the goddamned gun away. Now.'

And she was looking at him so pleasantly. The anger had gone from her face. She looked so striking. Not young any more. Not when you really thought about it. That was just one of Louise's tricks. One of her many tricks. Hal Jamieson wondered how he'd ever managed to keep her all these years. How she hadn't just swept off whenever she felt like it. When you looked like that, when you had that intelligence, that charm, you could do almost anything you wanted.

'I tried, Hal,' she said. 'You've got to give me that. I tried. The problem is I'm not going to jail. I can't do that. I'll do anything not to have that happen to me. Believe me. Anything.'

Hal Jamieson could feel the exasperation starting to buzz inside him like an angry wasp.

'No one's going to jail, Louise, no one's coming to any harm. That's the point of this conversation. That's why we're talking here. This woman is not a threat to us, any more than Michael is.'

Joni Lascelles said nothing. Found that something inside wanted to stop him saying that, some hard, cold thing inside her would have been very happy with the way Louise Gostelow saw the world.

'You don't *know* that,' Louise snapped. 'All along, you just trust things. Just say, that'll be fine, that'll be cool. Back then, back twenty years ago, we could have solved all this then. But you wouldn't do it. You had to do *the right thing*. See where it's got us.'

There was a tension in the room that they all could feel. It sat in the air and Joni Lascelles knew, knew straight away, that they didn't talk like this, not ever, not until now. That something had opened up this frankness like an old wound, and neither of them knew where it was going.

'Can't just kill people every time they get in your way, Louise,' Jamieson said, staring out of the window, out into the grey-green forest, not wanting to look at her, to see the intense concentration on her face. 'Killing people is not some kind of off-the-shelf solution you can buy like ant powder in a supermarket, sprinkle around you, then wait for all the bugs in your life to disappear.'

'No?'

'Not in my world.'

She picked up the gun from the table, started rolling the cylinder round, pulled a box from her handbag, put a shell in one chamber. Jamieson swore, then started to get up from the table.

'I said, put the fucking gun away, Louise.'

And felt a big hand on the back of his shoulder push him back down.

'I think you should stay where you are, Mr Jamieson,' Baxter said, and there, in that moment, something became clear to him, something that had been buzzing around in the back of his head for an hour or so.

He leaned back into his seat, took a deep breath, turned and looked at the big man in the shiny grey suit. Baxter didn't smile, didn't say anything.

'Excuse me?'

Jamieson stared at the guy, the sort of stare you had access to when you owned corporations, owned people, the sort of stare that made someone uncomfortable, without saying a word.

Baxter went a little red in the face, looked like he was sweating, and said, 'I think you should listen. I think you should stay where you are. Make this as easy as possible.'

He wasn't liking this, Hal Jamieson thought, he wasn't comfortable with the whole thing.

'How much she paying you, Baxter? How much? No problem. I'll double it. Where the hell you think her money comes from these days? How much you want?'

Baxter looked at him, unsmiling, hesitated, then said, 'Sometimes things are not just a matter of money, Mr Jamieson. I'm sorry. I didn't want to say that. You made me.'

And that much Hal Jamieson could believe. That much made sense.

'Ah,' Jamieson said. 'So she's fucking you *and* giving you money. Guess it's hard for me to compete on one of those fronts anyway.'

'I think you should be quiet and listen,' Baxter said. 'I really do.'

'So how long you guess this gonna last? You think this servant mentality's gonna serve you well with her in the future?'

Jamieson was starting to get mad now. Felt he could get madder than he'd ever been in his whole life, and it was not just at Baxter, it wasn't even at Louise, it was at the whole damned thing, himself included, the way it had all panned out.

'How long? I mean, I made twenty years or so, give or take a few little hiatuses in there from time to time. But I'm a bright guy, Steve. May not have your physique and the rest. But I can keep the money coming in. And that's important to Louise. Louise *likes* money, Steve. Only fair to warn you of that.'

Baxter let a thin smile come on his face, looked at him and said, 'Money isn't gonna be a problem, Mr Jamieson. Not when you're gone. There's gonna be *plenty* of money to go around.'

Then Hal Jamieson just shut up, just went quiet, felt his blood go thin in his veins, finally felt it all come home. Looked at Louise and felt drained by the years, the wasted years.

'This is the end, Hal,' she said, and she wasn't smiling then, she said it in the way she used when she fired a housekeeper: more sorrow than anger. 'This is what you should have made happen years ago but didn't. This is what I told you to do when we drove here, all those years ago, when they were in the back of the camper, and it could have been so easy. Now it all comes round. And after this I get to relax. I get so that I never have to worry about the cops, about jail, ever again. You see, everyone just gets closed out, everyone who knew what happened then. You, him, the girl, *everyone*, and I get to be free. And the joy is it's so neat. You can lose people out here in the woods, just drive out into nowhere, you don't even need to dig, they just *go*. And you, I don't even need to do that. I don't need to get involved in some inheritance problem. This is your cabin, Hal. You bought this for fucking. You got a pretty girl here. You get arguing. You got guns. You know what? I get sympathy out of this too. How'd I get better than that?'

Jamieson tried to think through the tangle of ideas shooting through his head.

'You can't just *kill* people like that, Louise. You can't even be thinking about this.'

'Really?' she said. Then checked the revolver, pushed it across the table to Quinn. It sat in front of him, a dull leaden colour on the shining wood. He didn't look at it.

'Remember the Barn, Michael?' she said. 'Boy, were they some times. Not quite this place, that's for sure, but we enjoyed ourselves there. That right?'

'That's right,' Quinn said, smiling, some crazy look on his face, and stared at Joni sitting across from him, an expression on his face she couldn't even begin to read.

'The games we used to play there. You remember them, Michael? You remember that game with the little switches, the on-off thing? Had that fancy name?'

'Wasn't a game, Louise,' Quinn said in a monotone voice. 'Thought you understood that. Wasn't a game at all.'

'Schrödinger's cat. That right?'

'Not a game,' Quinn said, and his voice was wavering, had that juvenile whine Hal and Louise had last heard two decades before.

'I get to think about that from time to time,' Louise said, 'and you know I may be bright, I may be smart, but it seems to me I never really did get it. Seems to me it was just like Russian roulette. Either the shell was in the chamber or it wasn't.'

Hal Jamieson looked at her across the table and said, in a tone he didn't want to sound like pleading, 'Don't do this, Louise. We can go back. We can forget this ever happened. Whatever you want, the money, Baxter, I don't care. Just don't *do this*.'

She waited for him to finish, then, without thinking, waved the idea away with her hand.

'We're not going back, Hal. There's no such place as *back*. You never learned that, did you? So pick up the gun, Michael.'

'The gun?'

'You heard.'

Quinn leaned forward, not knowing which way to look, saw Baxter pulling something out of his jacket pocket, pointing it at him, as he reached for the handle of the gun on the table.

Joni struggled to speak. Her mouth was dry. Something was spinning inside her head. The words just didn't appear.

'One shell in there, Michael,' Louise said. 'I spun the chamber. Even I don't know if it's there or not. Uncertain enough for you?'

'Not the same, Louise,' Quinn said. 'This is not the same at all.'

'Sure, it is. You remember what you said back then? We're all just little bits of stuff bouncing off each other. Everything. Everything we say, everything we do, it all just comes down to that. So whatever happens is going to happen anyway. *What the fuck?*'

And it grated on him. 'That's wrong, Louise. Something being predetermined that's not the same as something being *preordained*.'

'You say so. What the hell. Put the gun to the pretty girl's head, Michael.'

Quinn looked across at Joni Lascelles and wondered what he was really seeing, when he listened, when he let the colours talk to him. The face of a five-year-old child? The shape of golden wings fluttering behind her? This is *not* the same, he said. This is *not* right. And inside he heard his blood roaring, felt the heat racing through his veins.

'Put the gun to the pretty girl's head and pull the trigger, Michael. Who knows? Maybe we get a new universe right here and now. Maybe it's got the good fairy in it and she's got a magic wand. Maybe we're all in hell. Won't know until you pull the trigger. Go pull the trigger, Michael.'

'Please . . .' Jamieson said across the table. 'It's not too late, Louise, please . . .'

It was Quinn who answered, as he pointed the barrel straight at Joni's head, with its halo of blonde hair, the white skin of her forehead no more than six inches away from the grey metal.

'It's always too late, Hal,' Quinn said. 'We all should've learned that. It's always too fucking late.'

And she seemed so calm. She was fixing him with eyes that didn't show fear, didn't show hatred, didn't show doubt. Michael Quinn and

Joni Lascelles looked across the bright shining table into each other's faces and felt something, some kind of recognition, some kind of acknowledgement of a common bond she didn't even want to begin to think about pass between them. Her eyes were so strong, so bright, so fixed. They went right through him. They bore into him, as if this picture, this bright gleaming skull, this craziness, was the last thing she wanted to take with her out of this world.

'Close your eyes,' he said.

And it was a small choice, or maybe a big choice. Right at that moment, Joni Lascelles just didn't know. The world was tearing apart at its seams around her, and she could feel herself falling into the debris of its dissolution. So she closed her eyes, thrust her hands deep into the pockets of her jacket, and thought of some small, perfect planet a million miles away from this place, these people. And as she did, she could hear her own breathing, quiet, shallow, patient, hear the small noises of the room, the air from the heating system, the gentle ticking of the refrigerator, hear all these everyday, ordinary noises that lived beneath the world start to come to the foreground of her life, take on some real, discrete existence of their own.

'Pull the trigger, Michael,' the woman said, and it sounded as if her voice came from outside the room, sounded as if it came from somewhere out in space.

Then there was a noise, an explosion, so loud it seemed deadly in itself; the air was torn apart by something hot and noxious, and redness fell on her world, redness and the sound of screaming.

TEN

Magic

'... as if the plague was not the hand of God, but a kind of possession of an evil spirit, and that it was to be kept off with crossings, signs of the zodiac, papers tied up with so many knots, and certain words or figures written on them, as particularly the word Abracadabra, formed in triangle or pyramid, thus:-

ABRACADABRA
ABRACADABR
ABRACADAB
ABRACADA
ABRACAD
ABRACA
ABRAC
ABRA
ABR
AB
A

DANIEL DEFOE,
Journal of the Plague Year

Atherton and Redwood City, San Mateo and Burlingame, Paul Avenue, 22nd Street. Tom Cordobes looked at the names on the map and wondered where the train really would stop. Where the endgame might begin.

And tried to figure, once again, what the kid was doing, for this was surely a kid, a college kid, all cleverness and jive, and what this was about was *proving it*. Proving he was smarter, proving he was better than the old guys, the guys who fought, who didn't smoke pot, who worked and slaved and kept the line. It made it personal and for Tom Cordobes that was just fine, that made it all the better. When things got personal, they got real.

The carriage bounced its way along the CalTrain line, past places he'd only seen from the road and now could scarcely recognise. This was a different viewpoint. Things looked reshaped, transformed from here, and that wasn't a concept that interested Tom Cordobes much. He liked to know what he had to know and keep that close by him for when it was needed.

Occasionally, the radio crackled and Cordobes would think to himself: this kid isn't as smart as he thinks. He's following the line by car, he's just mirroring me out there somewhere along 101, past Redwood City, past the airport, following the shoreline along the Bay, past South Francisco and Candlestick Park, all the way into the city. And he thinks this old military junk is better than it is. He doesn't know about radios and how they play tricks on you. He doesn't know about the blocking effects of concrete and power lines. He doesn't understand atmospheric conditions. He thinks he knows more than he does, and that's dangerous, that's always dangerous.

But then, after Burlingame, something changed. The weather started to alter rapidly and soon the carriage was swamped by fog, like a cloud that had just descended from the sky and decided to hug the ground for a little while. It was cold. There was some winter chill behind it, and maybe even a rumble of thunder some way off, and that odd combination made the train seem stuffy, airless. Cordobes threw open all the windows in the empty carriage, tried to get as much air in as he could, sat down, feeling displaced, made uncomfortable by the every which way motion of the carriage. The inactivity got him down. He tried to think about what the kid might have up his sleeve. Then gave up. It wasn't worth the effort. He tried to think about what Langton might be doing. Drafting his resignation letter probably. Either that or thinking of some way Cordobes would carry the can for him. Palo Alto was a small police department. It didn't have the resources, it didn't have the facilities to start running things over the city lines into other people's territory. All Langton could do once the kid took the thing out of home ground was call on some big shot in the city, wait until the guy stopped laughing, then throw himself on his knees and beg for help. If he got real lucky, it was possible, in the forty minutes or so it would take the train to get from San Jacinto into the city, that they might get enough of their act together to meet the train. Possible, but not likely. And in any case, the undercover stuff took time. You couldn't just throw it all together in a couple of minutes, else it would look obvious and then where were you? Back at the beginning. Back with the kid coming on the radio and saying,

'I told you so . . .' Then phoning some asshole in the media and giving them directions on where to find the body.

No. The more he thought about it the more he knew what Cy Langton was doing right at this moment. He was in his office, just sitting tight. Not phoning anybody. Not bothering a soul. Just waiting for Tom to fix things, waiting for Tom to call through and say, 'It's OK.' One way or another. That was what Cy Langton would be doing, and maybe it was the smartest thing of all.

Cordobes stared out of the window, into the thick, grey blanket that now gave no more than ten yards' visibility or so. He had no idea whether he was still in open ground or a built-up area. You just couldn't tell. And then, out of nowhere, the radio barked at him, and Cordobes picked the thing off the seat.

'You there, Tom?'

There was a sound behind the voice: traffic? No. A foghorn. That could put the kid anywhere near the waterfront. Great help . . .

'I'm getting bored, kid. I bore real easy.'

'Yeah. Well, you're going to stay bored, Tom. You're going to get no excitement whatsoever out of all this. You just hand over the money, and then the boy goes free.'

'*Do not give me that crap!*' Cordobes yelled into the transceiver. 'I'm not some fucking moron. The kid's dead already. You think I don't know that?'

There was a pause and then he said the oddest thing, something Cordobes couldn't interpret at all.

'The kid's alive, Tom. You better believe me. I *kept* him alive, not that you're ever gonna get to know about that. But I did it. If it weren't for me, he'd be dead right now. And maybe not just him either.'

'Yeah,' Cordobes said, and wondered what this meant, wondered if there was something to use there.

'Up to you to keep him alive now, Tom. I've done all I can. Believe that or call me a liar, don't matter, it's true.'

'So?'

'So you get off at 22nd. You don't stay on all the way. By my watch that makes it your next stop. You get off, you take a cab, you go to the corner of California and Powell. You don't do anything stupid, like phoning for people or anything like that. You don't have time, Tom. None of us has time. You just go there. You wait. I'll talk to you.'

Cordobes could feel his temper starting to nag like a bee sting with all this.

'Which fucking corner, asshole? Got four corners at a junction like California and Powell. *Which fucking corner?*'

The radio was silent for a while, then the voice came back.

'You know, Tom, you got a bad work attitude. I just don't figure how they picked you for this job. I *know* what a junction is. I *know* it's got four corners. I didn't specify a particular corner, Tom, because it just don't matter. It don't matter at all.'

Cordobes tried to work it out and couldn't. Then realised how much he hated the tone in the kid's voice. Thought he'd remember that tone, that cold smartness there, for a really long time, long enough to keep this going until somewhere along the line you got some kind of conclusion. But you couldn't figure it out. You *couldn't*. All you could do was go along with it, see what happened, take your opportunity. And pray the kid wasn't as smart as he seemed. Pray that he wasn't just improvising, and dancing faster than any out-of-condition cop pushing forty could hope to match.

The CalTrain service pulled into 22nd and it was like stepping out into a bowl of thin icy cold soup. The air just hit you, took the breath out of your lungs, wiped a smear of chill heavy sweat right over your body. He shivered and knew then what the kid was doing. It was so thick here that you didn't have any choice. You *had* to improvise. When you could hardly see your arm in front of your face, you just didn't have any choice. Any plans you might have had just went clean out of the window. They were unworkable in this dank grey world where it was easier to hear something than to see it, and even the sounds, the everyday street sounds, voices, the traffic, the cable cars, the foghorn off in the distance, that all came through muffled, warped, reshaped by the fog until you couldn't begin to guess where in the real world it all came from. When you got down to it, all you had left was your brain, and if that was the way the kid was playing it, then Tom Cordobes didn't have much in the way of choices but to follow him.

He found a short line of cabs, dim yellow in the half-light of the fog, climbed in the first, lugged the sports bag onto the seat beside him, placed the radio on top. It just crackled and fizzed now. It sounded like a kid's toy.

The driver turned to look at him, turned to stare at the walkie-talkie which was threatening to ruin the low fidelity sound of his in-car music system and its less than perfect rendition of the Doobie Brothers. The man had long greasy hair down to his shoulders, a huge drooping moustache that joined up with his beard, and a fading tattoo on his cheek. Even in the gloom of the day he was wearing shades, a Ray-Ban aviator copy that looked like big black teardrops on his face.

'California and Powell,' Cordobes grunted, then tried to find some place on the bench seat where the springs didn't hurt too much.

'You in a hurry?' the driver grunted.

'I'd prefer to be moving, if that's what you're saying.'

The cab driver shrugged, threw a magazine over into the back seat. Cordobes looked at it: you could have used it as a trainee manual for rookie gynaecologists.

'You want to read my beaver book, man?' the driver said. 'Might improve that temper of yours.'

Then the car pulled slowly out into the street, and inched its way into the sluggish stream of traffic. Cordobes reached down, felt the gun behind his leg, ripped the plaster away, then pocketed the weapon. Improvising. Thinking of what might happen. Trying to second guess the kid. And it occurred to Cordobes that, whatever was going to happen, it had to happen now. No one, not even the kid, however smart he might be, could control things in this kind of situation. He had to come for the money. He had to try to get it. He had to show his hand. You couldn't run around the city in weather like this without losing your grip before long.

The cab started to climb uphill and Cordobes strained to peer out the windows. You could just about make out the office fronts and the odd store, the neon lights of the sex shops round the back of Union Square: 24 Hour Naked Girls, no cover. Then a sharp left and the hill got steep, so steep your backside slid into the back of the seat, you could feel the cab bumping over the cable car lines, the road got broader, you lost sight of the other side. The cab came to a halt, the driver put on the hand brake, kept his foot on the pedal just in case. The incline was really steep here, and just opening the door he could see, from the thin grey line of the inclined pavement, that it was something to think about, something to be taken into consideration.

'You sure this is California and Powell?'

The big black teardrops turned and stared at him.

'I am a licensed San Francisco cab driver, *sir*. You bet I'm sure.

375

That'll be two fifty and I'm sure I don't have to explain to you how hard I worked for that, I really did.'

Cordobes threw the guy three and got out while the driver just stared, glumly, at the bills. It was like being on the side of a mountain, the street seemed to run uphill at forty-five degrees to the horizontal. He struggled a couple of yards, looked up, saw the signs: California and Powell. Then tried to picture in his mind what it was like here when the fog blew away. Nothing came. You wandered a little way down one side of Nob Hill you got to Chinatown. As if to confirm the fact, Tom Cordobes could smell it in the air: the acrid, flowery scent he'd first encountered on the other side of the world, in a city where, for a brief while, he'd been king. If you wandered down the other side, you got to Union Square, Market Street eventually. The other two corners he just wasn't so sure about. Powell pointed on, all the way down through North Beach almost to the garish little tourist traps around Fisherman's Wharf. California just seemed to run all the way from around Embarcadero down on the waterfront back out the other side of town, one long straight street on the map, but right here it was just a switchback, went up and down, up and down.

And there was the cable car, too. Not that Tom Cordobes knew anything about cable cars, not that he felt anything towards them except an antipathy that was close to hatred that the city should allow anything as old and slow and awkward as that to block up the street and slow down the cars. Look to the front of most any traffic jam in San Francisco and what you always got, in Tom Cordobes' book, was some fucking cable car or a big yellow bus taking kids to school. Three cheers for the productive society.

He waited for a couple of cars to slow-dance their way through the junction, their headlights bright white orbs in the greyness, then stepped into the street and listened. It was there. Underneath the street, humming, singing, like the bass string on some giant musical instrument that ran through the spine of the city, the cable, taut and singing, hauling and heaving the cars up California, and wherever else they happened to go. There was a bell, the metallic clanging softened in the greyness of the fog, then the car loomed up suddenly out of the gloom, he stepped neatly back onto the sidewalk, and let the big wood and iron monster creak and roll past him. They let these fuckers crawl around the place like mechanical roaches any damn time they choose, he said to himself, and fell to wondering about the city, its strangeness, the way it always made him want to get the hell out, get back into the nice, flat suburban plainness of Palo Alto, and leave all this craziness, all this crap behind.

There were people around too. Grey figures that moved slowly past him, trying to peer through the fog, trying to work out where they were, where they might be going, trying to avoid the cracks in the pavement, and keep from stumbling into the road. It was that bad. It was as bad as he'd ever seen it and in a way he could only feel half sorry for the kid. Trying to pull a bag full of two hundred thousand dollars from under his nose in these conditions was not going to be easy, not without getting real close, and real close was the place where Tom Cordobes did his best work, always had.

When it came, it was so loud, so disorienting, that it took him by surprise, made the cold sweat get even chillier. One moment the street was still, he couldn't see or hear a soul. Then the air was rent by a single word, yelled at the top of someone's – the kid's – voice.

'*TOM . . .*'

Cordobes reached for the gun automatically, felt the metal, cold under his hand. The fog made the sound go weird. You just couldn't tell what was coming from where. The direction, the sound, the timbre of the kid's voice, it all just got mixed up in the atmosphere and seemed to come at you from all directions.

'TOM. YOU HEAR ME?'

And he still couldn't pinpoint it. Still couldn't even begin to make a guess about whether it was ahead of him or to either side.

'Yeah,' he yelled back. And tried to think, tried to work out why the kid wasn't using the radio any longer, why . . .

Because that would give him away, Cordobes said quietly to himself. Because all I'd need to do was home in on the static, the constant static, not something intermittent, something that was hard to pin down, like a voice.

'Tom. Put the bag down, then walk to the other side of the road.'

The kid sounded different. Sounded worried. Scared. Cordobes smiled inwardly. The kid had a right to be.

'We been here before. Which goddamned side?'

There was some hesitation. Then the kid came back, and it sounded like he was somewhere different, and he sounded different too, like some of his confidence was coming back. Like he knew what he was doing.

'I said this before, Tom. Don't matter. Put the bag down, go stand at the opposite corner. And one more thing . . .'

'Yeah?' He wished there was some way he could take a pop into the fog, just line it up where he thought the voice was coming from, feel the slug of lead disappear into the grey pillow of nothingness and find something through the gloom.

'When you get to the other side, whichever side you choose, you get to find something. Underneath the street sign. You use it. You keep on using it all the time. *All the time.* You understand? That means we're done. We're through. We're on our way and so are you.'

'What kind of thing?'

'Something lets us know where you are. What you're doing.'

'Yeah?'

'You're wasting time, Tom. Don't you know that?'

And this was the kid back to himself, he thought. This was the jumped-up little fucker he'd been spending the best part of the day yelling at down the radio. This wasn't the one who spoke first. There was more than one of them. There *had* to be. That was the secret of the trick, like some old sleight of hand pulled out of a card book. And if he could just peel back the greyness, peel back the sludge in front of his eyes, he'd be close enough to pop them, all of them, right there, close enough to hold them in his fist and squeeze the life out of them, drop by drop.

'I can't hear you walking, Tom.'

Cordobes listened out for traffic. The street was really dead. There was no wind. No sound except the far-off honking of horns and someone up high somewhere, giggling. These times the city just gave up on itself, said, what the fuck? and slowly fell into a party. The business guys down the finance district went for their lunch-time cocktails an hour or so early. The ones who were doing a little two-timing with some accounts clerk booked in for a couple of hours in some short-run 'hotel' and played the horizontal tango so loud it drifted out of the open window and mixed up with the sighs and groans of someone doing the same thing on the other side of the street. The city just shrugged its shoulders and gave up on itself, and if someone was playing some little drama down on the street, some little drama about life and death, then, so what? *We* should care?

Tom Cordobes dropped the bag, with its two hundred grand (minus a fifty for the cab driver) inside, heard it thud to the stone pavement and felt glad to be rid of it. Then he set off walking straight ahead of him, down California, down towards Embarcadero, down towards the ocean, listening all the time, listening for the scurrying of feet behind him, something, anything, you could take aim at. But they won't move till you get to the other side, Tom Cordobes said to himself. They won't move until you find the fucking thing and how are they going to know?

It wasn't easy even walking in a straight line. He set off right by the street corner. When he got to the other side, passed over the cable car line, whirring, singing underneath his feet, he was a good yard or two down, had walked at least a couple of degrees off ninety when he crossed. It was so quiet now it made him feel good. He could feel the kid(s) all aquiver out there, he could smell their nervousness in the fog, and all that did was make him feel better and better and better. Sometimes you didn't need to know where you were going, you just needed to know that something was going to take you there, something you could roll and flow with and wait until the moment comes. And this would be his moment. Something told him that, something told him even before he found what they'd left there.

He stubbed his foot on the thing first and that almost gave the game away. But not quite. There was no noise, just the dull sound of his shoe touching metal, and the greyness swallowed that up straight away, gave Tom Cordobes time to bend down, pick the thing up, very slowly, very carefully and look at it. You could buy this crap for a dollar or so a hundred yards down the hill in Chinatown. Imitation cable car bells, big ones, almost the size of the real thing, the kind of shit the tourists loved to take home, loved to polish and give a little brassy glow to their lives. And that was smart of the kid(s). You just bought four of them, left one at each corner at the foot of the street sign, where no one was going to find it, not unless you were looking. Then you kept out of the way. You got close enough to see which corner he was going to occupy – those people brushing past him in the gloom just had to have the kid(s) among them, *had* to, but there was nothing he could do about that. Couldn't arrest every goddamned passer-by. Then when you knew where he was, you just got him to drop the bag, got him to walk to the other corner, pick up the bell, then stand there like some jerk in a Santa Claus outfit, ringing the bell while they walked off with the cash, knowing all the time that if he started to move, they'd hear it, they'd hear him coming, and it was

379

all over, they just disappeared into the fog and they were gone. Good plan. And it couldn't be their only one, just the one that matched the weather. You needed other plans. And, most of all, you needed people. This was not something you could do, something you could even attempt, on your own.

Tom Cordobes smiled down at the brass bell and thought: that *is* clever when you think about how little time they must have had to make this thing up. Real clever. And he did nothing. Waited there, feeling the tension slide across the chill damp opaque air, listening to the hum of the wires underneath the street.

Eventually, the kid, the real kid, broke.

'We're not hearing you,' he yelled, and he sounded angry, he sounded mad.

He waited a good ten seconds, then yelled, 'Can't find it. Help if I know what I'm looking for.'

You couldn't hear anything out there, but he could guess how they were feeling now. They were shit scared. They had a right to be. Until he rang the bell, they didn't dare move an inch.

He listened to the wire tautening, humming under the street, wondered how long he could leave it.

'You find it now, Tom,' the kid yelled, and this time he sounded really frightened, sounded like he was losing it. 'NOW. Or the deal's off.'

And then the bell began to ring, loud and clear through the opaque fog, and he could hear them moving, dashing, racing across the street, not knowing where he was, not knowing that he was almost there himself.

The bell was still ringing and it just got louder and louder and he thought he could see something now, way off down California, the lights of the cable car, labouring its way up the incline, and he wondered when they'd realise, when the movement of the car would be enough to make them guess.

Then Tom Cordobes was across the road, the gun was out of his pocket, the magic gun that cured the world, and like three ghosts, their shapes appeared out of nowhere, hovered around the bag, picked it up, turned to scurry and stopped.

'It's the fucking cable car,' someone said in a low, flat voice, and at that Cordobes fired, heard something like fabric, tearing, ripping, somewhere, saw the first ghost jump then go down, go down hard, felt the gun leap again in his hand, fired once more, not a good shot, a little wide, saw the second one jump, saw his head jerk. Someone was screaming, '*Jesus fucking NO . . .*'

And it was the sweetest sound, because Tom Cordobes knew now that it wasn't going to be hard to take all of them down, take one at least alive, then lean on him, squeeze him, put him through some things he wasn't likely *ever* to forget – *you know, Tom, you got a bad work attitude, I just don't figure how they picked you for this job* – as long as he lived. It was going to be easy to do this because the dumb shit he hadn't hit was still there, still trying to get the second one away, holding him up on his feet, yelling and screaming just pleading to get caught.

Tom Cordobes started to walk across the rest of California, started to point the gun at the third guy, the one who was waiting – the real guy, and he wondered how he knew that – and began to think about what he was going to say, how he was going to handle this, when all of a sudden the world turned crazy and went upside down, some savage, shrieking pain hit him in the legs, the little pistol went pirouetting away into the greyness, and he felt himself lifted, floating, flying through the air for what seemed like an age, then falling, crashing hard into the grey stone of the street, something making a snapping noise somewhere in his legs, something starting to stream down his face, taste salty in his mouth.

The world turned black for Tom Cordobes. When he came to – *how long? how long?* – he found himself staring straight into the face of a uniformed San Francisco cop who was feeling none too pleased about the dent in his fender or the fact that there was the smell of spent cartridges on the air. He looked at Cordobes and said, 'You weren't just jay-walking there, were you, buddy? You got some real fucking explaining to do once I get you and your pal to hospital.'

Cordobes tried to speak but something made it come out all wrong, and in any case the cop wasn't listening, he was looking at the grey bundle over on the street corner, shaking his head.

He came back, said to Cordobes, 'That guy looks even worse'n you do, son.'

And started to work the radio.

Tom Cordobes remembered the sound of the siren but he was out by the time the ambulance arrived. The sound of the bell, though, that was different. The sound of the bell, so muffled, so insistent in the fog, that was still ringing in his head when he came to, five hours later in the hospital. Ringing so loud he thought it might stay there forever, might never really go away.

ELEVEN

Lady Macbeth

The shot had taken most of Michael Quinn's head off. He'd had time
to swing the gun round, point it at Louise as best he could, and pull
the trigger. But this was her universe, this was some place she owned.
The chamber was empty and he managed to pull on two more empty
ones before Baxter got his act together, loosed off one shot that missed,
then a second that took him out completely, went in straight through
his right ear, lifted off his scalp, pushed out his brains and a whole
scoop of blood, threw it in the air, landed most of it on Louise
Gostelow.

Joni opened her eyes and there was nothing you could do but look
at where the screaming was coming from and it was coming from
Louise. The blood and grey stuff covered her head and shoulders and
her face was smeared with it, the gore dripped down her forehead,
was in her eyes, on her lips, stood red and livid in the crevice of her
mouth. It made her look like some horror painting, the lines by Goya,
the colouring by Dali. Joni Lascelles felt she was watching this all from
some other place, some distant location, and found that somewhere
inside her there was a little black feeling that said 'good', a feeling she
didn't want to encourage, but didn't want to crush either, a feeling
that was more intense than fear, and wouldn't even let her see how
crazy that was. This was the crude black thing she'd sought when she
first came here, the coldness she thought of as revenge. And they were
wrong. It didn't smell sweet. It smelled like an abattoir: it smelled of
meat and blood and some salty odour, like iodine or ozone, and after

a couple of seconds you had to close your mouth to stop it getting inside you.

She looked across the table, trying not to breathe too deeply, felt her stomach rise, then fall again, for no reason at all. The force of the shot had lifted Quinn off his seat and onto the floor. The gun was still there, the barrel pointing nowhere. She looked at it, felt Jamieson's attention, found his face, they exchanged glances, wondered what there was to know, what to trust, in that shared moment.

Then Baxter was past them, scooping up the revolver, his hands shaking, his face a mix of rage and fear and anger, and looking at them.

'You *fucking* move I'll kill you now,' he yelled. 'You hear me?'

Jamieson nodded, and it was for both of them.

Baxter looked at Louise and said, 'Holy shit.'

Then walked over to the sink, picked up a couple of towels, walked over and gave them to her. Joni watched the way he moved, watched for some tenderness there. But it was absent. What drove him was fear, not just of the situation, fear of Louise too. The big man was as much a victim as any of them, and he knew, it was written on his face as he watched her mop her head, mop her eyes so she could see.

'That's what happens, Louise,' Jamieson said blankly. 'That's what it looks like. What you expect? A little red hole and some stage blood?'

And Baxter strode over to him, leaned down, looked in his face and said, 'One more fucking word. That's all it takes. One more fucking word.'

Jamieson threw up his hands, shrugged, looked at Joni, and said nothing. He looked at the body on the floor. It seemed so inert, so pathetic. Hal Jamieson had spent most of his life trying to stay away from dead things. It wasn't the sight that offended him. It was the waste. And even Michael was a waste. Even Michael deserved a chance to try to prove himself. Had proved himself, Jamieson thought. Proved himself right then in a way that had cost him his life. Was that deliberate? he wondered. Was Michael really trying to even something out? Felt some guilt at the end? Would Michael even know the answer himself? It was impossible to decide. Whatever you made of Michael's view of the world, you couldn't deny it applied to him. He really did bounce around, from point to point, from atom to atom, and eventually it bounced him clean off the planet altogether.

She'd stopped screaming. She was wiping the gore from her face with her sleeve, a constant, spastic rhythm, and with each wipe it seemed a little of the surface of Louise Gostelow came away too, revealed something that lived inside her, something that maybe was the real her, the one that did the talking these days. Hal Jamieson watched her trying to clean herself up and saw a middle-aged woman trying to cling to some distant, half-remembered thing that was never quite true in the first place, saw the lines in her face as she wiped Michael Quinn's blood and brains from her skin, watched something graceless and alien and lacking in humanity move inside her body. And if he'd known the right words at that moment he would have said them. If he had the right words that could have made Baxter explode, just straight away, turn with the gun, take him out, one clean shot – which was not the way with Michael – Hal Jamieson would have been happy to have left the world that way. Because leaving the world was surely something that was going to come and seeing Louise like this, seeing the mask lift from her face, meant it really didn't matter that much any more anyway.

He watched her wipe her face, watched Baxter throw her a box of Kleenex, watched her use up one tissue, pick up the next. And realised how truly crazy this was, how far this whole thing had now gone. She had Louise's shape, her hair, though caked in blood, her clothes, spattered and stained, her voice, and, eventually, her face. The face he recognised, loved, the face that seemed to mark her like a malediction through life. But this was not Louise, this was *not*, Hal Jamieson said to himself. This was someone else, someone Desert Rose switched on him all those years ago.

Then she walked over to the kitchen cupboard, took out a cloth, wet it, started dabbing away at her clothes, dabbing away at her dress, her blouse, manically, over and over again. And it was so like this Louise to think of the practical things, so like her to think about the cleaning up there was to do. Objects mattered to this Louise, he realised, they mattered a lot, much more than people. And maybe it was his fault for providing this Louise with so many objects, maybe that, and the acid, helped turn her. Maybe things would have been better if they'd stayed poor, if they'd had to face up to some kind of vicious reality, the sort that other people met. If things hadn't turned out to be so *charmed* the night they chose that particular universe all those years back in a dirt cellar in Palo Alto.

Louise – *this Louise* – wiped something away from her mouth, looked at Baxter and said, in a voice so cold, so flat, so devoid of emotion, 'Do it. Take them outside and do it. We got enough shit on the floor in here.'

And Hal Jamieson thought again. Thought that maybe you could do all this to yourself just by trying, just by being in this cold and shivery space you inhabited day in, day out. You didn't need anything, not Desert Rose, not some crazily indulgent husband, to help you on the way. Then looked at Joni Lascelles, hated himself for allowing her to be brought into this, looked at her and tried to find some hope inside her eyes.

TWELVE

Aftermath

The end may justify the means as long as there is something that justifies the end.   LEON TROTSKY

Two days after Tom Cordobes and Michael Quinn were taken into hospital and the media circus really started to get hot, a blue and white VW van pulled into a half-deserted camp site just outside Fort Bragg, way north of the city, on the long, slow coastal route into Oregon, on Route 1. There were five people inside: Hal Jamieson, Louise Gostelow, Paul Dunsany, Margaret Zalinski and the child who now bore the name of Joe. They didn't talk much and when they did it was about the little things: food, gas, where to stay, which road to take. Each morning Jamieson would walk to the gas station a half-mile down the road to buy some cigarettes, get the newspapers, then read them quietly on a bench on the sand dunes, letting the cold, clear Pacific salt air blow through him, half hoping that somehow, through some unseen process, it would make him, make them, whole again. And maybe, in a way, it did.

Cy Langton was right. Newspapers liked things in black and white. They liked winners and losers. And the losers in this story were the cops. The cops who had fouled up the investigation all along. The cops who had fouled up the handover. The cops who failed to get a hold of whoever did this thing, except for one kid with a bullet wound to the chest who didn't have much, didn't have anything to say for himself, except it was him and him alone (and nobody, however hard they tried, seemed able to prove otherwise). Failed to find out what happened to Miles Seymour, whether he was alive or dead, in pieces somewhere or other (but you had to be careful what you wrote about this one, you had to use phrases like 'investigating connections' because the truth was there was no evidence they could throw at this Quinn kid to link him to the death of the hippy boy, no evidence at all, and the only way they could charge him would be if he confessed). And Michael Quinn was very specific about what he would and would not admit to. As far as the Seymour case went, it was him and him alone, he said, and if you wondered where the money went, officer, well, you ask yourself this: some cop leaves two hundred grand in a yellow Adidas sports bag on the sidewalk in San Francisco then goes shoot the guy who's supposed to pick it up, are *you* going to be surprised when the money just sort of disappears into the fog? It became, for a week or two, some kind of city myth: who *did* get the money? Some bum now relaxing by a pool in Maui with a couple of nicely tanned chicks? A street cleaner? Maybe even a cop?

The myth just grew, however much Tom Cordobes tried to tell people there *was* more than one person, he saw them – *in that fog, Tom, c'mon* – not well, but he saw them. Three of them. And he wounded one too. Sure, he did. *Sure, you did, Tom.* And the newspapers just loved it when Tom hobbled out of hospital on crutches, looking slow and old and pathetic. Loved running the pictures and captions that said, *you remember the guy they trusted to bring the kid home? Take a look at him now, folks. Take a look at the crutches, the way his Zapata moustache hangs down on his face, take a good look and think, my, isn't it nice we can sleep safe in our beds tonight, with cops like this out there to look out for us?*

It moved from personal tragedy to general comedy in little more than the space of a week and the one who suffered most was Tom Cordobes. The problem was the story was no longer about some English boy getting kidnapped. The story was about the cops screwing up. And the more the media kept asking why, why, why, about the operation Cy Langton had botched into place that day, the more they forgot about what started it. Pretty soon there were more cops investigating the internal procedures of Cy Langton's department than there were chasing Miles Seymour and his kidnappers. Pretty soon after that, Miles was forgotten, and the case turned into a series of head to heads, between the Palo Alto police and the rest of the world. And between Michael Quinn and Tom Cordobes. So that when Quinn came to court, in the summer of 1976, he made sure to give as much damning information as possible about Cordobes, the way he'd behaved, the language he'd used, how, if everything had gone OK, he would have been able to get back to where the kid had been hidden.

Except he couldn't. Because Cordobes' bullet had rendered him unconscious for four days, and when he finally did wake up, when he finally did come to, the police questioning was so hard, so intense, so aggressive, as the appeal court was to agree nearly twenty years later, that cooperation just sort of went out of the window. Even if there was something left in his memory for him to cooperate with, and he wasn't agreeing that was the case. So no one ever did find out what happened to Miles Seymour and the funny thing was, by that time no one really cared. No one in America at least, though there was a six-year-old girl in England, going to a succession of boarding schools that kept asking for her to leave after only a few months, who remembered, who kept waking up in the middle of the night, sweating, seeing a small, shining figure, with bright-gold wings, somewhere in the middle distance of her imagination.

And while all this was happening, the VW camper was moving, moving, slowly north, from Route 1 to 101, then onto 199, through the Collier Tunnel and into Oregon, finally, after three weeks, three weeks in which it seemed clear that no one in particular was looking out for anyone else in this case, finding the courage to hit the big way north, I–5, take it all the way through Eugene, past Portland, over the border into Washington. Finally to Seattle. Which looked grey and flat and characterless in the spring drizzle and for some reason they couldn't explain, just felt, not like home, but somewhere they could rest. Somewhere they could stay. Somewhere things might work out. A place you could firm up those phone calls on the road to back home, the calls where you explained that you'd done this thing that young people did back then, this thing called 'dropping out'. That it was important to you. That it mattered so much that you had to do it whatever the hurt it caused back home, to the folks who were paying to put you through college, and couldn't do much else but shake their heads in wonder at the way these kids just gave it all up. Dropping out. This was America, this was 1976. Like Hal Jamieson said, you could just fall through the floor of the nation, wake up somewhere else, look at the pillow next to you and find a stranger who'd done exactly the same thing, and usually for less pressing reasons.

They'd got Paul's head wound stitched by some country doctor way out in the sticks in Mendocino, who'd looked a little suspicious when he saw the line of flesh that cut across his face and partway into his scalp, but it went away when Hal showed a few bills. The doctor said he needed hospital. That there was some evidence of concussion. That he needed looking at. And knew they wouldn't take any notice. Knew they'd just keep on running, let the wound heal, hope it would turn out all right. Which it probably would. But concussion was a funny thing. You were messing with deep, dark stuff there, when you got inside someone's head. There was no way of saying the amnesia would be temporary, no way of predicting what might happen in the future. And he just said it because he had to, there was some unwritten rule in the Hippocratic oath that told you, if a bunch of kids turn up on your doorstep who look like they've been messing around with things they don't understand, just tell them, 'Don't be so fucking stupid, children. You get older, you get to understand that waving your life so close to the flame is just plain dumb, you get older and you realise that sometimes you can get burned in ways you just didn't notice or even feel at the time.'

The little guy, the one with the ringlets, the one who seemed to be the leader, smiled at him and said, 'Yes, sir.' And looked as if he understood, he really did.

Inside the little camper van, in that cramped, closed, sealed place that was their world during those snatched few months of the beginning of their new lives, the lines became drawn, invisibly, without anyone thinking, without a word being spoken. Hal and Louise would sit up front, driving, planning, thinking ahead. And in the back Margaret Zalinski would look after the boy – *Joe* – and Paul too, as he gradually came out of his wounded daze, came back into the world, piece by piece. By the time they reached Seattle, they were like two separate states, two separate families, sharing the same land, but with a border running between the two. By the time they reached Seattle, and the fog was clearing in Paul Dunsany's head, Hal and Louise were a couple, were locked together by some bond, part necessity, part complicity, that kept everybody else outside their lives. And she barely spoke to Paul Dunsany. Didn't want to know what he thought, what he remembered. Nor was he sure himself what was real, what was invented in his head. There was an image there he could not lose, the picture of him and Louise naked on a big white bed, in a big white room, and the sound of her, the sound of her voice, the liquid sound of their fucking, and when that image came to him he could close his eyes and bring it back so clearly, so purely, that he knew this had to be real. This had to have happened. This had to explain why she didn't

THIRTEEN

Beneath the Trees

Come children, let us shut up the box and the puppets, for
our play is played out.

WILLIAM MAKEPEACE THACKERAY,
Vanity Fair

'When I yell just run,' Hal Jamieson said quietly to her, invisibly, as
they walked towards the door. And there was no chance to say anything
else, not with Baxter behind them, waving the gun like it was something
magic. She nodded, looking forward, looking at the door all the time,
looking into nothingness, not focusing on anything. What was going
on inside her head was something even she couldn't describe.

'Get the door yourself,' Baxter said, and Hal Jamieson's mind was
working overtime. It was always working overtime.

Outside it was late afternoon under a flat grey sky. Stratus, the pilot
in Jamieson said straight away, a big flat layer of moisture sitting there
around six thousand feet, just letting through enough light to make
the forest look darkly green and dead. But the air was fresh, and after
the smell inside the cabin that was a relief, that was good. That ought
to help you think. It ought to.

They looked around, waited, half turned to watch Baxter trying to
figure how to handle this. Around the cabin the ground had been
paved and neatly manicured: a rock garden, a barbecue area, a place
where you could put a couple of tables during the summer. All Baxter
kept thinking about was evidence. How the cops got it. What it stuck
to. What you had to clean up afterwards, and how much, how very
much, he hated cleaning up.

He pointed over towards the nearest line of trees, beyond the parking
space where the Shogun and the Lexus were now stationary, gleaming
dully in the fading light.

'Go over to the trees,' he grunted. 'Walk real slow. You run, I shoot you now.'

So they walked and Jamieson shook his head slowly at the big goon's logic.

'So what's it worth, Steve?' he asked, talking into the greyness in front of him, not turning to look at the big guy when he spoke. 'What's it worth? One million? Two? You just name your price. Doesn't matter to me. You know how much I'm worth? Last estimate was four billion dollars, most recent I heard. After the first billion you kind of stop counting and leave it to those Forbes people. Hell, Steve. Far as I'm concerned you can take the whole damn lot. No use to me if I'm dead now, is it?'

The big man said nothing, then grunted, 'You sure do talk a lot, Mr Jamieson. For a dead man you sure do talk a lot.'

Joni Lascelles said, 'You should listen to him, Steve. You know what that woman's like in there. You know what she can do.'

Jamieson nodded his head and looked at her sideways. She didn't flinch. She didn't look away. There was a strength there, he thought, that maybe stayed hidden most of the time, but was ready, was willing to show itself, when she most needed it.

'She's right, Steve. You got to decide. You got to decide just how much my wife's ass is really worth to you. How much you get with her. How much you get with me. Or should I say how much you *think* you're gonna get with her. Louise is one smart woman, my boy. This thing goes wrong for you, I don't think she'll be carrying the can. She's run rings around better men than you. Hell, what do you think she's doing now?'

Baxter shoved him in the back, waved them towards a bunch of big pine trunks that stood huddled together, like giants trying to shelter from the light of day.

'Guess I should thank you for that, Mr Jamieson. Your big mouth just made up my mind.'

And Hal Jamieson cursed himself, couldn't even look at the English girl for a second or two, wondered how he could be losing his touch like this. Wondered if there really only was one thing left for it, and that was to try to tackle the guy and let the girl run away, take her chances. Which were probably pretty slim, but a whole lot better than any of his.

'You can turn around now,' Baxter said, and when they did they saw the shame, the grief on his face.

'Don't like doing any of this,' he said. 'Want you to know that.'

'Doesn't make any difference to us whether you like it or not,' Jamieson said slowly, judging how far away the big man was, how easy it was going to be to tackle him, to keep him still, to give her as much time as he could. 'We get dead whether you're crying your heart out or having the time of your life, Steve. Think on that.'

'Yeah, well,' said Baxter, and the gun was coming up now, lazily, as if he was only half thinking about it. 'Point is that sometimes you get one thing happening after another and it just leads to a place you don't get to control, however much you want it.'

'You could have a billion dollars, Steve,' Jamieson said, and thought, he's too far, he's just too far, and if I move it just brings things on.

Baxter stared at him and there was real hatred there, it stood between them like something dark in the air.

'What the fuck would a man like me get to do with a billion dollars?' Baxter asked. Then he shook his head, pulled the gun up, pointed it midway between them, thinking which one to take first, wishing, really wishing, he didn't have to make this decision.

And it was Joni who heard it first, heard the noise in the woods, like a beast moving through the brush, moving quickly, not far away, not far at all.

'Someone's coming,' she said and Baxter's eyes flickered, a little animal sign of fear.

'Shit,' he said, hearing it too, and they watched the gun wave crazily in the air, not knowing where to go.

'Someone's coming,' she said again, and when Baxter looked at her, he felt he was looking at something that came from beyond the world. She was smiling at him and her face, her head, seemed so huge, so bright and golden in the grey-green gloom of the forest. She was smiling, and she would not run, not from this man, not from them. Not from anyone. Baxter knew that Louise was right. What this woman meant was not some vague, unspoken threat. What she meant was retribution, and that was something you didn't, couldn't, bargain with. That was something that just followed you, everywhere, night and day, always stepping on your shadow until the moment you turned round and faced it, saw it out.

Baxter looked at her, reached forward, punched Hal Jamieson hard in the face, sending him sprawling back into the dirt-brown carpet of pine needles, pointed the gun in her face and said, 'You first.'

Then something struck out of the bushes, something moving so fast he didn't really see it, and Paul Dunsany was there, she could see him there, she could recognise him, feel the gratitude for his presence straight away, and feel something else behind it, inside her: some distant sense of puzzlement.

Baxter rolled back under the force of this screaming, kicking figure, hands clawing at his throat, and wondered for a moment if the guy was just plain crazy. Then remembered his days bouncing outside the night clubs down Pioneer Square, swatted him with one big fist, swatted him again, saw the body come away, the spectacles go flying into the dirt, heard his pain, watched him slump to the ground, watched the girl reach down for him, look into his face.

She saw the line of blood at the corner of his mouth, the fear, the fury in his eyes. And Paul Dunsany looked at the three of them, sprawled on the floor, in the dirt and pine needles of the forest, looked at Hal Jamieson, at Joni, and felt such anger that it made him shake.

Baxter stared down at him, so tall, so big, and said, 'You dumb fuck.'

Then pointed the gun at his head, grinned, because it was OK now, someone had made up the balance here, someone had come for him, and that made it OK. Baxter grinned and felt happy, felt secure knowing that it would be over real soon. And then his vision went furry, something stung him in the shoulder, pushed him back against the tree trunk, and sent the gun in his hand wheeling round and round through the air.

Jamieson was scrambling after it as fast as he could, trying to get these thoughts into some kind of order, work out what was happening, who was who.

'You don't need the gun, Hal.'

It was a strong female voice, with a broad, cutting, blue-collar accent. Margaret Zalinski stepped out of the trees carrying a hunting rifle under her arm. Joni looked at her, the hair cropped close to the head, the lined country face, watched her stride out towards them, so calm, so confident in the woods, and thought: the blueberry lady. And wondered. There was a missing piece here that would have to be returned. But not now. Not now.

She held Paul, felt the warmth, the humanness of him, took out a handkerchief, dabbed at the blood on his mouth and wondered at the provenance of the tears that stood, like liquid pools, in her eyes, wondered who they were for, and why.

Jamieson picked up the gun in any case, kept it on Baxter, hoped the big guy didn't realise he wouldn't even know how to unlock the safety catch.

'Margie?' he said, staring at her, trying hard to believe this could be the same person. '*Margie?*'

'Run a farm, you need to shoot,' she said, and he listened to the clipped, rural way she spoke, took in her solid farmer's face, tanned and lined by the weather, tried to match it with the girl he knew, so long ago, didn't get even halfway there. 'Goes with the job.'

She looked at Baxter slumped against the tree.

'Quit fooling yourself, asshole. You'll live. I'd used the goddamn Saturday night special Paul here gave me, things might have been different, but I took one look at that and I just knew I wasn't gonna hit you with it. All you got was just a dumb little hunting gun I use for rabbits and deer. Might have a hole in your shoulder for a little while but it'll heal. What I hear maybe you'll be getting free Medicare in jail for it soon.'

And the big guy just lay there, said nothing.

'Can you drive?' Jamieson asked him.

Baxter flexed his arm. There was really just some blood in the shoulder there and a big nasty ache but he could drive, he *would* drive, he'd do any damn thing to get the hell out of there.

'Yeah,' the big man grunted, not looking at them.

'Good,' Jamieson said and threw him a set of keys. 'You go take the Shogun. You go take it where the hell you like because it is yours. It is your pay-off, my friend. I do not hold anything against you, Mr Baxter. I do not hate you. I do not bear a grudge. But I do not wish to see your face ever again. Or all these things may change. Understand?'

The big guy nodded, shuffled to his feet, shuffled to the Shogun, and they didn't even look back as he drove off into the falling night, the three of them were too busy looking at each other, silently, full of wonder, taking each other in, with Joni Lascelles staring at them from outside this circle, knowing this was not somewhere she belonged, feeling the power of this reunion wash over her, leave her numb, exhausted.

Hal Jamieson turned to look at the cabin. The naked figure at the window was too far away to read the expression in her face, but in a way you didn't need to. She was so still, so pale in the fading light. Really you didn't need to at all.

'This is all done,' Jamieson said, and he couldn't take his eyes off her. 'Michael's dead, Paul. This whole thing is run through. You should go. You should get the hell out of here right now. Leave me to clear this up.'

Dunsany felt around his face, where it hurt, decided that Baxter didn't hit as hard as he might, tasted the blood drying in his mouth, and wondered if there was any getting through to Jamieson, whether this was just a closed book.

'Hal,' he said, winding his spectacles back on round his face. 'We were friends once. What we did we did together . . .'

'Jesus, Paul, you did *nothing*.'

'We were friends.'

Jamieson turned and looked at him, looked at him across the years, saw the naive, talented kid, with longer hair, that big billow of innocence around him, and hated himself for ever taking that away.

'I don't deserve to be your friend, Paul. You deserve better than me. Now what I'm telling you I'm telling you once. What is inside that cabin belongs to me, it is mine to deal with and mine alone. You are not involved. You cannot, you *will* not get involved. You understand? What you do now is you go away. You and Margie, you take this woman, you both tell her what you know, and you hope she has it in her to forgive us.'

Joni Lascelles struggled to find the words for him and decided there was nothing, nothing that could ease his pain.

'Forgiveness doesn't mean anything,' she said in the end. 'You don't want that from me. You don't *need* it.'

Jamieson smiled at her. Found it hard to believe this could really be the same person as the tiny, frail child he saw on the TV twenty years ago, a space in time that seemed so close still to him, that was separated from the present by nothing more than lines upon the skin and dollars in a bank account.

'You let these people talk to you,' he said in the end. 'Then you decide.'

'You'll be OK?' Margie asked, and he still couldn't shake off his amazement that this could be what time had done to her, to make her so strong, so certain of herself. 'I remember, Hal. I owe you. *We* owe you.'

Hal Jamieson looked at them and wondered how this would all fall through in the end, wondered if there was anything in his power that could change it, and if he had the strength to want to find out. 'You owe me nothing. You take this woman and talk to her. Tell her what she needs to know. You do that and I'm happy, I'm fine. And that's a big thing to ask. A real big thing. Of you. And of her.'

Then he walked off to the cabin, went in the door, and never looked back.

The three of them worked their way through the woods to the old Ford pickup she used on the farm, parked between two big pines that stood like a huge wooden gateway into the forest, the dark, endless forest that rolled off into nowhere. Then they got in and drove off, not talking much at first, knowing there would come a time, and each, in his and her own way, fearing the consequences when it did.

Hal Jamieson found her in the main bedroom. She was seated naked in front of the mirror, her hair wet, plastered to her head, rubbing herself with a towel. He walked over, took the towel off her, started to help, and realised, with some great lever of sadness turning in his head, that seeing Louise naked would never stir anything inside him again. She looked pale. Her skin looked old. Her eyes wouldn't fix on him. They just kept examining her body, her face, her hair.

'You came back,' she said. 'That's Hal. You always come back.'

She was looking at him, looking in a way he'd never really known before. As if she was begging for some kind of comfort.

'Sure, kid,' he said. 'I always will.'

'You think so?' she said quietly, and reached for the make-up drawer. He watched her rebuilding herself, slowly drying her hair, drying her skin, and felt himself trying to judge if it would ever be possible to rekindle some warmth between them, almost cursed himself for the thought. The old Louise came back as she worked. As she played with the mascara, as she worked with the powder. The old Louise came back and if she minded that he'd seen behind the mask, she didn't show it. Louise had been truly naked for the first time in her life that day and after that what people thought of you, what you thought of yourself, didn't matter much any more.

'You were always the best,' she said.

'Yeah.'

She worked on her hair and he just watched, watched the way she cared for herself, preened in the mirror. It was just about dry now and when she did something with it, when she'd spent fifteen minutes with a dryer and a brush and a comb, it would get back to normal.

'I don't mean that the way you think. I had so many men be good to me, Hal. But you just acted like . . .'

And she struggled for the words.

'I thought you liked me, Hal. I thought you saw a person there.'

Hal Jamieson looked at her reflection in the mirror and thought how frightened, how sad it seemed, wondered whether that was real or just a trick of the glass.

'I never saw a person there, Hal. I just got bored and tired and sick of things the moment I was born and it never changed. You made it get a little better but it's still like that. You know that, don't you? None of this means anything. You want the truth? You don't mean anything. I don't mean anything.'

'Yeah,' he said. Then walked over to the wardrobe, pulled out a checked shirt, a pair of slacks.

'You can wear these, Louise. We'll go away for a couple of days. Take the plane. I'll get someone to clean up this mess. We'll go away.'

And maybe she heard him, maybe she didn't. All Hal Jamieson could look at was the way she kept dabbing at her face, trying to get it back to the way it was, maybe the way it was when she was twenty and everyone in the Barn – *everyone* – was in love with Louise. Everyone found themselves lost in her beauty, her power.

Back on the road, at Snoqualmie, where they were driving back down towards the coast, Joni found the thoughts multiplying, getting so strong they might flood her head, might drown her.

'Paul?' she said. '*Paul?*'

BACK TO THE GARDEN

ONE

Margie's Farm

In my dream the pipes were playing
In my dream I lost a friend
Come down Gabriel blow your horn
Some day we will meet again

ROBBIE ROBERTSON,
'Fallen Angel'

They slept at the farm, in separate rooms, woke early, struggled for things to say to each other. Finally, Paul and Joe went outside, started walking the lines of neatly clipped fruit trees, looking for pests, looking at the state of the soil. For Joe it was just another day. Some people on the farm, that's all.

You just couldn't tell with the weather out here in this part of the state, on the flat, fertile land that stood between the mountains and the sea. Sometimes the microclimate took it into its head to copy the city. Sometimes it did its own thing. This day started gloomy and cool, with limited visibility, a dour, dark beginning. Then the wind struck up, the sky started to change, and a bright eggshell blue began to peek through, won the battle, and by ten there was hardly a cloud in the sky. You could see all the way down to the Sound, a good fifteen miles away in the distance, across farmland and forest, a rolling, tumbling landscape that was so green, so verdant, it shone, until it met the glittering water, the surface shimmering like the scales of some gigantic fish, all the way to the Olympic mountains, snow-capped, so vast, so remote in the distance.

The two women sat on the porch of the modern, stone-built farmhouse drinking coffee, strong hot coffee, and watched Paul and Joe mooching round the fields. It took an hour or so for Margaret Zalinski to fill her in on the facts. But facts were bare things, pebbles scattered on the beach at random, no pattern, no meaning to them. Explanations were different. Explanations were harder. Explanations couldn't come just like that, flat and out of nowhere. They happened over time. You had to invite them into your life, let them worm their way to the front of your imagination, then start to come to life.

She looked at Margie and tried to imagine some hippy kid of twenty years ago, getting pushed around, floating in the stream of little people winding its aimless way around America. It wasn't easy. Margaret Zalinski looked her age. Looked maybe older. Working the farm, spending all this time out in the open air, out taming the countryside, must do that to you. She had a full, mannish face, one that managed to look content, even cheerful, without ever smiling much. And a slowness to her person that could be disconcerting. She thought before she spoke, and the pauses were long sometimes. She didn't rush any-thing. Maybe it was through living on the farm. Maybe it was through caring for Joe and having to explain everything carefully, slowly, to make sure he understood as best he could. Margaret Zalinski was a different kind of person from her. Different from anyone she'd known. So careful, so wary about where she did and did not tread.

Joni watched the two men talking slowly in the apple orchard, looking at the trunks for signs of disease, checking the fruit, and said, 'You and Paul. You were together. Afterwards.'

Margaret Zalinski studied her and there was a half-smile there, almost overshadowed by the bright-blue spark in her eyes.

'You can see things,' she said, in the flat, monotone voice. 'I'll say that for you.'

Not really, she thought inwardly. There was nothing to see. You could *feel* it. You could feel how it would happen. The slow momentum of togetherness. People fall together for all sorts of reasons but maybe love is one of the minor ones. Comfort, the sharing of grief, plain, simple fear, maybe these are the more common reasons. Maybe these make more sense than any arcane mysterious thing called love, a thing that everyone talks about, no one seems able to define.

'What happened?' she asked.

Margie took a deep breath and looked at the day. It was so fine, so radiant, and the air felt so rich, so sweet you almost hated the idea of letting it back out of your lungs.

'Time happened. Nothing more. Just time. It was a slow thing, in any case. Nothing we thought about. And when you get down to it, Paul is a city creature. He just loves that music so much, loves that damned little studio. You can never drag him away from there. Never get him out of that life. And Joe and me, we didn't fit in the city. It wasn't where we *belonged*. The pace was all wrong for us. We didn't run like that. That make sense?'

She nodded.

'So Paul helped me buy this land here. Helped me buy this house. All he took from that money was enough to buy that little houseboat of his, take a lease out on the studio and put some recording equipment in there. The rest he just gave to me and told me to get on and use it. And that wasn't the end of it either. First few years we were out here things were really rough. If Paul hadn't been helping us, God knows what might have happened. He's a good man, you know? He was going to tell you, bring you here, even though he thought it meant the end of you and him. Then Louise sent him the message, saying she'd taken you and I guess everything sort of moved in a different way. He's a good man. It's inside of him, and I don't think it does him any favours sometimes.'

'I know that,' she said. 'I knew that from the beginning.'

'We did too. He helped us a lot, and it cost him too, until we got things established. After a while, you get to know your work, and it starts to come good. I took the stall in Pike Place, sold direct to those happy little tourists who pay me straight on the nail for my dried blueberries and some apple tea, not taking off any fifty per cent god-damned margin like the store people do, and it came good. In the end. And by that time I was gone from the city, except for driving in most mornings and spending the day in Pike Place, which was fine, which was enough. And Paul and me were friends. Good friends. Better friends than we were lovers if you want the honest truth.'

'Maybe it's easier,' Joni said. 'Maybe friendship just needs less.'

And there was one of those long pauses while Margaret Zalinski thought about it.

'I don't think so,' she said finally. 'Relations between two people never come easy, not if they're worth something. There was time that came between us but there was something else too. Something we felt about what happened. Some kind of guilt we both had. Not that I thought Paul should have felt guilty about *anything*. He don't remember that much but I do. I *know* he had no idea there was a child involved in this. I *know* he would have gone straight to the cops if he had. But he doesn't accept that. Either it just isn't there inside his head or something just told him he had to feel guilty in any case, whatever. I don't know. I *do* know you can't have two people love each other if they're both grieving over the same thing. Both feeling the same blame. You can't lean on each other in equal measure and hope not to fall over. Life doesn't work like that, and you want the honest truth, I think that drove us apart as much as the fact I just couldn't stand the smell of the city, the way they treated Joe in the streets. We just got dumb there and it drove us apart. You get what I'm saying?'

Joni wondered whether she did. It wasn't something you could *get*. It was something you had to feel.

'Perhaps,' she said.

'That's an honest answer. And honest answers are sure-fire ways of killing things between people these days. You want another truth? Anyone ought to feel guilty about this, it's not Paul, not Hal Jamieson, not that goddamned wife of his. For sure not Michael Quinn, not that he had it in his head to feel guilty about anything. It's me. I got more out of what happened than anyone. None of this happened, you know where I'd be? Waitressing in some diner somewhere, living in a trailer park with four snotty kids and a husband who came home and beat me up every night. I'd got myself booked with a first-class one-way ticket for that life until this happened and you bet I would have got there bang on time.'

'You're a smart woman, Margie. That wouldn't have happened.'

'Nothing to do with being smart. You think that none of the women that happens to are smart? Not for one moment. It's got to do with luck and fate or some such thing. Quinn got something right there. Way beyond me what he was saying about it, but he got something right. You got some choices, you got some things where you got no choice at all. What bounced me out of all that was *him*. Joe was what happened. And it made my life. It *gave* me my life.'

Joni Lascelles wondered whether to ask, then knew it couldn't be left unsaid. 'You feel guilty about that?'

And she answered straight away, her voice rising a little, 'No, I do not. I ought to, but I do *not*. Not one little bit. That's what I got served and that's what I took. There'd been some way I could have stopped what happened, I would have done it. But I didn't have that opportunity. So I did what I could.'

'You did well,' she said. 'You did so well, Margie. I couldn't . . .'

She didn't want to say any more, she didn't want to think about it.

'Oh, yes, you could. Don't you go around thinking you couldn't. Know why? What happened to me, what I did, was something *I* wanted, not something I did because I thought I ought to. I did it because it gave me something and people still don't understand that; people see Joe and say, "Look at him, he's no more than a child." And I say, "Thank you." See, being a child is the best part of us, the best part till someone gets to start to poison it. Kids don't make bombs and they don't make drugs. Kids don't go to war and the only thing they know about hate is what we teach them. And you'd better believe that. You more than any of us. And, sure, kids don't do things that *are* important to us, we can't *all* be kids. But you ask me which way the balance goes and I know, I *know*, it goes in their favour. That we owe more to them than they ever do to us, than they *will* ever do to us. Someone says to me I look like I got a child in the house the rest of my days that makes me feel real lucky. It's like waking up each morning and feeling the day's been blessed.'

She said nothing, and Margaret Zalinski shifted in her chair, felt uncomfortable.

'Shit,' she said. 'I'm talking too much. What I said there, you best ignore that. I didn't have the right. What happens now, what happens with Joe, that's up to you. He's your flesh and blood. I got no rights over him. Haven't even got a piece of paper that says I'm his guardian or anything. You're his legal kith and kin. What you want to happen is what's going to happen. I won't stand in your way.'

Joni Lascelles watched them working in the orchard, so involved, so engrossed.

'Joe is your flesh and blood, Margie,' she said. 'Joe belongs with you.'

And something came loose inside her, the jagged, painful edge that had been gnawing away for as long as she could remember, saying that what she had sought of Miles was not the knowledge of his existence, but the benison of his forgiveness. What she had sought was something for herself, not something for him. This last, clinging remnant of her old self dissolved, floated away, and for a moment the distant shimmering of the water could have been gold fluttering in the wind, for a moment there may have been the sound of tinsel whispering across the years.

Margaret Zalinski was looking away, hiding her face, but Joni could see anyway. She could see how she let the tears just roll, a long steady stream, didn't try to choke them back, just let them come. And when the moment had passed, wiped them away with the back of her hand, turned back to face her, looking so strong, so handsome.

'What do you want me to tell him?'

'What can he understand?'

'More than most people think. We took him round a lot of doctors. Paul helped me there too. Didn't do much good. What happened is his brain got messed up somehow by that poisonous shit Quinn gave him and there's nothing they can do to change that now. How he is, that's how he's going to be, pretty much. He's slow. He retains what's important to him. He can read a little. Point is, he doesn't improve much. When I get old, I'll need to think about that, but I can put it to one side at the moment. You want to tell him you're his sister, he'll understand. He'd be real proud of that, I think.'

She didn't need to think about it much, but she waited anyway, she didn't want her to feel this was some snap, some instant decision.

'Tell him I'm a friend of Paul's. Just that.'

Margaret Zalinski didn't say anything for a good two minutes.

'Do I tell him he might be seeing you again?'

And to that there really was no answer. The simple truth was that Joni Lascelles did not know. Just did not. And did not understand the process that would lead her to knowing. It was all like a big blanket of fog in front of her, not frightening, not daunting, just opaque.

The two men were walking back to the house, talking slowly, looking as if they had been doing this for years, and for a moment she was jealous, of Paul, of Margie, for a moment something went red and hot inside her at the thought that they had watched him grow, from a child to a man, they had seen this miraculous transformation over the years and there was nothing left of it that she could share, no piece of magic that could warm her, offer some comfort.

They stopped on the dusty dirt path outside the porch and Joe put his hands on his hips and said, 'Signs of moth, Margie. We got moth.'

She looked at him, marvelled at him. He was a good six foot tall, strong, well built, with a tanned, healthy skin. And handsome too, a broad, pleasant, serious face, framed by dark, clean hair, cut short, the way she'd expect of a farmer. What had come down to both of them was something from their mother, she could see nothing of her father there. And to that had been added strength, real country strength, the strength you got on a farm. Joe was a good-looking man, even if he didn't think about it himself.

'Pretty girl,' he said, looking into her eyes with a curiosity so open it took her breath away. 'You want see the apples? City folk like seeing apples.'

He was squinting in the strong sunlight, not smiling, taking his gestures invisibly over the years from Margie, even down to the frankness that Joni found so disarming, even crippling, in its honesty.

She looked at Paul and could sense his nervousness, but that didn't stop him watching her, trying to see what was happening there.

'We have to go back to the city, Joe,' she said. 'Maybe another time.'

'OK,' he said and left it at that. 'You got a name?'

And he was smiling a little then, there was a line of good strong white teeth showing through, and Joe knew he was making a joke, liked his joke, felt familiar with it.

Four words, she thought, two lives. Two worlds, alive, beating, struggling to breathe, inside them.

'My name is Joni Lascelles,' she said.

And he laughed, so pleasantly, looked at the sky, rolled his eyes a little, as if to wonder, where *did* I hear that one, and said, '*Weird* name. You excuse me. I got to eat now.'

Then walked inside the farmhouse, started banging around in the kitchen, whistling, badly out of tune. And Paul Dunsany looked at the two women, went away, walked around the corner and started doing things that didn't need doing to the car.

'Can I hold you?' Margie asked, after what seemed like an age.

Joni walked forward and was surprised to find she was a good deal taller than her. Margaret Zalinski was a small woman. What gave her stature came from inside, was not physical, but it was real, you could touch it, you could feel its warmth and it was as strong as anything that was made of flesh and bone.

Joni Lascelles walked forward and opened her arms and then they embraced, silently, their faces buried in each other's hair, letting something pass between them that had no earthly name or form, but contained within it such power that they could only close their eyes and hold each other tight, then wait for the beast to release them from its awesome, unyielding grip.

409

TWO

Mount Olympus

The night before, when he'd done his best to clean Louise up, helped
her into some spare clothes, got her into the Lexus, Hal Jamieson had
driven straight to the GA terminal at Sea-Tac, filed a flight plan
for Hawaii, routing via San Francisco for a fuel stop. The flight
attendant took the plan, examined it and said, 'Have a nice break, Mr
Jamieson.'

Then smiled at them over the counter and wished he hadn't
bothered. They looked awful. They looked like dead people, he
thought. They didn't need a few days in Hawaii, they needed a new
life.

Jamieson flicked through the sheets of weather data on the board.
The cloud had come in with the night, right down to a thousand feet
in places, topping out at thirteen thousand, solid all the way. A good
old Sea-Tac instrument departure, getting vectored around by air
traffic, right and left, up and down, all the way, until that magic
moment when you broke free of the crap, came out on top, and
tonight it would be a bright, moonlit night once you got above the
cloud. Tonight the moon would be almost full and you could fly with
the stars, listening to the radio, letting the controllers tell you where
to go, free of gravity, free of the world. That was the biggest thing
Hal Jamieson got out of flying. It was the one moment in his life when
everything else in his existence – business, Louise, *life* – just fell into
the background and his head got taken over by that curious mix of

physical and mental disciplines, calculation and guesswork, that went into piloting a plane.

She stood on the asphalt and watched him check out the Citation visually from the outside, check the fuel, then unlock the side door, let the hydraulics roll it down, the steps unfolding on the way.

'It's a long time since I've been on the plane,' Louise said, as she climbed wearily up the steps.

'Too long,' he said, and turned on the power.

'Hal. We've got nothing with us. No luggage. Nothing at all.'

'I got a platinum American Express card, Louise. What more does anyone need? We just buy the stuff when we get there. And I just phone back home, get things sorted out so that when we come back, life gets back to normal. OK?'

She was strapping herself into one of the passenger seats – Louise hated flying up front, hated the way the dials and lights kept calling for your attention – and not looking what she was doing. She was examining her face in the mirror. It looked pale and tired and old and Hal Jamieson couldn't take it any more. He just pulled up the door from the inside, threw the lever, went up front, started sorting the plane out. By the time he'd unrolled his charts, the Jeppesen instrument plate, and a visual one for the Seattle area too, with the route of the customary instrument departure to the north carefully outlined in pencil over the complex ragged shapes of land and sea around this part of the state, she was asleep. Fast asleep, leaning back in the cream leather of the seat, her mouth slightly open, breathing a little noisily. He watched her for a while, wondered what dreams there might be going on inside her head, and hoped they were quiet ones, hoped Louise's private monsters might be giving her a rest for a while. Then Hal Jamieson called for start-up and began the run-through for getting the Citation airborne, winding up the engines, running through the pre-flight checks neatly printed on the card tucked into the pocket by the pilot's seat.

Traffic was pretty busy around Sea-Tac then but the controller handling him was feeling warm and friendly.

'It's real grey out there, Sierra Whisky, so we're going to lead you out of this by the nose before we hand you on to Portland. You're cleared taxi for one eight left, hold at Charlie.'

'Cleared one eight, Charlie,' Jamieson read back, rolled the throttle to get some momentum, cut her back when she was moving, tested the brakes, then followed the line of lights until he saw the big sign with the C on it. It took two minutes to run through the final pre-flight and call for departure.

'OK, sir, you are clear departure, three five zero to three thousand.'

The big silver bird rolled down the runway, the engines burned and she pulled eagerly into the air, Jamieson retracted the gear, then fought to keep her down. Even with full fuel, she was flying light and felt like pulling away. Running almost due north then climbing to three thousand seemed to happen so quickly that there was nothing between lifting the gear and then listening to the controller come back on with a new heading.

'We got some new inbound traffic just now, Sierra Whisky, and that means I'm gonna run you around a little, for which I apologise.'

And run him around he did. Jamieson got vectored back and forth through the zone dodging the big jumbos arriving from Tokyo and beyond, slipping between them a good thousand feet away in the opaque greyness, always painted neatly on the controller's radar screen, the squawk giving away his position, and his altitude too, always safe, always where he should be. Then they got back on track, back where Jamieson thought he should have been all along. Heading due west across the city, out towards Olympia, ready for a turn to the south, clearance to climb up to cruising altitude, to let the Citation rip and then tear on down the coast to San Francisco.

'Sierra Whisky, thank you for your patience, you are now cleared to climb to your cruise level on a heading of one niner five.'

'Copied, thank you, sir,' Jamieson said into the throat mike and reached forward for the bug that told the autopilot what to do, where to fly. It stood where he last left it, crossing the city, due west, and the altimeter was at five thousand feet. Jamieson looked at the little blue marker and wondered at his own laziness. When he first started flying, you did these things by hand. You guided the aircraft onto the right heading, you played with the throttle to get the right rate of climb, the right altitude. You *flew* the plane. Nowadays, it was all different. Nowadays, anyone could do it. You twiddled the bug on the autopilot and the plane just turned onto the heading. You dialled in the height you wanted, the speed you wanted to get there, and the computer just did the rest. Hell, if you got real lazy, you just programmed the route straight into your GPS system, let it talk direct to the autopilot itself, then sat back, watched the stars. Fucked some chick out of marketing. He'd done that one too. He'd done that one lots of times.

'Sierra Whisky. We are not showing your turn on our radar. Confirm your heading is one niner five.'

'Copied,' Jamieson said, then turned down the radio volume. Outside there was nothing but the luminescent greyness of the cloud, going on forever, opaque, and quite without shape. He remembered some of the tricks they'd played when he'd done his instrument rating. How they taught him to close his eyes and then try to guess what was happening to the plane. And how it was impossible in that greyness. You just couldn't judge things. Once you lost sight of the horizon – either the real one, or the artificial one on the panel of the little Beech trainer – the world disappeared. There was no way your body could tell if the plane was banking sixty degrees to the right, or thirty to the left. You could pull yourself straight into a stall and then a spin if you tried to fly in this kind of weather using your senses alone. Because they just didn't work any more. You had reached your limitations. And knowing your limitations was one of the ways you lived to fly another day.

Hal Jamieson looked at the blue marker sitting on two seventy degrees, looked at the altitude settled at seven thousand feet, glanced at the visual area chart, turned the marker ten degrees through north, felt the big metal bird move gently as the servos and hydraulics did their work and set the new course, undid his seat belt and walked to the back of the cabin. Louise was still asleep. And whatever dreams there were inside her head, they seemed to be OK, they didn't seem to be bothering her. Jamieson put a hand to her neck, felt the warmth there, felt the roughness of the skin, looked at the red marks that were still livid on the flesh where she had rubbed off the blood and brain of Michael Quinn. Then he kneeled down, felt her cheek, kissed her hair, let his head rest gently there, smelling her fragrance, something expensive, something he couldn't put a name to, and he didn't think about the greyness outside, didn't think about anything at all, just let the minutes roll by.

In the control tower at Sea-Tac they were going crazy, watching the little green dot, with Sierra Whisky's transponder code painted on the base, go all the wrong way, all the way it shouldn't, crossing Scenic Beach, heading on out over Duckabush, up into the Olympic range, yelling down the radio trying to get some response. But in the cabin of the silver bird, running smoothly through the greyness at seven thousand feet and a ground speed of 330 mph on the dial, there was no panic, no fear. Hal Jamieson held his wife's head and thought of nothing, absolutely nothing, let a big black vacuum fill his head and found that in the emptiness there was something that might have been peace: something with no grief or guilt, no fear, no pain. And when the Citation hit he felt nothing either. In a second they were gone, just a trail of blood and bone and debris nine hundred feet from the summit of Mount Olympus. So high, so remote, it took the accident investigation people from the FAA three weeks to recover every shattered piece of the plane, and the few remains of Hal Jamieson and his wife that had not been taken away by the animals, then try to piece things together, scratch their heads.

And finally shrug their collective shoulders, go for a beer, and say, *what the fuck?*

THREE

Fission (2)

Footfalls echo in the memory
Down the passage which we did not take
Towards the door we never opened
Into the rose-garden.

T. S. ELIOT,
Four Quartets

'Things sparkling.'

Five-year-old eyes flash through the window, fix on gold and silver mannequins behind the glass, moving to clockwork time, one with a baton in its hand, one bowing at a tiny violin.

'See, Florrie. Things sparkling.'

The pet name grates on her. She feels stupid here, in this foreign country, in this foreign costume, the white hems dragging around her ankles, stupid golden wings hanging on her back. Conscious of her awkwardness in this strange and unfamiliar place.

She looks at her brother, and something black and buzzing flits across her vision, then disappears into the dry afternoon air. She peers into the window, sees two small, ghostly figures reflecting back at her in the thin winter sunlight, their robes rustling in the faint, warm breeze. *So cute, so cute,* the passers-by said, and every word infuriated her. *So cute, so cute,* their mother had stopped, looked, admired them, taken out the little Kodak Instamatic, taken their picture in front of the window, said just a minute – just a Mummy minute, she thought – just wait here. There were things to do and it was so busy in the store.

She does not smile. She says, a little wearily, 'Yes, Miles.'

Then wonders if he will always be like this. Always the young one. Always someone to be cherished, cared for. And, without thinking, without having to make some kind of decision, accepts the idea, accepts the role, even at five. To care. To be present.

'They sparkle,' she says and looks at them again in the window, and thinks, maybe they *do*. Maybe they really do.

Somewhere, a mile away, in an old wooden house that has seen better days, Michael Quinn is coming out of the depths of an LSD trip and feeling tired and ill. He goes to bed, falls asleep, and has dreams that make no sense, dreams with angels in them – and Quinn remembers something from his old theology classes, remembers that demons are merely angels gone bad. Angels and some sad, savage violence that makes no sense.

Daniel Seymour drinks, but, in time, does not drink so much, finds that his anger dies within him (and with it his talent too), then, quietly, with some inner waking sense, begins to see his children for what they are, separate, individual pieces in the universal jigsaw, not parts of himself, his own private cosmos, owned, like goods and chattel. And with this realisation comes a peace to his marriage, a peace that resembles more a truce than genuine friendship, but proves enough to see the children into adulthood, when they win the freedom to create their own pain instead of inheriting it second-hand from others. Louise Gostelow marries a stockbroker from a good Roman Catholic family, works on her tan and her drink problem. Hal Jamieson winds up a product manager at Apple with great stock options and a reputation as Cupertino's wildest Valentino. Tom Cordobes gets busted by Cy Langton anyway, gets a job in security, spends long lonely nights watching the TV. And Roscoe Sutter, after spending so many years in the woods that smell of shit and eucalyptus

rassenfrassenrassenfrassenrassenfrassenrassenfrassen

driving passers-by crazy as he dodges the building workers trying to put together the new Gresham mall is discovered, one day in 1989, dead beneath the grey, scarred trunks of the few remaining trees, dead beneath a covering of ancient, piss-stained business pages from the *San Jose Mercury*.

Some things don't change because this is the – *a* – real world and, as a different Michael Quinn once said, preordination and predetermination are not the same thing.

She sees all this and it is not a dream. She sees it in her mind's eye as she stares out of the houseboat window, watching the water move,

416

grey and greasy, mirroring the flatness, the colour of the sky, rocking the boats on the lake gently, in a rhythmic, slow motion.

There is a suitcase on the wooden floor, an old suitcase, a familiar thing, though it no longer contains a gun bought in a Seattle back street by a different person an age ago, a gun that now lies on the bottom of Lake Union, the thick polluted waters already eating into the old, hard metal, peeling off its atoms one by one and mixing them into the semi-industrial soup of water and chemicals and dirt.

There is a suitcase on the floor, and in a side pocket an airline ticket. In some way she is there already. Joni Lascelles is working on London time, she is wearing business clothes, her head is hearing the sound of English voices, images of the streets come jumbling through her mind.

Outside, on the deck, Paul Dunsany is playing the old Martin flat-top acoustic, a slow progression of chords, gently picked, from major to relative minor, that ancient sequence, so close to cliché, so close to heaven, and she listens to the fluidity of the sound, the complex weave of his fingering, no voices, no melody yet, but that will come, she knows this somehow, though Paul Dunsany has never in his life written a song, something here is changing, some switches, levers, have moved inside him and they cannot be reset.

This is the coward's way, she says to herself, to walk away and leave the word 'perhaps' hanging in the air. To say, as circumspectly as she can put it, that there may be another time. There may be another chance. In the future, in that big grey airless place that no one can discern, that no one recognises until it's past. To leave unsaid the words of Margaret Zalinski, so true, so prophetic: that two people sharing the same guilt cannot lean on each other alone. To leave unsaid the cold, brutal fact: that she cannot look at him without seeing the reflection, hard and sparkling, of Miles, lovely Miles, Miles at the age of five, the real Miles, in his eyes. And however much she may or may not love him, however much goodness there is in his person, that is more than she can bear.

She picks up the suitcase and the airline ticket and walks out onto the small rear deck. Paul Dunsany, seated in a canvas chair, stops playing, and looks at her, not smiling, nothing there in his face that offers some kind of judgement.

'It's new,' she says. 'The tune. I haven't heard it before.'

'No,' he says, thinking about the old Martin, trying to remember

417

how many years it has shared his life, wondering why a piece of wood stringed with metal should carry such weight in his world. 'It's not new. I played that twenty years ago. I played that on an old Harmony Sovereign. In the Barn. I remember Louise watching me. I *remember* that.'

Some wounds never heal, she thought, and there was no understanding, no reasoning why.

He leans the Martin against the iron handrail that runs around the back of the boat, looks towards her, doesn't see into her face, and says, 'Too old, Joni. I'm too old for this. Rock and roll is something that means a lot when you're young, means *everything*. But there should be a rule in there somewhere, that says, when you get to thirty, you leave it behind. You grow up. You move on to bigger, wider, older things. And I never did.'

Then he stands up, walks so close to her she can feel the warmth of his breath, the scent of sweat on him, feels his arms hold her, allows herself to be kissed, feels ashamed of her reticence, her coolness, so obvious he doesn't need to mention it.

She touches the scar on his cheek. The dead skin. So smooth, so straight, and, as he stares into the golden halo of her hair, not daring to meet her eyes, she asks, wishing she did not care so much about the answer, 'What will you do?'

Even his voice sounds old today. So old, so lost. 'What can I do? What else is there? Pick up that guitar and throw it in the lake? Go drive a bus? Forget it all? Forget *everything*? I forgot too much already. If I'd remembered some more, maybe a lot of this would never have happened.'

'It's not your fault,' she says, and already, when she looks at him, she sees another, she sees the halo there, and the pain, sharp and bright, stabs at her from the past. 'This time, these feelings, they'll pass.'

'You could be a part of it,' he says, and touches her, she feels the gentle skin of his hand against her face and she can almost believe it until something registers the desperation in his voice. 'Maybe not now, Joni. But some time. When you're ready. When it's right. We could both get better. There are things here that are a part of you, not just me, not just Joe any more. And those things may hurt, they may cause you pain, but that's how it is, and the pain won't be different because you're some place else. It will still *be* there, and no one else to share it with either.'

418

All of which is true, and she knows it.

'It's not about pain,' she says. 'If it was just that, Paul, I could stay right now. It's about remembering. And forgiveness.'

Then touches his lips as he tries to speak.

'Not forgiving you, Paul. Forgiving me. And that's my problem. You know that. You must do.'

Across the lake a flock of ducks scatters and skims over the water, noisily, in a crowd. Little is moving at this time of the morning. The city around the lake seems to be asleep, seems too exhausted to climb out of bed.

'Paul,' she says, and draws away from him, has to. 'It's something only I can do. And you helped me realise that. Without you it couldn't have happened. But from now on it's up to me to make it work. You made me know I could be healed. But you can't heal me. And I can't heal you. We're the same in some ways. All of us who were a part of this, except for Margie, and she . . .'

The picture of her on the farm, the close-cropped hair, the inner strength that would never go away, started to come alive inside her head.

'She's different. Different from any of us. She could find herself through Joe. But we're not like that. We have to find it for ourselves. Or we don't find it at all. That's the way it is. Does it make sense?'

He shakes his head. 'No. But the best things never make sense. I can live with that. I love you. I think you love me. That doesn't make sense, but I can live with that too.'

And she remembers the night, the early hours of 1996, when they coupled, so frantically, so physically, in the street, off Pioneer Square, something so strange, so shocking to her, that now, at this distance, it seems unreal, it seems as if it never happened, though she knows it did, and she knows why too. And that it failed. That whatever stood between them is something that no amount of love, spiritual or physical, can wash away.

'Some time,' she says, hating herself, and touches the scar again, photographing it for herself, storing the look of it in her memory. 'Some time.'

Then kisses him, and stares across the grey flat slab of water, mindlessly watching some seaplane manoeuvring on the far side of the lake, watching the way it tries to cope with the swell, the tide, the invisible, endless, unfathomable shifting of the waters beneath it.

Joni Lascelles walks up the narrow gantry, off the houseboat, walks to the road, waits for a passing yellow cab, flags it down. Behind her, floating on the wind, she can hear the Martin, rolling gently, from C down to A minor, over and over again, a sound, a sequence, an interval so sad she knows it will stay with her all the way across the Atlantic, maybe beyond that, maybe forever, major to minor, young to old, life to death, vitality to decay, so slowly, so relentlessly, so inevitable, spaces in time that seem to flow in rhythm with the breathing of the world itself.

Three hours later, the salt smell of the ocean fading slowly from her lungs, Joni Lascelles leaves the big grey city, knowing she will never return.